BIG AL'S WRECKING AND SALVAGE

Also by Michael Hodjera

BIG AL'S WRECKING AND SALVAGE

MICHAEL HODJERA

BIG AL'S WRECKING AND SALVAGE

iUniverse books may be ordered through booksellers or by contacting:

iUniverse
1663 Liberty Drive
Bloomington, IN 47403
www.iuniverse.com
844-349-9409

Because of the dynamic nature of the Internet, any web addresses or links contained in this book may have changed since publication and may no longer be valid. The views expressed in this work are solely those of the author and do not necessarily reflect the views of the publisher, and the publisher hereby disclaims any responsibility for them.

Any people depicted in stock imagery provided by Getty Images are models, and such images are being used for illustrative purposes only.
Certain stock imagery © Getty Images.

ISBN: 978-1-6632-2216-9 (sc)
ISBN: 978-1-6632-2217-6 (e)

Library of Congress Control Number: 2021908779

Print information available on the last page.

iUniverse rev. date: 05/07/2021

Special thanks to Gail Barta for her assistance in preparing this manuscript for publication.

for mom and sis

THE FORTUNE'S FOOL

I

Home

My name is Rose Thorne. It's true. My adoptive parents gave me the name. They had a sense of humor, I'm told. Sadly, I didn't get to experience it first hand. They died in a car accident when I was 3.

I was raised by their parents on my dad's side, my Grandpa Kurt and his wife, Thea. Thea died a couple of years later in '45, so it was left to Kurt to bring me up. Since his health hadn't been all that great since he'd retired, his daughter, my aunt Trish, stepped in to keep an eye on him and to help raise me.

We lived a few miles east of Rattlesnake Junction, an hour's drive northeast of Tucson near the Apache Reservation. It was your typical American small town. It had a population of about 20,000, shops and businesses along a main drag, a movie theater, and about the same number of eateries as there were churches. We had an elementary school, a high school, and a junior college with a brand-new football stadium behind it.

Grandpa Kurt, Aunt Trish, and I lived in a ranch-style tract house with a red terracotta roof. It was built on a quarter acre of desert sand at the foot of the Akecheta Mountains of eastern Arizona and stood by its lonesome at the end of a cul-de-sac. It contained three bedrooms and two baths, one of which I shared with Aunt Trish, a den, a dining room, and a living room. Attached to the main house was a big two-car garage that was also Grandpa Kurt's workshop.

For as long as I could remember he'd worked on old cars in there. I'm pretty sure I inherited my love of all things automotive from him.

The house had started life as a model home, an example of what the other houses in the tract would eventually look like. But the rest of the development never materialized. The official story is that the construction company ran out of funds. Aunt Trish, who is a paralegal in town and who tends to know these things, said it was the other way round. It was the funds that left town, carried off by the chief accountant on the project, a guy named Slocum, never to be seen again. It was fine with me that the development never got done. I didn't mind that we were the only ones out there. I kinda preferred it that way.

The cul-de-sac sat at the end of a piece of nicely paved road complete with new sidewalks, streetlights, and fire hydrants. Everything but the houses. From home, it was a twenty-minute straight shot into Rattlesnake Junction down a gentle slope.

Though our house sat on a quarter-acre lot, it felt like a lot more because it was surrounded by nothing but miles and miles of desert in every direction. The area behind the house was wilderness, a warren of arid, sand-colored hills and canyons that rose to a jagged peak, Eagle's Crest, to the southeast. There were no fences, so I had no difficulty imagining it all as our backyard. For all practical purposes, it was.

When I wasn't at school or working at my part-time job in town, I liked to explore those hills, usually with Grandpa when I could tear him away from whatever he was doing in the garage. Nobody knew more about the desert than Grandpa did.

2

School

At school, the kids called me Rosie the Riveter because they thought I looked like a younger version of the woman in the famous World War II poster. It had been ten years since the end of the war, and everything relating to it was still fresh in everyone's memory. The artwork depicted a woman with a bandanna around her head showing off her biceps. The text read, "We Can Do It." I could dig it. I was a can-do kind of girl myself, even at sixteen. As long as I got to work on cars and go on long hikes around the countryside, they could call me whatever they wanted to.

Even I could see the similarity when I looked at myself in the mirror. What I saw looking back at me was a freckly-faced girl of average height with chestnut-colored eyes and red hair fanning out in all directions. The hair was where the bandanna came in, especially when I was working around a car engine. In those days I was apprenticing part-time at Ted's garage on Main Street, so I had to be careful. The stories of mechanics getting scalped because their hair got caught in the machinery were legion. That wasn't gonna happen to this girl.

I guess reaching up into cars from the grease pit had beefed up my arms some, too, like the Rosie from the poster. The other apprentice at the shop, Ernie, once made a comment about "my guns". I'd never given my arms much thought. But looking in the mirror, I could kind of see the similarity there as well.

It was generally acknowledged that I could beat up all the girls and probably half the guys at my school. The older girls used to pick on me in junior high because I was different from the bobbysoxers and never cared two cents what they thought of me. They learned soon enough that if they didn't want to show up in class looking like Raggedy Ann, scraped, bruised, and black-eyed, they'd better think twice about trying to push me around. I never started a fight. But word got around pretty quick that I was more than ready to finish one, if it came to that. When I got to high school the junior and senior girls still gave me a wide berth.

So, sure. Rosie the Riveter. Why not? Better to be her than those prisses who flounce around in frilly dresses and petticoats and didn't know a differential from an exhaust manifold. I think most of them were a little afraid of me.

Not that I went around looking for trouble, mind you. That wasn't me at all. I was happy being who I was and doing what I was doing. Mostly, I kept to myself and didn't bother anyone.

Working on cars kept me out of trouble, for the most part. Grandpa had been my auto mechanics mentor since I was old enough to lift a crescent wrench. He'd owned a Ford/Mercury/Lincoln dealership before he retired. He'd done well enough selling cars to buy the house at the end of Ocotillo Lane and provide a comfortable life for us. He kept telling Trish that she didn't have to work as hard as she did. But Trish had always enjoyed what she'd done, helping people who couldn't afford a full-on lawyer to handle their cases. Her job had the added appeal of keeping her up to speed on the latest scuttlebutt in town.

3

Work

Grandpa Kurt'd been working on a '48 Studebaker in the garage at the house for as long as I could remember, and he'd let me work right alongside him. I had studied at the feet of a master. I got good enough to land the job at Ted's Auto Repair when I turned sixteen and got my driver's license. Ted had me doing oil changes out of the chute, like any apprentice. But three months later I was doing tune-ups. Pretty soon I'd be doing rebuilds.

Ernie was Ted's other apprentice. He was a pimply-faced kid, a couple of years older than me. He had lank, thinning hair plastered to his scalp with baby oil. I could tell by the smell. He wasn't even out of his teens, and already he was well on his way to baldsville, poor guy.

Still, he was a good mechanic and a decent enough fellow. He didn't razz me the way some other kids did. He never called me Rosie, for instance, at least to my face. Instead, he referred to me as the engine witch. I took it as a compliment. I liked to believe it was on account of how good I was getting at sussing out engine problems. It got to where I could tell what ailed a car just by asking the owner a few questions and then listening to the sounds the car was making. There were sounds that were easy to pin down, like a stuck valve or bad wheel bearings. But my abilities went beyond that. I liked to think I had a sixth sense when it came to auto repair.

Of course, there were car problems that were beyond my diagnostic abilities. Like when a car got towed in DOA. I wasn't a psychic like Madam Roux. But in general, I was right more often than not. Hence, the moniker engine witch. At least I hoped so.

4

Crackpots

As I progressed, it must have gotten less fun for Grandpa Kurt to train me. I felt a bit sorry for him.

"Check this out, Rose," he'd say, showing me a gnarled lump of metal and wiring.

I'd take a look at it and say, "That's the new carburetor Chevy's putting on the Bel Air this year." Or, "That's the distributor cap from a '46 Packard."

He'd straighten up, sigh, and just stare at me. There'd be a slight smile at the corner of his mouth, so I knew he wasn't mad at me. I'd grin back kinda sheepishly. I couldn't help it that I was a genius mechanic.

Grandpa Kurt would go back to what he was working on. "Hand me that Phillips screwdriver, would you?" he'd say as he ducked back under the hood.

I obliged of course. Just because I had a swelled head about how good I was getting didn't mean I wasn't still in awe of what Grandpa Kurt could do. I knew enough to know I still had lots to learn. I may have had an elevated opinion of my abilities now and then, but I wasn't a complete nincompoop.

The Studebaker was always half torn down, or half rebuilt, depending on how you looked at it. Grandpa wouldn't hesitate to take out something he needed for another project. And just as often he'd be installing something he'd found at a flea market or brought home from the wrecking yard.

He loved to go to the wrecking yard if only to chew the fat with the proprietor there, Big Al. What was remarkable was that Grandpa could have the car in driving condition in under an hour, regardless of the state of disassembly it was in, whenever he needed to go somewhere.

While I aspired to be a mechanical genius, he truly was one. Before he'd taken over the dealership he'd been a lowly grease monkey like yours truly, learning the ropes, paying his dues in the lube pit. By the time he took the reins at the dealership he knew all there was to know about every car he sold.

He was also kind of a nut. I say that with a lot of affection and with all due respect. He could bend your ears for hours on end about the goings-on at Roswell in the late forties, space aliens, flying saucers, and moon men. More peculiar yet was his firm belief that the earth was flat. I think he got a lot of it from Big Al at the wrecking yard. Those guys were two peas in a pod. They would scale summits of BS when they got together until black was white and the sun rose in the west. There was no stopping them once they got going.

It could be said that Grandpa Kurt never heard a harebrained theory he didn't like, and Big Al had an endless supply of them. Consequently, I didn't know how I felt about Big Al. I was pretty sure he wasn't a good influence on Grandpa. But they were such fast friends, I mostly kept my opinions to myself.

Besides clinging to ideas that were outdated by the 15th century, Grandpa was a pretty cool guy. At age 70 he had a lanky, slightly stooped frame, probably from spending so much time bent over open engine compartments. He was partial to Levis, bleached and frayed by time and Tide, and white T-shirts. TownCraft was his preferred brand, purchased at JCPenney's department store downtown. On cool evenings when we ventured up the hill to look at the stars, he would grab an old Pendleton off the hook in the garage or a jean's jacket he'd had since before the war. He kept his steel-gray hair so short it was almost a buzz cut. I tried to get him to grow it out a bit so he wouldn't look so much like a drill sergeant, but so far my suggestions had fallen on deaf ears.

He had that way of standing when he was deep in thought, hands on his hips, head cocked to one side, as he studied his Red Wing work boots. To others, he seemed stern, but I knew better. He was really a softy underneath it all.

5

The Desert Almanac

Grandpa Kurt and I made it a point to hike the hills behind the house every few days. He taught me how to read the desert, pointing out places where skirmishes had taken place the night before. A snake and a fox. A coyote and a bobcat. He taught me to identify the trails of scorpions and lizards, moles and rats, jackrabbits and roadrunners, as well as the minute scrapings of beetles and bugs. During the day the desert slept. At night, it came alive.

We rarely hiked at night. For safety's sake, Grandpa said. You never knew what you might step on out there. I think Grandpa sometimes forgot I was old enough to look after myself and still imagined me to be the pint-sized elf that had been his workshop gofer a few years before. It was a common error among parents of teens, I guess.

We did venture as far as the top of the hill behind the house any time a meteor shower or an eclipse might be on tap. Fortunately for us, Aunt Trish loved to stargaze too. That meant we always had a well-stocked cooler on hand. Once we were situated in our aluminum folding chairs, draped with blankets to ward off the evening chill, she'd serve up snacks and lemonade while we stared in wonder at the star-strewn universe.

There wasn't much light interference this far away from civilization. So we had an unobstructed view of whatever celestial hijinks were promised for that particular night. We'd hang out and wait, hoping for the unexpected. A shooting star, a comet, or even the exhaust streaks from a high-flying supersonic jet. The plane itself would be a barely visible speck against the indigo sky, the rumble of its engines just an afterthought echoing across the hills and valleys.

Knowing he had a captive audience, Grandpa Kurt would hold forth about Area 41, UFO sightings, and the high probability of life on other planets. Most of it was pretty outlandish, but also kind of intriguing, especially as we sat there, stared up into the depths of an endless, unfathomable universe. Who could say what was and wasn't possible under a sky like that?

But inevitably he'd trot out his flat earth theory and dust it off, often prefacing his pronouncements with "Big Al says"—as if Big Al was the supreme authority on the impossible and his word was gospel. Coming from someone as level-headed as Grandpa Kurt in most other respects, it was troubling. Since I was as aware of the vast body of literature that stood in direct opposition to what he was going on about as the next high schooler, I was always ready to pounce with my book learning like a mongoose on a rat. I didn't mean any disrespect, but I debunked his ideas without mercy. When I presented my case, Grandpa Kurt would smile that inscrutable smile of his and remain silent, lost in thought. I think he was secretly pleased that I was challenging him. It proved that I was doing my homework. But I could tell I hadn't disabused him one iota of his crazy, regressive notions. The earth being flat? I mean, this wasn't the Middle Ages anymore, was it?

Regardless of what was on the agenda astronomically, rarely an evening's viewing went by when we didn't see half a dozen or more shooting stars. If we got out while it was still twilight, we'd have bats dive-bombing us on the way up the hill. This inevitably inspired a lecture about navigation using sonar.

Sometimes in the spring and summer months, when Grandpa and Trish were busy, I'd just roll out a sleeping bag on the chaise lounge on the patch of dichondra directly behind the house and fall asleep looking into the depths of space. I dreamt of adventures and exploits beyond our solar system. With Grandpa's help, I had found my way to Heinlein and Asimov and so became conversant with the notion of a life lived in an expanded context, unlimited by space and time. On these occasions, I would be confounded all the more by Grandpa Kurt's adamant refusal to accept the essential and basic concept of a spherical Planet Earth. I was old enough to know that people could hold contradictory notions simultaneously. Everybody had blind spots that would not yield to reason, but this was absurd. Here was an obviously intelligent, technically adept and learned man who inexplicably and frustratingly clung to an outdated notion that would forever limit his idea of what was possible. It just made no sense.

6

Big Al

I was a kid the first time I met Big Al. I remember being slightly intimidated by the big man with the ruddy complexion. Trish told me that he probably had a lot of Irish in his family tree because of the short red curls, darker than mine, and the flushed face.

"With a light skin complexion like that he shouldn't be spending as much time in the sun as he obviously does," she said disapprovingly. "You shouldn't either, young lady."

"Does that mean I'm Irish, too?" I asked.

"With that hair and skin, I'd say it's a good bet," she replied with a smile. "But there's a smidge of down south in there, too."

"How do you mean 'down south'?"

"Mediterranean maybe. Mexican or South American. That's your saving grace when you're out in the sun, and you're in the sun a lot. Just that touch of olive. It's why you don't burn. It's in those beautiful chestnut eyes of yours, too."

When Grandpa took me to the wrecking yard that first time, Big Al was wearing a gaudy Hawaii shirt, open at the front, over a white T-shirt, jeans, and scuffed work boots. I came to realize, over time, that this was his standard work outfit. All that changed from day to day was the design of the shirt. One day it was palm trees, panel trucks, and hula girls. The next, erupting volcanoes and crashing surf. Whatever it was, it was saturated with color to make your eyeballs bleed.

"Who do we have here?" were his first words in my direction.

"This is my granddaughter, Rose," Grandpa Kurt said with a hand on my shoulder.

"Well how do you do, young lady," said Al, bending at the waist and holding out his hand. His breath smelled faintly of booze and pipe tobacco.

"Fine," I said uncertainly.

I had been hearing about the legendary Big Al for a couple of years now, and it was a bit of a let down to actually meet the man. Of course, with the kind of build-up he'd gotten from Grandpa, Hercules as portrayed by Steve Reeves would have been a disappointment.

"Grandpa Kurt says you believe the earth is flat," I blurted out. I'd been harboring a secret animosity toward him ever since Grandpa had started spouting that nonsense back at the house. I blamed him for it.

Al seemed taken aback. He glanced beseechingly at Grandpa Kurt. When he saw no help forthcoming from that quarter, he turned his eyes skyward, scratching his stubbled chin. It sounded like someone taking a rasp to a piece of mesquite. "I didn't say flat, exactly," Al said, hedging. "Flattish would be more accurate."

"But science tells us that it's round," I persisted. "How would you explain the sun rising every morning and setting at night? It's all about the earth being round as a bowling ball and circling the sun."

Big Al frowned. "I know that seems logical," he said slowly. He scratched his jaw some more. "And if it helps you to understand it that way, I won't try to dissuade you."

I couldn't believe this guy. "But you're still claiming the earth's flat?" I said flatly. "Despite all evidence to the contrary?"

He just shrugged sheepishly.

"But it's not a matter of opinion," I practically shouted. "It's a proven scientific fact. Everybody since Pythagoras and Aristotle has known the earth was round." I'd done my homework.

"Yeah, well," Big Al said, grimacing as if he was passing a kidney stone. "You know the old expression, 'appearances can be deceiving'." I could see even he was embarrassed at the lameness of his explanation.

"That's a bunch of hogwash, and you know it," said I, thoroughly disgusted. "Can't you do better than that? You're an adult, for godsakes."

"Now, now," said Grandpa Kurt aghast, awakening to the perilousness of the situation. "Mind your language, young lady. Show Big Al some respect, please. It seems we've gotten off on the wrong foot here. Why don't you go rummage through that heap of parts over there and see if you can scare up that exhaust manifold we need."

"Hold on a minute, Kurt," said Big Al, grateful to finally see a way out. He seized it like a drowning man might a life preserver. "I think I've got what you're looking for over here. For the Studebaker, right?"

He took Grandpa aside thinking I wouldn't overhear what they were saying, even though they were barely six feet away.

"Didn't we agree that what we talked about amongst ourselves wasn't for general consumption?" I heard Big Al say. "It's just between you and me and the deep blue sea. 'Ears Only'." He tapped one of his ears to make his point.

"I'm truly sorry, Al," said Grandpa Kurt contritely. "I didn't think there'd be any harm in telling the girl. You saw her reaction. I doubt she'd tell anyone else. And even if she did, they'd just write us off, you and me, as a couple of old coots with too much time on our hands."

"Speak for yourself," grumbled Big Al.

I had the sense he didn't really care one way or the other that one of his nutball theories had come to light. There were plenty more where that came from.

"You know I've got a reputation to uphold," Big Al said reasonably. There was a hint of amusement in his voice. "I can't have people thinking I'm off my rocker. They might start taking their business elsewhere."

"Oh? And where exactly would that be? You know as well as I do you're the only game in town as far wrecking and salvage goes."

"You got a point there," said Big Al with a self-satisfied grin.

15

"Besides," said Grandpa Kurt. "People believe what they want to believe. You'd know that better than most."

Grandpa Kurt became a little more reserved in expressing his contrarian opinions on a number of subjects after that. But it would have been clear to anyone who spent more than five minutes with him that he hadn't given them up altogether.

As the years went by, I must have accompanied Grandpa Kurt to Big Al's a hundred times. It was like an advanced course in auto mechanics and automotive history combined just being around those old rusty, and in many cases, compacted clunkers. It felt like I learned something new every time I went, and I figured that made me a better car mechanic. It also started me dreaming about the kind of car I might one day want to own. It was a little like Christmas every time we went to Big Al's Wrecking and Salvage. You never knew what you'd find there. Or find out.

7

The Anomaly

Things had been unusually busy at Ted's in the autumn of '55. Consequently, I didn't have as much time as I liked for hiking the backcountry. I still got out as often as I could, though.

One day at dusk I'd been wandering the hills not far from the house when I spied the last rays of sun glinting off something in the undergrowth. Grandpa had decided to stay home to finish up rebuilding the Studebaker's carburetor for the twentieth time. So I was on my own.

I approached cautiously, thinking somebody had left a canteen or a wadded up ball of tin foil behind. The sky continued to darken as I went to have a closer look. When I was about twenty feet away, whatever it was jumped straight up in the air with a piercing sound like a squeal and skittered behind a rock. The movement was so unexpected, I sat right down on my keister. I never got a good look at the thing, but I had the impression of something smooth and curved, bullet-shaped, about a foot long. It might have been a beetle except I'd never heard of one that size.

I cautiously checked around the rock but found nothing. By now it was too dark to see anyway. So I gave up the search and went home wondering if I'd imagined the whole thing. I didn't mention the sighting to anyone.

That is, until the second time it happened. Ted had to go out of town and closed the shop early. Trish usually picked me up at the garage on her way home from work in the late afternoon. But since I was out early, I got Ernie to bring me home. With plenty of daylight left, I decided to go for a stroll in the hills. Grandpa Kurt was busy in the garage again, so I ventured out on my own.

I'd been walking for about twenty minutes when I heard a scuttling noise somewhere ahead of me. An animal rooting around in the brush was my first thought. A lizard, perhaps. Or a jackrabbit. I moved forward cautiously in case it was a rattler I was dealing with. Something metallic was moving through the sage. I scrambled after it. When I got close, the thing made a chittering sound and vanished behind a large sandstone boulder. Dang!

I decided that this was something I needed to talk to Grandpa Kurt about. This would be right up his alley, I thought, as the go-to guy for the strange and the uncanny. Anybody else would have told me I'd been seeing things.

"It was shiny and smooth," I told Grandpa Kurt when I got home. "And it moved fast."

Aunt Trish, who had arrived home by that time, was drying dishes at the sink. She said, "Maybe it was one of those toys they're advertising on TV. You know, for Christmas. A battery-powered, radio-controlled this or that."

"There was nobody else around," I said. "I checked for footprints. The thing was rooting around in the bushes like an animal. Except I swear it was made of metal. It was shaped like an armadillo but smaller. It was like a small, silver armadillo."

"I don't like the sound of that," said Grandpa Kurt. "Did it have legs?"

"I didn't get close enough to see."

"How about wheels?" said Aunt Trish. "What you're describing kind of sounds like one of those canister vacs that GE just started making. They're round at the base with a chrome swivel top. Maybe it was something like that you saw."

"I suppose," I said. "The size would have been about right. But it didn't move or sound like any vacuum I've seen. Besides, there's nothing to clean out there. Or too much. It's a million square miles of nothing but sand. Not to mention there's nothing to plug into anywhere."

"I'd say we've got ourselves an honest to goodness mystery here," Grandpa Kurt said with gusto. "Why don't we go out there and take a gander." He grabbed the armrests of his easy chair and pulled himself upright. "What do you say?"

"Right now?"

"There's still a couple of hours of daylight left. Why not? You said it was up the draw about twenty minutes. Right?"

"Give or take."

"We've got time to poke around for an hour and still be back by suppertime."

He went to grab a couple of flashlights out of the utility drawer next to the fridge. On the way he invited Aunt Trish to come along. "Gonna be an adventure," he said with a mischievous grin. "We might find ourselves a new species. Or a vacuum gone rogue. You never know."

"It's tempting," said Trish. "Especially if it's a new GE, seein' as I'm ready to retire the old Hoover. But I think I'll stay and get supper ready instead. Maybe next time."

8

Hot On The Trail Of ?

I took Grandpa Kurt to where I'd seen what I thought I'd seen. It turned out to be more like a half hour's walk up the arroyo instead of the 20 minutes I'd calculated. Eventually, I spied the boulder I'd seen the mystery object disappear behind.

"It was rooting around this rock," I told Grandpa.

"I don't see any tracks per se," he said thoughtfully. He circled the sandstone boulder, carefully studying the terrain as he went. "But something has stirred up the sand here and then smoothed it over. You see that?"

It did indeed look like the ground around the base of the boulder was uniformly smoother than elsewhere.

"It's been swept clean, I'd bet on it," Kurt said. "But there aren't any brush marks. Something stirred up the sand here and then covered its tracks. I don't know of any critter that cleans up after itself like that. What we're looking for is man-made, whatever it is. Has to be."

"Can we figure out where whatever it is went?"

"This smoothed over section doesn't seem to start anywhere or lead anywhere," Kurt said, a note of frustration creeping into his voice. "It's confined to this area around the rock."

"Could it have taken off? Like a bird?"

"Well, that's more likely than it just vanishing into thin air, I'd say. Though not by much. If it is man-made, where would such a thing have come from? There's no military base around here where they might be testing some kind of new gadget. There's nobody around here at all. Hell of a thing."

Kurt took off his floppy hat and scratched his bristly gray hair.

"Let's see if we can find more traces like this. Might as well, since we're here."

We began to wander around independently of each other to cover more ground. I ventured further up the arroyo, while Grandpa moved laterally from one side of the narrowing ravine to the other. I didn't see any other spots like the one we'd seen. But I did find something interesting.

I went back to get Grandpa Kurt. "There's a cave a little further up," I told him when I found him.

"There are caves all over this area," Kurt pointed out.

"This one's different," I said. "I think you need to have a look at it."

Grandpa Kurt gave me the hairy eyeball. But he knew me well enough to know I wouldn't send him on a wild goose chase.

We walked up the canyon together. As the walls narrowed, the sun sank toward the horizon behind us, bathing the sandstone cliffs in reddish light. Our shadows extended like fingers in the direction we were walking.

"There," I said.

Grandpa Kurt stopped and glared at the opening that stood before us. "I'll be," he said.

He was noticing what I had earlier. The opening to the cave was a perfectly formed cylindrical arch about twelve feet high.

"It looks like it could be a big drainage outlet," Grandpa Kurt observed. "But there's no reason for one to exist here in the middle of nowhere."

I was about to say maybe the military had built some kind of lab or test facility nearby and that this might be connected to that, but I caught myself in time. I didn't want to set Grandpa off on a tangent about secret government projects and skulduggery that ordinary citizens weren't supposed to be privy to. It was getting late and I thought it best if we stayed focused.

We moved cautiously forward until we stood at the entrance to the oddly symmetrical cavern, glaring into the blackness. There was no telling how far back it went.

"We don't have much daylight left," Kurt observed with a tinge of regret as he looked back down the canyon the way we'd come. The last rays of sun shone weakly on his face and the air temperature was dropping rapidly. We'd been out here longer than expected. It would probably be dark by the time we got home. "I'm sorry to say this'll have to wait for another time."

"How about tomorrow?" I said.

"Don't you have work after school?"

"I'll call in sick," I said.

9

Into The Unknown

As it turned out, it was Grandpa Kurt who got sick.

He collapsed while standing at the sink in the kitchen. His legs just gave out, and he sprawled backward on the linoleum. Trish, who happened to be home for lunch at the time, grabbed for the wall phone and dialed for an ambulance. It arrived 10 minutes later. He was taken to the clinic in town. But it was quickly decided he needed to go to a hospital in Tucson.

The doctors in Tucson said he'd had a heart attack. And though they were reassuring to a fault about his chances for recovery, I was left to ponder the unthinkable: Grandpa Kurt might not always be around. When my adoptive parents and Grandma Thea had died, I'd been too young to fully understand what had happened and how it might affect my life going forward. But Grandpa Kurt had been a part of my life for as long as I could remember. I couldn't imagine him not being there.

I put our discovery in the hills on the back burner and focused on Grandpa Kurt. I skipped school the next several days and rode into the big city with Trish to spend time with him, trying to cheer him up during his stay at the hospital. On the second day, he asked me to bring in an alternator he'd been working on in the garage and some tools. What good was it having survived a heart attack only to die of boredom afterward, was how he put it. The nurses weren't thrilled to have to work around greasy car parts and tools when they attended him. Something to do with sanitation standards. This might be why he was discharged a couple of days earlier than expected.

"The doctor said I'd need to take it easy for a few weeks," he told me when we got him home. I knew that meant he'd have to limit his time in the garage for a while. It also meant we probably wouldn't be doing much hiking in the backcountry in the near future.

As he reclined on the sofa in the living room, he must have known what I was thinking. "I'm talking hypothetically here," he said. "But should somebody in the general vicinity want to, say, head back out in the hills without me, I wouldn't be averse to it as long as they promised me they'd be careful. I'm curious about that cave, too, and I wouldn't blame you for not wanting to wait up on your old granddad. You're old enough now to make your own decisions. However, I would blame myself if anything happened to you. Are we clear?"

I just nodded. I sensed another exploratory mission in the offing in the not-too-distant future, especially now that I had Grandpa's blessings.

"Report back to me, OK?" Kurt said, supporting his head on the sofa's armrest. He was pale and winded after the trip home. The TV was on, but the sound was off.

"Aye, aye, sir," I said with a smart salute.

It took a couple more days before I got home early enough to make the trek. Putting my army surplus jacket on over a wool sweater, I grabbed a canteen full of water and a flashlight in case I didn't make it back before dark. With the end of the year fast approaching, the days were getting shorter, and it was getting noticeably colder sooner.

Forty-five minutes later I was standing opposite the cave entrance. Besides a couple of lizards, a king snake, a high-flying red-tailed hawk, and a rabbit I'd flushed out of a creosote bush, there hadn't been much sign of life on the way in.

The desert was still. Like it was holding its breath. Those back canyons could be as silent as the tomb when the wind died. But at that moment, in front of that cave, it felt extra eerie. I knew from experience that a silence like this could descend when there was a larger predator about. The thought gave me the heebie-jeebies, even though it had been a couple of years since I'd spotted a mountain lion in these hills. I told myself I was getting spooked for no reason. I wasn't going to wimp out after coming all this way. Besides, I needed to have something to tell Grandpa when I got back.

I took a swig from the canteen and fumbled around my utility belt for my flashlight. Finding it, I flicked it on and started forward, into the dark.

As the light from the entrance receded behind me, the air grew stiller yet. I could hear the blood pumping in my ears as the sand crunched under my boots. I caught sight of the skeleton of a deer in my circle of light and jumped. Maybe this *had* been the lair of a larger predator once upon a time. I glanced around nervously, but saw nothing else out of the ordinary. The bones were bleached white and crumbled as I nudged them with my boot. Probably decades old.

I continued on. The cave's dimensions never varied as you'd expect from a natural formation. It was the same size all the way in, about 12 feet high and about the same distance across. For the most part, it ran straight as an arrow into the mountainside.

Grandpa and I had been in agreement that the cave was man-made when we first saw it. So far I hadn't seen anything to change my mind about that. It was so symmetrical there was no way it could be a natural phenomenon. As to what its purpose might be, there wasn't a clue. Maybe it was a mine shaft. But the ones I'd seen had wooden timbers as supports, short gauge railroad tracks leading in and out, and evidence of digging and blasting, none of which was present here. This was just a hole bored way back into the mountain as if by a giant sand beetle.

It all added up to me feeling generally creepy, even though I'd seen nothing so far that was at all threatening.

I must have been about a quarter of a mile in when I heard a faint whirring sound ahead of me in the dark. I brought my flashlight to bear, but again I was too late. Whatever it was had scuttled out of range. I'd never gotten my light full on it, but I was left with the impression of something close to the ground, shell-like and smooth, the twin of the thing I'd seen nearer the house. And--I couldn't be sure about this--it had seemed to hover.

It was all too strange. To be honest I wanted to get the heck out of there, drop everything and run. Instead, I stood perfectly still. I made myself a fixture of the cave, which was hard to do because the hand holding the flashlight was shaking, casting a flickering light like a silent movie projector on the walls. I wasn't about to turn the thing off, though. So I just stood there, shaking. And waiting. I got my breathing under control and slowly started to back out the way I'd come in. When there was no further sound or movement in the tunnel ahead of me, I turned and made a dash for the entrance to the cave.

"You didn't see what it was," Grandpa Kurt said when I told him what had happened in the cave. He couldn't hide a note of disappointment.

"I just heard something," I said. "And by the time I brought the flashlight up, whatever was there was gone."

Kurt seemed to digest this for a while without saying anything, his brow furrowed.

"I don't like it," he said, frowning. "I'd be happier if you didn't go back out there by yourself."

I just kind of nodded.

But I was already thinking about my next visit to the cave. I'd be carrying a knife this time, that's for sure. And the Daisy BB pistol I'd gotten on my 14th birthday. No way was I going back into that cave unarmed.

10

The Silver Armadillo

It was a Saturday. With no school or work on the schedule, I got an early start. Trish was gone. She often went to the Legal Services office on Saturday to work on her cases because it was quieter there than during the week, she said, and she could concentrate. Grandpa Kurt was still asleep. The heart medication he was taking caused him to sleep in, something he'd never do otherwise. He was usually the first one up.

The morning sun was on my face as I trudged up the canyon, so I kept my eyes on the ground. I startled a rattler into rattling, but it was too far away to be a threat. I knew to make enough noise while I was hiking to give advance warning of my presence.

I stopped to catch my breath. It was still chilly enough from the night before that my breath condensed. We were heading toward Thanksgiving and soon there'd be frost on the ground in the morning, though it rarely hung around long. I preferred hiking in the cold to hiking in the heat any day.

I had on a fleece-lined jeans jacket over my 501s and was wearing my sturdy hiking boots. I was lugging a small pack this time around. In it, I had my canteen, my BB pistol, a sandwich, a butcher knife from the kitchen in case I needed extra firepower, and a flashlight with extra batteries. Today I was determined to find out where that tunnel led.

I made it to the cave entrance without incident, pausing long

27

enough to take a drink of water and fish my flashlight out of the pack. It was as quiet as it had been the last time I'd been there. Not a creature was stirring. The big black hole into the hillside gaped out at me. I took a big breath. It was now or never.

I stepped into the opening. The first thing I noticed was what wasn't there. Namely, my footprints from the day before. The sand in the cave was as smooth as if it hadn't been disturbed in a hundred years. This gave me pause right off. Someone or something had removed my tracks. I felt the fine hairs on my neck rise. There was someone here, or had been recently. Maybe they were watching me that very moment.

I shone the light around, but there was no sign of life.

I looked over my shoulder back out the entrance. The morning light was inviting. Give up this craziness and go home, it seemed to be saying. Straight ahead in the inky depths lay the unknown. I'd come this far, I reasoned. I'd keep going until I had a reason to turn back.

A half-hour later, I was still going. When I passed the point where I'd stopped the day before, I became aware of a buzzing sound. It came from up ahead. I slowed down and stopped at a point where the tunnel began to angle to the right. I stepped over to the far wall to get a view of what lay ahead.

It was there in the middle of the tunnel, oblivious to my presence. It was much shinier in the light from the flashlight than it had seemed the first time I'd seen it near the house. One thing was clear immediately. It wasn't an animal. It was some kind of machine or mechanical device I was looking at. Its shell was highly reflective, like polished chrome. And it hovered an inch or two off the ground as if the laws of gravity didn't apply to it.

I'd found the silver armadillo.

It could have been something out of War of the Worlds or The Day The Earth Stood Still. From what I could tell, it was sweeping the tunnel floor. Any imperfection in the surface magically vanished as it passed. All that was left in its wake was smooth, unspoiled sand

and dirt. Trish had been right, I realized with a start. It really did appear to be some kind of vacuum cleaner. Except it made the fancy Electroluxes and Hoovers of the day look like they were out of the Stone Age. If this really was just a vacuum, it was the vacuum of the future.

The mystery of my disappearing footprints was solved. It seemed to be the job of this thing to keep the floor of the tunnel in pristine condition. To what purpose or for whom I couldn't begin to guess.

It seemed to have gotten over its initial shyness because this time it paid no attention to me or my flashlight as I carefully ventured out of hiding and into the open. It just went about its business sweeping the cavern from side to side, ignoring me completely.

Beyond the silver armadillo was what looked like the end of the line. There was a rock wall that filled the tunnel and that was it.

I ventured forward, holding my flashlight before me like a sword as I approached the thing. I left the BB pistol and the kitchen knife in my pack because whatever it was didn't seem to be dangerous. I knew from past experience that the thing tended to be on the shy side, and I didn't want to startle it.

I saw my reflection in the shiny surface getting larger as I drew nearer. I must have gotten too close for comfort because it suddenly made a beeline for the back of the cave. I thought it would come to the wall and stop, but it didn't. It just disappeared as if it had been absorbed by the rock.

I straightened up blinking. I thought maybe something was wrong with my eyesight. From where I stood there was no place for the thing to have gone.

I approached the rock wall at the back of the cave on high alert. And then I saw it: a side slot in the rock face. It was about six feet tall and a couple of feet wide. Looking straight on, the rock wall seemed to be one continuous surface. But that was an illusion.

I cautiously drew up to the opening and peered inside.

ll

Rose In Wonderland

was looking at a fair-sized room, perfectly square, made of concrete. My first thought was: bomb shelter. There were two elevators in the middle of the room. This was some fancy bomb shelter, I thought. The elevators went straight up through the ceiling.

My shiny little friend was nowhere to be seen.

It was dead quiet in here. Maybe that was a bad choice of words. The opening I'd entered through was still there behind me. I could leave anytime I wanted. And so far I hadn't seen anything scarier than a fancy hovering Hoover. And even that was now gone.

The obvious question was where?

I walked the periphery, checking down low to see if there wasn't another optical illusion lurking somewhere or some other exit along the bottom of the wall, a cat door, or something like that. But there was nothing. Unless it could make itself invisible, it hadn't sneaked past me back into the tunnel.

I found myself standing in front of the elevator doors. It was the only remaining explanation.

I took a closer look. They were just your average elevator doors, the kind you'd find in a hotel or department store. And like those elevators, it had a button on a panel that separated the two doors. It was too high up to have been much use to the armadillo, I figured, unless it could levitate, which was entirely possible. I knew nothing about the thing or its capabilities. All I knew was that it wasn't too high for me. Without thinking too much about it, I pressed the button. Almost immediately there was the familiar "ding" and one of the doors slid open.

The elevator was empty. No sign of the silver sweeper. Maybe it had used the other elevator. The lights were on inside, so I didn't need the flashlight. I stashed it in my pack and stepped in. There was a control panel to the right of the door looking outward, just as you'd find in any elevator.

There were two buttons on the panel. The ground floor button and another above it that read "Logistics." I was thinking I should have paid closer attention in English class. As far as I could remember it was one of those fancy words that could mean a lot of things. If it went up to the top of the chunk of rock I was under, it might offer up a decent view of the desert to the west, I figured. Maybe I'd be able to see all the way to Phoenix.

I pressed the top button and the doors slid shut. The elevator began to ascend, slowly at first and then faster. Suddenly we were hauling bananas. After a minute of steady acceleration, I started to get a little worried. What the heck? I thought. By now we would have been through the top of the mountain. But we weren't slowing down. I concentrated on my breathing to stay calm and tried not to think of what might await me when the elevator finally stopped. What else could I do?

We continued to shoot upward for what felt like hours, but was probably more like twenty minutes or so. At long last, the elevator started to decelerate. It took several more minutes for it to come to a complete stop. How fast had we been going? A hundred miles an hour? Two?

Finally, there was the familiar and somewhat reassuring "ding" and the doors parted.

The first thing I noticed was the sky. It was a kind of a murky, opaque black. It didn't have any stars in it per se. Just flashes of light darting this way and that. If they were shooting stars they weren't like any I'd ever seen. The more I looked, the more they appeared to be distant vectors running from point to point. As I stood there just outside the elevator doors, the startling realization began to dawn on me that I was actually still indoors. I was within some vast cavernous space.

Mouth hanging open, I stepped out of the elevator and onto a metal mesh landing. The space I was in was so enormous I couldn't see the end of it. It just went on and on into oblivion. I could have been in outer space. The absence of stars was the only giveaway that I wasn't. That, and just a feeling that I was inside something and not in the wild blue yonder.

There was something else. I was breathing. And everybody knew that you couldn't breathe in space.

There was a massive light welling up from below, beyond the railing straight ahead. I took a few tentative steps forward and the surface of Planet Earth in all its breathtaking splendor gradually came into view. It was as if I was gazing down from the edge of space. I'd seen footage of X-15 tests at Edwards Air Force Base on TV showing the supersonic aircraft as it rocketed out toward the stratosphere. That's how the sky looked from where I was standing. Above me there was blackness. And below me, there was a blindingly bright, hazy layer of atmosphere. And below that, stretching into the distance, desert. Except I wasn't in any kind of experimental aircraft. I was standing on scaffolding.

There was something that nagged at me about the view. It took me a while to understand what it was. From this height, you'd have to be seeing the curvature of the earth quite clearly, like in those X-15 newsreels. But there was no curvature visible from where I stood. There was only a chunk of the planet that seemed to end at the border to the south and stretched to the state line far to the west. A big chunk, granted. But still a chunk.

And that chunk was flat as a pancake.

12

The Fortune's Fool

"Pretty impressive, hunh," said a voice over my left shoulder.

I nearly jumped out of my skin. A tall woman had appeared at my elbow. She was a few years older than me and strong. Muscular. Like an Olympic athlete. Her blonde hair was cut short. She had on baggy army pants and a black T-shirt under a khaki vest with a lot of pockets.

"My name's Gillian," she said. "I'm with Security. I make sure people from The Bubble don't get out and start poking around where they shouldn't. Case in point." She looked at me meaningfully. But there wasn't any real anger or hostility there. In fact, she was looking at me as if she seemed kind of interested in who I was. I figured she didn't often get visitors up here.

"What is this place?" I squeaked. I didn't sound like myself. I couldn't help it. My brain was short-circuiting. I couldn't begin to comprehend what it was I was seeing.

"We're on the Fortune's Fool," she said simply, as if nothing could be more obvious.

"The what?"

She sighed and started again. "We're on a space freighter named the Fortune's Fool. Don't ask me why they decided to call it that. It's a colonization ship."

"A ship?"

"As in spaceship," she said in a "See Jane Run" kind of way. She knew she had to go back to the basics in this situation.

"But. . . ." I just indicated the vast empty space all around us.

"Yuh. It's big." She saw that she had to clarify further. "You know the moon?"

I just looked at her

"That spherical thing that goes around the earth?"

I nodded stupidly.

"The ship's roughly half the size of that. Think of a giant disco ball hauling A through space at 99.998% of the speed of light."

I didn't quite know what she was referring to. But I got the gist. I looked down, fighting vertigo.

"You OK?" she asked, a look of concern on her face.

"Not sure," I said. I couldn't lie.

"Take a deep breath. Maybe it'll help if I gave you some background. Here's the deal. We left Planet Earth about a million years ago, local time. Up here it's been about 250 years. A little more to be exact. Ever hear of Einstein's Theory of Relativity? The closer you get to the speed of light the more time slows down relative to your point of departure?"

I looked down at the bright slab below me, which looked like a scale topographical map of a section of the Earth's surface. "Where's the rest of it?" I asked.

"You mean Planet Earth?"

"This isn't all of it."

"You're right," said Gillian. "What we have here is a piece of it that's roughly the size of Arizona. In fact, it is Arizona for all practical purposes, down to the smallest detail. That's where you live. You're a Settler."

None of this was making much sense. And what was starting to make sense was too disturbing to contemplate.

"I come from down there?" I said. "But that's not possible. The world is big. Bigger than Arizona."

"Localized Personal Reality Matrix," she said simply. "LPRM." She pronounced it like "lap room."

She saw that I wasn't getting it. Probably because I was looking at her like a dog does at a human who's talking, mouth hanging open and all. My tail wasn't wagging though. I just hoped I wasn't drooling.

"LPRM fills in the blanks. It makes everyone think they're on Planet Earth, when in fact they're on a re-creation of a small part of it. You may think you're flying to London, for example, but that's an illusion. 'There', wherever you go becomes, 'here.' You could go to Indonesia, Siberia, or Antarctica, and it really would be like being there. But you aren't there. It's all happening right here. Or more accurately, down there."

"Lap room," I said like a myna bird.

13

The End Of The World In A Nutshell

"**O**ur home planet was mapped down to the molecule before we left all those years ago. That data became the raw material for the SN reality utility that we've been using here. SN stands for Super Natural. A clever piece of branding. The point is, we needed enough elbow room to pull it off. Someone came up with 114,000 square miles as the ideal amount of space. It coincided with the total surface area of Arizona. That could be why it was chosen to represent the North American continent. Who knows for sure what the Designers were thinking?"

"Wait a minute," I said. My brain was starting to catch up to what this woman was telling me and the first stirrings of logic sputtered to life again. "Are you saying there are more places like this here. In this spaceship?"

"Yup. You got it," Gillian said, grinning at me appreciatively. "There are eight more levels like this one on board this ship. They're stacked like flapjacks above and below us here."

I was having enough trouble coming to terms with the idea that I'd been living in some kind of simulation all my life. And that the Arizona I knew was indeed as flat as one of those flapjacks Gillian had just mentioned, proving that Grandpa Kurt and Big Al had been right all along. The earth, or what we knew of it, really was flat. But to try to imagine nine levels the size of Arizona stacked on top of one another was a bridge too far.

"It's a lot to take in, I know," Gillian said sympathetically. "But you made it here. In fact, you're the only person to ever make it out of the Bubble. To the best of my knowledge, anyway. For that in and of itself, I think you deserve the full scoop. Don't you?"

"The ship's really that big?" I asked after several minutes of silence.

"Like I said," Gillian said. "Half the size of the moon. And this warehouse section makes up less than half of the available space inside the craft."

"And the rest?"

"Contains everything necessary for large-scale long-range space travel. That includes maintaining a habitable environment: breathable air, water, and food, that sort of thing. Then there's all the staff tasked with maintaining optimal conditions in the Stacks, as well as all Stack-related LPRM functions. Add to that the ship's crew, maintenance personnel, engineers, botanists, biologists, physicists, chemists, and any other scientists you could think of, folks in manufacturing and food production, ship's security, repair staff, and the systems personnel responsible for ensuring that everything runs smoothly at all times, and you start to get an idea of the scale of what goes on here. You'd be amazed by how much effort goes into maintaining nine culturally distinct realities simultaneously. It's a logistical nightmare. That's why there are cities of technicians and social scientists assigned to monitoring and maintaining the Stacks. And I mean that literally. It requires three technicians per capita to keep everything sorted out and to keep it real in all nine levels."

"But there are only seven continents," I pointed out. "Why are there nine levels?"

"Smart girl," said Gillian. "It's because of Asia. It constituted the bulk of the world's population when we left and contained more distinct cultures than anyplace else. So it was assigned four levels."

"Four?" It still wasn't adding up.

"Antarctica was left out because it didn't have a significant enough number of folks to warrant including it. So with Africa, Europe, North American, South America, and Australia each having one level, that makes nine altogether.

"You wouldn't believe the amount of horse-trading and wrangling that went into figuring out who and what to include. It went on for the duration while the ship was being built."

"How long was that?"

"About a century. Toward the end of the twenty-first century, when things were getting really dicey on the planet, people woke up to the fact that tough compromises would have to be made if anybody at all was going to survive. It was decided that a ship would be built. It was generally considered to be our best shot at survival."

"And when did the ship actually leave Planet Earth?"

"At the end of the 22nd century, 2195 to be exact," Gillian said.

I took a deep breath. "So what happened?" I asked. "Why did we have to leave?" I dreaded hearing her answer almost as much as I wanted to know what she had to say.

Gillian gave me an appraising look, maybe to gauge my ability to take in what she was about to impart. She plunged ahead. "In a nutshell? Overpopulation."

"You mean like too many people?" I squeaked.

Gillian nodded. "And the environmental degradation that was produced as a result. You see, all the things that had brought unprecedented wealth and power to select countries in both the East and the West in the 20th century began to work against the survival of the human species as a whole in the 21st century. The entrepreneurial spirit, the profit motive, the ever-increasing demand for resources, territorial expansion—all of these began to take a serious toll on the quality of life on the planet, animal, plant, and human.

"It was in the first half of the 2000s that it became clear the problems on Planet Earth weren't going away. In fact, things had begun to deteriorate at an ever-accelerating rate. In spite of that, it took hurricanes, rising tides, drought, famine, fires, disease, countless wars, and masses of people dying from pollution-related ailments for people to realize the jig was up. By the end of the first century of the new millennium, things had gotten so bad that even the die-hard holdouts recognized that the best that could be hoped for was to get a small selection of Earth's population off the planet before everyone was dead. The nations of the world put aside their differences, in itself a small miracle, and rallied to build the Fortune's Fool in geosynchronous orbit. It took another century before the job was done, and we were underway."

"So what year are we in? Really?" I asked.

"2444."

"Wait a minute," I said. "Then why is it 1955 down there where I come from?"

"The Powers That Be decided that we should run the couple of hundred years prior to the big crash in 2100 over again. Basically to keep everybody in shape intellectually and psychologically on the long haul through space. If you overlook a couple of nasty World Wars, a Cold War, racial strife, and mounting environmental degradation, 1900 to 2100 was one of the most exciting and productive periods in human history. In the 1950s you're right at the start of an incredible technological revolution."

"And this technological revolution as you put it, wasn't enough to save us?"

"Unfortunately, no. In fact, faith in tech was one of the things that helped do us in. Everybody sort of expected science and technology to get us out of the mess we were in. There were strides made to be sure. But it was all too little too late."

"So if, as you say, we're reliving 1900 through 2100, is it just coincidence that we're in the mid-fifties?"

"Not quite. Right now we're 55 years into the second run through. And the reason we're running the fifties again is that this happens to be a time period when American optimism and confidence were at their peak. That's not to say everything was copacetic in the fifties, mind you. Racism was rampant and attitudes toward women were appalling. In many ways, it was the Dark Ages. But because of the prevailing conviction that the future was bright and anything was possible, it seemed as good a starting point as any for the new colony, at least according to the Designers. The pessimism that would set in later wasn't on the horizon yet, except for a few academics."

"Does that mean we're going to be landing soon?" It was amazing to me that I was ready to even begin to entertain what I was being told. But I'd been to a lot of Saturday matinées and had read a lot of sci-fi. And here I was, wasn't I? Looking down on the world I'd grown up in from a height of what? A couple of hundred miles? Who was I to argue?

"We're about two and a half years out from our final destination," Gillian said.

"Which is?"

"A relatively young planet called Epsilon 4."

"OK. But could we back up a second? So what actually happened to cause enough problems so that we had to leave in the first place?"

"Besides overpopulation? Let me see. Greed. Inertia. Myopia. Hubris. Denial. In other words, human nature. The signs had been there for well over a century before people started to come around. And by then it was too late. All that was left to do was to pull up stakes and get out of Dodge as quickly as possible."

She fell silent while we admired the view.

I looked at her. "You're serious about all this," I said. "This isn't some kind of sick joke."

"Scout's honor," she said, holding up her hand in the universal scout salute.

"So now that I've seen all this, are you going to have to kill me?"

"Nah," said my host. Her brow wrinkled. "But I have to tell you. The protocol for this particular situation, though we've never had to use it before, calls for us having to erase your short term memory. You won't remember any of this. Other than that, everything will be the same as before."

She saw my look. "Don't worry, it's a painless procedure. You won't feel a thing. How long before they miss you back home?"

"Not for another few hours," I said. "Aunt Trish is working and won't be home until tonight."

I don't know why I trusted Gillian. Maybe because of her

no-nonsense demeanor in delivering the Cliff Notes version of the end of the world. It was like there was no room for BS in her personality. Or maybe it was the mean-looking ray gun she carried, along her thigh. I'd never seen anyone quite like her before. The closest I could figure was that she was some kind of futuristic cop.

"Are you a cop?" I asked.

"Sort of. As I said, I help with ship's security. But never mind that. If nobody's going to fret about you for a while I can show you around a little before I send you back. How does that sound?"

14

Above And Beyond

We lingered a while longer at the railing. Looking down, I could make out the mountains east of our house. They were like the wrinkles of an elephant's hide. But we were way too high up to see the house itself. Rattlesnake Junction was barely a smudge. Tucson was a larger smudge to the southwest, and there was Phoenix to the north. Everything else was swallowed in haze and clouds.

I expected to see an elevator shaft rising from the hills behind the house to the catwalk we were on, but there was none.

"As soon as you cleared the mountain you were airborne," Gillian explained. "It helps to think of the elevator as a rocket. Only it isn't a rocket. It works by magnetic induction. LPRM made sure no one could see the elevator on the ascent."

"You called the people down there Settlers. What does that mean exactly?"

"It means you'll be settling Epsilon 4. You're like the pioneers that settled the American West and the Fortune's Fool is kind of like your personal wagon train across the prairie, so to speak. You are the most important thing about this mission. Our priority is to get you to Epsilon 4 and then get you safely situated there. That's our primary goal. Otherwise, this two hundred and fifty-year journey across the galaxy would have been for nothing."

"Why aren't we, us Settlers I mean, in on it? It seems we could have been helping out all this time instead of living in some kind of dream world. That's what we've been doing, isn't it? Sleeping walking through a repeat of what to you is ancient history?"

"That's one way to look at it," said Gillian. "I think the Designers thought there was a survival advantage to this arrangement. They felt your innocence would give you an edge. Knowing you're on a spaceship creates its own set of social and political interrelationships. There's a command hierarchy, for instance. Everybody has their place within that hierarchy. Down there, you don't have any of that. The political and social institutions you have are identical to the ones that were there in the 50s."

"Except they're not," I pointed out. "They're created by this lap room you've been talking about. They're not really real. Nothing outside of Arizona is. Right?"

"True. But they're represented as accurately and faithfully as possible. National politics, world events, in fact, anything that doesn't happen in Arizona is replicated down to the smallest detail and amplified through your news sources, communications, and other cultural touchstones just as it was then. Aside from that, it's strictly hands-off."

"Why Arizona?"

"Besides being the optimal size to fit in the hold? I'd have to say it's probably because the terrain is supposed to be somewhat similar to Epsilon 4, your future home. They say it's a lot like the American Southwest used to be a few hundred million years ago give or take."

Something about the way she said this last part made me think there wasn't much left of the original American Southwest back on Planet Earth.

She seemed to read my thoughts. "The world as you know it no longer exists. It's just a lump of rock now, free from life forms. Not much different from the moon. The atmosphere's gone. The air's unbreathable. Life can no longer exist there."

We started to walk along the gangplank. I noticed again the lines of light I'd seen earlier in the darkness above.

"Those are trains and shuttles that connect to all parts of the ship," Gillian explained, falling easily into the role of tour guide. "There's a tram station up ahead."

I could see an elongated building a couple of hundred yards away. A train was leaving the station while we looked on. It reminded me of pictures I'd seen of the monorail at the new Disneyland theme park in Anaheim, California. It was weird to think that Disneyland, and California itself, only existed as a simulation. That would make the Disneyland we knew a simulation of a simulation.

"So this lap room as you call it has been manipulating time as well as space," I said.

"Indeed," said Gillian. "LPRM works across four dimensions. Instead of just recreating exotic locales, for instance, it's a time machine. It can recreate all the features of a time and place that we have temporal data for."

"Do you know how weird it is to me, knowing that?"

"I'm sorry," Gillian said sympathetically. "But remember, you weren't supposed to see this. If you hadn't ended up here, you wouldn't have been any the wiser until the moment you were transferred to the surface of the new planet, along with everybody else in the Stacks. It's only OK for me to tell you these things now because I know you won't remember any of this when you leave here."

15

The Captain

I was still wrestling with the notion that I'd been living on a piece of Planet Earth that was in the trunk of some kind of outrageously large space vehicle, traveling at close to the speed of light. And I was doing my darnedest not to think of the other eight levels stacked above and below this one.

"Stay behind me," Gillian said with sudden urgency. She got in front of me and shielded me with her arm, while she cleared her gun in one fluid motion. A blast of light singed a section of the gangway about four feet ahead of us, sending sparks flying.

Gillian fired a bolt of light, and I swear I heard something that sounded like, "Ooof!"

"Got 'im," said Gillian with satisfaction, blowing on the end of her weapon as if it were a '45 in an old Western, which it definitely was not. She held the ray gun at the ready for a moment longer, just in case.

"What was that?" I asked.

"A Grey," she said matter-of-factly.

"A what?"

Gillian seemed to be running a quick calculation in her head and came to some sort of conclusion. "Maybe you heard about the space aliens that were supposed to have crash-landed in New Mexico in the late Forties? Little gray creatures with big almond-shaped eyes?"

"Sure," I said. "My Grandpa Kurt and his friend, Big Al, are always going on about Roswell and space aliens."

Gillian stopped in her tracks. "Wait a minute," she said. "Big Al. You said Big Al, right?"

I nodded, wondering where this was going. "Big guy. Red-faced. Loves Hawaiian shirts. Owns a wrecking yard in Rattlesnake Junction? That's where I'm from, by the way."

Gillian's face clouded over. "I guess it could be him. Sure sounds like him, minus the shirts of course." She shook her head and pursed her lips in disapproval. "I thought it was only a rumor."

"What about Big Al?"

"Never mind," said Gillian, obviously peeved. "But It figures. Trust me."

"Who's Big Al to you?"

"Let's just say he's the one that makes the rules around here. And rule number one is, stay out of New Arizona. Never engage the Settlers in any shape or form."

"You mean he's some kind of big deal up here?'

"He's the head honcho," said Gillian, still seething. "He's the captain of the Fortune's Fool."

16

Shades Of Gray

Big Al, Grandpa Kurt's best friend, was the captain of the massive spaceship we were on? I guess it wasn't any more far-fetched than anything else I'd heard in the last half hour. I needed to focus. I needed to get my feet under me.

"About this 'Grey' you were mentioning," I said.

"The one that was taking potshots at us? They can be pesky buggers. Small but tough as nails. They can take a direct hit at half pulse and get back up a minute later, dust themselves off, and go on about their business like nothing happened."

"So did they crash-land in the desert in New Mexico in the late forties, like people say?"

"Yup," said Gillian. "As you can see, they're still around. They're definitely not an LPRM simulation."

"But how are they here now? How did they get on the ship in the first place?"

"They stowed away when we took off from Earth. They've been with us ever since. They fall into two categories: the good Greys and the bad Greys. The good Greys are actually very useful. The others are a nuisance. But we try to be tolerant."

"Didn't one just try to kill us?"

"Kill might be a bit strong," Gillian said. "Their weapons can cause damage, so you want to steer clear. But they're such lousy shots, they're not much of a danger to anyone but themselves."

47

We continued our walk toward the tram station up ahead. I found myself staring into the rafters in case another ambush might be forthcoming. The sun was there, almost directly overhead. But like, everything else, it wasn't the real sun. It was a much smaller version, not more than a couple of hundred miles away from what I could tell. It wasn't significantly brighter nor warmer at this altitude than it had been on the ground.

"It's a facsimile," Gillian stated. "It doesn't actually do anything but generate light. From the ground, it's supposed to look and act like the real thing. But the weather, the air temperature, the seasons are all controlled from up here."

I continued to peer into the darkness above us, trying to see what else was there.

"The next level is several hundred miles away," Gillian said. "The modules that control the climate down below are located between here and there. They're housed behind bulkheads, so there's not much to see. We try to keep the immediate area around the bubble clear, of course. If you're into tech, we can grab a shuttle and go higher."

I wasn't sure whether I was into "tech" or not.

"You might be more interested in the command and control center. We could take a peek at where we're going from the Viewing Deck. We're just coming up on the system that contains Epsilon 4."

"When did you say we were due to arrive?" I asked.

"Year and a half, give or take," said Gillian.

Something beeped. I swear it sounded like "In The Mood" being played by a munchkin orchestra. "Just a minute," Gillian said. "I've got to take this." She turned away from me and started talking to somebody who wasn't present. I didn't see a headset, but obviously there was one. It made sense given her position with ship's security.

I could tell from her end of the conversation that there was a problem.

She turned back to me after a few seconds and said, "Something's come up. We're going to have to cut our tour short." She began to steer me back the way we'd come.

"What's going on?" I inquired.

48

She sighed. "There's a slight problem at the command center."

I could tell there was more to it than she was letting on. "Everything going to be OK?"

She looked around. "I suppose it wouldn't matter if I told you. The Greys are the least of our worries right now. There's been a kerfuffle brewing for a while between the two major factions on board the ship. It boils down to a power struggle. Lately, it's threatening to boil over. It's too complicated to go into right now. But suffice it to say, the threat is serious. It could potentially disrupt the mission if it gets out of hand. We can't afford that, especially this late in the game. The next couple of years are going to be crucial."

She looked around again, scanning our surroundings on high alert. It felt like we might be under attack at any moment. But everything looked like it had a moment before. She made an obvious effort to calm herself.

"I'm sorry," she said. "But we've got to get you back home."

I got a last long look at the bright vastness below before I was ushered back to the elevator. Gillian must have pulled out some kind of electronic gizmo as we were running and zapped me with it.

The next thing I knew I was in the tunnel again. The elevators were nowhere in sight and I had no recollection of them, of Gillian, or anything else I'd just heard or seen.

THE BUBBLE

17

Business As Usual

Grandpa Kurt wasn't too surprised to hear I'd gone back to the cave without him. But I could tell he was disappointed he hadn't been able to go with me. When I got home he was back in the garage tinkering on his Studebaker again, his doctor-advised prohibition against working on cars obviously forgotten.

He straightened up when I came in and wiped his hands on a rag. "So?" he said. He could tell from my clothes and gear I'd been out hiking. It wasn't hard to guess the rest.

"There was nothing there," I told him truthfully. But even as I said it something tugged at my memory. Nothing emerged. "I must have gone a mile into the hillside. And there was nothing."

"But you got to the end of the tunnel, right?"

"Yeah," I said, seeing in my mind's eye a wall of solid granite. "It just came to a dead stop."

"And the thing that sent you in there to begin with, the silver armadillo, you didn't find it?"

What he said stumped me at first. Then gradually I seemed to remember what he was referring to. It was the reason I'd gone back up to the cave to begin with, I realized. And I think that elusive realization was what tipped me off. Something *had* happened in that cave. But for the life of me, I couldn't conjure up what it was. It bugged me, but that didn't help. "Nope," I said.

"You OK?" he asked me. "You look a little pale."

"I'm fine," I said. "I'm just glad you're back home and not in the hospital anymore."

"Maybe when I'm feeling a hundred percent, we'll go back up the canyon and take a look around together," he said. "What do you say?"

I nodded. But something told me this might not be such a good idea.

My adventures outside the Bubble were forgotten. Mostly. Aside from a few weird dreams about being suspended high above the desert and talking to a shadowy someone, that was it. The dreams quickly faded when I got up to start the day.

Grandpa Kurt continued to improve from his surgery. I think what I'd told him about the cave dead-ending back in the mountain had taken the wind out of his sails because exploring the cave hadn't come up again.

I'd been hanging out with a tall skinny guy off and on since the beginning of my junior year. His name was Rory. He was what was called a "brain" at school. He wore glasses, white T-shirts, and black jeans and was considered uncool by the other kids. He was an outsider, like me.

It was no big deal. We liked some of the same things is all. Like going to movie matinées on Saturdays. He liked science fiction and horror movies, and I did too. The Saturday matinée at the Rialto played flicks like Superman and the Mole Men and The Thing From Another World. I had posters from my favorites plastered all over my room. War of the Worlds, Red Planet Mars, When Worlds Collide, 20000 Leagues Under the Sea, THEM, The Creature From the Black Lagoon, and several lesser-known offerings like Cat Women of the Moon and Zombies of the Stratosphere.

We tried kissing one time. Kids were going steady all around us, and I guess we wanted to see what the fuss was about. Not much, it turned out. I don't think either of us was ready for it. He tasted like garlic and Juicy Fruit gum, and I probably smelled like motor oil. If romance was all about somebody sweeping you off your feet, this wasn't that. When that did happen someday, I figured this kissing business would make more sense.

We went to the county fair that fall and ate cotton candy and caramel apples. Rory won a big panda and proudly presented it to me. But then I was stuck lugging it around for half the night. I eventually wised up and asked him nicely to take it off my hands for a while. He carried it until he was gasping and sweat was popping out on his forehead. I guess chivalry was not dead after all.

We were on our way to the Ferris wheel when I spied a familiar face in one of the booths. It was Big Al from the wrecking yard. I went over to say "hi." He explained that he was moonlighting at the fair. They needed people to man the booths, and he had volunteered.

"How's your Grandpappy doing?" he asked. He looked the same as always. Big smile on his face and the red of his "Irish" skin clashing with his bright-colored Hawaiian shirt.

"He's OK," I said. "He's getting back into the swing of things."

"Tell him to stop by the yard. I got something for that Studebaker of his."

"I will," I said, and Rory and I continued on our way.

Meeting up with Big Al like that jogged my memory. There was something about him that it felt like I knew or should know, but I couldn't quite put my finger on it. I had a momentary image of being in a world within a world, like one of those Russian nesting dolls. Suddenly I was having trouble breathing.

"Are you feeling alright?' Rory asked me, concern on his face.

"Fine," I said. "Just fine."

In reality, I was still feeling queasy, like when you're high up and looking down. Vertigo. That was it. But that quickly changed into a weird kind of exhilaration. Suddenly I felt like I was on top of the world. All-powerful. Was I getting religion in my teens? I hoped not. I'd never had much use for it and didn't want to start now. But I couldn't explain what I was feeling or why. What was happening to me?

That night I found myself thinking of things I hadn't given much thought to before. Like where did we come from? Where were we going? Who were we exactly?

I saw Big Al's ruddy smiling face in my mind. For some reason, I thought he might have the answers to at least some of these questions. As to why this would be so, I had no idea. All I knew was that I needed to talk to him. And the sooner, the better.

18

Rockin' Pneumonia

ut the conversation with Big Al didn't happen for a while. Grandpa's recovery was slower than hoped. So a trip to the wrecking yard was postponed until he felt stronger. In the meantime, I stayed caught up with my classes and did my work at Ted's after school as usual. But everything seemed a little off. I found myself daydreaming a lot, both at school and at work. When Ted called me out for absent-mindedness a couple of times, I decided I'd better shape up.

In history class I found myself questioning what I was hearing, wondering whether it was really true. I had the nagging feeling I was getting only part of the story. The American revolution, Abe Lincoln, the World Wars, all of it. Then I'd have to shake myself out of it. What was I thinking? Was this some kind of rebellion against authority I was experiencing, this not trusting or believing what I was being told? Or was it something worse? Was I becoming unhinged? I hoped not. In those moments it seemed even more urgent that I talk to Big Al.

What helped to keep me sane during this period of time was, of all things, music. A major sea change in popular music was in full swing in late '55. As the year was on the cusp of turning into '56 I'd started listening to the radio. While Grandpa and Trish were in the living room watching Jack Benny and Steve Allen, I was in the kitchen with my ear pressed to our Marconi radio.

It had started with a single by an unknown singer from Tennessee that had been released earlier that year on Sun Records in Memphis called "That's Alright, Mama". I'd been following everything Elvis did since. I knew, for instance, that he'd recently gone over to RCA from Sun and that he had a record due out on that label in just a few weeks. In January to be exact.

The music was the perfect companion to my own restlessness. It was new and wild enough to distract me from my brooding questions and doubts. It grabbed my attention and held it.

My interests began to shift from B movies to rock n roll. And it wasn't long before the posters in my room began to reflect that change. Images of Elvis, Jerry Lee, and Fats Domino joined The Creature From the Black Lagoon and THEM on my walls.

I dragged Rory out to see Blackboard Jungle just before Christmas, knowing in advance that all the rock 'n' roll in the movie was right there in the opening credits. He didn't get it, didn't understand my excitement. This didn't bode well for our relationship, I remember thinking at the time.

There were other changes happening as well. A dazzling new crop of cars was rolling out of Detroit. Engines were getting beefier. Colors were getting bolder. And the designs themselves were getting longer, lower, sleeker, and shinier. You didn't have to look any further than the miniature portholes and swept-back fins on the latest Buicks and Oldsmobiles to see that they drew their inspiration from movie rocket ships.

Rock 'n' roll and V-8 engines seemed made for each other. They both got the adrenalin pumping. I'd had my driver's license since I'd turned 16. But Grandpa Kurt had convinced me to save my money and hold off on getting my own car until I turned 17. And when I did, you can bet I was paying special attention to the cars that came into the shop as possible candidates for a first car. I was leaning towards a T-bird or a Vette, all the while knowing they were way beyond my budget. Even Ford's mid-priced Fairlane and the Chevy Bel Air were out of range. A used car would be the best I could hope for, I figured. But a girl could dream.

And dream I did. Who said my car would have to be an old stock car anyway? Instead of settling for an old clunker from the late thirties or forties, I could use my automotive chops to build a street rod from scratch, using parts from the shop and from the wrecking yard. I'd need Grandpa's permission, but it could be done. I knew the small initial financial investment would have to be supplemented by an outsized expenditure of time and energy on my part. But that was OK. I was ready to put in the hours if it meant having a car like no other. It would be a fun challenge and right up my alley as a master mechanic. And, I thought, with a little diplomacy it might be up Grandpa's alley too. I knew that if I could get him involved, anything was possible.

"Are you crazy, Rose?" Kurt exclaimed when I broached the subject. "I'm not going to help you build yourself a street racing death trap."

"I'm already a good driver. You know that. Have I ever done anything crazy behind the wheel?" I knew it was the wrong angle as soon as the words were out of my mouth.

"What about that wheelie you pulled in cousin Tony's coupe a few years back? Remember? At the Fourth of July barbecue?"

"I was testing the clutch," I protested. "My foot slipped. And besides, I was fourteen at the time. I could barely reach the pedals. I've matured a lot since then."

"Uh Huh," said Grandpa Kurt. "You weren't supposed to be anywhere near that car."

"But that was three years ago. Have I ever gotten a ticket or done anything crazy in a car since I got my license?"

He couldn't deny it was true. Not only was I an outstanding mechanic, I was a cool head behind the wheel. Nothing rattled me.

"Time goes by faster when you're aged," I said philosophically, just to pull his chain. "Three years to you is like twenty to someone young, like me."

"Kind of like dog years," Grandpa Kurt said with a chortle.

"Woof," I said with a laugh.

"Aged, huh?" Kurt said. "OK. I told you we'd get you a car when you turned 17. And I know you've been patient. Tell you what. When Ted starts letting you do rebuilds, we'll see where we stand with getting you something to drive."

I nodded. I knew I had him. He wanted to build a street rod as much as I did.

19

The Birth Of The Roadrunners

I didn't just like listening to rock 'n' roll, I was itching to play it. I got a Silverstone steel-string guitar from Santa that Christmas. The action was really high, and it was a bear to play. My fingers didn't actually bleed, but they came darn close.

I knew pretty quick that the sound of the acoustic wasn't what I was looking for. I needed something with more oomph. I lucked into a used Gibson ES-295 one day at the local pawn shop for $65. I was well aware it was the guitar that Scotty Moore played on most of the sessions at Sun records. It was a lot of moolah for a high school kid like me. But I'd been saving my money from my job at Ted's for the better part of a year by then. It was meant for college, I knew. But I wanted the guitar badly enough to shell out some of my hard-earned savings for it.

It wasn't until I got it home that I realized I'd need an amplifier as well. I hurried back to the same pawn shop and found a blond Fender Princeton that was all chafed and banged up for 20 bucks. It looked like it had been dragged behind a truck across 100 miles of bad road, but it sounded pretty good. Between the guitar and the amp, I could produce a sound that I liked.

I knew this was just the start, the first step down rockabilly road. Going electric I'd need other musicians to play with. Not having that many friends, the problem seemed daunting at first. But that changed when I joined the marching band at the high school. There wasn't much call for a guitarist, so I became a cymbal player. I was really only scouting out potential members for the band I was forming anyway.

None of the guys there took me seriously when I told them I was forming a rock 'n' roll group. They just looked at me like I was speaking in tongues. They couldn't wrap their minds around a girl wanting to play rock 'n' roll. It made their brains explode.

But there were a couple of girls in the marching band who perked up at the mention. One was a black girl named Melissa Jordan. She played the tuba. The other was an Apache Indian named Tina Shining Cloud from the nearby San Tomas reservation. She played the flute mostly but could sing and play various traditional percussion instruments as well. Tina had the most musical experience of the three of us, being a regular player at tribal functions on the Rez. But she liked rock 'n' roll as much as I did. And seeing our set up, she thought she could contribute the most as a drummer.

With Melissa on tuba, Tina on a big skin drum she'd brought with her from the Rez, and me and my hollow-body Gibson guitar we weren't exactly rock 'n' roll. But we were getting there. We made a surprising amount of noise, the three of us. With a few adjustments, it felt like it could work. Melissa had aspirations to get an upright bass and Tina wanted to get a real drum kit eventually. But we actually sounded pretty nifty, I thought, just as we were. I doubted there was anyone around who sounded like we did and, rebel that I was becoming, I figured that for a good thing.

Tina was the only one of us who could sing for beans. The other thing that recommended her for the post of lead singer was that she could project over the noise of the instruments without the need for extra amplification. That meant we were ready to play right off the bat. A dedicated amplifier and speaker for vocals wasn't going to be in the cards for a while yet, I was pretty sure.

And we discovered it wasn't essential anyway. All it took was plugging a microphone directly into my guitar amp through the extra input. It wasn't very hi-fi. But the roughness of the sound seemed to suit the music. Plus, it took some of the pressure off of Tina's pipes.

Now she could be heard halfway down the block without breaking a sweat.

We were playing anything we could put a backbeat to. It turned out we liked a lot of the same music. We listened to any blues and R&B we could get our hands on. A lot of it was called "race music." We loved Big Mama Thornton, Big Joe Turner, Ruth Brown, and Etta James. And we found we shared a love of Sister Rosetta Tharp. But looking back on it now, I think I was angling more toward rockabilly right out of the chute. I loved that Sun records sound. It's what my guitar seemed to want to play.

We called ourselves the Rattlesnake Junction Roadrunners, which we later shortened to The Roadrunners.

So between school, work, and band practice, I was staying pretty busy. In the meantime, Grandpa Kurt had slowly but surely gotten his feet back under him and was his usual self again.

I still hadn't talked to Big Al, but by now even my reasons for needing to talk to him had faded from memory and with them any sense of urgency. I was curious what Big Al had for Grandpa Kurt's Studebaker and to see whether he had any parts for my soon-to-be-built street rod. But that was it.

20

My Conversation With Big Al

We finally got around to visiting the wrecking yard on a Saturday in February. It had been a frosty morning, and the chill lingered until late morning when the sun emerged in full force from the tule fog. Not long after I'd gotten my driver's license, I'd rescued an old Fiat hardtop that had been towed into Ted's one night and abandoned there. I figured it might be useful as a second car for grandpa, and figured I'd be able to use it too. We worked on it and got it to run. I had a car to drive when I needed it, and grandpa didn't have to put the Studebaker back together every time he needed to run into town for groceries. Unfortunately, it was always breaking down. It wasn't that we minded fixing it. It was that the cost for parts was starting to mount up. We agreed we'd sell it at the earliest opportunity. But for now, it was how we were getting around, he and I.

It was close to noon when we drove in the gate at Big Al's. We did a slow circuit of the stacks before pulling up in front of the low, flat building near the entry that was Big Al's parts emporium and also doubled as his office. Sometimes we ran into Big Al among the neatly stacked auto carcasses. Not today.

He came out the front door with a wide smile on his face for Grandpa Kurt. It had been a few months since Grandpa's last visit, but he acted like it had been years. Nothing like a major health scare to inspire an appreciation for those near and dear to us. Clearly, Al was pleased as punch to see Kurt. He was wearing a gaudy Hawaiian shirt covered with painted illustrations of paneled station wagons arranged against a neon blue ocean backdrop. I wondered whether he'd actually ever been to Hawaii.

Big Al looked to be in his fifties or early sixties, if I was any judge, and had the appearance of having been around some, so I figured it was possible he'd made it to the islands at some point. I personally didn't know anyone who had ever been. I guess that gave him an exotic air, though in all other respects he looked like a local yokel. I thought of what Trish had said about his probable Irish heritage. By now I'd gotten to like Big Al as much as anyone, but I sincerely hoped we weren't related. He had on his utilitarian scuffed tan work boots with thick lug soles that were probably a must working around broken glass and jagged, razor-sharp pieces of metal all day.

He motioned Grandpa Kurt over and showed him a matching pair of Studebaker side mirrors he'd found. Kurt looked like he'd won the jackpot. In the meantime, I wandered off with my eye out for prospects for a future vehicle for myself. But all the auto bodies in the immediate vicinity were lost causes.

When I got back to the shed, Big Al was there alone. "You're grandpa's doing some window shopping," Big Al explained. "He's down in the rows somewhere."

I nodded feeling kind of awkward without Grandpa around.

Then out of the blue, Al said, "Kurt mentioned you'd found something in the hills behind your house, a cave or something." He said it casually, but he was looking closely at me as he said it.

"Yeah," I said. "I mean, no."

"So," he said mildly, hands on his hips. "Which is it? Yes or no?"

"Nope," I said. For a second there had been something. But then it was gone. It was the weirdest thing. For an instant, I saw two versions of the cave in my mind. One dead-ended in the rock wall. The other contained a couple of elevators. I couldn't swear which version was real.

I didn't want to seem like a complete idiot, so I said, "I mean yes, there was a cave. But, no, there was nothing in it."

"You sure?"

I nodded my head. The scenario with the elevators seemed too bizarre to be believable. I chose the more likely option.

"But you poked around some, right?"

I didn't know why he was so interested. "Uh huh," I said, straining to see if I could locate Grandpa Kurt out in the stacks. Revisiting my visit to the cave was not something I wanted to do. It made me really uneasy for some reason. Just thinking about it was starting to make me nauseous.

"You don't look too good," Big Al said. "You need a bathroom? There's one inside." There was a look of genuine concern on his face.

"No," I said, "I'm alright." I gulped a couple of times. "What about you?" I said trying to change the subject. "Have you always worked in the wrecking and salvage business?"

"Nah," he said smiling broadly again. He reminded me of a politician with his white teeth and ready smile. He had a knack for putting you at ease. I could see why people liked him. He was a likable guy. And he always had a twinkle in his eye, like you and he were in on a secret. "I've worn a number of hats in my life," he said. "But I have to say this is my favorite job. It's peaceful and uncomplicated. And it's always interesting to see what little treasures the tide washes up on my little personal beach here."

Suddenly I saw an image of myself looking down on this landscape from a great height. Someone was standing at my shoulder telling me something about Big Al. Something important. No. Saying HE was important.

"Have you ever been the captain of a ship?" I blurted.

His eyes widened for a second. I could tell I'd surprised him.

"Like a sea ship," I clarified.

He nodded slowly, still smiling, and said, "I've done some captaining. Not a sea ship exactly."

I was about to ask him what he meant when Grandpa Kurt returned lugging a chrome fender behind him.

"Let's see if this'll work on the Studebaker," he said, propping it up on one end and wiping his brow. "Oh, and Rose here is on the lookout for some parts for a car she wants to build. I told her I'd help her put something together as soon as she starts doing rebuilds for Ted."

"That right?" said Big Al, seeming to appraise me in a new light.

"I have a feeling that's going to be happening soon," Grandpa said. "I have it on good authority that Ted just lost his main engine guy. Greener pastures."

This was the first I'd heard of it. I hadn't seen Felix around the shop for a week or so. I'd just assumed he'd gone on Christmas vacation early. I felt my cheeks glowing. I was going to be promoted to building engines!

"She wants to build a dragster, I think," Grandpa was saying. He chuckled, and Big Al chuckled right along with him. "But some kind of street-legal rod should do."

"I'll keep my eyes peeled for prospects," Al said amiably. "I might even have a straight frame back there somewhere. I'll need to check. I'm assuming you'll be looking for something with eight cylinders?"

"Straight 6 would do fine," Kurt said. "It's OK if it doesn't crack 10 seconds in the quarter-mile," he added, to make it clear where he stood on the matter of me having a hot rod as a first car.

"Well, well, well," said Al. "Let's see what we can come up with."

I just sighed. What was the point of building a street rod if it didn't have eight cylinders, preferably in a V-8 format?

It's no fun being a teenager. The grownups hold all the cards. Big Al seemed to know what I was thinking. He gave me a big wink when he knew Grandpa wasn't looking. So I had reason to hope.

21

The Roadrunners Big Debut

Grandpa settled up with Big Al, and the two of them toted the chrome fender back to the Fiat. It barely fit with the two of us in there. But it worked with both ends sticking out the side windows in the back seat further than was strictly legal. But we made it to the house without getting stopped. When we pulled into the driveway, we saw that Aunt Trish was home. Her cute two-tone turquoise and white T-bird coupe was parked in the driveway.

"What's Big Al's story anyway?" I asked Grandpa Kurt as we hauled the Studebaker fender into the garage.

"I've known Big Al for years now," Kurt said thoughtfully. "But I honestly can't say I know much about the man. It's not that he's secretive exactly. He just doesn't talk a lot about himself. It's obvious he's been around some. He seems to know a lot about a lot of things. He can hold forth for an hour on any topic you could name. I don't know why he's here, in this town, to be honest. He could be governor of the state if he wanted to be."

"Maybe he ran afoul of the law back east somewhere," I suggested helpfully, "and is hiding out here in desert country."

"He's been here a long time," Grandpa said dubiously. "I may not know the details of his past, but I've known him long enough to have gotten a pretty good sense of his character. He's a good guy. You become a pretty good judge of people when you've put in as much time in retail as I have. And it's not like he's inconspicuous. Everybody knows Al."

"Maybe he just wants a simple life. And the wrecking yard is a way to make an honest living and still be his own boss."

"That sounds about right." Grandpa Kurt said. "He seems to think there are big changes in the offing for the entire planet, but he's never been very specific about what those changes might entail."

"He's not one of those 'end of the world' nuts, is he?"

"I don't think so. He's a firm believer in science, as far as I can tell." He saw the skeptical look on my face. He knew what I thought of Big Al's "scientific" theories, regardless of how much I might like the man personally.

What Grandpa didn't realize was that I was no longer quite as skeptical about his theory that the earth was flat as I had once been, though I couldn't have told you what had happened to change my mind.

In the meantime, the Rattlesnake Junction Roadrunners, now just the Roadrunners, had their first gig booked. It was a dance to be held in the high school auditorium on the second Friday in March.

We were pretty nervous, it being our debut performance. But there was more to it than that. Women combos were scarce in the fifties, never mind that one of us was black and the other American Indian. And no matter how much we told ourselves it didn't matter, it mattered. It was a big deal to be playing in front of an audience for the first time. We had no way of knowing how people would react.

My bandmates were determined not to leave anything to chance. Melissa brought along her brother, an all-American tackle who was home for the weekend from the University of Arizona. And Tina brought along six of the biggest Indians I'd ever seen. Three were her brothers. And the other three were friends of theirs from the Rez. So even if anyone was inclined to mess with us for being girls playing rock 'n' roll, they had more than a half dozen reasons to think twice.

That didn't prevent us from getting some hard stares, especially from the jocks and their girlfriends. The girls didn't like it that their boyfriends were focused on us the entire evening, even though their boyfriends displayed nothing but contempt for us for being the upstarts they considered us to be. I recognized a couple of the girls as bullies that I'd had run-ins with in junior high. I couldn't deny a certain satisfaction in seeing them stew.

But as it turned out, there were a lot more kids who seemed to like what we were doing. The greasers, the Marlon Brando and James Dean types, and their girls seemed to be digging our music. It was still early days for rockabilly and rock 'n' roll. There just wasn't that much of it around. So maybe it was just that they weren't too picky about the package it came in.

After a couple of numbers during which everybody just stood around checking everybody else out, the dance floor began to fill. Pretty soon the hall was moving and grooving. The Roadrunners were off and running.

At a certain point toward the end of the first set, I noticed that the tuba was starting to take its toll on Melissa. Huffing air in and out like a bellows between songs, it was clear she was on the verge of collapsing. So we called an early break.

"Man," Mel said, gasping for breath. "I'm gonna have to get me that stand-up bass, and soon. I don't know if I'll be able to make it through the next set, let alone the next gig if there is one."

"Just lay back a little," Tina suggested to her. "We're all a little nervous here and trying too hard. You're doing great. They love you. Who else has got a tuba doing the bass parts this side of the border?"

I could tell Mel was listening to what Tina was saying. But I knew it wouldn't be long before she was hitting her old man up for the cash to buy that upright bass.

22

Off And Running

Word spread, and pretty soon we were playing regularly around town. Mostly it was parties, but we continued to get gigs at the high school and even a few at the local junior college. We played at the reservation a few times, too. The home crowd would go nuts for Tina. Somebody passed the hat for her and pretty soon she had the drum kit she'd been hankering for. But every now and then she'd trot out the big skin drum for old time's sake to thundering applause.

We had something. It took hearing it a lot of times from a lot of different people for it to eventually sink in. Four months after we'd started rehearsing we had time booked at a local recording studio. It was the size of a two-car garage. In fact, it *was* a two-car garage that had been remodeled. But it was big enough for us to set up in, even with the control booth taking up a quarter of the space. I thought of it as Rattlesnake Junction's answer to Sun Records. I'd seen pictures of Sun, and that studio didn't look much bigger than this. There was a mixing desk in the control booth with a bunch of knobs on it and a two-track tape machine.

We'd written a couple of songs by then. But we started off by recording our version of "Blue Suede Shoes" and "Trying to Get to You," songs that had come out on the first Elvis RCA release. Tina stuck to the tribal drum and Melissa was honking away on the tuba while I was flailing away on the Gibson. I'd stumbled on that

71

distorted sound that Link Wray would popularize a couple of years later on "Rumble." One of the tubes in my amp was on the blink and created this buzzing, fuzzy kind of tone. The volume suffered a bit, but when I turned the amp up to ten it sounded like Godzilla on a rampage. With Tina's raspy vocal delivery and her Sacajawea looks I figured we couldn't lose.

It didn't happen for us overnight, but we became known around town over the course of the next few months. We'd developed enough of a following with our weekend gigs that most everybody in town had at least heard of the Roadrunners. We sold 500 singles the first week. It would take a little longer for us to reach a wider audience, but that was OK. We were high school juniors after all, so there was a limit to the amount of promotion we could realistically undertake.

I got the job rebuilding engines at Ted's just before our first gig. True to his word, Big Al joined forces with Grandpa Kurt to build me a worthy street machine. Grandpa's reluctance to build me a car that was too powerful and too fast somehow fell by the wayside as the challenge of creating a world-class street rod from the ground up took hold. His single-minded determination was enough to give even me pause. Grandpa wasn't one for half measures, much as he liked to preach moderation. I think I inherited a little of that single-minded focus from him, especially when applied to something I cared about. Maybe more than a little.

Big Al notified Grandpa Kurt when a '41 Willys arrived at the wrecking yard. The body was pretty banged up, but the frame was straight. Kurt had Al pull a 331-cubic-inch engine out of a '53 Chrysler that had been rear-ended by a locomotive or a semi, take your pick, and then been tossed in a cement mixer. There was nothing wrong with the engine, however. The Chrysler Firepower Hemi was the biggest stock engine out there. I knew it was going to be fun to work on.

Big Al had found a recent transmission that was in decent shape to go along with the Chrysler Hemi. But it was. . .an automatic. Naturally, I would have preferred a stick shift. Stick shifts were what most racers used. It gave you more control if you were in an endurance race like the Formula One. But I wasn't planning on doing any Formula One racing anytime soon. Drag racing, now that was another matter. The trans being a Dual-Range Hydra-Matic made specifically for the Willys meant it was about as up-to-date as it could be. But unless you had the shifting dexterity of Juan Manuel Fangio, the Hydra-Matic would probably more than hold its own in the quarter-mile. All you had to do was put the hammer down and let the Hemi V-8 do the rest.

The gauntlet had been thrown down for Grandpa and me both with this project. Whether we'd rise to the challenge was entirely up to us.

Big Al brought the Willys body, the engine, and the transmission over to our house on his flatbed truck which had the Big Al Wrecking and Salvage moniker on the side over a cartoon illustration of a rocket ship blasting off against Saturn in the background. Maybe it should have jogged my memory, but it didn't. I just thought it was cool.

The Willys was rolled down the ramp. The engine and transmission were lowered by crane from the flatbed and then rolled into the garage on a dolly. Total cost for the car and engine? $150, thanks to Big Al's more than generous special discount.

"I can't tell you how much I appreciate this," I told him with total sincerity. My dream car was now sitting in the garage of my house. In pieces, granted, but it wasn't hard to imagine the finished product. At least for me.

"Can't wait to see what you come up with," Big Al said, beaming first at me and then at Grandpa Kurt.

"Me too," said Kurt. "I don't want to build anything Rose is going to get hurt in. There's safe and there's fast."

Big Al smiled wryly. "Well, it shouldn't come as a surprise that if you drop that Chrysler V-8 onto that lightweight Willy's frame, you're going to have a guided missile on your hands. It'll be the fastest car in town, maybe in the state." He laughed.

Grandpa Kurt sobered up. "We just have to make sure it'll be safe if I'm going to allow Rose anywhere near the driver's seat."

Sure, Grandpa, sure.

Things went on as usual. If you call playing in an all-girl, multi-ethnic band in the fifties, usual. But we had a lot going for us. We had Tina. She was awe-inspiring. Not many people would have disputed that. She was the Indian princess of story and legend. She had high cheekbones, silky black hair, a ramrod straight posture, and she hardly ever cracked a smile. When she sang and played you had the feeling she wanted to raze the town to the ground, thereby accomplishing what her forebears had been unable to. I'm not ashamed to admit I had a crush on her early on. Who wouldn't?

And we had Melissa whom I knew better than Tina, at least at first. We'd had a couple of classes together and, while we hadn't actually hung out socially, I was well aware she was a star student. She was on the debate team and had been elected school treasurer. She was rail-thin and had mocha-colored skin. At school, she always wore glasses. But when we played, she stashed the specs and became a whole different person. She did something with her hair too, styling it up into a gravity-defying pompadour. She became a rockabilly queen. Even before she got her upright bass.

Last but not least, there was me—a redhead with wild curly hair and freckles, a real "paleface" to boot. I'd sometimes tie up my hair in Pippy Longstocking pigtails for a kick. But regardless of what I thought of my looks, I seemed to have my share of fans as well. They were mooning over me at our shows just as much as they did over Tina and Mel. I didn't think it was my dazzling guitar pyrotechnics either—I was no Scotty Moore. But I was learning. And who's to say? Maybe I'd get close someday if I kept at it. We were discovering, too, that even a modicum of fame could skew people's perceptions, making you seem better than you actually were.

Of my experience beyond the Bubble, there was nary a trace left. The experience had been almost totally banished from my mind. I still had weird dreams on occasion. And sometimes things I learned in class would trigger odd memories and even weird physical sensations for no apparent reason. A couple of times I got vertigo just sitting at my desk. But as time wore on I learned to take the strangeness in stride, thinking it was just something I'd have to live with. I didn't see any other option.

23

The Rex

Work started on the Willys immediately.

Grandpa rolled up his sleeves and dug in. He was an artist with a blow torch. He sliced off the extraneous parts of the body and chopped the top a few inches, so the car had a raked look, back to front. He cut into the hood and sides of the engine covering so that the engine, when installed, would be revealed for all the world to see. But he kept the front of the car and its fenders intact so that it would still hopefully be identifiable as a Willys.

The body was going to be as light as he could make it. To that end, he got rid of most everything inside the car as well, except for the front bench seat. He took out the door panels and headliner. He tore out the old dashboard and replaced it with a chrome instrument panel. Plus he had it in mind to put a tachometer on the dash under the rearview mirror.

After a couple of weeks of work, we had a stripped-down body, evenly sprayed with rust primer. The body was resting on top of an overhauled and steel-reinforced chassis designed to handle the torque the engine would produce once it was in place and hooked up to the transmission.

Grandpa Kurt was about as motivated as I'd ever seen him. Getting so involved in the project seemed to be the best thing for him, though. It was helping him heal. You could see the transformation after those first two weeks. His hospital visit and any worries about his health were mostly forgotten when he was lost in his work. He'd been treading water for years with the Studebaker. Futzing around with it no longer held the appeal it once had. It was basically just something for him to do. This new project was a whole other thing.

While Grandpa was working on customizing the body and strengthening the chassis, I was busy with the engine. I cleaned it up and customized it as much as our budget would allow, adding a four-barrel carburetor which kicked the output up to about 300 horsepower. Big Al was more than generous in supplying parts. He got me a chrome blower that looked new, but which he claimed was used. He didn't charge me for it. Since the engine was going to be visible I wanted to add as much chrome as I could, and he helped with that, too. Being fairly new, it didn't need a lot of work other than the enhancements. It purred like a big kitty right off. This was a good thing because school, work, and the band were cutting into the amount of time I could spend on the car.

Even with the V-8 yet to be installed, the car looked mean. I liked how the rear of the car swept down toward the front. It looked like it was moving just sitting there. There was something primordial about it, especially with the rust primer. It conjured up, in my mind at least, the biggest, baddest predator of them all, Tyrannosaurus Rex.

I began to call it the Rex.

Grandpa went about his business with a big smile on his face, humming a tune. Now and then I'd catch snippets of something from The Wizard of Oz. It was apt. We were kind of on the yellow brick road with this project, off to see the wizard. We didn't exactly know where we'd end up, but it sure was exciting getting there. I couldn't wait to see the V-8 mounted on that rail. When the engine was where it needed to be, it would just be a matter of putting the finishing touches on the body and drivetrain.

Reluctantly, I turned my attention to my schoolwork and getting through the rest of my junior year. Meanwhile, the band was as busy as ever. As summer drew nearer we were getting inundated with requests to do parties and school functions at an accelerated pace, both at the high school and at the junior college. The fact that our 45 had been out for a while by then and was getting played on local radio didn't hurt the demand for the band.

Plus, it was the spring of '56. Rock 'n' roll was in the air everywhere. New music and new stars were arriving over the airwaves all the time. The Roadrunners picked up new songs as quickly as they came out, and our repertoire expanded by leaps and bounds.

24

The Rex Lives!

"I think we're ready to drop the engine on the frame," Grandpa Kurt announced one Saturday morning.

The engine was resting on a pedestal next to the car. It looked big, shiny, and new. While, in contrast, the body looked like an ancient vessel, something dredged up from the bottom of the sea, waiting for the engine to bring it to life. It wouldn't be long now.

"Wanna help me hoist it into position?"

"Sure," I said.

I helped him secure the straps from the engine hoist. That done, Grandpa used the hydraulic lift to raise it off its perch and pivoted it expertly over the body of the car. When he had it lined up, he lowered the V-8 onto the frame.

Grandpa Kurt took his time. He went around checking the alignment from every angle to make sure it was going onto the engine mounts just right. When he was satisfied, he released the tension on the lift and let the frame take the full weight of the engine. Then he quickly disconnected the straps and moved the hoist out of the way, so we could have a good look at it.

The contrast between the new chrome-plated engine and the primered body couldn't have been more stark. Or interesting, I thought. I knew right then I didn't want to finish the body any further. I wanted to drive it just the way it was.

"It's one of a kind, that's for sure," Grandpa Kurt said, voicing my own thoughts.

Now that it was approaching completion, it was almost scary. I knew what Doctor Frankenstein must have felt at the moment of truth with his monster.

"I've ordered some chrome pipes for the exhaust," Kurt said. "My treat. But the custom wheels are something I thought you might like to decide on yourself. I'm sure you'll have your own preferences on that."

I did. I knew I wanted mag wheels all around. The front wheels would be smaller, like the forearms on a Tyrannosaurus. And the rear wheels needed to be massive for traction. The slicks they used at the drag races were treadless and made of soft rubber. They couldn't legally be used on the street. So I planned on getting some cheater slicks. They had some token tread on them to make them street legal but were wide enough to give me the added grip I'd need.

Something seemed to be preoccupying Grandpa Kurt.

"What's up, Gramps?" I said.

"I'm wondering whether this is such a good idea,"

He was having second thoughts? Now?

"It'll be OK," I said as casually as I could. "I know how to drive."

"I know that. Nobody around here knows more about cars than you do. Excepting me, of course. And you've been driving since you were old enough to peek over a dashboard, never mind you got your driver's license a year ago, give or take."

"Then what is it?"

"The way this car is going to look and drive when it's done could make it a trouble magnet. It could attract the wrong kind of attention, you know? Guys'll want to challenge you in it. They won't be able to help themselves. I'd never forgive myself if anything happened to you."

"I can keep my head on straight," I told him. "I'm not going to let anybody get to me. I've learned a few things about how to get by growing up in this town. Nothing's going to happen."

Grandpa continued to look solemnly at the car. He heaved a sigh.

"OK, OK," he said. "I've always trusted you to know what you were doing, even when you were young. And I never regretted it. You're a good kid, Rose." I think Grandpa Kurt was misting up. This wasn't just about building a car. He was acknowledging that I was growing up and becoming my own person. I loved him more than ever right then

"I won't let you down, Gramps," I said.

25

The Rex Debuts

The school year came to an end with a flurry of gigs, and then things rapidly tapered off as the summer doldrums hit. The weather was getting hot, most days at or above 100 degrees, and folks were content to stay indoors with the air conditioning on full blast. There were still parties to be played on the weekends, but there wasn't much going on either at the high school or the junior college. And we weren't old enough yet to be playing the bars around town.

Nevertheless, our band rehearsals continued all through the summer. Melissa finally got her upright bass. She had a summer job as a carhop at Sally's Drive-in. When she had the money in hand, we all went over to Slocum's Music which supplied the local schools with band instruments. We found a nice used double bass that Mel immediately gravitated toward.

Tina took a summer job at Penney's to make some extra money. She already had a drum kit and a car. But like Mel and me, she was saving money for college further down the road. We were all planning to start at the JC where tuition was free before considering other higher learning options. But all that seemed a long ways off.

I was staying busy, too. I added hours at Ted's and was making decent money. I was putting most of what I was earning in my own college fund. The rest I was putting into the car. I pictured tuck 'n' roll upholstery for the bench seat. Grandpa wanted to help out, as he had with everything else, but I insisted I wanted to do that much on my own.

The rest of the time was spent hiking in the backcountry or just waiting for parts for the Rex to be delivered. We were getting most of our accessories from a new company, American Racing. We ordered a chrome radiator and some chrome bars for bumpers. All that gleaming metal really stood out against the dull, unfinished look of the body.

"It's you," Grandpa Kurt mused one day.

"You mean I'm like a rusty old '41 Willys?" I said.

Grandpa laughed. "Think of it as a self-portrait in metal and chrome. Look. It's even red—like your hair!"

"Primer red," I pointed out. I crossed my arms and tapped my toe, waiting for his next feat of metaphorical ingenuity.

"It's one-of-a-kind," Grandpa said, proceeding undaunted. "It's got power to spare, but it's also down to earth with that primer finish. And with the chrome accents, the radiator, the engine, the pipes, and the bumpers there's plenty of sparkle there, too. Sparkle and strength for all the world to see. And I have the feeling the world *will* see it one day."

I got a little choked right then. Grandpa could be a charmer when he wanted to be, I had to admit, I felt pretty good about his description. I already felt a strong connection to the car. It really *was* a work of art, one that Grandpa and I had worked together to create.

In early September, the wheels arrived. The big cheater slicks on the back made the rake of the body even more pronounced and mean looking. The body looked like it was huddling protectively over the big shiny Hemi V-8. The chrome pipes flowed down the sides of the engine, collecting in two larger channels underneath the car that ran out the back.

In unguarded moments the cave in the arroyo still tugged at my memory. It was like an itch I couldn't scratch. I went back there occasionally on my hikes, but stopped short of venturing into the cave again. I didn't bother to tell Grandpa about these excursions. There was no point.

It was a couple of weeks into the new school year when we introduced the Rex to the world.

Grandpa Kurt held the driver's door open for me with a smile and a gallant sweep of his arm. I settled in behind the wheel and took stock. The shiny dashboard gleamed back at me. I could see my reflection in it--carrot-colored hair curling over my forehead in ringlets under my ball cap, while the rest of it flared out behind me like flames out of a tailpipe. Or so I liked to think. I winked at my reflection. We were about to make some serious noise.

I found the pedals and made sure the car was in neutral. I turned the key and waited for the engine to catch. When it did, you knew it. The whole car seemed to lift a couple of inches on the chassis as the engine turned over, The blare from the unmuffled tailpipes was loud enough to shake the house. I tached the engine a few times to get used to the feel of the car and the outrageous noise. It felt like I was in a rocket, ready for blast-off.

I put the transmission into drive and the car lurched forward out of the garage and out into the sun without any help from the accelerator. The idle was enough to get the thing moving at a brisk clip. I applied the brakes. The engine continued to rumble under me.

"How does it feel?" Grandpa Kurt shouted to me, leaning in through the passenger window.

I just nodded, speechless.

Aunt Trish came rushing out the front door, thinking the house was being shelled.

"We might have to muffle it a little," Grandpa Kurt shouted at me, grinning. "They'd arrest you if you drove into town sounding like this." I could tell he was as excited about the car as I was.

Trish came over. "The dishes are migrating out of the cupboard," she shouted over the noise. "And I think the chandelier in the dining room is coming out of the ceiling. There's plaster all over the dinner table."

When she saw the car that Grandpa and I had built, she went silent.

"It's really something, hunh?" Grandpa called to her as soothingly as he could while shouting. "We'll turn it off in a second. I promise."

26

Gunslingers

The street racers were gunning for me from the first day I took the Rex out. I ignored them, like a good girl. But no teenager is wise at all hours of the day.

The first time it happened I was on the outskirts of town on my way home. Rattlesnake Junction peters out pretty quickly where the town suburbs meet the desert. The houses and businesses quit and the desert starts. But the blacktop goes on toward the east hills for several more miles to where the development that was to include our house was supposed to have been built.

They were waiting for me at the side of the road, Tommy Strickland and his ever-present buddy, Chet. I guess Tommy needed someone to mark the event, a witness to his impending victory. They were seated in the brand new Bel Air Tommy's parents had bought him as an early graduation present, the engine idling. Tommy's ride was cherry, I had to give him that. It sat back on its hind wheels with its nose in the air. Kind of like Tommy himself when he strutted around campus. While the Rex was tilted forward, his car was tilted back in what was sometimes referred to as a "dump." Whatever you called it, his car was pretty tough. Maybe the coolest at the school.

Tommy's folks were rich. Or as rich as it got in the Junction. His father owned an interstate trucking business that must have brought in some dough. The Chevy was two-tone blue and white, with shiny reverse chrome wheels. Tommy's car was a swan, all factory customized and pristine. When he revved it up, it sounded like a finely tuned machine. Mine, on the other hand, was a snorting, spitting dragon that looked like it chewed up asphalt for breakfast. It was pretty noisy, despite the glass pack mufflers Grandpa had installed on it to make it street legal.

The Bel Air had its nose pointing in the direction I was going. When I got within range, Tommy floored it, spewing pebbles and burning rubber my way. I swerved to avoid his car as he crowded me over the broken centerline.

As I've hopefully demonstrated so far, I'm usually a fairly even-tempered teen. It took a lot to set me off. But this demonstration of jackassery crossed the line. First, there was the getting pelted with dirt. Then there was the getting blinded by a cloud of smoking rubber. And now he was forcing me over into the oncoming lane. It was more than any self-respecting girl could take. Not that there was anybody coming in the opposite lane or anything. We were the only traffic on the road for as far as the eye could see.

That was probably also why I was willing to give my displeasure some free rein, if I'm completely honest. Instead of slowing and backing off like he probably expected me to, I put the hammer down and zagged out and around him. This maneuver put me right next to him in the oncoming lane. While my cheater slicks were fighting for purchase, we were accelerating at about the same rate. The Rex was putting out so much power my rear wheels were spinning freely, and I was fishtailing all over the place.

I could tell Tommy was giving it all he had. But he wasn't gaining any ground on me. Seeing him there next to me, about to bust a vein trying to stay ahead, I started to relax for the first time. I let up on the gas just enough to allow my slicks to find purchase and dig in. When they did, I was slammed back in my seat, and I swear my front wheels lifted off the road. When I looked over, Tommy and his car were nowhere to be seen.

I found him in my rearview mirror, eating gravel and trying to keep control of his car. It was a losing battle. He went into a sideways drift that sent him off the road. I took my foot off the gas pedal, watching the drama unfold in the mirror. I was praying he wouldn't roll it. It could have meant serious injuries or worse. But the sand along the road was hard-packed, and he just slid sideways parallel to the roadway until he came to a stop about fifty feet into the chaparral.

I slowed and turned the car around. I wanted to make sure everyone was alright. But Tommy was already veering back toward the road, fighting his steering wheel all the way. I rolled down my window as he emerged on the asphalt again. I could tell before I said anything that he was not happy. At first, it looked like he might try to ram me. But even as far gone as he was, he knew he'd be the loser in any demolition derby-style encounter with my car. He swerved at the last minute and settled in alongside me. Chet had his window down in the passenger seat, and Tommy was yelling something across him that I couldn't make out. Probably just as well. I doubt he was complimenting me or the Rex. Chet was staring straight ahead, stony-faced, obviously bearing the brunt of Tommy's tirade.

I rolled my window back up, confident that I wouldn't want to hear what Tommy had to impart. They had started it after all. I gave a small wave before hitting the brakes to let them surge on ahead. Then I whipped the car around in a 180-degree turn and resumed my drive home, obeying the speed laws as if nothing untoward had happened. It was clear Tommy's pride was hurt more than anything. And aside from the scratches and scrapes on his Chevy, he was going to be just fine.

I watched my rearview mirror as the boys shrank in the distance on their way back to Rattlesnake Junction, whipped. I'm pretty sure I imagined the tail-tucked-between-their-legs part.

27

Rumble

Tommy started circulating a story around school about how I ran him off the road and scuffed up his car. But the only people willing to lend an ear to his grousing were the rich guys he hung out with and their girlfriends. Their opinion, shared by some of the jocks crowd and a few other assorted girl hating lame-os, was that girls belonged anywhere else in a car but in the driver's seat. It didn't help that I could play electric guitar better than any guy on campus. Now I had a brute of a car that could beat their best.

Tommy and his car were at school the next day. He'd cleaned the Bel Air up a bit but had yet to buff out the scratches and touch up the paint. Somehow it didn't look quite as pristine as it had before.

I was pretty sure I hadn't seen the last road race challenge I'd have to deal with. And I was right. But for the most part, I kept my head and refused to rise to the bait. Still, it got to be a weekly thing--guys pulling up next to me at stoplights, engines revving, grinning like idiots. Or congregating where I happened to be parked just to insult me or my wheels. Cheap thrills. But I noticed they kept a safe distance while taunting me, trying to impress each other with their sarcastic wit. I think they were a little bit scared of me, the smart ones at least.

Occasionally, guys got pushy. That tended to happen after school in the student parking lot. Once a knucklehead named Rudy came up on me as I was getting into the Rex. He tried to grab my hair while three of his buddies looked on, snickering, but standing well back. I just stomped his instep and elbowed him in the gut before getting into my chariot and peeling out while he rolled around on the ground moaning. I'd had more experience fighting than most of the guys at school. And that by the time I was 15.

Once I went to visit Tina at Penney's after school. There were three hoods checking out my car in the lot, looking in the windows and gawking at the custom wheels. These guys were older, obviously not high school students. They clearly had more time on their hands than was good for them. They looked the part of car jockeys, slicked-back hair, Acme T-shirts with the sleeves rolled to show off their muscles and to hold their Marlboros, jeans with the cuffs rolled up and keychains dangling from their pockets. I knew they were trouble the minute I laid eyes on them. But I also wasn't going to turn tail and run.

"These your wheels?" one of them said as I approached, looking me up and down. I took him to be the leader of this merry band.

"Yup," I said without slowing. "Comin' through."

As I made for the driver's door, the lead guy stepped in front of me. "I got an idea," he said. "How about you take us for a spin around the block. Show us what you got." He shot his buddies a leering gaze.

"Not going to happen, chum," I said, reaching for the door handle. "Move over."

Next thing I knew there was a switchblade in his right hand, attached to one of those dangling keychains. "Or how about you hand over the keys, and we'll show YOU how it's done. My guys here'll keep you company in back, while I take the wheel."

I appraised him for a minute like I was sizing him up for a seersucker suit. His smile widened. He was confident I was going to do the sensible thing and capitulate. Instead, I kneed him hard in the nuts. He wasn't expecting it, and he was wide open. The knife clattered to the pavement. He went down on all fours, crimson-faced, gasping for air. He'd made the mistake of thinking the switchblade was a nuclear deterrent: no one would go up against him while he had it in his hand. It had probably worked in the past. Not this time.

I moved to get around him, but he caught my ankle, slowing me down just enough for the other two lunkheads to grab an arm each. I twisted and spun, kneeing one in the groin, and pulled him headlong into the other one. I knew how to fight dirty when I had to, especially when I was outnumbered and outgunned.

Meanwhile, the leader was getting his wind back. He teetered to his feet and started to limp toward me, the blade flashing. I knew I wouldn't have time to open my car door and get in before getting sliced, so I ran around the front of the car, getting it between me and the maniac with the knife.

Of course, by now his other two flunkies were on the move too. They came around the car from the back end, while the leader followed me around the front. I knew I was running out of time.

Then I saw a blur of movement on the other side of the Rex. Tina had come up on them so fast nobody had registered her arrival before it was too late, She was carrying a brand new Louisville Slugger, probably snagged from the Penney's sports department on her way out the door of the store, and she was swinging for the fences. The baseball bat took out the guy with the knife first, hitting him square across the shoulder blades. The knife went flying and the wind was knocked out of him. But he still managed to turn around to face Tina as she wound up for the next swing. This time the bat caught him in the jaw, and he went down for the count.

This new development gave the other two pause. I managed to land a quick one-two punch to the guy closest to me before he had a chance to react. And while my punches didn't knock him out, they dazed him enough to stop his forward motion. When they saw Tina, the Apache Princess, coming for them with the bat, fire in her eyes, they deflated like popped party balloons. They hightailed it, leaving their leader behind on the field of battle, out like a light.

Tina looked at me. "You alright?" she asked.

"Thanks to you," I said.

"I have brothers, remember?" she said. "They taught me how to fight. It's still the Wild West for Indians at the school."

I didn't know what to say to that. She'd probably had it tougher than I had growing up, but she never let on. This was the first time in memory that she'd ever revealed something personal about herself to me.

28

The Ambush

realized that I had to be more cautious and less of a hothead going forward. I'd always had a sixth sense about trouble brewing. But I needed to be able to back off and find back up when the occasion called for it, something I'd been reluctant to do in the past. Self-reliance was my middle name. But this had been a warning about what could happen. Things might have turned out really badly for me if Tina hadn't shown up.

We became better friends after that, Tina and I. Realizing we were both fighters, and outsiders to boot in our own ways, gave us something else besides music in common. Of course, as an all-girl rock n roll band in the fifties, we already were in a class of our own.

At gigs, there were usually guys ready to take up the slack and dissuade people who wanted to hassle us. Tina's brothers, for example, were a regular fixture at our shows. As was Melissa's brother, when he was home from college. And when those guys weren't around, we had fans, especially those of the greaser persuasion, who could be plenty intimidating on our behalf when the situation called for it.

I didn't like having to rely on the boys for protection. I didn't like it at all. But I wasn't an idiot about it. We had other things to think about besides our safety. Like getting through the next set. We were as aware as anyone that we weren't exactly living in enlightened times as far as male/female relations were concerned. I had to acknowledge, though not without a lot of resistance, that if I wanted to be able to focus on playing music and not have to worry about what might happen later off-stage, I had to get over myself and my tough-guy image and learn to accept what help was offered.

There were still unforeseen circumstances that cropped up once in a while. Usually, they weren't anything I couldn't handle myself. But there was one night at a Christmas dance that comes to mind. I was busy lugging my gear out to my car after the gig when Bel Air Tommy and two of his pals showed up and boxed me in. To be honest, I was more concerned about my guitar than anything. Those hollow body electrics can be fragile. I didn't know what I'd do if mine got busted up.

Consequently, I got knocked around a bit before I managed to push the guitar and amp under the car, out of harm's way. After that, I gave as good as I got. Eventually, some fans from the dance saw what was happening and came over to help out. I'd been doing pretty well on my own, but it was nice to be able to take a breather, especially after having just played a three-hour gig.

Tommy and his friends got worked over pretty thoroughly that night. They looked like they'd gone a couple of rounds with Rocky Marciano when it was all over. Their fancy clothes were torn. They were bruised and banged up. Try as I might, I couldn't feel too sorry for them. Three guys against a girl? It was pretty low, even by their standards. Either they were still obsessed with recovering their lost dignity after our race months ago, or they considered me a different species from the other girls and therefore exempt from the rules of good behavior that applied to them. In any case, it was their problem, I figured, not mine.

Not that I couldn't be poised and lady-like if I set my mind to it. I cleaned up pretty good. But hey, I didn't have anything to prove to those guys. They were pathetic as far as I was concerned. They'd been beaten by a girl. Again. And this time, I was pretty sure, everybody would hear about it.

The upshot? I didn't hear anything from the "elite" contingent on campus again for the rest of the school year.

In general, I was getting razzed less and respected more. By now most of the guys on campus were willing to concede I was a decent guitar player, especially as the Roadrunners continued to release records and had achieved a level of renown as a band. Nothing succeeds like success. Most of the girls on campus still weren't sure what to make of me. I was fine with that.

There were still the jocks who had the musical sense of a beer keg, and their girlfriends, who may secretly have liked what we were doing, but wouldn't have been caught dead admitting it. The girlfriends tended to give me a wide berth, even as they talked me down amongst themselves. They weren't brawlers. They wouldn't have stood a chance against me, and they knew it—some of them firsthand from back in junior high. Plus, by now it had gotten around that I worked at the repair shop. What kind of girl worked in the lube pits? My kind, that's what.

Oddly enough, no one messed with the car. I'd have figured that would be the first target. But then, it wasn't that easy to crack. I had a lock on the gas tank, so there was no pouring sand into it. But I honestly don't think anyone tried. There was a respect for machinery in our culture that was sometimes lacking when it came to humans. So I cruised around town in the Rex relatively unharassed.

Anyway, now that the band was gaining a level of notoriety, folks seemed more inclined to wave or give me the thumbs up as I rumbled by than to hurtle insults.

29

A Day At The Races

There was a drag race in February of my senior year hosted by the Elk's club which was open to all comers. Surprisingly, Tina started pressing me to sign up for it in that portentous way of hers.

"You should do it," she said, stone-faced. "Your car must be allowed to run free. Like the wild palomino." I hadn't known her long enough yet to tell if she was joshing me or not. I was 80 percent sure she was. But I didn't want to offend her, so I decided to err on the side of caution and take what she said at face value.

I'd never actually opened up that Chrysler Hemi in a real race. And I have to admit I'd always been a bit curious about what that would be like. I'd been good about obeying the rules of the road, mostly. But the idea of an actual legal, real-life race on a paved quarter-mile track was pretty compelling

"The spirit of the Rex needs to be honored," Tina told me seriously. "Like a challenger for the dominance of the herd, it longs to be tested. It requires worthy opponents to reveal its true mettle." Her intensity could be just a little unnerving.

Truth be told, I didn't require that much convincing. The more I thought about it, the more it started to seem like it could be fun to sign up.

I finally talked to Grandpa Kurt about entering the race. He considered my request for a long time, looking at me and then at the car and back. Finally, he nodded gravely and said, "OK, I think you're ready. But you better listen up. When you come off the line, you need to baby the accelerator. Don't just stomp it. Your wheels'll be burning like a prairie wildfire otherwise. You won't have any traction. You might even blow a tire. So easy on the gas pedal off the line. Got it?"

I didn't mention that the showdown with Tommy, as well as a half dozen or so other street races I'd been drawn into since then, had shown me as much. I already had a pretty good idea of what I needed to do to stay in a race. But since I didn't want to hurt his feelings I just nodded. "Sure," I said. "Thanks for the advice, Grandpa."

Kurt and Aunt Trish were there when I showed up at the drag strip that Saturday. It was a little-used, arrow-straight patch of concrete just outside the city limits to the north. I'd done a couple of hours work at Ted's that morning, finishing up a valve job for a local mucky-muck who needed the car by Monday. He had the clout to send a lot of business our way if we got the job done in a hurry, is the way Ted explained it to me. Naturally, I had to oblige.

Two or three hundred spectators were already there when I arrived, scattered across some football bleachers that had been carted over from the high school for the occasion. A $3 admission was being charged for the use of the bleachers, which offered the best view of the quarter-mile track. The money was going toward the cash prizes, $300 for the winner, $200 for second place, and $100 for third. It was a warm day for February, and the track was starting to shimmer with the heat rising from it like a desert mirage.

The field featured a dozen custom cars. Everything from souped-up Model As and Model Ts to stock late model Chevys and Fords, the preferred wheels of the Ivy League crowd. There were two basic racing categories: modified racers and stock cars. The Rex was naturally in the former category with its blown, four-barrel, big block engine resting on a chopped and reinforced customized frame. The car's vintage Willys heritage was still obvious from the front grille and headlights to the cab and swept-back rear end. It still had the soul of a Willys, and I was proud of that.

Both categories were to be pitted against their respective kind. Stock cars were racing stock cars and custom cars would go up against other custom cars. That was really the only rule. That was fine with me. I was just here for the fun of it. I knew I was probably going to get creamed by the local hot rod jockeys and the out-of-towners with their fancy rigs. I was at peace with that.

The event was akin to the county fair, only on a smaller scale. There were banners and flags flying in the late morning westerly breeze. There were concession stands that sold corn dogs, popcorn, hamburgers, ice cream bars, and sodas. People that wanted something stronger brown-bagged spirits they'd brought in with them. This was supposed to be an all-ages event.

People were milling around the cars, gawking and chatting with the owners. I was the only high schooler in the modified category. Tommy and Chet were there with Tommy's Chevy which was entered in the stock car category. The scrapes and scratches from our encounter at the start of the school year had long since been repaired, of course. You wouldn't have known they'd ever been there. The car was showroom perfect. The boys ignored me.

I went over to where Grandpa and Aunt Trish were huddled. Melissa showed up with her dad, who I knew as Mr. Jordan. I'd met him previously when he brought Mel to our rehearsals, and I'd seen him a time or two at our gigs standing at the back of the room, tapping his toes. He was a burly bear of a guy who had a sweet disposition and a ready smile on his face. Melissa was the apple of his eye. He was proud of her and since she was one of the best students at school he had every right to be.

"I love the races," he beamed. "I've heard so much about this car of yours, Rose. If you can drive halfway as good as you can play the guitar, you'll give 'em a run for their money, sure." He seemed like a big little kid. His enthusiasm was infectious.

Grandpa volunteered to show Mr. Jordan the Rex. Meanwhile, Tina arrived with two of her brothers, Ray and Billy. Introductions were made to Aunt Trish, who was totally overshadowed by the young men. The sun came out again when the guys excused themselves and wandered off to check out the cars.

"I'm glad you came," I told Tina.

"You doing OK?" she said, inspecting me, a look of concern on her face.

"I was feeling some nerves," I told her. "But I feel better now with family and friends around."

"Today you let the horses run free," she said, making a lateral chopping motion with her forearm while standing straight and proud. "All here shall bear witness."

I almost burst out laughing. But I caught myself in time.

30

Gone

They put me up against an older guy. No surprise there, since I was the youngest participant. He was thinning up top, overweight, probably in his mid-thirties. I could have been wrong. I was a bad judge of age. He could have been in his twenties. Or forty-five, for all I knew.

I could tell he wasn't thrilled to be going up against a teenage girl. He was over by the judges' stand arguing and pointing over at me, flapping his arms like a tom turkey trying to get off the ground, his face as red as a ripe pomegranate.

He had a nice looking '32 Ford, though, I had to admit. It had more of its original frame than mine did. The engine wasn't sitting on a rail like mine was, so I couldn't tell what he was running. It sounded impressive, though. It had stock wheels, the rear ones slightly oversized and the front ones on the small side. They gave the car a jaunty foreword angle. A little like mine. Except I wouldn't have called my car "jaunty." Whereas his looked kind of cute, mine looked like it carried a big chip on its shoulder.

This might have been closer to the truth than I wanted to admit. Much as I tended to downplay winning, I wanted to win. Especially since my competitor was over at the judges' table belly aching about me to anyone who would listen.

I had to get my head in the game and stop thinking about Elmer Fudd over there. In my previous road racing experience, I never had much time to worry about who I was going up against. They just appeared, and it was sink or swim. Racing had never been a planned event for me, until today. Now, for better or worse, I had a little time to think about things. For one thing, there was an audience in attendance. It was like doing an outdoor concert. Only this time I was driving instead of playing guitar. There were more than a few kids from the school there. Some were fans of the band. And a few of them wanted to see me fail, like Tommy and his ilk.

My racing competitor came back to his car, which was idling at the starting line next to mine, muttering to himself. When he saw me, he stopped talking to himself. "Might as well go home right now, little girl," he said. "You and that piece of junkyard junk shouldn't even be out here."

"Nice to meet you, too," I said with a smart salute as I climbed in behind the wheel of the Rex. I had the window rolled down and called out, just to be neighborly, "What are you running?"

"Wouldn't you like to know," he fired back. "You'll find out soon enough, don't worry, seein' as you're still around." He tached his engine to prove his point as he settled in behind the steering wheel.

I'd seen my share of attitude from street racers, but I was taken aback by this guy's complete lack of manners. Wasn't there supposed to be a level of professional camaraderie and sportsmanship on display at a real race like this? Apparently not.

I was caught a little off guard when the flag went down. I stomped down on the accelerator harder than I intended, and immediately broke the slicks loose. The Rex was fishtailing like there was oil on the track, which there wasn't. I was going nowhere fast.

Needless to say, Elmer shot out ahead of me. He kept his cool. There was barely a wisp of smoke coming up off his wheels as he tore off down the track. He'd succeeded in rattling me, which had no doubt been his intention, and I imagined him smirking as he quickly opened up a big lead.

After a second, I caught my breath and settled down. But a second is an eternity in the quarter-mile. Nothing to be done about it now except to ease off on the throttle, even though it meant letting him expand his lead even further. Finally, the cheaters caught. I did a neat little wheelie as I came after him.

And come after him, I did. He was halfway down the track by now, powershifting away, hitting the clutch without letting off the gas. Without a clutch to worry about, I just moved the big shifter on the floor to change gears. With the modifications that Grandpa had done on the trans, the automatic behaved like a stick shift without the clutch. With every gear I selected, the front end would lift off the ground a few inches.

I passed him about two-thirds of the way to the finish line. I could see the look of panic on his face when he wasn't able to locate me in his rearview mirror. But by then it was too late. I was past him and gone.

I won four more heats that day before I was eliminated by a gas dragster from Rawley. There was no shame in losing to that fire breathing, drag-racing demon. I'd made it into the semi-finals by then and wound up third for the day in the modified category. I was handed a cashier's check for a hundred dollars on the podium and drove home in my chariot, beaming.

31

Whole Lotta Shakin'

The earthquakes started toward the end of my senior year in high school. They weren't massive movers, at least not at first. Just shakes and shudders once or twice a day toward the end of a particularly warm spring.

It made things tricky at Ted's. Especially when we had a car up on the lift. There were times when we just had to drop everything and run for it. We never lost a car, but it got hairy a few times with a couple of tons of metal bouncing and bobbing around six feet in the air.

Glasses and cups would migrate out of the cupboard at home and measures had to be taken to keep them inside. Mostly it was just a matter of applying a little duct tape here and there.

But cups and glasses weren't the only things jogged loose by the tremors. The kinds of dreams I'd had after the cave incident came back with a vengeance. I was getting that odd sense of vertigo again at inopportune moments.

Once it happened as I was giving a book report in front of English class. I got ushered to the nurse's station. But by then the sensation had subsided.

And then there was a time when the feeling came over me in the middle of a performance. I actually went down to my knees while I was playing a solo. The audience thought it was part of the act. I went with it and pretended it was. The response was so positive that

103

I considered including it or something like it as a regular feature of our sets. Those kinds of theatrics were common in early rock 'n' roll. Look at Little Richard, Chuck Berry, or Jerry Lee Lewis. It was more fun doing it when I felt I had control over the situation, though.

That sense of unreality that I'd had early on came back too. There were extended periods of time when I felt like I was living in a dream, nothing around me what it seemed.

Something was coming to a head. I knew it in my bones. The earthquakes were part of it. Though what was coming to head or why remained stubbornly beyond my grasp.

Besides the fact that I felt a little crazy a lot of the time, everything went on as before. I went to school. I went to work. And when I wasn't doing either of those things, I was getting ready for the next show with the band, working on a new song or just hanging out at home or in the car, listening to the music coming in over the airwaves. As a torch-bearer of the new sound, I felt it was my duty to know what was going on.

And when I had a minute, I tinkered on the Rex. I tuned it and retuned it. I buffed the chrome plating on the engine, the gas tank, the bumpers, and the radiator to a high shine. The Rex's fame had spread by then. The least I could do was keep it presentable.

There was a moment there when I was even considering painting it. But I came to my senses in time. That rust primer finish was part of what made the Rex, the Rex. It was part of its distinctive charm, striking fear into the hearts of anyone who might be inclined to take me on. Consequently, on the racing front, I finally had a little peace, even though I knew there was a guy in a garage somewhere trying to build a machine that could beat the Rex. Or, better yet, a girl.

That was OK. If I'd had anything to prove, I'd done it at the Elk's drag race. Besides, I had other things to think about, like school and playing music. Not to mention going nuts.

I really was genuinely worried about my sanity. It's hard to take anything too seriously when nothing seems real. I'd find myself just laughing to bust a gut for no reason. I had enough self-confidence not to wig out completely. Somewhere behind what I was going through there was a reason. It lived there in the shadows. I had the feeling that if I could just get quiet, let things settle enough, I'd be able to figure out what it was.

32

Zapped

It took a visit to the wrecking yard for things to start to come into focus. As the shifting and shaking persisted, I felt I needed to talk to Big Al. If anyone might know what was happening, I thought, it was him. I didn't know why I thought that. It seemed absurd on the face of it. But there it was.

I drove out to the wrecking yard one day after work. It was early March and the days were getting longer. The sky was still light when I pulled into the yard and drove up to the shed that was Big Al's office. I didn't see anyone, but the gate was open. So I figured somebody must be around.

I turned off the ignition and got out of the car. There was a scurrying noise when my boots hit the ground, and I saw something small and shiny disappear into the stacks. I blinked. I thought I was seeing things. But there was also a strong sense of deja vu. I'd seen something like that somewhere before.

All was quiet. The office was dark. And Big Al was nowhere to be seen. Being among the stacks of wrecked cars and trucks with no one else around was just a little spooky. Images from those cheesy Saturday matinée fright fests I'd attended at the movie theater weren't much help.

I saw a squat figure emerge from the banks of twisted metal. It was the size of a five-year-old. But it was no child. The silver bug-like thing had vanished. And the daylight was starting to fade from the sky.

The thing teetered on its hind legs like a human. But it wasn't like any human I'd ever seen. It had gray skin, a big head, arms and legs that were way too skinny for it to be a costumed person, and large slanting eyes. I had to shake my head to clear it. It looked like comic book illustrations I'd seen of the aliens that were supposed to have crash-landed next door in New Mexico. I had to stop myself from breaking out laughing. This had to be some kind of joke, right? Somebody somewhere had to be pulling the strings. But something told me it wasn't a joke.

When I looked closer, I saw that the thing was carrying something that looked a lot like a gun. It raised a three-fingered hand with the weapon in it and pointed it in my direction. But before it could pull the trigger, there was a brilliant flash of light to my left. It was like a lightning bolt, rendering the stacks of wrecked cars in stark relief. I was momentarily blinded. I fell to my knees in the dirt waiting for my eyesight to return, halfway expecting to be used as target practice by the little gray moon man.

When my vision cleared I was looking up at a tall woman who looked strangely familiar, though I would have sworn she wasn't like anything I'd seen before.

"Hi again," she said.

Then she zapped me.

33

Gillian

"You remember me?" asked the woman.

I nodded. It had all come back to me the instant she did whatever she did to me. "Sure," I said. "You're Gillian, the warrior woman. From topside."

"Warrior woman," she said showing some teeth. "I like that."

I remembered it all: the cave—with the elevators this time—the rocket ride literally out of this world, the scaffolding, looking down on the piece of the planet I'd been living on and which was in fact stored in the cargo hold of an unimaginably large spacecraft called the Fortune's Fool.

"What are you doing here?" I said. "Didn't you say something about fraternizing with the Settlers? It being prohibited and all?"

Gillian laughed that. "Normally, yes," she said. "But the truth is we may need your help."

"My help? What could I do to help you?"

"You remember the Greys?"

"The moon men. Sure," I said. "Like the one that's over there, dead."

"Not dead," Gillian said without looking over at the Grey crumpled in the dirt like a limp rag. "Just knocked out. It's like I told you on the gangway. They're hard little buggers to hurt. Not that we want to hurt them. They're protected. They're an invaluable resource, actually. Most of them anyway. There's a few that are a real nuisance.

The rebellious ones pride themselves on being a pain in our collective ass. Even so, they have the same rights to life and liberty as anyone else on the ship. Even though they aren't officially crew members."

"It sure looked like he wanted to shoot me with that ray gun of his," I pointed out.

"I'm not saying the delinquent Greys are harmless," Gillian said. "They've put folks in the hospital more than once. But those incidents have been rare, especially when you consider how long we've been underway. They're such lousy shots. Plus, the military tech they insist on using is pretty ancient. Still, we have to make sure everybody who might come in contact with them understands the risks."

"I'm guessing they're not supposed to be here in Arizona. New Arizona, I mean. So why are they here?"

"It's kind of embarrassing, actually," said Gillian. She wasn't exactly blushing, but close. "We think they snuck in on the elevator with the captain on a recent visit. In some empty oil drums. This is exactly the sort of thing that our rules about crew members entering the Bubble were intended to prevent. But the captain's the captain."

"You're talking about Big Al."

"Captain Alfred Wertmueller," said Gillian. "The man you know as Big Al. He's been a great captain. The best. So his staff tends to cut him some slack when he goes off on his little moonlighting jaunts. They're well aware he likes to come here for recreational purposes. But he thinks it's a big secret."

"So how long have these Greys been here?"

"Not long," Gillian replied. "A few hours. They shouldn't have gotten too far."

I thought of the cave and was puzzled. It was at least twenty miles away from here.

Gillian saw the look on my face. "The Captain--Big Al--has an access point right here in the yard. That's how the stowaways got in. Surveillance footage tells us there are five of them."

She glanced over at the fallen intruder. "Four more to go," she said cheerfully,

"What can I do?"

"Help us look for them. Keep an eye out. Take this." She handed me a small metallic gizmo that had what looked like a miniature TV screen on one side. "You can call us on this if you see one. I strongly advise against engaging the Greys on your own."

She saw the incomprehension on my face as I took the contraption from her.

"It's a wireless phone," she explained. "Battery operated."

"OK," I said, turning the thing this way and that. It was super lightweight.

"You listen here. And you talk here." She pointed to opposite ends of the device.

"You push this button to get one of us on the line. Got it?"

"Where's Big Al now?"

"He's back in the stacks trying to track down the other Greys as we speak. I can't stay. I've got work up top that can't wait. But it's important to contain these guys. We don't want mass hysteria on our hands. Will you help?"

"I'd like to, but I have to be home soon. It's getting late, and I've got school tomorrow."

"No problem," said Gillian. "Come by when you can. We believe they're all still here in the salvage yard. But you never know. Al's going to keep the place locked up to keep them contained. They're not great climbers."

34

Big Al's Wrecking And Salvage

"I have a question," I said.

"Just one?" Gillian quipped.

"For now," I replied evenly. "What is the captain of a spaceship the size of a small moon doing running a wrecking yard?"

"I can't speak for the captain," Gillian said. "But the truth is there's not much for the captain of a voyage like this to do. It's all automated. As long as everything's operating within tolerances, all is well. From what I know of Captain Wertmueller, he's not the kind of guy to sit staring at a computer screen all day just to look busy. And he's not big on micromanagement. He trusts his people to do their jobs. So why not set up shop in the Bubble? He's fascinated by junk. And he loves old cars. So voilà!" She spread her arms wide and did a full turn in place like a Disney princess. Given her stature and her military gear, it was pretty funny. "He's as happy down here as a pig in. . . . Well, let's just say he's really happy here."

"It sounds like you know him pretty well," I said.

"It's my job to monitor excess and egress from the Bubble. The captain likes to spend time down here. So by default, a big part of my job is to look out for him, make sure he doesn't get into trouble."

"Does he get into trouble a lot? He looks to me like someone who can handle himself pretty well."

"And you'd be right about that. And no, he doesn't get into trouble. Intentionally anyway."

"So you have to guard against unexpected circumstances."

"Right again. No one could have predicted that the Greys would find a way into the Bubble, despite all the measures we have in place to prevent that from happening. They're sneaky little buggers, that's well documented. But we don't really need any complications now that we're coming into the stretch. We've got enough on our plate topside right now. And getting ready for the final approach to Epsilon 4 is only part of it," she added cryptically.

"More complications?" I said remembering my hasty departure from "topside" which Gillian had facilitated all those months ago.

"You could say that," she said grimly. I decided now wasn't the time to press her on it.

A light bulb went off in my head. "Do the earthquakes we've been having have anything to do with our coming to the end of the journey?"

"Yes. In fact, they do," said Gillian, seriously. "We've been decelerating gradually for the last couple of years. It takes time to slow from 99.998% of the speed of light without using up a lot of fuel. But now that we're approaching the star system that is our final destination we have to hit the brakes a little harder. Unfortunately, there's no way to dampen the vibration the engines make when they fire. These are some big ass engines. So you get tremors here in the Bubble. It's unavoidable. The good news is that the earthquakes are temporary. They'll taper off as we come into orbit. Hopefully, our breaking procedure hasn't been too disruptive for you down here."

"Not really. Just a few broken dishes. And one or two hairy moments in the shop."

"The shop?"

"The garage where I work. It's an automobile repair shop."

"I see," said Gillian. She smiled.

"You know," she said. "You've got it pretty good here. You're lucky."

"How so?"

"Well, despite the best efforts of our competent and extensive staff to replicate history accurately and precisely, human nature hasn't entirely cooperated."

I waited for more.

"We knew there'd be some variance in the historical narrative, despite our best efforts to keep everything constant. But what the scientists and social engineers hadn't counted on was the degree of social evolution that would occur during our two and a half centuries underway. You see, even recreating the events and conditions of the twentieth and twenty-first centuries precisely, there has nevertheless been a greater than expected deviation in behavioral norms from what was predicted. And your ability to do what you're doing as a female in 1950s Arizona is a perfect example of that."

"You mean I wouldn't have been working as a grease monkey in the original version of history?"

"Less likely, let's just say."

I wondered if that would apply to building my own hot rod and playing in an all-girl rock 'n' roll band with Mel and Tina. None of that had been exactly easy. But as I could attest, not impossible.

"Despite our best efforts to keep things the same, they changed, And for the better, I'd say."

"Actually," I said. "There has been some disruption since the earthquakes started. But it's been more up here than anywhere else." I tapped my head.

"How so?"

"When the earth began to shake a few months ago I started to remember things. I got flashes of being up top, above the Bubble, looking down."

"Really?" There was a look of concern on her face.

"Strange dreams, mostly. And then there's the vertigo."

"Damn it," Gillian said with uncharacteristic vehemence. "They told me there wouldn't be any side effects to the memory suppression protocol. But there are always side effects, I guess."

"In fact, I came here tonight to talk to Big Al about what was happening to me," I said. "I had a sneaking suspicion he might have some answers."

"Well, you suspected right," she said with a laugh.

"But now that I remember what I remember, I just have more questions."

"Of course you do," Gillian said. "But before you start, let me tell you how sorry I am that we had to put you through all this. I'm sorry we had to erase your memories to begin with. But the security breach you represented made it necessary. You were actually the first case on record of someone finding their way out of the Bubble. I personally think they need to rethink their approach. Your experience demonstrates it's not a perfected science. I apologize."

Gillian was being so gracious about it, I couldn't be too peeved. Besides, it wasn't my style to hold grudges.

It was almost pitch dark outside by now. The sunset was just a dark red line on the horizon.

"How long is it before we get to where we're going?"

"Another year or so, give or take."

"So," I said, taking a deep breath. "Everything we learned in history class about the twentieth century, the world wars, the A-bomb, the Cold War. . . ."

"They all really happened and have been faithfully reproduced by the Localized Personal Reality Matrix," Gillian finished for me. "Nobody said the history of the human race was pretty. LPRM has recreated the history of 1900 to 2100, warts and all. The idea was not to re-engineer the human race to be anything other than it is, or has been. Mankind would have to survive on its own merits in the new environment, or not survive at all.

"The fact that a measure of human evolution has taken place during the time we've been underway is encouraging. It indicates we may manage to avoid some of the pitfalls of the past after all, and not just repeat past mistakes. Maybe the human experiment will succeed this time around where the first one failed.

"Love your wheels, by the way," she said.

35

Ep/ilon 4

I came back to the yard the next day after work. It was about 5:30 in the afternoon. This time Big Al came out to greet me as I pulled in. Besides his usual Hawaiian shirt, he was sporting a dark blue skipper's hat with a gold anchor stitched on the front.

"Ahoy," he said by way of greeting as I stepped out of the Rex. "Gillian told me you came by last night. Sorry about our alien buddy trying to take a potshot at you."

"No harm done," I said. "Have you been able to round the rest of them up yet?"

"There's one still unaccounted for," Al said. "But I'm looking. Lots of good hiding places in here. Too many."

I nodded, surveying the stacks. Finding a two-foot alien among the hundreds of defunct cars and trucks seemed nigh impossible. But then again maybe Big Al had some way to track the things. He seemed to have handy gizmos for just about any purpose.

"Wow," said Big Al, taking a step back. "You guys did an amazing job on the car." He took his time inspecting the Rex from every angle. "You had a chance to see what she'll do?"

"A time or two," I said modestly.

"I'll bet," said Al with a knowing grin. He took off his cap and scratched his wiry close-cropped red curls.

"I came by to see if I could help you find the other Grey."

He nodded. "I've got it pretty much covered here," he said. "But you can help by keeping on the lookout around town. There's a chance our friend may have gotten out of the yard. The perimeter fence is in need of repairs in a couple of places. Don't go out of your way, though. Just keep your eyes peeled. If you see anything out of the ordinary around town, use the phone Gillian gave you."

"The phone," I said. "Right."

"Just press the button and give a holler. You'd be doing us a great service."

"Does that mean you're not going to zap me?"

"Zap you?"

"You know, so I'd forget all about. . . ." I nodded my head upward.

"Nah," said Big Al with a rueful grin. "Gillian told me you'd had some side effects from the procedure. You're one of the unlucky few who are somewhat resistant. You're one in a million our scientists insisted. I'm sorry about how what we did affected you. That wasn't supposed to happen."

"Special. That's me," I said, maybe a bit more lightheartedly than I felt. Thinking I was going nuts hadn't been all that much fun. "I'm guessing you'll want me to keep what I remember under wraps, though. Right?"

"Er. If you wouldn't mind. Go ahead and tell Kurt. But we're not quite ready yet to have the details about our transgalactic voyage become general knowledge. At least until the time is right. All will be revealed eventually, of course, I can assure you."

"So Grandpa doesn't know about you and the ship?"

"Not expressly. But he may have guessed some of it from our conversations."

"I'm not sure he'd believe me if I told him what I know."

"You'd be surprised," said Al. "He's one of the most open-minded people I've met down here. We're going to need folks like him. And like you too, when we come in for a landing."

"How's that going to work, exactly?"

"'Landing' is a figure of speech of course. There's no way this oversized Christmas tree ornament could ever be landed anywhere. It was never designed to. It was built in space, and in space it shall remain. When we pull into the new solar system, we'll go into orbit around our destination planet. It doesn't have its own moon. So we'll effectively become its moon.

"Oh, and it's a bi-solar system," he added. "Our final destination, Epsilon 4, is roughly equidistant from two suns. That means the planet is warmer, in general, than planet Earth was. Uniformly tropical, in fact. And it's much younger than Earth. It's a lot like Planet Earth was hundreds of millions of years ago in its geological development. Indigenous life hasn't progressed much beyond the oceans, at least as far as we can tell from way out here. But there may be surprises once we get there. You never know."

"So when we get into orbit around this Epsilon 4, what happens?"

"We shuttle everyone down to the surface."

"You'll just get on the horn and announce that we've all left a dying Planet Earth and been onboard a spaceship for the last 250 years, and now it's time to disembark through gate 2 and settle on a new planet?" I said incredulously.

"Well. Maybe not quite like that. There'll be a stretch of time when we recreate the living and working conditions our passengers are used to on the ground. That means building towns and cities from scratch. Creating infrastructure. Roads, energy, water, and waste treatment facilities. And we have to do it to spec. Everything has to be like it was here on the ship. Or as close as we can get in the new environment without having to do a lot of terraforming. That way we hope to avoid any significant disruption during the transition process."

"Seems to me the transition will still be pretty traumatic anyway. I don't see how it'll be avoidable. It's going to shake people up."

"We'll be using some advanced psych technology to smooth over the rough edges. Basically, everyone will be asleep for a while."

"Asleep? For how long?"

"A few months. Maybe a year. When you wake up again you'll be on the ground, living and working in places that look a lot like the ones you left behind in the Bubble."

I stared at him. "You're going to recreate Ted's? The school? Our house? What about Kurt's workshop?"

"Essentially, yes. Especially Kurt's workshop." Big Al was grinning. "Prepare to be amazed." He seemed to be enjoying himself. He was like a proud parent excited to see how the kids would react to their presents on Christmas morning. "The idea is to make the transition as seamless as possible for the Settlers. Which means you. Minimal impact is the goal."

I couldn't say I was entirely at ease with this approach. Keeping everyone in the dark about what was about to happen, let alone all that had happened to bring us to this point, left a bad taste in my mouth, I won't kid you.

I guess big Al could see I wasn't exactly thrilled because he said, "If there was another way to do this, believe me, we'd do it. It was decided a long time ago that this was the way to go for humanity to have the best chance at survival. There's a lot at stake here. And we only have one shot to get this right. We've got some amazing tools at our disposal to ensure things go smoothly."

As amazing as what was used on me to make me forget my experience up top? I thought sarcastically. But I didn't say anything. It was all too big for me to get my head around. I didn't like it that we'd been kept in the dark. But what use was it to start grousing about it now? That horse had left the stable a long time ago. What other option was there realistically, but to let things play out?

I gave Big Al the hairy eyeball. "When all this is over and done," I said. "Will the truth be known? All of it?"

"Yes," said Big Al, as serious as I'd ever seen him. "Everyone will be privy to the whole and complete story. You have my word on that."

36

Existence As We Know It

I almost wrecked the Rex a couple of times on the way back to the house because I was having a hard time concentrating. I had a lot to think about. Like what was the point of doing anything if the world as we knew it was about to end? And that didn't even take into account that the world as we knew it was not the world we thought it was in the first place. Everything was up in the air, so to speak. Why go to school? Why go to band practice? Why even bother going to work? It would all just be going through the motions until the big moment.

I started to get philosophical about it, never a good sign. I told myself this was the way life was. You came into the world without having much say in the matter. And you never knew when it would all go away. It was part of the deal. Uncertainty was woven into the very fabric of things.

But the converse was also true. Why *not* go to school? Why *not* go to band practice? Why *not* go to work? Were things that different now from the way they'd always been? You just had to get on with your life, regardless of what lay ahead.

In the best of times, it could still all end tomorrow. Everyone knew that. But you didn't just sit around gnashing your teeth about it. You did what you could with the time you had. And at 18, I had plenty of time ahead of me, if I had any say in the matter. So it made sense to continue to hone my skills, both as a musician and as a car mechanic. I took this tack, resolving to let tomorrow take care of itself.

I managed to keep the car on the road long enough to get it into Grandpa's garage.

"What happened?" asked Grandpa Kurt when he saw me. I must have looked wilder than usual. I caught a look at myself in the entryway mirror and barely recognized myself. My flaming hair stood out in all directions. And I was pale as a ghost. I looked like I'd stuck my fingers in a socket.

What happened? Where to begin?

"The car's obviously OK," Kurt observed, giving the Rex a quick once over while trying to guess at the source of my current state when I couldn't immediately express myself verbally. "You've still got all your limbs. You flunk chemistry? Somebody back over your guitar? You lost your best friend? You fell in love? What?"

"Grandpa," I said. "Did you ever feel like the world wasn't what you thought it was?"

"Every day," said Kurt. "What are you getting at?"

"What if you found out that everything you'd believed all your life was wrong?"

"Is this some kind of existential crisis we've got here? Is that what this is?"

"No. I'm talking literally. What if you discovered that nothing you held to be true was true."

"Why don't you just come out and tell me what's on your mind, girl? I promise I won't dismiss it out of hand. You know I wouldn't."

"We're inside a giant spaceship," I blurted out.

"What's inside a giant spaceship?"

"Everything. Planet Earth. Or what's left of it. We've been traveling through space at close to the speed of light for 250 years and replaying the last 200 years of world history on a loop since we left Earth to keep us busy. We're on our second go-round."

Grandpa scratched his head. But to his credit, he kept his cool. "And the source of all this new information is. . . ?"

"Gillian. She was the first one I met up top."

"Up top," he parroted uncomprehendingly. It was unfair to tell him like this. But I suddenly felt I needed to get it all out or explode.

"And today Big Al."

"Wait. Big Al? As in Big Al's Wrecking and Salvage? What does he have to do with this?"

"Everything," I sounded pathetic, even to my own ears. "He said you'd be more receptive to the idea than most."

"That we're all on a giant spaceship? He must think I'm a complete idiot."

I could see he was getting kind of agitated. "He said you'd think about it for a while," I said uncertainly. "And that it would start to make sense to you."

"Boy, isn't he the optimist?" Grandpa muttered. "How gullible does he think I am?"

"You did go along with his idea that the earth was flat," I pointed out.

He just looked at me for a long moment. "Alright," he said, regrouping. "It's true I've heard some harebrained theories from him. I've even tried a few on for size. But this is going too far. And here I thought I had the market on crazy cornered in this family."

"How can I prove it to you? We're coming in for a landing soon, and the cat'll be out of the bag anyway. So either you believe it now. Or you'll find out when everybody else does."

I could have taken him back to the wrecking yard to hear it from Big Al himself. But unless Big Al volunteered to let him ride back up the big elevator in the sky with him, which I seriously doubted he'd do, it would just have been more talk. More harebrained theories, as Grandpa put it. If there was a way to convince Grandpa that what I was saying was true, I sure didn't know what it was.

As it turned out, the problem solved itself.

37

Mascot

Grandpa Kurt shook off the funk he was settling into. "Listen," he said in a conciliatory tone. "What do you say we go over to the Tastee Freeze? We can talk about this over a hot fudge sundae. I'm buying."

"Are you trying to buy me off?" I said. "That hasn't worked since I was ten."

"I'll go get Trish. We'll make it a family outing, like old times. It'll be fun."

The three of us ended up piling into Trish's T-bird and driving to the Tastee Freeze a mile down the road, me squeezed into what passed for a back seat in the '56 coupe.

Rolling into the lot, it was clear something wasn't right. People were screaming and running in every direction. It took me a minute to pinpoint the cause of the problem. Standing in front of the bushes directly across from the drive-thru window was a Grey, probably THE Grey. The one that got away.

"What the hell is that!" exclaimed Grandpa Kurt.

I don't think Trish had fully registered what we were looking at yet. She was seeing what we were seeing, but her brain wasn't processing it.

The thing couldn't have been more than twenty feet away, so it was pretty unmistakable. At least to someone who had seen one before.

"It's a Grey," I said matter-of-factly.

"Wait. Is that thing real?" Grandpa said. "It's not the new drive-in mascot or something." He was looking at the Tastee Freeze sign and back at the alien, trying to connect the dots. It wasn't quite working.

So far the alien had not moved. It might have been a statue, planted there like that. But the way it was standing and where it's attention was directed suggested it was reading the menu over the drive-thru window with singular concentration. Was it about to place an order? It was the weirdest thought: did space aliens have a thing for soft ice cream?

"Don't go any closer," I said, pulling the small metal device Gillian had given me out of my jeans. I hit the button on it, and when Big Al answered, I said, "It's here. At the Tastee Freeze on Route 22. Up toward the mountains."

"The drive-thru near your place?"

"That's the one."

"Are you in a car?"

"Yes," I answered. "Grandpa and I are with Trish in her T-bird."

"Good," said Big Al. "Stay where you are. Do not. Repeat. Do not approach it. I'll be there in a minute."

Grandpa Kurt was looking out the front windshield, his mouth hanging open. Trish was staring straight ahead with a frown on her face. She was still trying to decide if the thing we were seeing was real. Since the Grey hadn't moved, it was really hard to tell. I could sympathize with her.

"Best if we just stay put for now," I said, squeezing the gizmo back in my jeans pocket.

"What is that thing. . . ?" Trish said, still staring straight ahead.

The Grey was kind of cute. If you didn't know about the ray guns they tended to carry.

Just then it moved. It seemed to tear its eyes away from the menu and looked down at the ground. Perhaps it was contemplating its financial situation or currency exchange rates. It seemed oblivious to the commotion it was causing just by being there. Most of the people who had been inside the joint were now in their cars. Engines were revving all around us, and tires were spraying gravel everywhere. People couldn't get away fast enough. The take-out window had been abandoned.

"That thing is alive?" Trish said in amazement. Now that the issue had finally been resolved, she seemed to take the matter in stride. She wasn't screaming. Not yet, anyway.

"You remember what I was telling you about the giant spaceship? The one we're really on?" I said to Grandpa Kurt. "Well, that spaceship is kind of infested with these critters."

The manager of the drive-in was now approaching the Grey with what looked like a butterfly net. His assistant was cowering behind him. When they were about ten feet from the alien, it calmly raised its ray gun and fired. It was just like in the movies. A beam of light went out and hit the manager. He went down like a sack of turnips. Meanwhile, his assistant was in the process of hightailing it back to the cover of the restaurant. The guy was no dummy.

The Grey pointed his ray gun at the retreating assistant but held fire. Maybe he didn't think he was worth the ammo. Or maybe he had to wait for his gun to recharge.

Beside me, Aunt Trish gave a choked gasp. She was eyeing the fallen manager and the butterfly net fluttering dismally in the breeze next to him on the gravel.

"Don't worry," I told her. "He's probably alright. I have it on good authority that their weapons aren't fatal."

"How do you know so much about these things?" Trish asked incredulously, staring at me in her rearview mirror.

"I don't," I said. "Or rather, I didn't know I knew. My memory had been erased. But now that's changed, and I know what I knew before. Again." I sounded pretty pathetic, even to my own ears.

Aunt Trish just looked at me in the mirror, speechless.

Grandpa Kurt snapped out of the daze he was in and turned around to face me, or as close as he could in the tiny car.

"You've seen these things before?" he whispered, trying not to attract the attention of the alien with the gun standing near the front of the car.

"Over at the Wrecking and Salvage," I said. "Big Al can tell you all about them. I just called him. He's on his way."

"That thing you had against your ear is a phone?"

"Cool, hunh?"

Grandpa brought his attention back to the space alien. "Damn," he said as if from a deep trance. "I've been wanting to see one of these things my whole life. I thought that ship had sailed."

38

Showdown

I could tell Grandpa Kurt was going over what I'd told him about the world-within-a-spaceship, reviewing it in light of current information. "So what you said about the spaceship," he finally said, still staring out the windshield at the Grey. "That's on the level?"

I nodded, but he didn't see me. "It turns out a lot more happened to me when I went into that cave up the arroyo than I thought," I said. "But I honestly didn't remember any of it. They erased my memory like I said, so I wouldn't blab everything I'd seen and cause a panic. I just got it back last night—my memory—when I went to visit Big Al in the junkyard."

"If that's true, why did he or whoever it was, restore it?"

"He said he wanted my help in tracking down this little guy. A bunch had gotten loose at the wrecking yard. He'd rounded up the rest, but he thought one of them might have escaped. Looks like he was right."

"And that thing you were talking into was some kind of communications device?"

"That's right. It's a wireless phone, kind of like a miniature walkie-talkie."

The Grey was now looking at the T-bird with curiosity, cocking its head this way and that. It started toward the car.

Trish inhaled sharply. "It's coming this way," she hissed.

"Just stay calm," I said. "It's like those wild jungle cats. If you don't move, it can't see you." I was pretty sure that was nonsense, but I didn't want anyone to panic and become a target. Besides, the T-bird was less than a year old, and I didn't want it covered with blaster burns.

Fortunately, we weren't forced to make the decision on whether to stay put or make a run for it, as Big Al's tow truck roared into view at that moment. It pulled into the Tastee Freeze parking lot kicking up gravel and dirt as it slid to a halt.

The Grey must have known the jig was up, because it suddenly changed course and made a beeline for the bushes. Too late. Big Al had rolled down his window before his truck had come to a complete stop. He had a ray gun of his own, it turned out. He drew a bead on the retreating alien, his tow truck's suspension still rocking and bucking under him, and pulled the trigger. He hit the bull's eye. The alien went sprawling face down in the dirt near the edge of the parking area and lay motionless.

To the three of us inside the T-bird, it was like seeing a movie western play out in front of our eyes. Only in this case the bad guy was two feet tall, had gray skin, and was from outer space.

"He'll be alright," I found myself saying, mimicking what I'd been told on previous occasions. "They're tough little buggers."

39

The Promised Land

"So," said Grandpa Kurt when we were back in the peace and safety of his garage. Trish had retreated to the kitchen. That was her refuge in times of crisis. And I guess seeing the Grey qualified. She wasn't as anxious as Kurt to know more right then.

"If we're on a giant spaceship, then where the heck are we going?"

"We're heading to an earth-like planet across the galaxy to start all over again," I informed him.

"What happened to the old one?"

"In the tank. Uninhabitable."

"Why don't you tell me what you know?"

So I told him about the ecological collapse that led to building a spaceship big enough to carry a sampling of humanity to a new home 250 years distant at close to the speed of light. And how we'd been cycling through the last 200 years of human history to pass the time until we arrived at our destination. And I told him about the 8 other levels above and below us that contained a cross-section of the different cultures that had existed on Planet Earth at the time of the ship's departure.

"And us Arizonans were selected to be among the Chosen People. How come?"

"Apparently Arizona was the right size," I said, recalling what Gillian had told me months ago. "And its climate's roughly similar to where we're going. At least, so it was believed when we left. That may need to be amended as new information comes in."

"But how could they pull this off? Making us believe we're in the fifties. And then recreating the broader historical context we're living in? How's that even possible?"

"Localized Personal Reality Matrix."

"Which is?"

"It's an advanced algorithm, is what Big Al said. Don't expect me to tell you what that is. But it's enabled us to experience the world and everything that's happened between 1900 and 2100 down to the smallest detail."

"Everything? The World Wars? The Cold War? Roosevelt, Truman, and Eisenhower? Jesus! Even Khrushchev?"

"Everything."

"And when somebody traveled to Baltimore. Or Paris. Or Timbuktu?"

"LPRM," I said. "For further details you'll have to ask. . . ."

"Yeah, yeah. I know," said Grandpa. "I'll have to ask Big Al."

"Alfred Wertmueller, actually. Captain Alfred Wertmueller."

"Captain Who?"

"Big Al is really Alfred Wertmueller, the captain of the ship we're on, The Fortune's Fool."

It was a lot to take in. But Grandpa was doing the best he could. He was giving it the old college try. After all several minutes of contemplative silence, he said, "So we only think we're living in the 1950s. But it's really a simulation."

"It's as close an approximation of how things were in the fifties as the technology will allow."

"Jesus."

"That about sums it up," I said. "And this is the second time we've repeated the 1950s. That makes three go-rounds in all if you include the original."

"It's one well-worn decade."

"In a well-worn couple of centuries."

"So it's actually. . . ."

"2444. Or more like 45 or 46 by now. I'm not sure."

Grandpa swore some more. "I can see why they wanted to keep this under their hats," he said. "They'd have had a full-blown mutiny on their hands otherwise. As things stand, if I understand this correctly, there's nothing to be done but ride it out. It's pointless for everyone to get riled up about it, even if they wanted to. It's too late. And in the meantime, we--those of us who have this privileged information--have to take it on faith that the people responsible know what the hell they're doing." He paused and shook his head. "If it were anybody else but Big Al. . . ."

I looked over at Grandpa Kurt. "Do we trust Big Al enough to go along with all this? And not say anything to anyone?"

Grandpa Kurt mulled this over. "Yeah," he said finally. "If we're coming in for a landing, I don't see as we have much choice. But even if that weren't the case, I'd still be inclined to give him the benefit of the doubt. He's one of the finest people I've ever met.

"Of course, if I didn't happen to know Big Al personally I'd either be panicking right now or just extremely pissed off. Not that it's gonna make a heck of a lot of difference one way or another. If what you're saying is true, this has all been planned down to the smallest detail for decades, hell, centuries. I doubt anything any of us could say or do would change much at this point."

We sat quietly, contemplating our predicament.

"When exactly did you say we get to this Promised Land?"

"Soon. In the next year or so, I was told. I don't know exactly when. And maybe that's the idea. They don't want us knowing too much. It's gonna happen when it happens. You know the earthquakes we've been having? It's the big ship putting on the brakes."

Grandpa nodded. "Hell of a thing," he said. "And when we get to this new planet?"

"We'll go into orbit around it. The ship will become like a satellite. A smaller version of the moon. From orbit, we'll be shuttled down to the surface."

"And the human race will start all over again from scratch."

"Not from scratch exactly. There's some pretty advanced technology onboard that is supposed to help us jumpstart the settlement process." I didn't mention the fact that we'd all be asleep for a year, give or take, while preparations for our arrival were being made. I felt Grandpa had enough to chew on right then. Maybe Al would fill him in on the details later. Or maybe not.

"So we won't be living in tents, like the Mongolians."

"I don't think so."

"Who's to say we won't just mess everything up again?"

"I think that's up to us. The hope is that when we learn about what happened on the original Planet Earth, we'll make different choices. I guess the people who planned this mission felt this was our best chance. Or maybe they didn't have time to think through all the angles. They just needed to pack us up and get us out of Dodge."

"And now we're coming in for a landing. I guess we'll find out if we can do better this time around and if their faith in us as a species is justified."

40

What About Gas?

Knowing that everything was about to change in unimaginable ways made even the most mundane things compelling all of a sudden. Everyday tasks were suddenly precious and amazing. I started to pay attention in my classes. And every gig the Roadrunners did was like the last gig we'd ever do. It was hard to imagine the band continuing once we touched down on the surface of a strange planet. It seemed survival would be the number one priority, not entertainment. And besides, who knew if there would be any place to plug into down there?

I even felt funny driving around in the Rex. Would it get shuttled down to the planet along with the rest of us? Or would it fall by the wayside during the transition process? And if it did make it to the planet's surface, where would the gas to run it come from? Gas came from dinosaurs that had been dead for millions of years. If Big Al was right, the destination planet, Epsilon 4, was a pre-dino kind of place. And as far as anyone knew, there was going to be nothing there to greet us when we arrived but a few fish.

The first chance I got to ask Al directly about it, he said, "All we really know is that it is a very young planet. It contains the same conditions for life that existed on Planet Earth before things went bad. There'll be ocean critters almost certainly. We don't expect to see much besides plants on land yet. Evolution won't have progressed that far.

"If the planet is as young as you say it is," I said. "Then it'll look a lot different from this." I gestured all around me. We were surrounded by stacks of rusted and mangled metal. But he got the gist. I was talking about New Arizona, not the wrecking yard.

Big Al smiled. "You're right about that," he said. "It'll be volcanic, most likely. Which is something we didn't know for certain at the outset. And the place having two suns means we can expect the climate to be dry desert in the interior, like Arizona, but tropical along the coasts all the way to the poles."

"Is that why you like to wear those Hawaiian shirts? Because they'll suit our new environment?"

Big Al burst out laughing. "I honestly hadn't thought of it that way," he said when he was able to speak again. "For me, this is a fashion choice, something to help me blend in. But you've got a point. If we're right about Epsilon 4, the whole planet could look roughly like a volcanic island, lots of hardened lava. Like the island of Hawaii, in fact. And if that's the case, these shirts I'm wearing could set the trend."

"So the shirts are like a uniform to set us common folk at ease?" I was just needling him, but he took it seriously.

"That's not what I meant," he said. "You do realize that you are the reason we're making this trip. You're the most important thing on this ship. Don't forget that."

"We're the prized cargo. I know," I said. "But we were not supposed to know anything about what's really going on." I guess I was still bugged about all we hadn't been told and the fact that I couldn't even share what I knew with my friends, including my fellow Roadrunners.

"Our survival is going to depend on cultural coherence across the board," Big Al told me levelly. He may have been wondering if I was still on board with this secrecy thing or if I was getting ready to jump ship, so to speak.

"I know. I know. And the best way to do that is to keep everyone in the dark, no exceptions," I said.

"That's right," said Al soberly. "It wouldn't have been the same if everyone had known about the mission from the get-go. The emphasis would inevitably have shifted in the process. It would have become a ship's culture where everything was geared to getting to where we were going in the most efficient manner. Instead of a variety of social and political systems, we would have had a monoculture based on a traditional command structure organized from the top down. And that would have run counter to everything the Designers intended, which was to preserve as many of Earth's institutions as they could in their original unadulterated form and deliver them to a point across the galaxy."

I remembered Gillian mentioning something along these lines when I met her up top on my first journey beyond the Bubble. The idea still didn't go down without leaving a sour aftertaste in my mouth.

"Do you really think you would have been happier as a passenger or crew member than as a teenager growing up in 1950s America, free to pursue your own personal interests and inclinations? Because that would have been the alternative. It might have been interesting for a while. Before the tedium of regimentation and the rigors of long-range space travel set in."

Putting it in those terms took the wind out of some of the resentment I'd been nursing. I was already starting to feel nostalgic for everything I knew and loved, and it hadn't even ended yet. Who would I have been without the music and the cars and Rattlesnake Junction? A space cadet? A private in someone's army? No, thanks.

Big Al continued. "The idea was that we, I should say you, would have a better shot at survival in the new circumstances with a richer, more varied life experience behind you, one that emphasized self-reliance and independent thinking over following rules and ship's protocols. I guess only time will tell if we were right."

I nodded. I was starting to get it through my thick skull that this wasn't just about my own wounded pride. It was a lot bigger than that.

"So," I said. "What do you wear up there on the bridge?"

"I've got a uniform and everything," said Big Al, with a wry grin. "I'm decked out like a four-star general most of the time. Gotta maintain a certain image, you know. Half of the job is to inspire confidence in others, to make it seem like I know what I'm doing. It gets tiresome as hell. That's one of the reasons I like it here so much. I can let my hair down."

"So to speak," I supplied.

"So to speak," he agreed with a chuckle, removing his cap and scratching his curly stubble.

I idly wondered how many ship's captains had come and gone on the long journey from Earth. Five? Six? More?

"What about my car," I said. "Will I be able to take it down to the surface too?"

Big Al chuckled. "Priorities, right? I don't see why not. Not after you went to all the trouble to build it."

"With your help," I reminded him. "What about gas?"

"With all the volcanic activity there's bound to be some kind of fuel available, something we could use or adapt for use in the kinds of vehicles we have here. It won't be fossil fuel based, but that may be just as well. As you move into the future, your cars will evolve. You'll invent other, shall we say, less impactful means of propulsion. But we don't want to get too far ahead of ourselves. Right now, some kind of gas is the way to go to get everything up and running in the shortest amount of time. So that will be a top priority right off the bat."

41

Carbon Copies

So," I said casually. "Was there a real Elvis once upon a time?"

Big Al looked at me like what-the-heck? "Elvis?" he repeated.

"You know. Mr. Rock 'n' Roll? Heartbreak Hotel. Hound Dog. Don't Be Cruel."

"I know Elvis," Big Al said cryptically.

I figured my change of topic must have given him whiplash.

"Rock 'n' roll has to be hundreds of years old by now, along with everything else," I said.

"I think Elvis is as real as he can be 400 years after the fact," said Big Al, thoughtfully.

"And that means?"

"Not as real as he used to be, maybe," he said smiling as if at a private joke. "But real enough. The music you're hearing over the airwaves is 100 % genuine though. It's all from the original sources."

"So an impersonator is taking his place, right? Has to be."

"You'd be surprised to what lengths the Cultural Continuity folks will go to find stand-ins for the stars and hitmakers of the day. They take their work very seriously. There's a whole section devoted to getting it right. It's the size of a small city."

"Like some kind of talent agency?"

"Yeah. Except they do everything. They don't just find people who look and sound like the stars of yesteryear. They develop the acts and all that entails. The people they select receive comprehensive training in all pertinent aspects of whomever it is they'll be representing. When the talent's ready, concerts are booked, interviews given, magazine covers shot, the works. It's all about historical accuracy."

He regarded me a moment. "But sometimes something new comes along," he said. "Take you guys, for example."

"Us guys?"

"The Roadrunners band."

"You know about us?"

"Sure. Hard not to."

"And what makes us so different?"

"Well, for starters, you're not prefabricated. You're the genuine article. And that makes you special. Your fame is spreading. Your music is becoming known. One day you may come to eclipse many of the folks you look up to right now."

"But aren't we landing soon? Doesn't that mean the fun will all be coming to an end?"

"Just because we're landing doesn't mean that everything will come to a screeching halt. We're hoping it won't. We're going to need artists and musicians more than ever to boost morale and maintain continuity as we move from the ship to the ground. We're going to need homegrown talent, not just the canned variety. When people realize that their heroes, musical and otherwise, have been dead for centuries, they're going to be looking around for replacements. Count on it. They'll be looking to original artists like you to speak to their experience."

"So we're just going to take up where we left off when we land?"

"I sure hope so," said Big Al sincerely. "We'd like nothing more than for things to go on just as they have been up until now and for everything to evolve naturally from there. We can't expect it all to go off without a hitch, of course. This has never been done before. But the sooner things normalize the better, once everyone's down on the surface."

"Elvis is doing a show in Phoenix," Tina White Cloud said casually during our next rehearsal.

"Count me in," said Melissa enthusiastically.

They looked at me, surprised I guess, that I hadn't chimed in yet. They must have been wondering what was taking me so long to get on board. I suppose knowing Elvis wasn't really Elvis had something to do with that.

I couldn't say anything about what I knew to be true though. I didn't think Big Al would appreciate it. It wouldn't stay a secret much longer, granted, but it wasn't my place to spill the beans. That was best left to the geniuses upstairs.

Still, I couldn't help but wonder how the news that we'd been living an illusion would go over when the time came. Would there be mass hysteria? Nervous breakdowns. Looting and shooting? I sure hoped not.

"Sure," I said finally, "Let's get tickets."

They looked at me kind of funny. But the moment passed, and we started into the next number on our playlist.

We made the pilgrimage to Phoenix on concert night. Melissa's dad was the chaperone. None of us had ever been further than Tucson. Consequently, having a dad along was a condition of our going.

I left the Rex at Melissa's and joined her and Tina in the back of Mr. Jordan's new Olds 88. It was big and comfy. A real cruiser. I'm not sure what Melissa's dad thought of Elvis. But I had it on good authority he was a Fats Domino fan, as were we. So I figured he'd find something to like in Elvis' music. He even looked like Fats a bit, if I squinted. As a big supporter of Melissa and her playing, I figured he had to have an ear for the music. I imagine he thought of our outing as a kind of field trip for us budding musicians. Potentially valuable career experience.

We got to the auditorium a couple of hours early. Even so, there was a line around the block. Luckily we had tickets in hand, thanks to Grandpa Kurt having ordered them for us in advance.

The show itself was pretty dang exciting, even knowing it was all staged by the Big Talent Agency In The Sky. They'd done a fine job of recruiting an Elvis stand-in. He looked and sounded like the real deal. Nobody was asking for their money back, I can tell you that. Even the ringers for guitarist Scotty Moore, bassist Bill Black, and drummer DJ Fontaine were spot on. Not only did they look like them, they played like them.

For Tina and Melissa, the event was like a religious experience. It confirmed everything we were doing musically. My own life-changing experience had happened months earlier when I stumbled upon those elevators in the cave up the canyon behind the house. And that transformation process was still in progress.

Still, it was all pretty cool. The real Mr. Swivel Hips or not, the show cemented our resolve to keep playing. It was all about the music, right? That and street rods.

At least for yours truly.

42

Paul And Des

The Roadrunners were booked to play the Rotary Hall in town the next Friday night. Our covers of Heartbreak Hotel (our A-side) and Don't Be Cruel (our B-side) were receiving a lot of local airplay and our audiences were growing. I drove over right after work at Ted's. I could have driven home. But I would have had to turn right around and drive back into town.

As it was, I had my guitar and amp in the Rex, all ready to go. It was early but that was OK. I needed a breather after school and work. I could nap in the car for an hour if I felt the need.

One of the things I liked about playing the Rotary Club was that they had a decent PA system. Usually, Tina had to sing through my guitar amp. The microphone we'd gotten for her was just like the one Elvis used on stage. It had been expensive by our standards. But it was worth it just for the look.

The stage was a raised platform, a couple of feet higher than the rest of the floor. It was directly to your right as you came in the door from the parking area. There was a good-sized hardwood dance floor in front of the stage. The rest of the place was occupied by upscale dining tables and leather padded chairs. The place had more the feel of a swanky restaurant and dance club than an informal meeting place for the town's business owners and professionals, which is what it was supposed to be. Business must have been good.

I was surprised to find I wasn't the first one there. As I approached the parking lot I saw a brand-new Cadillac convertible parked at the entrance to the building. I pulled in next to it, wondering who it could belong to. I knew most of the cars around town by now but had never seen anything like this one. It was pink, and I knew for a fact that Cadillac didn't offer pink as a stock color.

The only pink Cadillacs I knew about belonged to actors or actresses way out west. And those I'd only seen in magazines. And then there was the Caddy convertible owned by Elvis himself. That association alone was enough to cause my imagination to take flight. What if the "One and Only" or rather the stand-in for the "One and Only," had made the trip over from Phoenix to catch our show that night? It gave me a rush of excitement to think of it. I realized, of course, that I was getting carried away. There was probably a more mundane explanation for the presence of that particular car at the Rotary. And that explanation most probably had nothing to do with our band.

I took a deep breath and opened my car door, sleep forgotten. I had been considering bringing in my gear right off the bat, but there was plenty of time for that. I had to know who the owner of the Caddy was before I did anything else.

My heart was pounding as I pulled the front door open. I reminded myself that even in the unlikely event that the owner of the Caddy was the Elvis we'd seen in Phoenix, he wasn't the real Elvis. But he'd been good. He'd had talent. The week before he'd brought the house down in an auditorium filled to the brim with 3000 screaming fans. To those fans, he was the real thing. He was as real as it was ever going to get for any of us.

I was blinded coming in the door out of daylight. So I stood there inside the entrance, waiting for my eyes to adjust while the heavy doors slowly swung closed behind me. Gradually, the bandstand came into focus to my right. And then the tables and chairs to my left. The dining tables were made of some kind of dark wood, mahogany maybe, lacquered to an expensive sheen. They glistened in the dark.

Three people were standing on the dance floor before me. There was a Rotarian I recognized from a previous gig at the hall, a Mr. Bryant. He managed the venue. His first name was Ben or Burt or something like that. He was OK. He'd been jittery at first about having rock 'n' roll in his hallowed hall. But the audience had been well-behaved, and the show had come off without a hitch. So we got invited back.

Bryant was talking to a couple who had their backs to me.

The front doors finished closing behind me with a solid thunk that brought the conversation in progress to a halt. The trio turned to look in my direction. I pegged the couple for the owners of the Caddy right off and heaved a sigh of relief. The man was fit, tanned—and probably in his fifties or early sixties. The woman was striking, tall with straight jet-black hair. Her age was impossible to pin down. She could have been twenty-five or fifty-five. I felt like a bunny being considered for a meal by a mountain lion when she looked me over. Her eyes were like searchlights. Her high cheekbones and erect posture reminded me of Tina. She could have been an older version of our drummer, except that her skin was so pale it was almost translucent.

I took another look at the man. He was impressive in his own way. His salt and pepper hair was trimmed short. He oozed charisma, like a big-time movie star. There was nothing menacing in his stance. But in the confident way in which he carried himself, you could tell he was used to commanding a room.

The manager of the club motioned me over. "Here's the guitarist in the band right now," he told his visitors. Then to me, he said, "These good folks are here to meet you."

The man stepped forward and extended his hand. With a soft Southern drawl, he said, "Paul Galahad. Call me Paul. This is Des."

Galahad's hand was warm. Des' was as cold as marble.

"Pleased to meet you," I said uncertainly. "Is there something I can do for you?"

"We came down to catch the show," said the man who called himself Paul. "We heard your cover of Heartbreak Hotel on the radio and wanted to come see you and your band in person."

"Is that your Caddy out front?" I asked the couple.

"Yeah," said the man. "Always had a thing for Caddies. Can't help it. Even after all these years."

I felt like I was missing something. Like I was on the outside of an inside joke.

"Why don't we sit down," said Paul Galahad. "Got a minute to spare? We won't take up much of your time. I know how it is when you're getting ready to go on. It's nice to have a little time to yourself."

"Sure," I said. There was something about this guy. Like he was used to being the center of attention. It made me curious. "What do you do Mr. Galahad, if you don't mind my asking?"

"It's Paul," said Galahad. "I used to be an entertainer. A singer."

"What kind of music did you do?"

"Gospel, blues, country, rock 'n' roll, you name it," said Galahad, offhandedly. "A lot of Elvis stuff, actually. But I had to get out of the business."

"How come?" I was trying to picture this older guy playing rock 'n' roll. It wasn't as hard as I would have expected.

"I got tired of the grind. There were other things, too. Health issues and such. I couldn't have gone on even I'd wanted to. So my career and I had a parting of the ways. I left the old life and started a new one." He glanced at Des. "I haven't performed in a long time."

That made me even more curious, of course. Whatever problems he'd had in the past, he looked fine now. Better than fine. "Why don't you join us on stage tonight, if you feel up to it?" I said on an impulse. "We do other Elvis songs besides the ones on the record. We'd love to have you do a number or two with us." His reaction made me think I'd gone too far. "But if you really don't want to, that's OK. No pressure. I just thought. . . ."

His suntanned features had clouded over. He looked past me toward the stage area as if old, not particularly welcome, memories lurked there in the dark. The silence drew on. The club at this hour was quiet as a tomb.

Finally, he turned back to me, an unreadable expression on his face, and said, "Why don't we just wait and see what happens."

43

Miracle At The Rotary

The song he chose to do was Love Me Tender, a song the band had never done and didn't know. We'd performed about every song in the Presley repertoire except that one. It was nothing against the song, which we liked as much as anything Elvis did. We just leaned toward the upbeat numbers for our show.

So while Paul Galahad ventured over to take the mic from Tina, I was going over the chord changes for the song with the volume on my guitar way down. Melissa was watching my guitar like a hawk, picking up the progression as I went along. By the time he took his position in the center of the stage, I thought we had some idea of what we were doing. Enough to fake it, at least.

Since the song as it was originally recorded had no percussion, Tina left her kit and walked to the edge of the stage. She didn't venture too far, though. I wasn't the only one waiting to see what this stranger could do.

Nobody was paying any particular attention. We'd just done a pretty lively set and people needed a break to relax, get a drink, chat up their dates, or whatever. My guitar barely registered when I started strumming, even with the volume up.

When Galahad started singing the room grew quiet. All eyes turned toward the stage. His voice had an enormous presence. It filled every cranny and crevice of the hall.

I'd listened to that song hundreds of times on record at home. I knew every nuance. As I listened, I became convinced I knew that voice, except for the minor fact that it just wasn't possible. And yet, when I closed my eyes I heard that same voice, the one that was on the records. An image appeared in my mind's eye. Elvis.

True. It had some mileage under its belt, but it was the same voice. There was no doubt in my mind. How that was possible, I couldn't begin to fathom. But the longer he sang the more certain I became. It was all I could do to keep my place in the song and not just stare at the singer on stage with us. I even got choked up at one point. If you knew me, you'd know that never happens.

There was total silence when we finished the song. The man named Galahad just returned the mic to the stand next to Tina's drums and jumped down off the stage. Nobody even thought to clap. The crowd parted like the Red Sea until he stood next to his partner once again. Then the crowd filled back in and the murmurs started, building to a dull roar. The conversations were all variations on the same theme: Who was that?

I knew we had to do something. So I signaled All Shook Up, one of Tina's showcase songs and one that seemed particularly apt at that moment. As previously mentioned, Tina was no slouch in the vocal department herself. She could have given Wanda Jackson a run for her money. But she lacked the soul and the experience of the guy who had just left the stage. Even so, it worked. People started moving to the music, and that moment of amazement and incredulity passed.

I didn't see Paul Galahad or his impressive girlfriend again after that. They just disappeared. I figured they'd slipped out the back way and had driven off somewhere in that Caddy. His departure was as much a mystery as why he'd been there in the first place. My thoughts were a jumble.

We finished our set, one of our better performances I have to say, packed it up, and went home. But that night I lay awake for a long time thinking about that song and that performance. It followed me into my dreams that night.

44

The Original

Grandpa Kurt and I were back over at Big Al's the next day. He was looking to replace a rusty door latch for the Studebaker. As we wandered through the stacks, I told Grandpa about the concert the night before. He was only mildly interested. It wasn't really his kind of music. He preferred big band jazz. Duke Ellington, The Dorsey Brothers, Glenn Miller. Frank Sinatra was pushing it as far as he was concerned.

I was surprised when Big Al, who had been walking behind us, perked up. "This guy at the Rotary," he asked. "What did you say his name was?" He had stopped while Grandpa continued walking on ahead.

"Galahad," I told him. "Paul Galahad. He was with a woman, a looker."

"Desdemona," said Al fondly.

I just looked at him. "You know those people?"

"Sure," said Big Al. "I've known them a long time. Haven't seen them in years, though. They keep to themselves. How are they doing?"

"Good, I guess. Did I mention he jammed with us on stage at the Rotary?"

"No shi. . .kidding?" Big Al seemed genuinely surprised. "That's front-page news," he said. "He doesn't perform much anymore. Never,

146

in fact. He must have been in a rare mood. Or you must have been really convincing. You were lucky to have heard him."

"He had a heck of a voice," I agreed.

"There's that."

Big Al and the man who called himself Paul Galahad would have been about the same age, I figured.

"So how do you know him?" I asked.

"I make a point to know who's on my ship," Big Al said. "I'd been a fan. And we became friends. He's been around even longer than me, and that's saying something."

"He didn't seem that old."

"He does look pretty good for his age, doesn't he?" Al said with a laugh. "I guess we both do." I felt I was missing something.

"Alright," I said, getting impatient. "Spill."

Big Al scratched his jaw. "All I know is something happened to him a long time ago," he said. "It had something to do with his girlfriend, Des. Everyone thought he'd died. He claims she saved his life. Whatever the details, the upshot was that neither he nor Des age the way that most people do."

"What are you saying? That they're immortal?"

"I don't know about immortal. Just that they've been around a good long while. Centuries maybe."

"What?" I said. I didn't think I'd heard right. "Did you say centuries?" I could feel a headache coming on.

"I really can't tell you more than that," Big Al said turning serious. "Frankly, I never thought it my place to ask. That was between him and Des. I do know he's one of the most generous people I've ever known. That, and as you observed, one hell of a singer."

"You must have some theories," I insisted.

"Oh, I've got theories alright," said Al. "But you'd think I was crazy if I told you."

"Crazier than all of us being on a giant spaceship headed for another planet?" I said. "Try me."

"You got me there," Al said with a grin of admiration or annoyance, I couldn't say which. He looked up to see where Grandpa was. He was well out of hearing range, engrossed in searching the stacks for more Studebaker parts.

Al turned back to me. "He's the original," he said simply, in a low voice.

I blinked at him. "The original?" I repeated.

"He's the King," said Al. "The one and the only."

"The king of what?" I asked, truly baffled by now.

"The king of rock 'n' roll, of course. The man himself. Elvis."

I was stunned into silence, a relatively rare occurrence for me.

Al was looking at me with a bemused expression. "Told you it was going to sound nuts."

"How? How do you figure?"

"I've known the man for most of my life. You pick up things. Snippets here and there. A few references. A few things no one could possibly know. Unless they'd been there. He was careful not to divulge his true identity, but he's not a secretive person by nature. In the length of time I've known him, he couldn't help but let a few things slip. I never questioned him directly. I valued our friendship enough to not ask. I didn't want to sour things between us.

"But I'm as sure as I can be of anything. It's him. The man himself. The king of rock 'n' roll."

45

The Kid

"**A**nd then there's the kid," Big Al continued.

"They have a child?"

"I don't think it's their child. They seem to be looking after her. But the kid could just as easily be looking after them."

"What do you mean by that?"

Big Al shrugged. "It's just a feeling I get when I see them together. It's like the kid is on equal footing with them, regardless of appearances."

"How old is she?"

"She looks about your age. Maybe a year or so younger. But that's the thing. I've known her for as long as I've known Paul and Des, and she's always looked about the same. The trip's been hard on her, harder than it's been on most. She's as frail as I've seen her. But the point is, she hasn't gotten any older."

"So she's an immortal too," I said like it was no big deal. "A teenage immortal." But I was shook. I was thinking, how is any of this possible? I could almost buy Elvis as being an immortal. That's because I was confident his music would live forever. If it didn't, there was no justice in the universe. And what Big Al was telling me now squared with what I'd felt to be true when I heard that voice on stage at the Rotary--that Paul Galahad was the original Elvis. The picture was still hazy, at best. But the idea wasn't as far-fetched to me as it should have been. I knew nothing about Des and this young girl Al was talking about, however.

"The girl's something else, no doubt about it," Big Al went on. He could see me squirming with what he was telling me, but he seemed to be enjoying my discomfort. "She's darling, just sweet as you please. But when you take a closer look, there's more going on there. Even as sickly as she is right now, she's a real tempest. A powerhouse."

"What do you mean?" In for a penny. . . .

"I dunno," said Big Al looking off into the distance. "There's something really old there. I mean ancient." I became aware that Big Al was looking directly at me. "Come to think of it, she's a little like somebody else I know."

I shook my head. Was he messing with me? "What? What are you saying?"

"You're a little different yourself, aren't you?"

He was trying to divert the conversation from this kid he was talking about. Sure I was different from most girls my age. It didn't take a genius to know that. But I wasn't going to let him get away with the misdirection.

"So this kid. . .," I said, folding my arms and waiting to hear more. I was prepared to wait all day.

Big Al chuckled, seeing I wasn't about to be dissuaded. "You remember that theory I mentioned?"

"The one about Paul Galahad being the original Elvis?"

He nodded. "Well, I have a theory about her too."

"OK," I said. I was thinking, Here we go again. "Are you going to share it with me?"

I could see Big Al was conflicted. He sincerely didn't know whether he should say more. Maybe he thought he'd said too much already.

"My lips are sealed," I said to reassure him. "You can bet I won't be mentioning whatever you tell me to anyone." If this was as out there as the Paul Galahad theory, they'd have me in a straight jacket before you could say Jack Sprat, if I dared repeat any of what I was being told to anyone else.

"My theory?" said Big Al. He seemed to have made the decision to trust me. "She's older than they are. Her memory goes back to before the problems began on Planet Earth. Back to a time before civilization even, when the continents were still in the process of forming." He stopped himself. He seemed to need to collect his thoughts before continuing, "Behind the ingénue facade, she's a formidable force. What she allows us to see is the proverbial tip of the iceberg. Paul and Des trust her, so I've always trusted her too. She's never done anything to indicate she might pose a threat to the ship."

"Go on."

"I think of her as a stowaway of a whole different order. She's not like the Greys. She's like something straight out of mythology. Like a fugitive from Olympus. Only I doubt she's Greek."

"OK," I said, not sure what to make of what he had and hadn't told me. "So why were Paul and Des at our show the other day?"

"I can't speak for him of course, but knowing him I'm pretty sure he just wanted to see you perform," said Al. "He must have heard your music around and been impressed enough to seek you and the band out personally, nothing more. It could be you remind him of himself in his younger years. I could easily imagine him being tickled enough by what you and your band are doing to want to see you firsthand.

"This is Elvis' time," Big Al went on. "This is when it was all happening for him. This particular period in history has got to be near and dear to his heart. And he's getting to experience it all over again. For the third time, in fact. He gets to eavesdrop on his own personal history incognito, from the sidelines, without the heat of the spotlight on him. It must be a real kick for him."

"Don't you think he'd want to experience it as a performer too?"

"From what I know of him, I doubt it. He was at the beginning of his career here. It was all ahead of him. The world was his oyster in '56 and '57. It was all new, and he was at the top of his game. But all that changed later on."

"How so?"

"When the novelty and excitement of those early years had worn off, he was stuck with having this larger-than-life image to maintain and live up to. He became, quite literally, a prisoner of his success. He couldn't go anywhere or do anything without being noticed and besieged. The pressure of having to perform nonstop and keep up his persona 24 hours a day, year after year, did him in in the end. But all that was yet to come, starting with his being drafted into the army in '58."

"He's going into the army?"

"You heard it first," Big Al said and laughed. "But you're not going to see that part play out. There's not enough time before we get to where we're going."

"Does he know about us coming in for a landing?"

"Sure. He, Des, and the girl are kind of VIPs on the ship. They spend as much time out of the Bubble as in it. They know the whole deal. They signed on for the ride at the very beginning, so they know all about the project. They were there before the plans were written up for the Fortune's Fool. They were there before things began to go south on Planet Earth even. And they saw the decades of hemming and hawing that followed, while everything went to hell."

I just nodded, taking it all in. "So you don't know where they might have gone?"

"Not a clue."

Later that night I was passing a small apartment complex on the way home when my heart skipped. I spied that distinctive pink Caddy nosed into one of the parking spaces in front of the place. It was there the next day too. And the next.

I was delighted to think the dynamic trio had chosen to set up shop in the neighborhood. It was a huge deal to me knowing Galahad and his friends were still around. And now there was this whole other mystery surrounding the three of them, courtesy of Big Al. I figured the captain had seen a few things in his time, and it would take a lot to impress him. Yet he seemed to be in awe of Paul Galahad and his family, or family-like unit. I wanted to know more. If they were going to be around for a while, maybe I'd have a chance to get better acquainted and everything would come clearer.

There were twelve units in the apartment complex, five downstairs along with the main office, and seven upstairs. They formed three sides of a rectangle that opened onto a swimming pool that faced the highway. I felt a charge every time I went by on my way to and from school. But the idea of actually stopping and knocking on their door was a bridge too far for me. There was just no way I could have done it. What would I have said? "Howdy. I just wanted to welcome you to the neighborhood" and then hand them a fruit basket like the Hospitality Hostess. Nope. It wasn't my style to intrude.

There were pushy folks who might have done something like that. But I wasn't one of them. And from what Big Al had said, these were people who valued their privacy.

46

Free For All

We were booked to play the county fair that October. The fairgrounds bordered the town to the north, and as usual, the place was lit up like Christmas. The Ferris wheel was turning lazy circles high above the other rides and attractions that fanned out around its base. Beyond these were pens containing prize-winning livestock, hogs, cows, goats, roosters, and just about any other domestic animal you could name. And behind those, way out on the periphery, were the bull and bronc riding corrals flanked by grandstands. It was a Friday night, and there was a good turn out. Alternating cheers and groans could already be heard emanating from the rodeo section, even though it was still daylight.

I wasn't into rodeo that much, so I stuck to where the rides and concessions were. The stage was set up under a canopy at the base of the Ferris wheel, conveniently located near the food court. We were due to go on at sunset, so I had time to grab a bag of caramel corn on my way to the stage.

When I got there, I looked out over a crowd of a couple of hundred people, kids and adults alike. Grandpa Kurt and Aunt Trish were there, I noticed. And I recognized a few of my classmates who were regulars at our gigs. Fans, I guess you could say.

We launched into our first set, and more people began filtering in. We were a curiosity, and they were there mostly to gawk at first. But eventually a few began to dance around on the asphalt. The PA set up here wasn't on par with the one they had at the Rotary Club, but from the reaction, I'd say we were getting our message across.

There are a few bad apples in every bushel. In this case, they were a trio of dunces from out of town. These were older guys who seemed to be having a hard time wrapping their heads around the idea of an all-girl rock 'n' roll band. It didn't help that one of the band members was black and the other a purebred Indian, no matter how amazing they looked and how well they played.

They'd just come over from the rodeo section, and it was clear from what they were wearing that they fancied themselves quite the cowboys. They had the look down—pointy cowboy boots, hats, western shirts complete with silk neck scarfs, and big shiny championship belt buckles to top everything off. But everything was brand new. These guys had probably never ridden a horse.

They were pretty full of themselves. We were trying to get through the last couple of songs in our set, and they were doing everything they could to drown us out with their whistling and hollering. It wasn't long before a few of our fans took issue with their behavior. They confronted the newcomers, and before you knew it, a full-blown rumble was in progress.

I gotta hand it to our fans. I may have mentioned before that they weren't the kind to take sh—guff—from anybody, regardless of how seasoned they thought they were. And certainly not from a bunch of yahoos wearing fancy hats, trophy belt buckles, and snakeskin boots. If these dudes were looking for the opportunity to mix it up, they got their wish that night and then some from our wiry ragtag group of fans.

As the flashpoint for the free-for-all, we thought it best to remove ourselves posthaste and ducked into the wings to prevent things from spiraling even more out of control. Also, to get a better view of the proceedings.

I saw one of the cowboys jostle Grandpa. I came up off my folding chair like a shot, ready to defend him. But then I saw Kurt elbow the guy in the gut and kick his legs out from under him in an elegant sweep, as cool as you please. The guy went down and wisely stayed there. I took my seat again. Grandpa obviously didn't need my help.

It was right about then I noticed a waif-like, honey-haired girl standing by herself just below the stage a few feet in front of me. She was so pale she looked like she should be in a hospital, not traipsing around the rowdy fairgrounds on a Friday night. The only animated thing about her was her mouth. She was chewing gum a mile a minute. She was obviously as amused by the goings-on as we were. I invited her to take a seat next to us. She didn't need any further coaxing. She flashed a smile and bounded up onto the stage like a gazelle, despite being nothing but skin and bones.

"Cherry," she said, extending her hand.

"Rose," I said, taking her hand, I seemed to recall having heard that name somewhere before recently, but couldn't immediately place it. "This is Melissa," I said, going down the line. "And Tina there on the far end."

Hands were shaken all around.

"I don't think I've seen you at our gigs before," I said. "This your first time hearing the band?"

"Yes," she said. "Live, that is. I've heard your 45 though. My uncle plays it a lot."

I was starting to get goose skin, like when a piece of a puzzle you've been working on falls into place. "Your uncle wouldn't happen to be, ah, Mr. Paul Galahad, would he?" I knew now where I'd heard the name before. Big Al. This was the legendary "kid" who wasn't actually a kid. This was Supergirl.

It may have been the power of suggestion, but there was something about her. Like her so-called uncle, she had charisma. Star power. Despite the fact that her skin appeared almost translucent, and she seemed thin enough that any passing breeze might whisk her away.

"I'm new in town," she said. 'I thought I'd come down to see what was going on."

"If you want to get a feel for Rattlesnake Junction, I guess this is as good a place as any to start," I told her. And because of her obviously fragile state, I added, "You don't need to venture too far.

If you stick around this bandstand long enough, you'll see just about everybody in town sashay by at some point."

"I really enjoyed your set," she told me earnestly. "Your singer reminds me of Wanda Jackson."

"She's been told that," I said, looking over to see if Tina had heard. But she was preoccupied watching the fisticuffs play out in front of us. "Thanks," I said on her behalf.

47

Hawaii

I offered to show her around town the following day, it being Saturday and a day off for yours truly. I admit my intentions weren't entirely selfless. The new arrivals in town had me dying of curiosity. As I mentioned, I wasn't normally the type to get involved in other people's business, but these folks seemed to be the exception.

She accepted.

I told her I could pick her up where she lived, but she told me that wouldn't be necessary. Maybe she didn't want me to know what I already knew. That she lived in an apartment complex along the road into town from my house. I didn't press the issue. She said she could meet me outside the movie theater in town, and I agreed.

True to her word, she was waiting for me curbside at the Rialto as I pulled up in the Rex. She was dressed in a gauzy dress, like something a ballerina might wear. She looked otherworldly. Like an anemic Tinkerbell. I got out and locked up the car.

"Nice wheels," she said when I joined her on the sidewalk. "You did an amazing job on it."

I was about to ask her how she knew I'd been a party to building the car, but she grabbed my arm and dragged me down the street before I could say anything. She was a couple of inches shorter than me. I must have had thirty pounds on her and I wasn't fat. Even so, she was surprisingly strong. I had to focus to keep up.

"Are you going to enroll in school?" I asked her.

She shook her head. "No time for that," she said. "Even if I wanted to. Which I don't. You know this is all going to end soon, right?"

"I heard."

"There are things to be done. Arrangements to be made."

I was about to ask her what arrangements she needed to make when she swung us into a dress shop. We emerged twenty minutes later, Cherry with a shopping bag full of new clothes. I wondered whether these 'arrangements' included updating one's wardrobe.

"Just in case," she explained. "I've been told things aren't going to change that much when we land. But you never know."

I just nodded. I didn't have money for shopping, so I just followed along. It was like she was the one leading the tour, not me.

"You had breakfast?" she asked me.

"A bowl of cereal," I said.

She seemed to know exactly where she wanted to go, without any help from me. She just pulled me along, a mad gleam in her eye, oblivious to the stares she got. We came to a stop in front of Henrietta's Café. It was the place I would have chosen if she'd asked me. We slipped into a vacant booth near the front. The café was a long narrow room with the counter on the right and red vinyl booths lined up to the left.

Cherry flopped down on the side of the table facing the street and studied the menu. Her face lit up. "They've got Spam!" she exclaimed.

"You going to have some?" I said uncertainly. What was so special about Spam?

"No," Cherry said. "I don't eat meat. It just reminds me of home."

"Oh? And where's home?"

"Hawaii."

I thought about that. I'd discovered that nothing really existed apart from what was represented in the Stacks. It was all an illusion. Maybe she didn't realize it. I found myself feeling sorry for the girl. She'd been living in a dream, not the real thing.

"Oh, the Hawaii I remember was real enough, thank you very

much," Cherry said as if reading my thoughts. "I remember it from before everything went to shit, and we were forced to hitch a ride on this rust bucket. It's really a shame what the human species did."

"You say that like you're not a member," I said casually. It was one of those questions where I was a little scared to know the answer.

"You got that right," she said, rolling her eyes. "No way I'd want to be tarred with that brush."

We went back to studying the menu. I decided on orange juice, hash browns, two eggs sunny side up, and toast. When the waitress arrived, Cherry said she'd have an English muffin with some jam.

"You look like you could stand to eat a little more," I ventured. Next to her, I felt like a weightlifter. Heck, Audrey Hepburn would have looked like a nightclub bouncer standing next to her.

She shrugged, unoffended. "Everything will be fine once we're down on the ground again. I know it will." It sounded a little like she was trying to convince herself.

"The place we're going to is supposed to be a lot like Hawaii," Cherry continued, a distant look in her eyes. "Lots of volcanic activity. Oceans for thousands of miles in all directions. If that's really the case, it's something I can work with."

The prospect sounded none too shabby to me.

"You think there'll be beasties? Octopi with a hundred eyes and long tentacles? Fish that can swallow ships?"

Cherry considered my question seriously. "Al says no," she said. "Too early in the evolutionary cycle. Regular fish, maybe, and lots of microbial life. A few bugs. We won't know for sure until we get there."

"No skeeters, I hope," I said. "I'm allergic."

"I doubt it. If Al's right, there's nothing on land big enough to suck the blood out of. So probably no mosquitos."

Our food arrived and we dug in. More accurately, I dug in. She barely touched her muffin.

"Do you miss Hawaii?" I asked her, knowing the answer before I asked it.

Cherry nodded thoughtfully, taking a dainty bite out of her

muffin. "Like crazy. But if we're lucky the whole planet will be just like the Big Island."

She gave me a searchlight look. It gave me a shock. It was like flames were flickering deep in her eyes. And for the first time, I had the dizzying certainty that she really was not quite human. Not even mostly human.

Suddenly Cherry stopped chewing. Staring straight ahead, she frowned. She picked up her napkin, dabbed her mouth with it for a second, and set it down. "We gotta go," she said.

48

Lazarus

"hat? Why?" I asked. My breakfast was half-eaten. Cherry didn't say anything as she pushed herself up from the booth. The matter was obviously not up for discussion. She reached into a small handbag she had over her shoulder and pulled out a wad of crumpled bills. Without looking at the denominations, she peeled off a few and threw them on the table.

She looked like she meant business. I hadn't seen her so intent, so I went along. I gave the remainder of my breakfast a last longing gaze and followed her out the front of the café, practically running to keep up.

We got to my car in record time. When we climbed in she said, "Drive." She said it in a way that brooked no dissent.

I drove us to the highway that led toward her apartment, thinking she'd forgotten something there or was late for some kind of appointment. But when I slowed to turn into her apartment complex, she said, "Keep going."

There wasn't much past the apartment complex except open desert. And, of course, my house at the end of the road. "Are you sure?" I asked. But she just kept staring out the windshield.

The road funneled down to the familiar barely used, newly paved suburban street that we lived at the end of. The house loomed up ahead.

I drove right up to it and pulled into the driveway, a twinge of concern in my gut. I was totally baffled. Stopping the car, I pulled the handbrake and got out. Cherry was already out of the car and tugging on the garage door. What the heck? I thought.

The door came up, and there was Aunt Trish in a crouch near the workbench. Looking closer I could see she was cradling Grandpa Kurt's head in her hands. She had such a look of anguish on her face, it broke my heart.

"I found him like this," she said, her voice quivering with emotion. "I called for an ambulance but no one's come yet. I don't how long it's been. There's no heartbeat."

I pushed in beside her and started using my CPR training, pumping his chest, holding his nose, breathing into his mouth, and then pumping some more. I went through the sequence about a dozen times with no result.

Then Cherry, who had been standing behind me, came forward. In a voice barely above a whisper, she said, "Let me try."

In a daze, I stood up, looking down at Grandpa's unresponsive form. I'd done everything I could do. I gently took Trish's arm and led her toward the door to the kitchen. Behind us, Cherry continued to stand there looking intently down at Grandpa Kurt splayed on the concrete floor.

"I'll call emergency again," Aunt Trish said. "They should have been here by now."

While she went into the living room, I went back to the door to the garage, which was still open a crack.

With my hand on the doorknob, I saw Cherry crouch over Grandpa Kurt. She had one hand on his chest and one behind his head. Something funny started to happen to my vision. I'd always had 20/20 eyesight, but right now Cherry was going in and out of focus. I blinked a few times, but it didn't help. She was at the center of an expanding sphere of light. The light overwhelmed her fragile form, and she disappeared in the brightness. I held a hand up to my eyes to shield them.

The transformation from Cherry to ball-of-light and back took about a minute and a half. All I know for sure is that by the end of that time, Grandpa Kurt was back. He started coughing and rolled onto his side. Cherry, meanwhile, was the frail blond girl again. If anything, more frail. She was now standing back at the entry to the garage. I hadn't seen her move. One second she was a glob of light hovering at Kurt's side. The next she was twenty feet away, looking on.

I tore the kitchen door open, relief flooding through me. I ran to Grandpa's side and grabbed his calloused hand, tugging on it to get him up off the concrete.

"Must have fainted," he said, a confused look on his face. He dusted himself off. From all appearances, he seemed his usual self.

"You OK?" I asked.

"Never better," he said. "Just getting old, I guess."

"Do we need to take you to the hospital?" I said.

"No, no. Not the hospital again. Anything but that."

"Aunt Trish might have something to say about that. She was worried sick. We both were."

Just then Trish was at the door, relief flooding her features. "Gramps," she said. "You're OK."

"Sure," he said. "No need to make a fuss. Just got a little lightheaded is all. I'm fine and dandy now."

"The ambulance is going to be here any second."

"Call 'em back and tell 'em to turn right around," he said, mildly annoyed. "There's nothing for them to do here. I'm fine."

Just then Grandpa Kurt caught sight of Cherry silhouetted in the garage doorway. He just stared at her. He didn't say anything, or couldn't.

"Grandpa Kurt," I said. "This is Cherry."

I dreamt that night that I was up top again, inside the spaceship proper. I was in the cargo hold where what was left of humanity was located. I could see the Stacks before me like shelves in God's pantry. There were boxes and storage crates all around me, piled so high they disappeared in the darkness above me. These were all the things that were being transported to our new planetary home. The piles of boxes went on for miles in all directions. Machinery, building materials, dry goods, and sundries, all brought with us from Planet Earth. I noticed that the lid on a nearby crate was open. I stepped up to it and found it empty. I looked down at the label on the crate. It read "Pele".

I awoke thinking of Cherry, the fire in her eyes, and how she had helped Grandpa Kurt. And I realized what Big Al had been trying to tell me when he referred to "the kid" as a special kind of stowaway. There was something else being transported to the new planet besides machinery and the hardware necessary to tame it and make it habitable for humanity. Something non-material, vast, and unfathomable.

49

Graduation Day

When I drove into town the following morning, I didn't see Paul Galahad's Cadillac parked in front of the apartment complex. I felt a jolt go through me. Somehow I knew they were gone.

Every day that passed seemed to confirm that fact.

Finally, when I was all but certain they'd left, I stopped in front of the place, found the manager, and asked him about the owners of the pink Cadillac. "They left," he said. "Checked out this morning."

"Did they say where they were going?" I asked.

"Nope. That they did not," he said.

"And they didn't leave a forwarding address?"

He shook his head and left me standing there while he went about his business.

I walked up the stairs to where the manager had indicated their apartment had been located. It was late afternoon, and the sun was angling toward the west, submerged in a bright haze that was coming off the desert floor. I stood in front of the door to the apartment they had occupied and knocked, even though I knew there was no one there. As expected, there was no answer. The place was deserted.

The earthquakes seemed to intensify as the spring of '57 turned to summer. My high school graduation ceremony arrived and my family was there. Grandpa Kurt and Aunt Trish were beaming. It was the kind of thing that adults got excited about.

The band had been busy as the end of the school year loomed. There were lots of parties. Not to mention the junior and senior proms and the all-nighter that was held at the Holiday Inn in Tucson. We seemed to be the hot ticket around town in those days before The Big Switcheroo.

As it turned out, my concerns about never seeing the dynamic trio again were slightly premature. To my amazement, Paul Galahad, Des, and Cherry showed up at my graduation, along with Big Al himself. I didn't know how to react. It was so unexpected, I was overwhelmed. I admit I might have started to mist up a little when I realized they were there. But don't tell anyone.

They looked fantastic, of course. Paul with his tan against a crisp white shirt, open at the collar, black slacks, and shiny black shoes, his salt and pepper hair slicked back, a little longer than before. Des looked a little like Morticia, pale as death and sleek as a seal in a form-fitting full-length black satin dress. Cherry was wearing a frilly lemon-yellow party shift, her hair done up in a ponytail. As usual, she was chewing gum at a hundred miles an hour. They looked like they'd just stepped off the silver screen. But even if they'd been dressed in rags, they'd have stolen the show.

We all went down to the Circle B Restaurant for a bite after the ceremony. It was a sprawling ranch-style affair with a Western theme, surrounded by corral-style fences adorned with longhorns, spurs, and horseshoes. The neon sign showed a buckaroo riding a bronc, flickering through a series of poses to imitate the movements of horse and rider. There was a wide, white gravel parking area to the right of the restaurant that wrapped around the back. Classy.

Of course, I wanted to have them to myself to ask the questions I longed to ask. But I could see that it wasn't going to be easy with Gramps and Trish in attendance. They weren't privy to Paul Galahad's true identity.

I did get to cut Cherry out of the herd for a moment as we were led to our table.

"I've been wanting to thank you for what you did for Grandpa," I whispered. "He doesn't know you saved his life. But I'll never forget it."

"It would have been hard on Big Al with Kurt gone," she said as if it had just been the reasonable thing to do to raise him from the dead. Maybe to her, it had been easy. But I suspected not.

I wanted to ask her a hundred questions. How did she do it? How did she know Grandpa was in trouble at the café? Who was she?

But I just thanked her again. "I can't tell you what an honor it's been for me that you came today. Do you think there's a chance we'll see each other again?"

Cherry stopped, all except for her jaw which was still working away at full speed. "I think there's a good chance," she said slowly. "We're kind of in the same business, you know."

Did she also have musical chops, as yet unwitnessed, I wondered? Or maybe she also had a thing for cars. She liked the Rex, I recalled. But before I could ask, we were at the dinner table scooting onto the vinyl seats, and the moment had passed.

"So how's the music coming?" Paul asked me in that down-home way of his.

"Good," I said. "We've been playing a lot."

"I noticed you've been getting local airplay," he said. "That's good. That's how it all starts."

The more I looked at him and listened to him speak, the less difficult it was for me to accept that this could be the true Elvis, a few years further down the road. Basking in that charisma, it was the easiest thing in the world to imagine.

"Like it started for you with Sam Philips at Sun?" I said.

Paul smiled, looking around to see if Grandpa or Trish had heard what I'd said. "You've been paying attention," he said quietly, with a certain satisfaction.

"How could I not?" I whispered back. "Why do you think I'm doing what I'm doing? There's only one reason."

"Oh, I'm sure you've got other inspirations, other folks out there on the circuit," he said modestly.

"Well, maybe Wanda Jackson," I whispered back, and he just laughed. "And of course Rosetta Thorpe. And Big Momma Thornton."

"Good choices," he said. "I'm normally not in the business of telling fortunes, but I see good things happening for you and your band."

"I don't know," I said. "A career in music seems like a long shot to me right now. We've been playing for over a year now, but it still feels like we just started."

"You're young. But that can work to your advantage in the business. Best to be ready so when it does happen it isn't too much of a shock to the system."

"I'll keep that in mind," I said. He was dead serious. So I took note.

"Hey, what are you guys yakkin' about over there," Grandpa said, finally acknowledging the conspiratorial whispering at our end of the table.

"Just talkin' music," the man who called himself Paul Galahad said. "I was just saying I was willing to bet Rose here is going to make quite an impact on the music scene with that band of hers. Maybe in the not too distant future."

I blushed.

Grandpa seemed somewhat mollified. "As long as she agrees to finish up her college studies," he said.

"No reason I couldn't do both," I pointed out. By graduating I'd proven I could get decent grades AND be a wiz of an auto mechanic AND play rock 'n' roll, all at the same time.

"Maybe so," Grandpa said, thoughtfully. "Maybe so." He knew how much I loved to play music. And he was a fan, despite his somewhat antiquated personal taste. He may not exactly have understood what we were about as a band, but he remained supportive of what we were doing. I loved him for it.

"Well," he said with a faint smile. "I suppose we'll see, won't we?"

"I'll be your manager," Cherry piped up beside me. The idea seemed to tickle her, I could see. But I didn't know whether she was serious or not.

"There's nothing I'd like better," I said, and I meant it. "Especially if it means you guys stick around here longer term." In the unlikely event she did take charge of our career, things certainly wouldn't be boring.

But if we were coming to the end of the journey, the point was probably moot. I figured we'd be too busy worrying about survival to think about things like rock 'n' roll and booking gigs. Then I recalled Big Al saying he foresaw even more of a need for our music than ever before after we landed.

I didn't know about that. But I decided to keep an open mind about the possibility, at least.

50

The Watering Hole

We were into summer now, looking to start junior college in the fall. I added a couple of hours at Ted's to supplement my income like I'd done the previous couple of years.

It also meant I had more time to myself, not to mention more time to hang out with my bandmate buddies. We'd written a couple of tunes and were getting ready to record them at the same studio we'd recorded the Elvis covers at, Iguana Records. So while the total number of gigs tapered off during the summer, the band was staying busy. Our covers were still getting airplay. And that meant our 45 was still selling copies at the record store. So offers to play shows and parties were still coming in.

Added to this was the fact that all of us had turned 18 during our senior year. That meant we could play at a select few bars around town that featured live music on alcohol-free nights for the underage crowd, plus the out-of-town gigs we'd had to turn down while school was in session.

We got a regular Thursday night gig in a place called the Watering Hole in Gila Springs. The town was a few miles southwest of Rattlesnake Junction on the road to Tucson. It was a biker hangout, and the crowd could be on the rough side. Thursday was an off night for the bar, so the management had decided to make it an alcohol-free night. They wanted us to play, hoping to bring in the younger crowd and maybe boost their weekday numbers.

A fan or ours, Lydia, was instrumental in getting us the gig. She was the daughter of the owners of the bar and a classmate of ours from school. I could picture her pleading with her folks to get them to offer a night at the bar just for her and her friends. After weeks, maybe months, of badgering, the beleaguered parents must have thrown in the towel and agreed to her wishes to keep the peace.

The problem was, the club owners couldn't very well deny their regular clientele of cowboys and bikers access on those nights. So the hardcore contingent was allowed in as long as they behaved themselves and drank sodas like the rest of us.

It was kind of funny to see the contortions those guys went through to get their hooch fix under the new rules. What ended up happening was that they'd sneak out into the parking lot and top off their sodas with some high test stuff they kept in their cars. Then they'd come back into the club feeling no pain and generally make a nuisance of themselves. They started harassing the kids and, of course, the all-girl band on stage. Security at the club had to be beefed up. Fights broke out.

Tina had to bring in her brothers and several of their friends regularly to dissuade the clientele from getting grabby. Which, of course, led to more confrontations and fighting. Bottles got thrown, furniture busted, and windows broken. Inevitably the cops would get called in.

The handwriting was on the wall. Our Thursday nights in Gila Springs were numbered. It was a matter of economics. With expenses for repairs and new furniture mounting, it became a losing proposition for the management to keep alcohol-free Thursday nights going. The outlay rivaled what they were taking in.

So it was no surprise when in late July, despite Lydia's protestations, the day arrived when we were not invited back to The Watering Hole in Gila Springs.

With the beginning of my first year at the local junior college fast approaching, the earthquakes were happening with increasing frequency. I took that to mean the Fortune's Fool was coming up on the star system where our new home resided. The brakes were being pumped big time. Besides Big Al, Grandpa Kurt and I remained the only ones who knew what the tremors meant.

I know I should have been more anxious. Everything was about to change. But I was more excited than anything. Grandpa and I were on the same wavelength about that. He'd been talking to Big Al, so he was up to date on the latest.

There was new information coming in as well as confirmation of what was already known. The planet was mostly water and contained one continuous continent along a north/south axis. It was probably somewhat similar to what Earth was like in the beginning, before the continents broke off and drifted apart. Most of the life on the planet was sea life as far as anyone could tell, and there was a variety of vegetation on what was mostly volcanic terrain.

"Did Al happen to mention when we're going to be landing?"

"He didn't give me an exact date," Grandpa Kurt said. "But he said we're just a few months out now. He said that when the quakes taper off and stop, it means we're there. The planet's gravity will catch us and pull us into orbit. There'll be no more need for the engines at that point."

It had been really hard to keep what I knew from my bandmates. I had started to say something about it more than a few times before I caught myself. It would be a relief when everybody knew what was going on. Keeping secrets wasn't my style.

But when the truth became generally known, it didn't happen quite the way I expected.

51

The Day The Sun Stood Still

The day the sun stopped dawned like any other. It was late fall of my first year at junior college and the temperatures still hovered in the eighties and nineties at midday.

But on this particular Saturday, it never got to midday. The sun got stuck just above the horizon at about 8 o'clock in the morning. The clock ticked on, but the sun just sat there on the eastern horizon like it had run out of gas.

The girls and I were at Henrietta's having breakfast at the time. We'd had a gig the night before at the J C, where we all now attended. There was an 11 o'clock curfew for live music at the school, so we'd gotten home at a reasonable hour. We were unusually well rested for the morning after a gig.

We'd gotten to the café just before 8. Henrietta's was a popular spot for breakfast, especially on weekends, and the place was packed to the gills. Some girls from the gig we'd played the night before were there and waved to us as we entered. We lucked out, arriving just as a booth was opening up.

We placed our orders and about twenty minutes later, our food arrived. We chowed down and yakked away as usual. Tina mentioned the possibility of us playing a dance at the Rez the following weekend. There was nothing on the books for that night, so Melissa and I said sure.

We were about halfway through our meal when we noticed a

few people standing around in the street outside the café, shading their eyes, pointing up at the sky, and scratching their heads. As we continued to eat, more people began congregating out there. It got to the point where the crowd was spilling into the street, disrupting the flow of traffic. Something was definitely happening out here.

"What do you think's going on?" Melissa asked. She put her fork down and turned in her seat to get a better look out the front windows of the café.

"Alien invasion?" Tina suggested.

A chill ran through me. Was it finally happening? Had we come to the end of the line in our voyage across space? Was the crew of the Fortune's Fool finally showing their cards? Was the big secret kept all these years about to be revealed at last?

I said, "We'd better check it out."

We settled our tab and followed the foot traffic out the door. Once we were outside, we shielded our eyes and looked up at the sky like everyone else seemed to be doing. We didn't notice anything awry. At first. There was no banner across the sky that proclaiming, "Welcome to your new home, earthlings. Prepare to disembark." It looked like a regular Saturday morning.

"What's happening?" I asked a bystander. "What's everybody looking at?"

"It's the sun," the man said. But he was pushed along by the crowd before he could explain further.

And then we got it. The sun hadn't moved since we'd arrived. It was now after 9 a.m., and it still looked and felt like 8 o'clock. The morning chill hung in the air when by now people should have been putting on sunglasses and trying to figure out ways to beat the heat.

There weren't any hysterics. People were just kind of in shock, wandering around in a daze. I couldn't blame them. One of the basic tenets of their reality had just been called into question. I knew the feeling. I thought to myself, wait till they find out we're not on Planet Earth anymore and haven't been for two hundred and fifty years. I couldn't imagine what kind of reaction that would produce. For now, people just looked confused. But there was no major panic. Not yet, at least.

"What the heck is going on?" Tina asked beside me. Even she seemed rattled, which almost never happened. "How is this possible?"

I just shrugged and said nothing. But I had a theory. Whoever was in charge of the sun moving across the sky day in and day out had fallen asleep at the wheel. But since saying that involved divulging privileged information, I couldn't just blurt it out.

"What?" Tina said. I guess I was just standing there thinking when I should have been panicking. I just didn't look worried enough to suit the circumstances. "You wouldn't know anything about this, would you? I mean, how could you, right?"

The jig was up and I knew it. I didn't know whether the sun stalling was a mistake of monumental proportions or part of some pre-arranged plan to start to acquaint everyone in the Bubble with what was really going on. But regardless of whether the sun stopping in the sky was intentional or not, the end result was going to be the same. The truth would come out. With every minute the sun failed to chart its usual course across the heavens, any justification I had for remaining silent was quickly eroding. I decided it was high time to fill the girls in.

"I think we need to have a talk," I told them.

We piled into the Rex without further discussion, and I drove them up to the house. Tina was scrunched in behind Melissa and me. It wasn't the first time she'd had to sit back there. The girls were amazingly calm. I had to give them a lot of credit for that. They weren't bombarding me with questions yet, though I knew they were about to burst. I don't know if I could have matched their restraint under the circumstances.

Nothing had changed, cosmically speaking, by the time we pulled into the garage. The sun was still where it had been a couple of hours ago. Kurt was at his workbench, the garage door open, so I drove the Rex straight in, stopping next to him. The girls climbed out of the car.

Kurt was surprised to see us all there. "To what do I owe the pleasure?" he said.

"Have you noticed anything unusual about the sky this morning?" I asked him.

He glanced out the open garage door and back at me. "What do you mean?" he asked. He was soldering a connection on a solenoid using his jeweler's loupe as a magnifier. "I haven't been outside yet. What's up?"

"The sun's stopped," I said.

He put down what he was working on and followed us out of the garage. Shading his eyes, he looked at the sun. He frowned. Then he looked at his wristwatch. "What the hell?" he said.

And then he got quiet. I figured he was thinking something along the lines of what I'd come up with back in town. Something was going on up top, outside the Bubble.

He looked at me and then at the girls. I could see the wheels in his head turning.

I said, "I think Melissa and Tina deserve to know what's going on."

52

Going Up?

started my story at the beginning. I told them about the silver armadillo and finding the tunnel and the big elevator in the sky. I told them about finding out about New Arizona and discovering that we were actually all onboard a giant spaceship heading to a new world because the old one was in the crapper.

"You know," said Tina brightening, which was saying something. She was usually so bright to begin with that she was almost hard to look at. "There's a medicine woman on the Rez who has been saying something like this for years. The way she told it, the Great Eagle would be transporting mankind to a new home among the stars. She is a revered elder, but oftentimes folks don't know what to make of her pronouncements. Everyone assumed it was all some kind of weird metaphor."

"Great Eagle is not a bad metaphor," I said. "Although in this case, it's more like the Great Bowling Ball in the Sky."

I told them about how we were coming in for a landing sometime soon and about how I figured something had gone on the fritz in the ship at large to cause the sun to stop in its tracks. Either that, or it was part of the plan to introduce the population to the notion that we weren't in Kansas anymore. Grandpa just kind of nodded in agreement. He was letting me do the talking.

"So what do we do?" Melissa wanted to know.

"Big Al's the one to talk to," I said. "It turns out he's the captain of the ship we're on, the Fortune's Fool. If anyone knows what's going on, it would be him."

"Big Al? As in Big Al's Wrecking and Salvage?"

"The same."

"My brothers told me about him," Tina said. "They go over there all the time to get parts for their cars. They said he was cool. They couldn't understand how a guy like him could be content working in a junkyard. I guess it makes sense if it's a sideline. His idea of fun, maybe."

"So what do you say?" I looked over at Grandpa Kurt.

"Let's take the Studebaker," he said. "I think we'll all fit."

A couple of minor adjustments under the hood, and the Studebaker was up and running. We drove over to the wrecking yard only to find it closed up tight. We hung around until we were positive there was no one around. Not even a pesky Grey.

"Must be serious if Big Al's not here," Grandpa Kurt remarked.

"OK," Tina asked. "What's Plan B?"

"Anybody up for a hike in the desert?" I asked.

About an hour later, equipped with flashlights and windbreakers we were standing outside the arched tunnel up the arroyo. The sun was still in the same place in the sky that it had been since morning. My watch said it was 4 pm.

We entered the tunnel and hiked in claustrophobic darkness for what seemed like hours before we rounded the final corner. We slipped through the crack in the rock, and there before us were the elevators. They looked just like they had the first time around—two steel doors, side by side, under a chute that went right up through the solid rock ceiling.

"Going up?" I said.

53

The World Beyond
The Bubble

nd up we went. Up and up. The mood was solemn. To everyone but me, this was a new experience. They were leaving the known world behind. I knew what they must be feeling. Nothing would ever be the same again.

"Aunt Trish is going to be worried about us," I said to Grandpa Kurt, breaking the silence. We must have been barreling along at a good clip, but after the initial acceleration, the sensation of movement had ceased. As before, the ascent was completely soundless.

Grandpa Kurt cleared his throat, bringing his attention back to what I'd said with some effort. "I left her a note saying we'd gone for a trek and might not be back for a while," he said quietly, as if reluctant to break the silence. "I told her not to worry."

I nodded. The minutes ticked by.

After a period of gradual deceleration, the elevator stopped and the doors opened onto the scene I'd witnessed the first time. There was the steel mesh landing in front of us, bordered by the metal railing. And beyond that was the familiar bright glow welling up from below.

Only this time it wasn't quite as peaceful up here. The metal walkways teamed with people running this way and that, dressed in different costumes. Uniforms, probably. Trams streaked across the sky in all directions.

No one was paying much attention to us. Too busy, I guess. Maybe they were trying to get a handle on what had gone wrong with the sun.

Smoke was descending from somewhere high up, and there was the acrid scent of burnt wiring in the air. But Grandpa and the girls didn't seem to notice. They were standing at the railing, transfixed. They were looking down on the world, their world. I joined them.

They were spellbound. Who could blame them?

They were looking down on Planet Earth as if from the edge of space. Except, of course, we weren't in outer space. There was air to breathe, and it was room temperature up here. I turned to look behind us, past the elevators, toward where the sun was still frozen in the act of rising in the east. This close to it, it didn't look quite as authentic as it had from the ground. And it wasn't putting out any more heat than it had the first time I'd seen it. Of course, I knew from that first meeting with Gillian that the heat was actually coming from somewhere else entirely.

I stopped a guy who looked like he was about my age who happened to be running by.

"What's going on?" I asked him. "What's happening here?"

He stopped and looked me up and down. Then he looked at the rest of us. "You guys from down there?" he said. He indicated the bright expanse below us.

I nodded. I seemed to be the only one capable of speech. "Is this about the sun not moving?"

He swallowed and nodded. "Sabotage in Systems Operations," he said.

"Sabotage?" I managed.

"You probably don't know," he said. "OK." He took a moment to collect himself. "There's a mutiny in progress. Xenecorp is trying to take over the ship."

"Xenecorp?" I repeated.

"The biggest corporate conglomerate on the ship," he explained.

He was a towhead, a little taller than me, lanky, sporting a buzz cut. "We're trying to sort it out. Say, you guys alright? Having the sun stop is serious sh. . .stuff. I can't imagine how it must be for you down there. It's gotta be disorienting as hell."

I had to agree.

"We should have things under control again soon," he said. "We're trying to kick-start the solar transit system as we speak."

"How do we get to the bridge?" I asked. I was hoping that's where we'd find Big Al.

"I don't think you want to go there right now," the kid said. "It's a war zone. You wouldn't be safe. Besides, the command center is sealed off. Nobody's going in or out."

"We're friends of Big Al's," I explained. "Can you tell us how we can find him?"

"You know Captain Wertmueller personally?" he said, awe in his voice. "Wow." He thought things over for a moment. "My guess would be that he's on the observation deck. With the command center locked down, he's likely overseeing the situation from there."

"How do we get there?"

"See that shuttle stop over there?" He was pointing to a tram station a hundred yards away to the south. "Hop on the next train and take it to the end of the line. Wait." He dug into his jacket pocket and produced what looked like a plastic card. "Take this token. It'll get you there with no problems."

"Thank you," I said as I watched him race off again.

"I mean it," I called after him. But I doubt he heard me.

54

Mutiny

few minutes later we were on the shuttle or tram or train or
whatever you want to call it. It was about half full, mostly with
people in military garb hoisting strange, dangerous-looking
weapons with snub nose barrels and weird wire rifle stocks. We got
braced by somebody in uniform as we entered. But the pass we'd
gotten from our blond friend seemed to work its magic, and we all
got on.

Taking off was like being shot out of a cannon. There was no
sensation of motion, but you could tell by looking out the windows
that we were hauling bananas. We blasted like a comet through the
interior of the ship. The glow of New Arizona receded behind us as
we left everything we knew in the dust.

It soon became apparent just how vast the space we were in was.
Areas of bright light came into view and just as quickly disappeared
behind us. They were probably cities, but we were going so fast it was
hard to tell. We did make a couple of stops in those areas of bright
light. More people in uniform carrying those weird stubby rifles got
on. We always got the once over when new riders got onboard. But
we must not have looked like much of a threat, three girls and an old
man. So nobody questioned us.

Even at the crazy speed we were traveling, it took about an hour
to reach the end of the line. The doors opened and everybody filed
out. We decided to wait until the last of the soldiers, or whatever

they were, had gotten off. We didn't want to get trampled. There was definitely tension in the air, and the smells of burning wiring and metal had intensified. I'd taken a shop class in junior high where we did a lot of wiring and soldering. It smelled like that times a hundred.

With everybody out of the tram, we stepped into what looked like a subway station with a concrete platform and high ceilings. People and things were heading in all directions, moving fast. No one was out for a leisurely stroll. The "things" were like the robots I'd seen at the Saturday matinées of my youth, mechanical contraptions of all shapes and sizes that moved around like they knew where they were going, just like the humans. I didn't see any Greys, but that wasn't surprising. I figured they were smart enough to keep out of sight under the circumstances. Unlike us.

The station itself was bright and airy on the inside. The tram seemed to be on a lower level of the station because all the escalators led upward. We followed the people in uniform and found ourselves in a spacious open area that looked like an airport terminal.

There was a kiosk in the center of the marble-like floor. I was hoping it was an information booth. We walked over to it.

The people behind the desk were too busy to notice us at first. But then one of them did and everybody stopped to look us over.

"You're not from. . . ," the closest person said.

"The Bubble. Yup," I supplied to move things along. "We're from New Arizona. We're here to see Big Al. We're on special assignment. He's waiting to hear from us." I knew I had to get their attention and figured a little exaggeration was in order. I didn't want to think we'd come all this way for nothing.

"Big Al," said the woman we were talking to. "You mean Alfred Wertmueller? Captain Alfred Wertmueller?"

"The captain," I said. "That's right."

"New Arizona," the woman mused. "I hear there's a problem with your sun."

"That's part of why we're here," I said.

"Give me a minute," said the woman. "Let me see if I can locate him."

She made swiping and poking gestures in the air in front of her. "You know he's pretty busy at the moment," she said vaguely. Her focus and movements reminded me of the famous mime, Marcel Marceau, who I'd seen on Ed Sullivan pretending there was something there when there clearly wasn't.

"Here he is," she said finally, still staring at empty space before her. "He's upstairs on the observation deck. Take the elevator in that corner and go all the way up. You're not carrying any weapons are you?"

"Nope," I said. We didn't even have a Swiss Army knife between us this time around.

The woman nodded as if she figured as much.

"Listen," I said. "I know you've got your hands full. And we appreciate your help. But can you tell us anything about what's going on. We heard there was some kind of mutiny in progress or something."

"I don't suppose it's revealing any state secrets if I tell you that you heard right," said the woman. "It's the corporate contingent again. History trying to repeat itself."

She paused looking at each of us, probably wondering how much detail to include in her explanation. She saw she had a rapt audience, so she continued, "Here on the ship the corporations were intentionally assigned a secondary role because of what happened back on Planet Earth. I don't know how much you know about it, but a lot of the destruction back then was the direct result of unfettered corporate overreach. Not all of it, of course--there was complicity at all levels. But a lot of it. Now we have Xenecorp, the biggest corporate entity on the ship, trying to hijack the ship in the eleventh hour. Unfortunately, they've got a lot of the military backing them this time around, not to mention their own superbly equipped militias.

"A fair chunk of our military, it turns out, would love nothing more than to have things be just like they used to be back when corporations ruled the world. But how things had been once upon a time was a big part of why we lost our home planet to begin with. The Designers intended for humanity to have a fresh start with this expedition. But the old ways keep reasserting themselves. There's no overestimating human hubris and the profit motive. Unfortunately, we had to rely on elements of the old corporate structures to maintain the ship and its systems on the crossing. You may know we had to leave in a hurry under less than ideal conditions. Now those early decisions are coming back to haunt us."

"So why is this happening now?"

"Xenecorp has managed to keep its long-range plans hidden until recently. As it turns out they've been accumulating giant caches of illegal weapons and munitions to supply their private militias for decades. Now they're making their move. The governing body of this ship, the Federation, was supposed to keep Xenecorp in check. But since the company was tasked with maintaining most of the ship's systems, the Federation has always been at a disadvantage when it comes to oversight and regulation. There had to be a level of trust involved in our dealings with them. That trust, it turns out, was misplaced. Xenecorp has made sure we've always been a step behind, And now the chickens are coming home to roost."

"If this Federation you're talking about is supposed to have been in charge of the ship, how did this rogue corporation get its own militias to begin with?" Grandpa Kurt asked.

"The corporations have always had a good deal of autonomy. Their employees live and work in their own cities and have their own local governments. The militias got their start as locally managed law enforcement agencies. Unbeknownst to us, they'd been expanding and consolidating for years."

"So now things have reached a point where this Xenecorp figured it could take the ship from the Federation?" mused Grandpa. "To what purpose? What do they hope to accomplish?"

"They want to set the agenda once we land."

"An agenda that favors the corporations?"

"As I mentioned, they want things to be the way they were on Earth before the cataclysm when corporations had carte blanche and called the shots. The Federation, on the other hand, has always been dedicated to the Designers vision of creating an environment for the Settlers that was free from corporate tyranny of any kind. So you can see how there might be a problem. The Federation is partly responsible. The Federation hoped that a spirit of cooperation would prevail on the ship, especially in light of how things had turned out on Earth. They turned a blind eye to the trouble brewing instead of tightening the screws, hoping Xenecorp would come around as we approached the end of our voyage. That hasn't happened."

That gave us something to think about.

"What are your chances of holding onto the ship, given what you've just told us," asked Grandpa Kurt.

"Right now? I'd say fifty-fifty."

55

Panorama

The elevators to the observation deck had transparent walls, so we had an impressive view of the interior of the ship as we rode up. I took a speck of light on the horizon to be New Arizona, but I could have been wrong. It was just a twinkle among a constellation of lights all around us.

It was like we were approaching a solid wall of metal panels as we proceeded upward. We knew they curved around to form a sphere, the outer wall of the Fortune's Fool, but from here the curvature was all but impossible to detect. Stuck to this metal wall was a rectangle that looked like a postage stamp. It grew rapidly in size as we drew nearer until it filled the transparent ceiling of the elevator. We were slowing rapidly.

Finally, our view was cut off by the four sides of an elevator shaft. After the previous vista, it felt claustrophobic. But the darkness lasted only a few seconds before we stopped, and the doors opened.

We found ourselves in something like a reception area. There was a curved desk in front of us backed up to a low profile curved wall. Beyond the desk and wall was a sight so boggling none of us could get a handle on what we were looking at first. It just didn't seem real. Floor to ceiling windows dominated the far wall. And in the middle of these was a gigantic, dazzlingly bright blue orb. The orb took up almost all the available viewing space, side to side, top to bottom.

Epsilon 4. It must have been.

The four of us moved toward the windows like zombies. We were barely aware that we were being scanned by some kind of light. A group of soldiers appeared before us, giving us the fisheye. They funneled us toward the curved desk.

There were three receptionists there. Two were occupied helping other arrivals. The third was a young man who seemed to be completely engrossed in what he was doing as we approached him. He looked pretty sharp in a shiny silver space age-type suit and tie. It was like a toned-down version of the flashy lame suit Elvis was wearing on the cover of a recent album. Except that while Elvis' suit was gold, this one was silver. He looked very clean-cut, like he'd just gotten back from the barber.

He glanced up and his eyes widened as he beheld three heavenly apparitions and a butler. Not really. We were three scruffy girls and one grandpa. From his reaction, I'm pretty sure he'd never seen the likes of us before.

"H-how may I help you?" he asked, after a noticeable pause.

"We're here to see Big Al. Um. Alfred Wertmueller, the captain," I said.

"And you are?"

"We're friends of his," I said. I stepped aside so the young man could get an unobstructed view of Gramps.

"And what is your name, sir?" asked the receptionist.

"Kurt Thorne," said Grandpa.

"Just a minute, please." The receptionist poked a finger at the air in front of him, like the reception we had talked to earlier had done. He looked mildly surprised at what he appeared to see there. He looked up at us again. "Go on in," he said. "Captain Wertmueller is expecting you. He's just around the partition here. You can't miss him."

"Thank you," I said, flashing him a winning smile.

"Anytime," he said, giving Tina the once over. I couldn't exactly blame him.

We rounded the corner and stopped dead in our tracks, awestruck again at the view of the blue pearl of a planet we appeared to be hovering over.

"Home sweet home," said a familiar voice in my ear. I turned to find Big Al standing there. I almost didn't recognize him. He was wearing a blue suit complete with epaulets, adorned with an impressive array of ribbons, stars, and other military decorations. He had on an official-looking dark blue brimmed cap, rimmed with golden embroidery.

"An outfit and captain's hat from the olden days," he explained modestly. "It's what a ship's captain wore in the nineteenth century. There's something to be said for decorum when it comes to getting things done around here."

"You certainly look the part," I assured him.

"I'll take that as a compliment," he said with a smile and turned to Gramps. "Good to see you, Kurt."

He took grandpa in a bear hug, oblivious of the stares of the people around us. I guess we rated as VIPs. I couldn't see him hugging anyone else around here, especially in that uniform. The girls shook his hand politely.

"So what brings you to my lair?" asked Big Al. "Wait. Let me guess. A small matter of Stalled Sun Syndrome. Am I right?"

We all nodded solemnly.

"Hell of a thing," he went on. "We got it sorted out, of course, The sun's moving again."

I couldn't contain myself. "But now the cat's out of the bag," I blurted out. "Everybody's going to be wondering what's going on. They're not going to be able to unsee what they've just seen."

"Don't be so sure about that," said Big Al amiably.

56

Showdown

Our little reunion was interrupted when a side entrance to the observation deck exploded, sending plaster and concrete spraying in all directions. People ducked and scattered. As far as I could see, no one had been injured, but the resulting hole in the wall was about twice as big as the original doorway.

Through the opening about fifty soldiers rushed into the room, fanning out, weapons drawn. The uniforms were different from the ones worn by the Federation. These were dark blue, while most of the Federation uniforms we'd seen so far were tan. The Federation soldiers faced the surly intruders without any signs of flinching or retreating. They deserved props for that. That entrance had been pretty impressive.

In the plus column was that neither side had started firing.

"Stay behind me," whispered Big Al to us.

A thin figure dressed in a more formal version of what the new arrivals were wearing strode to the fore.

"Alfred Wertmueller," said the figure in a surprisingly deep and authoritative voice.

Big Al turned slowly, keeping his eyes on us. Then he walked brusquely toward where the other man was standing.

"Dick Blythe," he greeted the other man amiably. "You could just have knocked."

"Cut the crap, Al," said the thin man. "It's time to hand over the codes. We've got Operations locked down so none of your people can get in or out."

"That means *you* can't get in either," said Al with a hint of satisfaction.

"It's only a matter of time," said the man. "We *will* get in. Even if we have to obliterate the whole wall to do it. We've got a photon cannon being wheeled into position as we speak."

"There's a lot of sensitive equipment in there, Dick," said Al calmly.

I could barely control a snicker at the way he said "Dick."

"Blow the place up, and you'd be cutting your own throat," he continued conversationally. "You know as well as I do the controls for the ship's systems are in there, including vital climate functions and general life support."

"You don't need to tell me. We built those systems and maintained them all these years."

"As per our agreement," Big Al pointed out, "Listen. You and I both know you're going to need the Settlers' help in getting yourselves set up down there. Without them, it'll be that much harder for you to gain a foothold. You haven't thought things through. But I'm not surprised. You weren't trained to think for yourselves. Xenecorp only ever provided you with enough information to get whatever job you were assigned done. The long view is what the Federation is about. We're the ones whose job it has been to understand how everything fits together on this mission to ensure we all have the best chance at survival."

"Enough chit-chat. Give me the codes, or I'll give the order to shoot. You won't live to see the culmination of your glorious mission. Would you prefer that?"

"It's not going to work, Dick," said Al reluctantly. "We can't give you those codes, and you know it. And if you try to blow those doors, you'll regret it. They're tougher than anything else in that room. You blast your way in, and you're going to destroy everything on the other side of the wall as well. You may think your weapons are pretty smart. But you can't defeat physics. You'll incapacitate the entire ship, including the shuttle transports that are supposed to get you and everybody else down to the surface.

"It's suicide, Dick. You want to kill yourself, go ahead. But don't take everyone else with you. Our best chance is still the Federation charter. We do our job. You do yours. Putting you and your bosses in charge would be the worst mistake we could make."

"What you think is irrelevant," said Blythe. "We've got all the manpower and weaponry we need to take over this ship. And that includes a fair portion of your own military, I might add. They've seen the light of reason. You should be worrying about how things will end for you."

Big Al didn't seem surprised at this news. Nor did he appear particularly worried. In fact, he smiled wryly to himself as if this exchange confirmed some long-held theory he'd been entertaining.

Melissa, Tina, and I just looked at each other wide-eyed. This was the whole ball game. Right here.

57

The Cavalry Arrives

The thin man continued to glare at the captain. The temperature in the room seemed to drop several degrees. Al maintained his poker face through it all. He was as opaque as a block of granite.

The tactical forces on both sides were giving each other the hairy eyeball. So far no one had lost their cool and gotten trigger-happy. But it was just a matter of time.

It was dead quiet as the soldiers sighted at each other down the barrels of their stubby rifles. The tension was so thick it would have taken a bandsaw to cut it.

Into this scene walked Cherry.

It was a shock to see her there. I knew from experience that she wasn't quite the "normal" teen. But to have her appear out of nowhere, so far away from where I'd last seen her was disconcerting, to say the least. She was looking even more pale and undernourished than I remembered. She was wearing a tattered terry cloth robe and fuzzy pink slippers that looked like a floppy-eared cartoon critter, but I couldn't tell which one. She was drying her hair with a hand towel as if she'd just gotten out of the shower. She seemed as unperturbed by the spectacle before her as if she'd walked into her own living room.

But her arrival had an undeniable effect on the room. The soldiers were glancing at her out of the corners of their eyes, trying to look at her and at each other at the same time. It was funny if you didn't know what was at stake.

Big Al acknowledged Cherry, and something passed between them. The man named Richard Blythe was suddenly nervous. It was as if the balance of power had shifted somehow, placing the intruders at some kind of disadvantage. It was baffling.

Big Al was well aware of the change in the room and said, "Better give some careful thought to what you're doing, Dick, and how it might affect the mission. Don't be so quick to believe everything your handlers are telling you. They have their own agenda and, believe me, they don't care what happens to you. I suggest you withdraw your troops from here and from the command center immediately, or I won't be able to guarantee your safety. As I said, you're out of your depth here."

Surprisingly, the thin man kept his mouth shut. He pulled at his collar, as if it had suddenly become too tight. It was clear he didn't want to show weakness in front of his men. But it was equally clear he suddenly wanted to be anywhere else but there. Something had shifted, and he seemed to know he couldn't follow through on his original plan for some reason. That was the only way I could explain it. What I didn't know was why.

The only possible explanation was Cherry. Her arrival was the only thing that was different. I knew she was pretty awe-inspiring. She'd proven that when she'd revived Grandpa Kurt. But why this group of surly armed men would be afraid of her, especially in her weakened state, I couldn't figure. She was a girl with healing powers. And these were professional soldiers with big guns.

The thin man made a downward chopping motion with his hand, and his team lowered their weapons in response. Without an additional word being uttered, he turned on his heel and strode out of the room through the ragged hole he'd created. His men followed him in an orderly fashion, one group covering the next, until the last man had disappeared through the opening.

"What just happened?" I asked Grandpa Kurt.

"Beats me," he said.

"Sorry about the interruption," Big Al said, corralling us.

"What was that all about?" I asked him, unable to contain myself.

"It's amazing how a little superstition can go a long way," he said.

"Cherry?" I said.

He nodded. "Let's just say her reputation precedes her. I'd never ask her to intervene on our behalf, no matter how bad things got. This situation is not hers to solve. It's our problem. She knows that and I know it. But they don't need to know it."

He grew serious. "Listen," he said. "I think you folks need to get back to New Arizona. I'm pretty sure we haven't seen the last of these guys. I don't want you exposed to any unnecessary danger. We've got the situation in hand up here. No need to worry."

From what I'd just seen and heard, I was just a wee bit skeptical about that. I peeked over his shoulder to where Cherry was standing in her housecoat and funny slippers. She gave me a little wave. She looked exhausted.

I ran over to her and gave her a big hug. She felt insubstantial, little more than the Terry cloth robe she was wearing.

"It's so good to see you," I told her.

"You too," she said.

We stood apart and looked at one another. I was genuinely worried about her.

I realized the others were waiting for me. "I better go," I said. "I hope we'll have a chance to talk later."

She nodded a little somberly.

"Until next time," I said hopefully, giving her hands a quick squeeze. "You take care of yourself. OK?"

Then I turned and ran to catch up with the rest.

"Give Paul and Des my best too," I called over my shoulder.

She nodded again. It was almost as if she no longer had the energy to respond verbally.

And then the wall intervened, and I lost sight of her.

58

Brave New World

"What was that?" Melissa asked.

Grandpa Kurt, Tina, Mel, and I were on the shuttle speeding back toward the Bubble.

I looked over at Grandpa Kurt. He remembered Cherry from the garage that morning but wasn't aware she had saved his life. I hadn't thought it necessary to enlighten him. I didn't know what he would make of that. Heck, I didn't know what to make of it myself. So I'd said nothing.

"Maybe that girl has special superpowers or something," Tina reflected. "There is something about her. I don't know. If one of the ancient ones were to return to earth, he or she would be like that girl.'"

"You mean kind of weak and sickly looking?" Mel asked

"No," Tina said with a note of impatience. "There's something else. Something around her." Tina paused, trying to find the words for what she wanted to express. Finally, she said, "She has the warrior spirit. Proud. Strong, Yet humble. Did you notice? Those soldiers all looked like they were about to piss themselves."

"Big Al said it was superstition," Mel pointed out.

I didn't say anything, although I tended to agree with Tina, especially after what had happened in the garage with Grandpa Kurt. But that was only part of it. I was thinking back to what I'd seen in Cherry's eyes on a couple of other occasions. Flames flickering in the depths. A feeling of vertigo, like I might actually fall into those flames if I wasn't careful. I thought I'd been hallucinating at the time. Now I wasn't so sure.

"On the other hand, maybe she does have superpowers," Melissa said warming to the idea. "Like Superman, only she's a she."

I knew she had superhuman powers. I'd seen proof. It stood to reason she might have other talents as well.

What had become clear to us all was that the tug of war we'd only heard about until now was real. The entity called Xenecorp and its militias were challenging the rightful authority, the Federation, and the outcome was far from certain. We'd just seen evidence of that first hand And it was beginning to sound as if those of us in the Stacks might be caught in the middle.

All I had to do was to imagine our own American military trying to take over our democratically elected government in the states to get a feel for what was happening onboard the Fortune's Fool. Of the people, by the people, and for the people. Right? That's what it was supposed to be all about. But if a dictator took over, be he a general or the president of some industrial conglomerate, all bets would be off. We'd all be living under tyranny. It would be like *Brave New World*, which I'd just finished reading for freshman English.

This struggle had been going on behind the scenes for who knew how long, unbeknownst to us poor ignoramuses on the ground in New Arizona. Now it looked as if things might be reaching the boiling point at the most crucial moment in our journey. And the worst thing was, there wasn't a lot we could do about the situation one way or the other.

I had to give the girls credit. They were handling things amazingly well, considering they'd just learned the truth about New Arizona and the ship and the 250-year journey just that morning. Now they knew it wasn't just some abstract idea that they could dismiss. They'd just seen proof positive that it was all true.

What was equally true was that we'd arrived at Epsilon 4. Which meant we were now in orbit around the planet that would be our new home. It had looked inviting. It was a big blue marble with clouds swirling on the surface. In other words, it looked a lot like what we'd been taught Planet Earth had looked like, once upon a time.

Having learned that we were coming in for a landing on a new planet, I thought it might be useful to brush up on geology, so I'd taken it as an elective. I'd also signed up for a course in evolution. I wanted to have some idea of what to expect when we landed. I saw now that it wouldn't have hurt to have a course in political science under my belt too, considering what was going on aboard the ship. I guess I'd just gotten my first taste of factional conflict. A crash course, you might say. Or almost.

With some effort, I brought myself back to the present moment, which had us speeding across the vast interior of the Fortune's Fool toward a growing speck of light in the distance: New Arizona. I started to think about what might lie ahead in the Bubble. When we'd left that morning, the sun was stalled in the sky. Big Al had mentioned the glitch had been taken care of. But what about the aftermath? I could only imagine what kind of chaos and upheaval we might be facing. How was Trish handling it? Or the folks on the Rez? And Melissa's parents? I guessed we'd soon find out.

59

Ignorance Is Bliss

It turned out everyone was handling it just fine.

In fact, no one seemed to know anything about the sun stalling in the sky that morning. The few people we talked to looked at us like we were crazy when we mentioned it. It was like it never happened. No doubt the folks up top had something to do with that. I wondered how many other times crises had been averted with little interventions like this one, little adjustments to what people remembered.

I thought about my own experience with having my memories edited. It still left me with a queasy feeling. I sure hoped that when we landed there wouldn't be a similar hands-on approach to what we did or didn't remember. The whole notion was really starting to get my goat.

I mentioned my concerns to Grandpa.

"Something to ask Al the next time we see him," Grandpa said. "But my feeling is he'll say they've done what they needed to do in order to minimize trauma for their prized cargo. Namely us. And you have to admit, they've done a decent job of it so far, judging from the overall result. Big Al has assured us it isn't going to be like this once we're down on the ground. It's going to be strictly hands-off. At least if the Federation has its way."

"So you're OK knowing we've been in a big lab up here?" I said. "With us being the rats?"

"I think that's a little harsh," Grandpa said. "I know Big Al. And I trust his judgment on this. He's always been upfront about what his goals for us are. It's Xenecorp's intentions that I'm not so sure about."

"I hope you're right about this."

"It's pretty impressive what they've done here when you think about it," Gramps said, "recreating what to them is the distant past. Our lives have been pretty good, all in all. Wouldn't you say?"

I could see his point. We did have a good life going. One I wouldn't have traded for anything in the world. Even if it had all been a kind of dream."

"No doubt it would help if we knew more," Grandpa said. "Or less, I'm not sure which. As it is we're kind of in the middle of the scale. We know more than nothing and less than a lot."

I couldn't suppress a dry laugh. "Ignorance really is, or was, bliss."

I thought for a minute. "Why do you think we get to keep our memories intact if nobody else gets to?"

"Again, I'm only guessing. But I think he thinks we can handle it. We're the lucky few. The cognoscenti. Plus, I think he considers us his friends and doesn't want to tweak our experience any more than he has to. Remember, we're due to leave the ship any day now. Then all will be known. Or at least as much as they want us to know."

"I guess I'd rather know what I know, than not," I said. "Better to be wise to what's going on and depressed, than be a happy Idiot."

Kurt raised a glass of apple juice in a toast. "Here's to happy idiots," he said with a grin.

"I wonder how things are going up top," I said. "I hope Al can get things sorted out before we land. I never felt claustrophobic in these wide-open spaces until I found out we were on a spaceship, I don't care how big."

Grandpa laughed. "I'm with you on that," he said. "Whether we agree with how all this has been handled, I'm pretty sure we don't want the other side to win."

Now that we were in orbit, the earthquakes had completely stopped. I think we were all kind of holding our breath—Melissa, Tina, Grandpa Kurt, Trish, and I—waiting to see what would happen next.

But in the meantime, even with big changes in the wings, life went on as before. There was school, and on the weekends we had gigs. We rocked and rolled like never before, maybe because we knew this phase of our lives was about to end and another was about to begin. We had no idea what to expect from here on out. We knew next to nothing about the details of our getting transported down to the surface. I pictured the lights suddenly going up, like in a movie theater, and all of us being herded toward the exits. Would a cosmic bullhorn, inform us the trip was over, and it was time to leave the ship in an orderly fashion? Would we then be crammed into giant shuttles? Probably none of the above. We knew we would be asleep during the actual move to the surface. Big Al had told us as much. But wouldn't we at least receive some forewarning?

If so, there would have to be some news soon, so we could prepare. Pack some bags, at least. I was trying to figure out how to get my guitars (I had a couple by now), my amp, microphone, mic stand, and cables into a package I could easily carry. But then what about things like clothes, shoes, records, toothbrush, etc? Big Al had mentioned he wanted to create our experience on the ship as accurately as possible on the ground. And he'd all but promised to get the Rex down too. I clung to those prospects for reassurance.

We were all a little on edge, I can tell you. It was like we were racing toward a cliff on an open plain. No one knew exactly where the cliff was and what might be awaiting us at the bottom.

As it turned out, we needn't have worried.

EPSILON 4

60

In The Beginning

The transition to the planet's surface was seamless. It had obviously been planned to the smallest detail. One moment we were going about our daily routines in New Arizona. The next we were on a new planet with no memory of how we'd gotten there.

Nevertheless, it was perfectly obvious that a drastic change had occurred. The scenery was entirely different. Instead of dry sandy desert, there was now black lava rock everywhere you looked. A crust of it stretched out in all directions as far as the eye could see. It rose gradually inland toward a smoking volcano in the distance about fifty miles away. And down a gentle slope to the west, emerald green waves crashed against the seashore. Whereas Rattlesnake Junction had once been a landlocked backwater, it was now a beach town.

Otherwise, everything looked just like it had before. The town's layout--the houses, buildings, shops, restaurants, schools, streets, and their relation to one another--was identical to the Rattlesnake Junction of old. The minute I noticed the shift, I ran out to the garage. The Rex was there, alongside Grandpa's old Studebaker. (Priorities, right?) From all indications, Big Al had delivered on his promise.

It was as if our humble desert town had won an all-expense-paid trip to a tropical paradise. It was difficult to object. The skies were clear and the air was balmy. There were clumps of tall grasses poking out of the lava here and there. And towards the ocean and around town there were trees that looked a lot like palms.

The most obvious difference from before was that there were two suns in the sky, one to the north of the median and one to the south. I sensed that we'd lost a few days. Or weeks. Or months in the transition. It was impossible to say. There was no point of reference. Still, I couldn't complain too much based on the results.

It was only later when we'd visited town and talked to a few people, that it became clear that Grandpa Kurt, aunt Trish, the band members, and I were the only ones who seemed to know this was not the way it had always been. If Big Al's goal had been to make the transition as smooth as possible, he had succeeded. Everyone else took their new digs for granted. And why not, since even the milk in the fridge was fresh? To those of us in the know, it was a feat of engineering and logistics that was nothing short of miraculous.

The junior college was now on the slope above town and had an expansive view of the ocean. Even the towns around Rattlesnake Junction and their distance from each other were replicated pretty accurately. The main difference was that now they too were beach towns. In the distance to the south, I could just glimpse a balmy Tucson, situated on the coast like a less hip Los Angeles. The Indian Reservation was there too, only now it was inland and uphill to the northeast.

I had to wonder where the other cultures from the Stacks were. Where had Europe ended up? Or South America? Or Africa? Where were the three Stacks that represented the Asian continent now located? I tried to imagine all those cultures in a similar tropical setting, equidistant from one another on the massive island continent we'd seen from the observation deck. There was obviously plenty of room for everybody. That meant no one was going to be stepping on anyone else's toes for a while. And if overpopulation was what ultimately did Planet Earth in, Epsilon 4 wouldn't be going down that road for a long time to come.

Naturally, I wanted to explore. But for now, I was still in school, so I couldn't venture too far from home. Home, it turned out, was about the same distance from town as before and also roughly in the same direction: east. But instead of being backed up against the sun-scorched hills of eastern Arizona, we were now further up the lava slope than anyone else. The top of the smoldering volcano was closer to us, but not by all that much.

We had an even better view of the ocean than the school, being higher up on the hill. In fact, it was a little cooler at this elevation than it was along the coast. This worked in our favor when the novelty of being in a perpetually warm and humid climate started to wear off.

Big Al's Wrecking and Salvage was where it had always been with respect to the other businesses and buildings in town, faithfully reassembled to the last totaled sedan. The only thing missing was Big Al himself.

I took the Rex to the wrecking yard not long after the change, hoping to find the place open for business and Big Al himself hanging out there again in his Hawaiian shirts. Now, more than ever, he'd fit right in.

But so far, no such luck.

6l

Those Who Remember

Being among the select few who remembered the way things had been brought the band closer together than ever before. Our gigging schedule took up where it had left off. We had been booked nearly every weekend through the rest of the school year and that hadn't changed.

It was interesting to see everything resting on a bed of black lava instead of desert sand. But getting used to it took less time than I would have thought. I missed the sand at first. But then I discovered that the lava flows were as interesting in their way as the desert had been. The hardened lava had a variety of textures and features, nooks and crannies. It was like a vast ocean that had solidified. The landscape was all smooth waves, crests, and gullies. And underground there were empty lava tubes, many big enough to walk upright in, that ran for miles inland.

One day the girls and I hiked about halfway up to the volcano. I drove in as far as I could go in the Rex. I soon discovered that the flat areas of the landscape were deceptive. I had to focus to keep from getting stuck. Cracks and crevasses would appear out of nowhere, big enough to swallow a car if you weren't careful. But we made it and managed to get back in one piece during the course of a weekend afternoon.

Big Al's Wrecking And Salvage

As it turned out, there were actually some honest to goodness dinos around. Surprise! The planet was older than anyone had imagined. But the ones we'd seen were big, slow-moving critters, herbivores from the look of it. They reminded me of brontosauruses. These came from somewhere inland. I was a little worried at first that we might be confronted someday with my car's namesake—a real T-Rex. But so far that hadn't happened.

At least there weren't any mosquitos. They'd been right about that. And from all indications, the Greys had remained aboard the ship. That was also good news. One less thing to worry about.

Gradually the story came out. It seemed that everyday people knew a little more about who they were, where they were, and how they had come to be there. Books that chronicled the last couple of centuries of Earth's history began to appear on shelves in libraries, schools, and colleges. Over the course of weeks and months the details about New Arizona, the abandoned Planet Earth, and our 250-year-long journey across the galaxy emerged.

The information was all broad strokes. Smaller details of what had happened after the fifties remained obscure, probably intentionally so. For instance, you couldn't find technical manuals on how anything worked much beyond the period we were living in. I, of course, couldn't wait to find out how music would evolve going into the sixties and beyond. But there was precious little info to be found on the subject and no actual recordings to listen to. It was hardly surprising. I could see the powers-that-be not wanting us to get ahead of ourselves. They wouldn't want the past as they knew it interfering with the future we were about to create for ourselves.

It was amazing how easily this new information was assimilated and became a part of our general knowledge. Maybe a little too amazing. What people were learning about themselves and where they had come from didn't cause widespread panic or even outrage, as you might expect. It was as if they had always known. Seamless was the word that kept coming to mind. I had to admire how slick the transition from spaceship to planet, from not-knowing to knowing, had been. These Designers had thought of everything.

I couldn't detect any evidence of behind-the-scenes manipulation beyond that. As far as I could tell we, the Settlers, were pretty much on our own on the surface of this new planet. But then, it had seemed that way back on the Fortune's Fool as well.

Melissa and Tina, for their part, were relieved that everything had gone so well. They'd been as worried as I had been that the transition would cause a major upheaval—gnashing of teeth and pulling of hair. Also, the pressure to keep what they knew under wraps was suddenly lifted, which was a huge relief. Everyone was, after a few weeks, basically on the same page, without the need for lengthy discussions, arguments, or explanations. It was weird, granted. But what was the alternative? Chaos? Fighting in the streets? No, thanks. And what would protests have accomplished anyway except to distract everyone from what needed to be done now that we were here?

Meanwhile, the Fortune's Fool was a nightly feature in the sky over Epsilon 4. It was closer than Earth's moon had been to Earth. But being smaller, it looked similar in size. It was quite a bit brighter, probably because it was made of metal and catching the light of two suns instead of one. And probably due to the way we were situated between the suns, every night was a full moon night.

Accepting the ship as a replacement for Earth's moon was not hard to do. It was easy to forget it was a spaceship we were looking at and not a big chunk of rock. It certainly didn't make it seem any less romantic, at least to the romantically inclined.

The sunsets were amazing, one sun setting just before the other each day. We were told the gravitational forces generated by each sun offset the other and kept Epsilon 4 navigating a small ellipse between them. Consequently, the climate and the length of days, etc., remained amazingly consistent year-round. Planting, growing, and harvesting could be done at any time. This meant our idea of "seasons" would soon have to be retired.

62

Normal, Approximately

With the approach of my nineteenth birthday and the beginning of my second and final year in junior college, I had to start thinking about what I'd be doing after I graduated from JC. I decided, since we were on a brand-spankin' new planet, that being an explorer would be something I could cotton to. You didn't necessarily need to be an egghead to be an explorer, I figured. You just needed some initiative, a decent set of hiking boots, some long-range binoculars, and a sun hat, as far as I could tell--and a healthy dose of curiosity about your surroundings. I had all those things.

It helped if you knew something about map making--cartography, it was called-- geography, and geology to get you started. So those were the courses I was enrolled in for the upcoming year. Eventually, I'd have to figure out how to make a living traipsing around the countryside. But I figured that could wait till later.

Life was too interesting right now to worry about careers, the future, and things like that. When we weren't in school or sleeping, we were playing rock 'n' roll. I was still working at Ted's. The music was starting to bring in some dough, both from the records and from playing out. But the work at Ted's was more reliable. Plus, I still loved cars and the perfume of eau de grease. Grandpa continued to tinker on his immortal Studebaker, while Trish continued to work at Legal Services in town and made sure the two of us didn't starve when she got home.

We made the pilgrimage to Tucson a time or two, just to see what

Tucson was like as a coastal city. Very hot and humid, it turned out. The new location was already changing the local economy in subtle ways. There was now more of an emphasis on tourism. And already there was a burgeoning fishing industry, which would have been hard to imagine in the olden days.

The same could be said for Rattlesnake Junction, only on a smaller scale. We became, over the ensuing months, a fishing village. New hotels were going up along the waterfront. Nothing on the scale of Tucson, though.

All the major cities of all the countries and continents represented in the Stacks were now located on the coast, just as Tucson and Phoenix were. But despite the similarities in climate and location everywhere you went, people still seemed to like to travel and see what things were like someplace else.

Since we lived near a large body of water now, we didn't have anywhere near the temperature extremes that we'd had in the desert. But the humidity made up for that. As time went by I was ever more grateful that we lived as high up on the hill as we did.

Sometimes those big lumbering, leaf-eating dinosaurs would saunter on by the house. We'd gather at the windows with our jaws on the floor, peering out at them. But like everything else, we got used to the sight. They were completely harmless. Sweet, even. But I couldn't keep myself from imagining they might have more toothsome brethren around somewhere, and whether we shouldn't be more worried.

It was reassuring to know that Grandpa had a decent sized arsenal. A couple of thirty aught sixes, a ten gauge double-barreled shotgun, a half dozen handguns--Colt 45s mostly, like you'd have found in the Old West. When I let my mind wander, I wondered what it would take to bring down a full-sized tyrannosaurus. I figured you'd have to place your shots carefully to do any damage in the short term. By short term, I mean before he chomped you in half and swallowed you in one gulp.

We never did come across any raptors, big or otherwise. But what we did get was an alien attack. At least that's what everybody thought at first.

63

The Invasion

I t was six months later that the attack came. Ships landed in droves around Tucson. We saw it on TV.

No one landed in Rattlesnake Junction. We were small potatoes, after all. No self-respecting alien invasion force would bother with us.

But it wasn't green-skinned critters with antennae that poured out of the ships in Tucson and Phoenix, taking control. It was humans. Humans in dark blue uniforms with the Xenecorp logo on them.

Those of us who knew about the standoff between the Federation and Xenecorp on the Fortune's Fool must have had similar thoughts: maybe things hadn't gone as well aboard the ship as hoped.

The band had been rehearsing in a music room at the college when the invasion came. A school administrator stuck her head in the door and told us what was happening, or as much as she knew about it. We packed up our gear and hightailed it over to my house.

Grandpa always seemed to be dialed into what was happening around town and the world at large. We learned from him that the occupation of Tucson was not an isolated event. The same thing was happening in the bigger cities all over the planet. Xenecorp had landed everywhere at once, taken charge, and declared martial law. So much for the hands-off approach to us Settlers. The only bright spot was that the invaders were spread pretty thin. As many as there were, they couldn't control every square foot of Tucson, for instance.

Nevertheless, they effectively set up roadblocks at all the entry and exit points around the big city.

"What's happening on tribal land?" I asked Tina.

She shrugged. "Everyone's arming up," she said wistfully. "It's bringing back a lot of bad memories. You've got all these bluecoats swarming all over the place, butting in where they don't belong and generally wreaking havoc. You see what I'm getting at? It's like the olden days. The Apache fought the blue coats then. And you can be sure we'll fight them now if it means protecting our freedom."

Melissa chimed in. "Dad says there's already talk of forming a resistance in town, in case those space goons decide to head this way."

"Well, we'll be ready up here, too, if it comes to that," said Grandpa grimly. "I've got enough firepower to handle a fair-sized raiding party. You girls know how to shoot?"

"Talking about shooting," said Tina. "You oughta give some thought to joining us at the reservation. You're pretty exposed out here on the flows. My Aunt Cassie has a guest house that my grandparents used to live in. You could stay there. You'd be as safe there as anywhere. No one knows more about guerilla warfare than the Apaches."

There was silence after Tina's speech. "She's got a point," said Grandpa finally. "We're kind of like sitting ducks out here on the flows. As tough as we are, we wouldn't slow them down much with their fancy ray guns and flying saucers if they decided to come this way. I'd want us all to have a fighting chance."

Tina looked at Melissa.

"I think I'll stay with my family in Rattlesnake Junction for the time being," Melissa said. A star student both in high school and in college, she was probably the smartest of our group, and the most sensitive. She was taking what was happening pretty hard. But she wanted safety for herself and her family. "Maybe I can convince them to come too," she said. "If you don't think anyone at the Rez would mind." She looked over at Tina.

"You kidding?" Tina said. "They'd welcome you and your family with open arms. They love the band on the Rez. I don't know if I ever told you, but they have a name for you, on account of your skills as a bassist. It translates roughly as Deep Thunder."

Melissa was obviously pleased with the moniker.

"The thing is, we need to stick together," Tina continued. "It's better for morale if there's more of us. Not to mention it'll be easier for us to practice if we're all in the same place."

More grinning.

So it was decided, at least for us Thornes. While we went and got our things, Tina made a couple of phone calls.

"My aunt knows we're coming," she told us. "The guest house is yours for as long as you want it."

"I'll go see how my family's doing," Melissa said.

"You've got my number," said Tina.

Melissa got behind the wheel of her dad's Buick, which she'd parked in the driveway before we went off to practice. Her dad let her use it when he was at work. She backed out of the driveway, the big V-8 purring. We all watched her as she became a speck against the dazzling backdrop of the ocean, heading toward town.

64

The Fall Back Position

When we arrived at the reservation, everyone seemed to be on the move. It was like the tribe was breaking camp, getting ready to head for the hills. Which was more or less what was happening. Tribal members were gathering weapons, ammunition, clothes, and supplies enough for a prolonged siege, getting ready to take them into the lava flows farther uphill.

"Looks like we won't be staying at auntie's after all," Tina remarked, deadpan, taking in the scene. "I think we're going directly to plan B."

"And what might that be?" Grandpa Kurt asked. The four of us, including Trish, were packed into the Studebaker, along with enough gear for a two-week stay.

"It's called 'find your own cave and stake a claim'," Tina said. "Before they're all taken."

On Tina's instructions, we drove uphill until we came to a solid wall of lava about fifteen feet high. Half the cars on the Rez were already parked there on the hard-packed sand below the ridge line. The lava here wasn't as smooth as elsewhere. It was lumpy and porous, with mounds and spires forming up here and there. Beneath and around the mounds snaked crevasses that formed narrow sand trails, protected from view and from the elements. All along these trails were hollows and tunnels, many tall enough to stand up in. This would make a great hiding place. No doubt about it.

In the middle of the lumpy, bumpy lava mounds there was a clearing, a flat, sandy area surrounded on all sides by a low-lying wall of porous black rock. It became the go-to place when everyone had staked out their temporary living quarters in the tubes and tunnels.

When it seemed like everyone was assembled in the clearing, the tribal leader, a man dressed unassumingly in jeans and a red and white Pendleton shirt, spoke. Tina was the only one of us who had any idea what he was saying. So she translated for us.

"He's offering a prayer of thanksgiving," Tina explained.

A stillness had descended over the tribe, and though we were in the back, we heard every word of the ancient language clearly.

"Now he's asking the spirits for protection for the tribe and help in repelling the invaders who trespass on our land and threaten our safety."

A question and answer period followed in which the tribal leader laid out a strategy for the defense of the tribe. Since this was done in English, I had no problem understanding what was being said.

Tribal members were going to be assigned as lookouts while groups of volunteers would patrol the peripheries. If the tribe came under direct attack, this clearing would be the fallback point. Everyone would gather here to make a stand. It made sense. The area we were in was like a natural fortification, offering excellent visibility for miles in all directions.

Paths snaked away from the clearing, lava rock rising high on both sides. We'd found the entrance to a lava tube next to a shallow hollow where Tina's family had decided to make camp. The tube we adopted contained several side branches that became alcoves where Trish and Grandpa and I could each have a bit of privacy. Our own rooms, in other words. Except for the muffled voices of our neighbors, it was absolutely still inside the tubes. And kind of cozy, especially when the candles and lamps we'd brought with us were lit.

Reports were coming in. Tucson had fallen, practically without a shot being fired. The invasion was so sudden and unexpected that no effective defense had been mounted. The invaders from the ship had just swept in with their sci-fi weapons and taken over. The radio and TV stations had been commandeered first. And the message beaming out was that we were now under the control of Xenecorp. Xenecorp had our best interests at heart, it seemed. Any resistance was strongly discouraged for our own safety. Though there had been few, if any casualties so far, the clear implication was that this could change in an instant if we put up a fight.

So far, Melissa and her family had not turned up in the lava tubes. I thought of her and her father preparing to do battle down in Rattlesnake Junction with pistols and rifles that were toys compared to whatever these spacemen had with them. The intruders had about 400 years on us in terms of weapons technology.

I guessed we'd eventually find out whether we stood a chance against them. The early conquests had gone unanswered because of the element of surprise. But I couldn't see folks lying down for these guys for long, no matter how intimidating they might be, or how impressive their guns were.

65

Danny

anny Two Feathers was a friend of Tina's brothers. Her brothers were well over 6 feet tall and weighed in the neighborhood of 250 each. We knew them from the Rez and from when they would show up at some of our hairier gigs as unofficial security. Danny, on the other hand, was about my height and weight. He was in the same year as me at the JC, having transferred in from a high school closer to the Rez. Now that we were in the lava tubes next to Tina's family, he was around a lot.

I liked him OK right off. Where Tina's brothers were full of swagger and bluster, he was serious and quiet. I knew from Tina he was a good student. Beyond that, I didn't know much.

"How do you figure what's going on?" he asked me one afternoon. He had come by to see if there was anything we needed.

"You mean with Xenecorp?"

"Yeah. Them."

I thought about it for a moment, wondering if I could share what I knew with him. I decided I could trust Danny. He wasn't the type to go blabbing to everyone in sight. So I told him what Al had told us on the observation deck that day months ago, without naming my source. About how Xenecorp was supposed to have been subordinate to the Federation, which by now everyone knew had been in command of the ship on the journey across the galaxy. Though most everything had come out in the preceding months, there were still a few key pieces of information that weren't generally known. Among these was the ongoing power struggle between Xenecorp and the Federation, which by all indications had reached the boiling point. Another was the fact that the legendary Captain Alfred Wertmueller and Big Al of Big Al's Wrecking and Salvage were one and the same. But this was something I intended to keep to myself.

"The company was responsible for building and maintaining the ship's systems on the crossing. But after what had happened on Planet Earth, they were denied any kind of leadership role. They were strictly support staff."

Danny understood. He and anyone who had studied the history of Earth's demise knew about the role of the big corporations in The Fall.

"I get it," Danny said. "It's understandable the Federation wouldn't want a repeat of what happened on Earth on this mission. They wouldn't want economics overwhelming sound judgment on everything else that mattered, like public health, education, and environmental policy."

"Exactly," I said, impressed that he'd gotten to the heart of the matter so quickly.

"But old habits die hard, right?" Danny said, staring into the middle distance. "After toeing the line for a couple odd centuries, they wanted to write the script again like in the olden days. They wanted to be the ones in charge like they'd been on Planet Earth."

I nodded. "It's not generally known, but the struggle between Xenecorp and the Federation has been going for a while," I said.

"Oh?" he looked at me then with an appraising gaze. "And how do you know all this?"

"It's a long story," I said. "But let's just say I got it from the horse's mouth a while back."

"And which horse would that be?"

"I happen to know the captain," I said.

"The captain of the Fortune's Fool? You know Captain Alfred Wertmueller?" he said with barely concealed amazement.

"Through my Grandpa," I added quickly. "They're buddies."

"No kidding," Danny said, with genuine awe.

I could tell he wanted to know the details. But that was as much as I felt comfortable revealing at the moment. I didn't have any right to tell anyone that the captain had been moonlighting at the wrecking yard in Rattlesnake Junction all this time. That was his business. It was something known only to a select few who had successfully managed to keep it under wraps until now. I sure wasn't going to be the one to spill the beans.

"Do you know what's going on with Captain Wertmueller?" Danny wanted to know.

"I don't," I said. "But the news can't be good if these guys are here now doing what they're doing. It can only mean the Federation failed in its efforts to stave off the mutiny on the ship. I don't know if that means something's happened to the captain or not."

We sat there for a while contemplating this grim prospect.

"I don't even know the guy," Danny said. "Captain Wertmueller, I mean. But I have a lot of respect for him and what he's done to get us here in the first place. I sure hope he's alright."

"So do I," I said. "So do I."

66

The New Normal

Xenecorp had things pretty much buttoned up in a few days. TV and radio, originating as it did from the major cities, had abruptly stopped sending out dispatches and updates on the invasion and instead was now exclusively broadcasting propaganda praising Xenecorp and its "liberation" of the planet. From whom or what was never mentioned. In fact, if you only listened to the radio and watched TV, you'd be excused for thinking there had never been an invasion to begin with. Everything was just hunky-dory. The future was sterling.

The broadcasts were all about amazing opportunities to get rich and how a luxurious and opulent life could be yours if you displayed enough initiative and worked tirelessly for the company. It sounded like the good ol' American work ethic that we all knew and loved, except there was no mention of personal, artistic, or political freedom. It was all about what Xenecorp would provide in exchange for your undying allegiance. Life would be better for everyone, the ads promised, if you kept your head down and went along with the program. Crime and poverty would soon become "things of the past". But "antisocial behavior" would not be tolerated. You had to read between the lines a little to understand that any kind of dissension, public protest, or indication of dissatisfaction with the current system would henceforth be lumped in with what was considered antisocial behavior. On the other hand, opportunities for advancement would be endless. Anyone could become a manager and even a CEO given enough time, enthusiasm, and dedication.

Interestingly, anything having to do with democracy or democratic institutions was omitted. There was no mention of elections. The idea of personal freedom rarely came up, except in terms of making consumer choices and living the good life as defined by Xenecorp. The emphasis was on unwavering devotion to the company, on acquiring the latest gadgets and gizmos, and the rewards of working for Xenecorp, such as public holidays and a couple of weeks vacation a year spent in a company owned resort or facility, of course.

Xenecorp TV programs always featured an impressive array of gadgets that we'd presumably be trading our freedoms for. I found the advertisements for lawnmowers particularly amusing since there weren't yet any lawns around to mow. In fact, the programming was nothing but wall-to-wall commercials for products and services that Xenecorp offered. The bombardment was so persistent you longed for the days when ads interrupted your favorite TV show for only ten minutes each half-hour.

No one was fooled, at first at any rate. It was all a transparent ploy to distract us from what was really going on: that we had been conquered and were now being occupied by an external force. But if they thought we'd be so bowled over by their piles of synthetic merchandise and technicolor TV fantasies that we'd just forget that we no longer had control over our destinies, they had another thing coming.

You had to admire how smooth these guys were. And how relentless. And who's to say that a few of the weaker minds among us weren't starting to cave under the onslaught of lies and misinformation we were constantly being subjected to? Who's to say, after being slammed day in and day out, 24 hours a day, by images of canned sunsets and beautiful people having the time of their lives, there weren't some folks in the crowd starting to wonder if life might not be so bad under Xenecorp after all.

Of course, the question was, what happened if you didn't play along? There were already reports of people going missing coming in on the grapevine. More often than not these were folks who had been openly critical of the new regime. The message going out was clear. Freethinkers need not apply. Xenecorp demanded zealots. If you didn't play along, you yourself became as disposable as the goods they were selling.

If all this sounds like an upscale version of what the Soviets were doing to keep their people in line, you'd be right. It was like the Soviet bloc, only with slicker propaganda and cooler stuff. But the brainwashing was pretty similar, as was the tendency of those who resisted the "generosity" of the new state to disappear, never to be seen or heard from again. I'd paid enough attention in history class to know how the brown shirts had taken over in Germany in the 1930s. I knew about what went down in Russia after the czars. And in terms of sheer firepower and with TV as a form of mind control, the dictators of the past had nothing on these space entrepreneurs. There had never been anything like this. These guys had mass indoctrination and the power of suggestion down to a science.

This was the new normal.

67

The Re/i/tance

The only bright spot was that the countryside had so far been left pretty much alone. Out on the fringes, and I guess Rattlesnake Junction fell into that category, we were still free to turn off our TVs if we wanted to, think our own thoughts, and go about our business much like before.

"They're spread too thin to bother with us," Grandpa Kurt was theorizing. "They don't have the manpower to be everywhere at once."

We were in the cave having dinner by candlelight: Melissa, Tina, Trish, Grandpa Kurt, and me. Melissa hadn't been able to convince her family to take shelter in the caves with us. But that didn't mean she wasn't hanging out with us every chance she got. We ate in silence for a while.

"What do you think they want with us?" Melissa asked. "I mean, they can do just about anything with their futuristic technology. Compared to them we're just this quaint throwback."

"That's a good question," Grandpa Kurt said. "Why bother to make the effort to try to brainwash us at all?"

"Yeah," Tina said. "They could just threaten to mow us down if we don't cooperate. That would get the job done." You could always rely on Tina for an unsentimental assessment of the situation.

"What they want is converts, not slaves," Grandpa mused. "They want us to go along with them voluntarily. They *need* us to go along for whatever reason."

"Maybe it goes back to what you said earlier about them being spread too thin on the ground," I said. "There aren't enough of them here to keep millions of people in line by force. It's more practical to do it this way."

"At least, for the time being maybe," Grandpa put in. "Maybe Tina's right. If this doesn't work they'll do whatever it takes to get us to do what they want us to. They hold all the cards."

"What do you think they want us to do for them that they can't do for themselves?" Trish asked.

"That's the $64,000 question," said Grandpa.

"I wish Big Al was around," I said. "We'd just ask him."

Everybody nodded.

"If they're taking the slow approach," Tina said. "Trying to win us over instead of just ordering us around, that might give us an edge. It could give us time to organize some kind of resistance. We could turn our superior numbers back on them."

"Have you seen their weapons?" Aunt Trish put in. "How could we go up against that and expect to make a dent?"

Tina was chewing on the simple meal of tortillas, rice, and beans that Aunt Trish had prepared. "Guerrilla warfare," she said. "The tribes basically invented it. Planning a strategy is the first step."

"We organize and figure out a way to take back Tucson," I said, getting excited about the prospect. There hadn't been much to feel good about since the invasion. And planning the demise of our conquerors was the first ray of sunshine in a while.

"It's dangerous," Trish said. "Too dangerous."

"Right now we're just talking," I said.

We all sat there looking innocent.

68

The Raid

I was a pretty good shot with Grandpa's .38. I often went out behind the house when I needed to let off some steam and plink pop cans. I'd been a big fan of TV Westerns before they were all replaced by Xenecorp's propaganda. So I had no problem getting into character. My favorites were the Lone Ranger and the Adventures of Wild Bill Hickok with Guy Madison and Andy Devine. And more recently Have Gun Will Travel. Paladin was my kind of hired gun.

But as much as I liked the .38, I found I truly excelled with the Winchester Grandpa Kurt had. It was a vintage Model 1873 that used .44-40 cartridges and had the shorter 20-inch barrel. I could hit a Coke can at 100 yards with it with no scope. It suited me fine.

It's what I took with me on that first raid.

We hadn't been the only ones plotting against our occupiers. Danny Two Feathers and Tina's brothers had already been working on a plan to conduct a late-night raid down Tucson way.

At the appointed hour I just showed up with the Winchester. They were loading into one of the big canvas-covered trucks they had on the Rez for hauling produce and workers from place to place. Tina's brothers just looked at me when I appeared. They gave me the hard stare for a few seconds. In the end, I guess they must have decided I made the cut because when I climbed into the back of the truck with the eight or so other rifle-toting Indians, nobody objected.

Not much was said on the way to Tucson. There was no mention of a plan or discussion about where we were going. I figured I'd find out soon enough.

It was kind of a big deal. We hadn't heard of anyone pulling a raid before. But that didn't mean it hadn't been tried. The bluecoats could simply have quashed any news about it. Still, it would have been hard to keep reports of a raid, successful or otherwise, from getting around. So there was a good chance we really were the first, for better or worse.

It took an hour for us to get to the outskirts of Tucson. We were running with our lights off. The Fortune's Fool was lighting our way, being the biggest and brightest object in the nighttime sky.

As stealthy as we were, I figured we'd get stopped before we got to the city limits. Having encountered no real resistance up until now, they'd quit using checkpoints to monitor the comings and goings to and from the city, but I figured Xenecorp would have some kind of surveillance gear in place instead. But we were far from the only folks on the road at that time of night. And from the outside, our truck looked totally innocuous. There was a steady stream of eighteen-wheelers hauling food, drink, and other supplies to and from the city. There were even a few passenger cars heading for town, coming from who knew where. The fact that there wasn't much traffic leaving the city made me think some kind of curfew must be in effect.

The driver of our truck seemed to know where he was going. We pulled off the main road onto a dirt track across the lava flows. It led toward a huge flat area in the distance that was lit up like a baseball stadium. We came across a sea of World War Two military vehicles parked along the roadway to our right, jeeps and transport trucks mostly. The closer to the lights we got the greater the array of military hardware we saw. In addition to personnel carriers, there were now tanks, anti-aircraft guns, long-range artillery, prop planes, a few fighter jets, and even some B-29 bombers.

Our driver pulled the truck off the roadway well before we reached the bright lights that lay straight ahead. We hiked in the last couple of miles, careful to keep out of view among the trucks and jeeps as much as possible. A couple of times we froze and ducked for cover when lights came down the road behind us. Our truck, which we'd left just off the road, looked enough like everything else here that it didn't attract any special attention.

69

The Depot

We made it to the circle of light in the center of everything. What we saw there was straight out of an A-list technicolor science-fiction extravaganza. There were spotless, gleaming pieces of hardware everywhere, that we could only guess the purpose of. The relatively featureless ones might have been shuttles. While the ones that were prickly with what looked like stubby cannons were probably fighters. And the big squarish ones could have been used to haul bulky equipment or transport large numbers of troops to and from the ship. These were contained within a transparent wall of shimmering light, about twenty feet high, that seemed to emanate from towers constructed at intervals around the compound. Someone tossed a rock to test the wall. It disappeared on contact. Nothing made it to the other side.

We peered out from our hiding place among a group of WWII armored trucks that looked like relics, even by the standards of the fifties. In fact, everything outside the circle of light was like a giant museum of twentieth-century military hardware. Or a graveyard of the same. It was so unsophisticated that they hadn't even bothered to fence this stuff off from intruders, like us. Compared with what was within the golden circle, it constituted no threat whatever. It wasn't worth worrying about. I thought of Big Al and how he would have a field day here, trying to figure out how to get some of this vintage equipment into his salvage yard. With a pang, I wondered how he was and if he had managed to survive the coup on the ship.

We all stared at the gleaming machinery for several more minutes, hypnotized. Then Jake, the leader of our merry band, abruptly stood up, turned, and strode back the way we'd come. The rest of the guys scrambled to catch up.

"What?" I said. "Aren't we supposed to be doing something here? Blowing something up? Where's he going?"

Danny pulled me aside. "This was supposed to be a recon mission," he said quietly. "We've seen what we came to see."

"We came all this way just to gawk?" I said incredulously. I'd lugged Kurt's Winchester out here for nothing.

"We're not equipped to do more right now," Danny explained levelly. "How effective do you think our pea shooters would be against that?" He indicated the sphere of light. "We don't even have anything to get us in there."

He had a point.

"You got any ideas?" I said.

"Nope," Danny said evenly. "But given time, somebody might come up with something."

The rest of the group was already a dozen steps away, on their way back to the truck.

"Can't we at least steal something out here?" I asked. "One of those old US military trucks? Or a tank? Surely they're not going to miss one of those. Don't you think a tank could come in handy?"

Danny gave a chuckle. I think it was the first time I'd seen him smile. "Maybe another time," he said as we half-walked, half-ran to catch up with the rest of the group. "Right now we've got to concentrate on getting back. If they don't come after us, that already tells us something. It means they don't have this area under airtight surveillance."

"If this stuff is so valuable to them, you'd think it would be more closely monitored," I said.

"It could just mean they're confident none of us Settlers could do much harm to their gear, providing anyone would dare to mess with it to begin with. Shows you how much they think of our abilities."

"That they're non-existent?"

"Exactly," he said with the slightest smile. "They haven't had cause to worry before now. It also means we'd better make it count when we do strike. They're not likely to underestimate us twice."

We took the same route back to our truck as we'd taken coming in. We walked past the same rows upon rows of good ole American military hardware from the war. It seemed like a darn shame that it was just sitting there, collecting dust. Of course, how much value any of this gear would be against what we'd seen back at the depot was an open question.

We got back to the truck without incident. So far nobody'd turned up to ask us what we were doing there, politely or otherwise. This was seen as a small victory in itself by the group.

No one said anything on the way back, me included. We were all digesting what we'd seen. And trying to figure a way to get into the depot, so we could do some real damage.

I snuck back into our cave without waking anyone, so there was no explaining to do. By the time I got up the next morning, Trish had left.

"She's gone to work," Grandpa said. "But after that, she says she's going back to the house. I'm thinking about heading back there today too."

I noticed there were fewer tribal members around. They must have decided it was safe enough for the moment to go home as well.

"We know where to go if the bluecoats show up in town," he said. "But right now there doesn't seem to be an attack imminent, and therefore no reason to stick around here. You're welcome to stay if you want."

As much fun as camping with family and friends had been at first, living in these dark subterranean tunnels was starting to get a little old, I had to admit. I'd started longing for my bed at the house. Not to mention my music.

"Give me a minute," I told him.

I met Tina outside our cave. She had on khaki shorts and hiking boots and her backpack on over a white T-shirt

"I heard you went out with the boys last night," she said. I could tell right away she would have wanted to go too if she'd known. We'd gotten to know each other pretty well over the past couple of years playing in the band together.

"It turned out to be a sightseeing mission, nothing more," I said, downplaying the incident.

She must have sensed my disappointment, however. "I'm betting you wish you could have shot something full of holes with that nifty old Winchester," she said. "Or at least gotten to blow something up."

"How did you guess?" I said, and we both laughed.

"But you do realize we've got to have some kind of strategy when the real shooting starts, right? We may only have one shot at this. And if we lose the element of surprise, we're probably done before we start."

"I know," I said. "I know." Was I the only hot head around?

"So," I said. "You heading back to the Rez?"

"Yeah. My brothers are busy loading up the truck right now. You're welcome to come. It's probably still safer on the Rez than it would be at your place or in town. There's a lot of injuns with guns on the Rez, and they know how to use 'em." She pantomimed sighting down the barrel of a rifle.

We broke out laughing.

"Better I keep an eye on Grandpa and Trish," I said. "The Rex could come in handy if we need to make a fast getaway. Maybe I'll cruise by the school and see if there's anything going on there."

"You think they'll have classes again after what's happened?"

"Who knows. It just seems like a good place to find out more about what's going on, classes or no, especially with TV and radio down for the count. What say we get together at my place for rehearsal in a day or two if nothing else happens in the meantime?"

"Sure," said Tina. "If everything goes south, get out quick as you can. I'll meet you back here."

70

News

I t turned out the radio wasn't as useless with Xenecorp in charge as we'd thought. On the way back to the house with Grandpa Kurt, we came across a station at the end of the dial that, as far as I knew, hadn't been there before.

The hosts were actually talking openly about the invasion and what was known about the takeover. We looked at each other, shocked to hear anything but propaganda coming out of the speakers.

"Gotta be local," Kurt remarked.

"Finally. Some real news," I said. "Seems risky for whoever's broadcasting."

As we continued to drive toward our house, the signal started to get spotty.

"Probably a low-powered setup," Grandpa Kurt speculated, "transmitting from somewhere back in town."

"You really think so?"

"I'd bet they're hunkered down in someone's garage or basement. A coverage radius of a couple of miles at best. Not enough to attract a lot of attention outside Rattlesnake Junction. And hardly worth bothering about, if you think you're convinced you're the lords of the universe."

"Still, they're tempting fate. They're taking a real chance."

"Maybe. But think about it. Those bluecoats don't consider us much more advanced than insects."

235

"And just as easily stomped out?"

"Their technology is centuries beyond ours. From their standpoint we're neanderthals. We couldn't possibly pose a threat to them with our pop guns and toy radio station.

"Since you put it like that."

We listened some more. We were obviously at the limit of the broadcast range when we got to the house. But in among the static, you could still make out what was being said.

I unloaded Grandpa Kurt and our gear, still trying to pick words out of the noise.

"You going somewhere?" asked Kurt.

"I'm thinking of heading back into town," I said, "Maybe I can find out more about the new station. Like where it is and who's running it."

Grandpa Kurt nodded. "Let me know what you find out."

"I'll be back in an hour or two."

I drove toward Rattlesnake Junction, the signal growing stronger as I approached the outskirts of town. It was definitely an amateur effort. But it seemed like a small miracle that such a thing existed in among the slick advertising onslaught to be found everywhere else on the radio dial.

But before I began my search for the phantom radio station, I had another destination in mind.

Big Al's Wrecking Yard seemed just as deserted and forlorn as it had been on my previous visits lately. The chain-link fence was still padlocked, and there wasn't any sign of activity in the stacks beyond. I pulled up to the gate anyway and turned off the engine. After a couple of minutes of taking in the silence, I opened the door to the Rex and got out.

I approached the fence. The only things that moved were the multi-colored flags that flapped lazily in the balmy breeze wafting in off the ocean. That and the occasional whistling noise as a gust of wind blew through the crevices and crannies of the old wrecks in the yard. It was spooky. I remembered the showdown with the Grey and wondered if there might still be any around.

I jumped when I heard a soothing voice at my ear. "Can I interest you in some genuine pre-owned automobile parts?"

I whirled around and found myself face-to-face with Big Al. He looked like he'd been in a barroom brawl. His face was bruised and his lip was swollen. There was a cut over his eye and his right forearm was wrapped with a smudged bandage.

"Don't you think you should get that looked at?" was the first thing I could think to say.

"This?" said Al, as if surprised to find a dirty bandage there on his arm. "This is nothing. Just a scratch."

"What happened?"

"Why don't we go inside," said Big Al quietly, looking around surreptitiously. "I'll tell you about it."

71

Big Al Returns

There'd been so many things I'd been dying to ask Big Al, I didn't know where to begin.

Aside from the lip, the bruises, and the bandage, he looked pretty much the same. He was in his civilian clothes. That is to say, he had on a Hawaiian shirt, faded jeans, and work boots. He pulled a half empty bottle of Wild Turkey and poured a healthy amount into a coffee mug.

"We held 'em off for as long as we could, kid," he said apologetically, taking a swig and grimacing. "We got everything prepped for you down here and rebuilt to spec as planned. And we managed to get everyone out of the ship and down to the surface without a hitch. But then the standoff collapsed. Turns out Xenecorp had more sympathizers among our security forces than we'd anticipated. People we thought were friends turned on us, and we found ourselves fighting on two fronts.

"It was a losing battle. In the end, we had to cut our losses and beat a strategic retreat. Most of our forces are hunkered down right now on the surface, in unoccupied areas of the planet. There's no shortage of hiding places in the wide-open spaces. I chose to come back here instead." He spread his arms in a mock grandiose gesture, taking in the yard and all it contained.

"Disguised as the proprietor of a wrecking yard featuring quality

238

used parts," I said, happy that Big Al's true identity had never become generally known.

"There are only a few loyal, hand-picked individuals that know about my sideline," Big Al said with a wink. "And those I trust with my life."

"Is there anyone else from the ship here?" I asked, thinking of Gillian.

"There are half a dozen of my associates back in the stacks right now. I didn't want too many of my people in or near the inhabited areas. It would be too risky for the Settlers."

"They sure are keeping a low profile," I said. "I was positive the place was deserted."

"That's the general idea," Big Al replied. He turned his attention fully to me. "So what have you been up to lately?"

I told him about us moving into the lava tubes after the invasion. And how most of us had since returned home.

"Grandpa thinks the reason they haven't been cracking down harder is that they need us puny humans for something. Something they can't do for themselves," I said. "We've been going round and round wondering why Xenecorp is using propaganda instead of brute force to keep us in line.

"Your grandpa is right," Big Al said. "They need workers in large numbers, at least in the short term."

I waited for him to go on.

"They're going to need raw materials if they want to establish a long-term presence on the surface. Creating the infrastructure they envision from scratch will require a lot of mining. They'll need all kinds of ore in fairly short order."

The picture was starting to come clear. "They need us to mine what they need."

"In the short term, yes. They've got enough supplies on the ship to last them a while. But those stores won't last forever."

"And what about after the short term?"

"With your help, they'll eventually get their automation going,"

Big Al said. "Machines will ultimately do the work they want you to do."

"Yes, but what happens then?"

"To those who toe the line, nothing probably," Big Al said. "They will always need good little consumers. As such you will remain a vital part of their plans. Plus, they'll need workers in the service industries doing the jobs they might prefer not to do themselves, not to mention a vast network of support staff to run their idea of a perfect society. And if you prove to be good workers and consumers, there'll probably be opportunities to progress through the ranks, though it's unlikely that as Settlers you'll ever land positions of real authority."

"Unlimited opportunities for advancement. Just like the ads say. Or nearly."

"They're on the level about that as far as it goes. Turning you into slaves would be counterproductive, a waste of manpower and resources. It's so much more efficient to have a voluntary, albeit brainwashed, workforce. That's why they're using the indoctrination approach. They're hoping it will get them the cooperation they need with a minimum expenditure of effort and resources."

"And if it doesn't?"

Big Al shrugged. "It could get messy. They're committed now. They'll do what it takes to survive down here, even if they have to apply direct pressure."

"Sounds like we'd still be slaves. But by another name."

"That's a fair assessment," Big Al said.

"This wasn't their plan from the beginning," he went on. "They'd figured on having months, even years, to get everything in place for a strategic assault of the surface. But things didn't work out that way. Their intentions came to light, and they felt compelled to act. They had to move up their timetable and that meant they had to improvise. Trust me, improvisation is not their strong suit."

"So this is it?" I asked Big Al. "It's all over?"

Big Al looked at me in surprise. "What? No!" he said, shaking his head like he couldn't believe I'd come to that conclusion. "This is just a setback. We fully intend to take back control of the ship. Make no mistake."

"So you're saying there's hope you'll be able to beat Xenecorp?"

"Absolutely," he said enthusiastically. "Their weapons are more sophisticated. And they have greater numbers. Granted. They might seem to be holding all the cards right now. But that'll change. Believe me."

I was happy to hear he was so optimistic. But for the life of me, I couldn't see any cause for optimism right at that moment.

"So what are we supposed to be doing in the meantime?" I was more confused now than before.

"Just keep doing what you've been doing," Big Al said.

"I've been going to school, working at Ted's, and playing with the Roadrunners," I pointed out, not seeing how any of those activities could help turn the tide. I was too ashamed to even mention we'd been trying to come up with a plan to attack Xenecorp's supply depot outside Tucson. That idea, small scale as it was, seemed pretty absurd compared to the greater forces at work.

"Then keep studying, keep working, and keep rockin'," he said jovially.

I asked Al if he would stop by the house. "I know Grandpa would love to see you," I said.

"I'll have to take a rain check," he said. "I'm in the middle of establishing secure accommodations for my people here on the surface. Things are a bit dicey as they stand right now."

I thought that was the understatement of the year. But I didn't say anything.

"Give Kurt and your aunt my best regards," Big Al said, accompanying me back to my car. "I'm sure we'll all have a chance to get together again soon."

72

Radio Rattlesnake

I stopped at the junior college and was surprised to find a few classes still in session. Officially, according to the receptionist in administration, the school was closed until further notice.

I went to the lecture hall where my English classes usually met. The professor was there, along with about 20 or so students in a room made to hold about 150. I took a seat and listened to a lecture on Aldous Huxley. My prof, Mr. Bernard, gave us a reading assignment that included passages from Brave New World before class was dismissed.

I waited for a student I knew, Miranda, near the exit.

"You know anything about the new radio station in town?" I asked her, expecting a blank stare.

As it turned out, she knew exactly what I was talking about. "Rattlesnake Radio?" she said with enthusiasm. "It started up a couple of days ago. There's a rumor it's broadcasting from the basement of the American Legion Hall, the one on Fourth Street near Central. It's not supposed to be common knowledge, but everybody knows anyway. It's kind of big news."

I thanked her and drove over to Fourth and Central.

The old adobe hall was nothing special, at least from the outside. Added to that, it didn't look like anything was going on. I peered through a couple of windows but could see no activity. It was dark inside. I went around to the rear, where there was a parking lot and a back entry. There was one car in the lot, a rust bucket from the late thirties.

I tried the door, and it swung inward. A short, dimly lit hallway culminated in stairs leading downward. I took the stairs and found myself in a basement corridor that ran the width of the building from the rear to the street, lit by bare bulbs. At the end of the corridor, an open doorway beckoned.

There was a disheveled guy in there at a table pushed up against a cinder block wall. He was seated with his back to me, talking into a microphone that was connected to what looked like a ham radio. The microphone must have been as old as the car outside. The metal was pocked and corroded, giving it the appearance of having been dredged up out of a lake after a decade or so underwater.

The DJ looked like a beatnik. Maybe that was a bit generous. A bum was more like it. He had long, scraggly light brown locks and a goatee. He was reading aloud from some pages in front of him.

I listened for a while without alerting him to my presence.

"A band of resistance fighters set fire to an abandoned government building in downtown Tucson today," he was saying. "They broke several ground floor windows and hurled Molotov cocktails into the building before fleeing the scene. The attack seemed to catch the bluecoats off-guard. Before a response could be mounted, the perpetrators had vanished from the scene. No arrests were made."

The beatnik newsman finally sensed me standing behind him. "And now The Coasters' 'Charley Brown,'" he said. The 45 was queued up on a turntable. He dropped the needle on it. The song seemed an inspired choice, given the vandalism he had just been reporting on.

He threw a switch to mute the mic and turned to face me in his rolling chair.

"Rose Thorne," he said. "To what do I owe the honor?" His manners were surprisingly genteel, considering his appearance.

"You know who I am?" I said, surprised.

"Everybody in town with an iota of sense knows who you are,"

243

he said amiably. "You're the guitarist for Rattlesnake Junction's best band. And if you aren't a household name yet, you should be."

I was blushing. He wasn't bad looking once you got past the facial hair. He was probably three or four years older than me.

"I heard the broadcast on the way into town today," I said. "I wanted to see what you all were up to."

"Radio Rattlesnake," he said, leaning back in his chair and spreading his arms magnanimously to take in his decidedly unassuming surroundings. "The only real radio station left on the planet." He proclaimed the descriptor with practiced authority. It was probably the station's tagline.

"Are you the only DJ?"

"Nope. There are about fifteen of us altogether, all volunteers. Six DJs and the rest support staff." He seemed to really see me for the first time, or pretended to. "Say," he said. "We happen to have some openings at the mic during the week. You interested?" He raised his eyebrows Groucho Marx-style. The pitch had a well-worn quality.

"Me? A DJ?" I said.

"There's no worthier calling right now," he said, "for anyone who cares about freedom of speech and freedom of the press."

I couldn't argue with that. It could well be a way to make a difference under the circumstances.

"It's a once in a lifetime opportunity," he said cheerfully.

To be in the hot seat, I thought. Sitting ducks if things went south. The DJs here would be obvious targets if Xenecorp did come a'callin'. What I said was, "I have zero experience in radio broadcasting,"

"There's nothing to it," he said. "You're used to working around microphones on stage. I can attest to that. I've seen the Roadrunners play at least a half dozen times."

"Oh?" I said. "Where?"

"I took in a few of the gigs you played up at the college," he said. "You even did a show or two at my fraternity."

"You're in a fraternity?" I said, unable to conceal my surprise.

"Was," he said with a dry chuckle. "Can you believe it? I'm reformed now. This was back in the days when being in a fraternity mattered. All of that went out with the invasion. I'm kind of embarrassed to admit it now."

"Doesn't everyone want to be in fraternities? Or sororities?" I asked innocently.

"Do you?"

He had a point. To conform to somebody else's ideal of how girls were supposed to look and act was not high on my priority list. "You got me there," I said.

"It was already pretty silly before all this other stuff started. It's completely ridiculous now."

"Hey," I said. "Maybe you'll need your frat brothers one of these days, when the time comes to take this planet back. You never know."

"Whoa! That's the spirit," he said. "Now I know we need you here."

"Oh?"

"If there's any chance for us to throw off the yoke of oppression and take the planet back from the bluecoats, it'll start here, in underground bunkers like this, with little radio stations like ours."

I looked up at the pipes that snaked along the ceiling. "Well," I said. "It's definitely underground."

"It may not look like much," Mr. Unkempt said. "But the fact is, people are looking to us to provide them with information they can't get anywhere else these days. We've got more and more listeners tuning in every day. You heard us and found your way here, didn't you?"

I couldn't argue. I'd been drawn to the station like a magnet to metal. It was difficult to overstate the allure that hearing the truth over the airwaves had after so long without.

"I'm not sure I could do this," I said.

He waved away my misgivings like gnats in front of his face. "Oh Pshaw," he said, pivoting back to the turntable and queuing up another track. "And now, ladies and gentlemen, I've got a special treat for you," he said. "This is Rattlesnake Junction's very own Roadrunners doing 'Heartbreak Hotel'. You're listening to the only

245

real radio station left on the planet, Radio Rattlesnake." The record started playing. He switched off the mic and turned back to me.

"Hey," I said with a sigh. "That's not playing fair."

He smiled a big smile. "Just give it some thought, OK? I'm serious about getting you on the air. We could arrange a time slot to suit your schedule, and you'd be free to do whatever you want during your on-air time, play your songs, play somebody else's songs, talk, interview relatives, your pet, whatever. There are many ways to serve the cause of liberty," he said stentoriously. "And if it turns out you can't join us here in the short term for whatever reason, just keep doing what you're doing. Nothing says freedom like loud, take no prisoners rock 'n' roll."

"Thank you," I said. "I think."

I couldn't help but notice this was the second time I'd been advised to continue playing rock 'n' roll in the last hour.

73

Parade

I was in the driveway washing my car when the first of the planes flew over. I use the word "plane" loosely. It looked like a flat silver wedge as it knifed through the air, making zero noise.

"It seems they've finally taken an interest in Rattlesnake Junction," Grandpa Kurt observed, scratching his jaw, a frown on his face as he stood in the driveway.

"You think they're here because of the radio station?" I said. They'd been broadcasting a lot of resistance-related stories lately, I knew. Everything from small-time vandalism in the big city to nighttime raids featuring homemade explosives.

"Anything's possible," said Grandpa with a shrug.

"I honestly can't think of any other reason why they'd be here all of a sudden."

I knew the station's programming pretty well by now. Since classes at the JC were now few and far between, I was spending more time in the basement at the American Legion. I'd let myself be talked into doing a music show, spinning discs for a couple of hours twice a week. News briefs about attacks against the bluecoats had been on the increase. The propaganda push, it seemed, was having the opposite effect from what was intended. It was just pissing people off.

"But we're not doing anything at the station we haven't been doing for months," I said.

"You might want to stay away from the Legion Hall for a while.

At least until we know more," Grandpa Kurt said. "I don't necessarily see them coming out here to the house to pay us a visit. But you never know."

"I need to check if everyone's alright," I said, coiling up the hose and turning off the faucet.

"I'll go with you, if you don't mind," Grandpa said. "I'm as curious to find out what's going on as you are."

I loaded Grandpa into the passenger seat and off we went.

Our first stop was the American Legion Hall. I made a cautious approach and ended up parking on Fourth Street well before the entry to the parking lot to be on the safe side.

I convinced Grandpa to stay put in the car while I ventured out to see what was going on. On the outside, the Legion Hall looked pretty much like before: abandoned. But inside it was a different story. The place was in chaos. The entire staff seemed to be there, hauling papers and equipment to an old van parked outside. I saw the DJ I'd met on my first visit to the station, Ace was his name. I took him aside to ask what was going on.

"The bluecoats are headed this way," he said.

"We saw a couple of aircraft fly over earlier," I told him. "It didn't look like much of an invasion."

"Well, the other shoe's about to drop," Ace said. "We've gotten word from Tucson that a convoy is on the way here. We plan on not being here when it arrives."

"A convoy? Coming to Rattlesnake Junction?"

"Looks like," said Ace. "It's not a massive mobilization. 10 or 12 vehicles at most. But they're coming fast. They could be here any minute."

I gulped and nodded. "Do you need help? What can I do?"

"You can take the transmitter with you," he said. "You live further away than any of us."

I didn't need to think about it. "Sure," I said. "I'm in."

"Just make sure you hide it really well. Just in case."

I had one of the guys bring the transmitter, the box that looked like a ham radio, to my car. We stowed it in the back.

"Remember," Ace said. "Keep this stuff under wraps. I wouldn't want you getting into trouble because of it."

"How am I going to get in touch with you?" I asked.

"We'll be posting cryptic messages on the bulletin board at the college. You'll know which ones are from us. Check there every couple of days. We'll try to regroup when we can. We'll tell you where to bring the gear."

I walked back to where I'd parked, and Grandpa and I headed back to the house.

When we got there, Aunt Trish was in the driveway waiting for us.

"You guys alright?" she asked before I'd come to a full stop.

"Yes. What's happening?"

"I got a call from the office. They're saying a squad of bluecoats showed up in town," said Trish. "I was worried they were there to raid the radio station."

"We just came from there," I told her. "No sign of them yet. But the staff was clearing everything out just in case. Have you heard anything else?"

"Nothing about the station," Trish said. "According to the grapevine, they seem to be in town as a show of force. They just had a little parade down Main Street, displaying their fancy artillery, or whatever it is. If they were trying to impress, it didn't work. Nobody could make heads or tails of what they were seeing. They might have as well have been parading Westinghouse appliances down the street."

"We're lucky they didn't give us a demonstration of how those things actually work," I pointed out."

"There's that," Trish agreed.

"I guess they still need us to like them," Grandpa said. "They're still hoping the propaganda approach will work, despite all indications to the contrary."

"What's with today's display then?" I asked.

Grandpa rubbed his jaw. "Might be their patience is starting to wear thin. They've tried the carrot approach. Today they wanted to show us what the alternative would look like."

"Just so long as they weren't heading over to the American Legion building," I said.

"Not as far as anyone could tell," Trish said.

"Are they still around?"

"Come inside," Grandpa Kurt said. "Let's find out. I'll make a couple of calls."

74

The Xenecorp Agenda

"It sounds like they've left town," Grandpa Kurt said, hanging up the phone. "They're on the road back to Tucson."

"So that was it?" I said incredulously, but also relieved. "They just did a drive through?"

"Looks like. For now."

We were sitting in the kitchen, eating cookies, Trish, Grandpa, and I. I took the phone and dialed Maggie Gonzales's number. She was as close to a general manager as the station had. She picked up on the second ring.

"What's happening with the station?" I asked. "We heard Xenecorp's left town."

"That's what we're hearing too," Maggie said. "They didn't bother to come by the hall. I don't know whether to be relieved or offended."

I laughed. "So everybody's fine?" I said.

"It was just a show, it looks like," she said. "A little military parade to cow the peasants into submission."

"Works for the Soviets."

"For being as advanced as they are, it all seems a little quaint," Maggie said. "They want us to know who's boss, but don't really want to ruffle any feathers."

"If the soft touch doesn't work, the jackboot might be next."

251

"What do you suppose is in it for them? It's obvious they're trying to win us over. But why?"

"They need a workforce," I said. "Voluntary, if possible. But if that doesn't work, I don't think they'll hesitate to use a more hands-on approach."

"But why? What do they need us for? Look at all the crazy gear they've got."

"They're going to need us to mine the ore they're going to need to get their idea of a perfect society off the ground. Eventually, they'll have their machinery do the job."

"You sound pretty sure," Maggie said. "And how did you say you know all this?"

"I didn't," I said. I told her what Big Al had told me at the wrecking yard without mentioning Big Al or his connection to the Fortune's Fool.

"You want to protect your sources," Maggie said neutrally. "I can appreciate that."

"The information's good," I told her. "Let's just say it's from a person of authority who has a personal stake in defeating Xenecorp."

I could see Maggie was bursting with questions. "OK," she said finally. "We just won't be able to name names. I can handle that. Our mystery person will be an official source who chooses to remain anonymous."

"He wants to help the Federation to take back control of the Fortune's Fool."

"Don't we all," Maggie said. I could almost hear her looking skyward over the phone. "What do you think the chances of that happening are?"

"He seemed optimistic," I said, sounding none too optimistic myself. "But then he strikes me as a glass-half-full kind of guy."

"So Xenecorp wants us to slave in the mines while they get their own gear in place. All this stuff about us achieving a better life, a higher standard of living, and so on, is bunk? A smokescreen?"

"Not necessarily, but it's definitely not the whole story," I said.

"Their utopia is going to need customers to function. And support staff."

"Great. We'll be servants."

"And consumers."

"So what's their endgame?"

"If I had to guess, I'd say they want to replicate the life they were used to on the ship right here on the surface. Up there they were given free rein to live what they considered to be a comfortable life, but it was all very contained because space was limited and because the Federation was there to keep them in check. Down here, they have the potential to expand outward in all directions. The raw materials that exist on this planet will enable them to do just that."

"In other words, they want to re-create the kind of conditions they enjoyed back on Planet Earth. But isn't that exactly what did Planet Earth in? Their idea of living the good life was all hunky-dory until their expansionist philosophy hit the proverbial brick wall. Resources ran out. Space ran out. But the momentum continued until it all came crashing down."

"In a nutshell."

"So the plan was that Xenecorp was supposed to stay on the ship once we got here?"

"I don't know. Maybe they were supposed to be assimilated gradually over time under the watchful eye of the Federation. Of course, now any grand plan the Federation may have had is clearly in jeopardy."

"Well," Maggie said. "This news will certainly give our listeners something to think about. People won't be happy. But at least they'll be forewarned."

She was quiet on the other end of the line. Finally, she said, "It sure would be helpful to get an interview with whomever you're in contact with. This information needs to get out."

"I don't think that'll be possible," I told her. "It's just too risky for my source. Exposure could be disastrous for him. And it might compromise what's being done to take back the ship. I will ask, though. I promise."

253

"I don't want you to get yourself or anyone else in trouble over this," Maggie said. "You don't want to betray any confidences."

I was relieved to know Maggie got it. Big Al's well-being was a priority for me. The final decision whether to come forward would remain up to him. Always.

75

Mobility

The bluecoat's military parade had made everyone jittery. Which was probably the idea. Anyone who had been lulled into a false sense of security by the lack of direct action on the part of Xenecorp was effectively reminded of the precariousness of our position. Xenecorp could do whatever it wanted, when it wanted to, and there wasn't much we'd be able to do about it.

Since Radio Rattlesnake had vacated the Legion Hall, it was time to reassess. We met at the Circle B Restaurant in the middle of a weekday afternoon. Besides a few bar patrons, there was no one besides us in the place.

Most of the radio station's staff members were assembled at a long table in the darkened recesses of a banquet room in the back. Here we could talk freely amongst ourselves. It helped that the waitress on duty was a fan of the radio station and someone we knew from school. She brought us sodas and fries, but otherwise left us to our business.

The topic that was foremost in everyone's mind was what to do about the station. Should we simply move back to the American Legion or find some other alternative?

"There's no proof Xenecorp even knows we were at the Legion Hall," someone said. "We could go back there and start broadcasting all over again, like before."

Maggie frowned. "Do you doubt they could've found us in

a heartbeat with their technology if they wanted to?" she said. "And doesn't it make you just a little nervous that they singled out Rattlesnake Junction for their little parade? How many other towns around here had that privilege?"

This gave everyone pause.

"On the other hand, if we assume they can find us wherever we are," someone else said, "then we might as well just go back to the Legion Hall. It's a good a place as any to broadcast from."

I decided it was time to wade into the conversation with my two cents worth. I put my hand in the air as if I were still in elementary school. "Why don't we go mobile?" I said. Grandpa Kurt and I had been discussing the idea just that morning at breakfast. "If we could pull out at a moment's notice, it could give us an edge if Xenecorp ever did decide to come after us. At the first sign of trouble, we could weigh anchor and head for the hills."

Most of the staff was nodding in agreement. They seemed to like this idea.

"All we'd need is a truck, a broadcast antenna, and a generator," I continued. "I think I know where to find the truck. Or at least everything we'd need to put one together on the cheap."

I'd almost stopped at the wrecking yard on the way over on the chance that Big Al was around, but felt that might be jumping the gun. I decided to wait to find out where everyone stood first.

It was quickly agreed that I check around for a suitable truck for a pirate station. I didn't mention Big Al, but I knew he'd give us a good deal if he happened to have what we needed. He might even know where to find a generator.

We agreed to assemble at my house in a couple of days to see how the plan was proceeding. I think after witnessing Xenecorp's show of force, everyone was relieved just to cool their heels with their loved ones. It was starting to sink in that we might have dodged a bullet this time. The station could well be in the line of fire if and when the shooting started. Even so, judging from the looks on the faces at the Circle B that afternoon, we were resolved, one and all. We were committed to having Rattlesnake Radio continue to broadcast in whatever form it took. It was understood that what we were doing was important and that the truth needed to be heard. I felt proud to be a member of this group of people who were ready to stand up to Xenecorp and the tyranny it represented, regardless of the odds.

76

The Ambulance

I stopped at the wrecking yard on the way home. The place was locked up tight and looked deserted, like last time. But I knew better than to let that deter me. I stopped the Rex, walked up to the chain-link fence, and waited. It wasn't long before Big Al strode out from among the stacks. It was always a relief to see him. And his appearance never failed to bring a smile to my face. All was not lost, his presence told me. There was still hope.

He didn't act like a fugitive. He seemed as confident as ever, and the shirts he was wearing were, if anything, gaudier and more likely to attract attention than anything that had come before.

"You heard about the convoy in town," I said.

He nodded. "Come on in," he said.

He unlocked the gate and let me through, taking care to lock it behind me again. He motioned me toward the office.

"I think it's smart that the radio station is going mobile," he remarked after I told him why I was there. "It might not stop them from finding you, if that's what they want to do. But it would slow them down."

"Do you think you might have a truck for us?"

He considered for a moment. I could see him going through the inventory list of broken-down dump trucks, wrecked semis, and rust bucket panel trucks he carried in his head. "I've got an ambulance in back that might serve," he said finally. "It'll take some work to get it running, I expect. But I could give you a deal on it."

"How much?"

"How does free sound?"

"Free? You sure?"

"I'm not here to make money, kid, in case you hadn't noticed. This is fun for me. This is the way I unwind."

"Even now, with the ship overrun and the wolf at the door?"

"Especially now," said Big Al, with a grin that suggested he might know something I didn't. Everything about his demeanor seemed to indicate someone who had not a care in the world—this one or any other.

"What else do you need?" he asked.

"A generator."

"Juice. Of course," he said. "I've got a power supply that's newer tech. It's a battery pack that charges off solar. You'll never need to plug it in. That goes doubly with two suns in the sky. I've also got a gizmo that'll scramble your location. It'll buy you time if they decide to come looking for you. They won't know where you are, unless they happen to catch physical sight of you. I trust you've got a hiding place in mind? A garage would do for the short term. But you might need a place away from town, if you can wangle it. The local garages and warehouses are the first places they'd look."

"We've got a spot for the family staked out in the lava caves above town," I said. "We'd just need to find one big enough to drive the truck into."

"If you're going to be in the tubes, you might need a broadcast antenna that'll work underground, or at least near the entrance to those caves. Come back tomorrow, and I should have what you need. How's that for service?"

"A-1," I said, and he laughed.

When I came back the next day, Al had the ambulance loaded onto the back of his flatbed truck. There were tarps next to it that I guessed were covering the other gear he had mentioned.

We caravaned back to my house. Grandpa Kurt was waiting for us as we pulled in. The two men greeted each other like the long time friends they were.

After the joyful reunion, Big Al lowered a ramp at the rear of the truck and offloaded the old ambulance, which looked like it hadn't seen action since the last war. There were burn marks on the body and there was some rust. The tires were old, but looked serviceable, and the lights on the roof were still intact.

"Does the siren work?" I asked.

"I haven't checked," said Big Al. "Put a charged battery in 'er, and we'll find out."

While Big Al and Kurt got ready to unload the rest of the equipment, I retrieved a battery from the garage. When I came back out I got my first look at what had been under the tarps. There was a metallic gizmo about the size of a Radio Flyer wagon and a couple of square wafer-thin panels, about 12 inches on a side. They looked like small window panes made of some kind of glass or plastic, transected by wire.

Big Al saw the question in my eyes.

"That's the power pack," he said, indicating the Radio Flyer-sized package I'd been looking at. These panels over here charge it." Seeing the confusion on my face, he added, "They collect sunlight, which is then converted to electrical energy, which is then stored in the power pack until you need it to run your gear. It's already dialed in to deliver your standard 110 volts so everything you plug into it should work fine." He must have thought our set-up was incredibly quaint, but he expressed nothing but enthusiasm about our endeavor.

I admit I was pretty excited by what I was seeing.

"I don't see any cables," I said.

"It's wireless," Big Al said.

I nodded like I understood, which was a stretch.

"This here is an antenna," Big Al continued. It was a thin gray panel that looked like a rubber placemat, about two by two feet. "It also connects to everything wirelessly."

"Of course it does," I said. I was starting to get just a little skeptical that I'd be able to figure out the set up enough to make it work.

"Don't worry," said Big Al, reading my misgivings. "It's basically plug-and-play. All you do is turn the power on here, and it sets itself up. It monitors and maintains itself. No special training necessary." He laughed. "It's a great little system if I do say so myself. It's portable, self-contained, and powerful. It has at least a hundred times more range than what you had before. But I'd start it on a lower power setting, so you don't attract too much attention right off."

I looked at the stuff on the ground, amazed. The whole set up could easily have fit in the back of the Rex.

I realized I was still cradling the replacement car battery, and my arm had fallen asleep. I opened up the ambulance's engine compartment, took out the old corroded battery, and installed the new one.

"Are you sure it doesn't run?" I asked Al. "It looks like everything's here."

"To be honest, I never got around to checking."

I nodded, got in the driver's seat, and turned on the ignition. The engine turned over continuously for half a minute or so. To everyone's surprise, it finally caught and kept running as I pumped the gas pedal. The exhaust belched smoke like the Queen Mary. But the longer it ran, the more the engine smoothed out and the less exhaust was produced. A tune-up was in order and a new muffler. But it seemed to run just fine.

I put the van into reverse with a clank and lurched backward down the driveway until I was out in the street. I had to double-clutch it to get into first. But after that, I was off down the road at a fair clip. I drove for half a mile before I turned around, the engine still chugging away like a champ. It sounded like a couple of the valves were tight, but that was easily remedied.

I tried the siren switch and surprise! It wailed away like a banshee. Not only that, but the two lights up top were flashing red right on cue. We had a full-on working ambulance. It was almost a shame to be using it as a mobile radio station. On the other hand, it would be a great cover for what we were actually up to.

It was a fair-sized truck. It had plenty of space in the back for a half dozen of us (or more in a pinch) even with the new transmitting gear loaded in.

I rolled triumphantly back up the driveway and pulled to a stop. Big Al was beaming proudly.

"Works like a charm," I told him through the open window. "It'll be perfect once Grandpa and I go over it."

77

A Brief History Lesson

Trish invited everyone into the dining room for sandwiches and ice tea. I took the time to contact Maggie from the station to tell her about our new mobile radio station set up. She couldn't wait to see it.

I had told Al about Maggie wanting to interview him personally, not expecting much. But Al took the time to consider the request. "I will talk to her," he said finally. "If she can guarantee my anonymity."

"You don't have to do this," I told him, concerned about the risk.

"It's worth it because of what's at stake," he said. "It's important that the facts are known, so everyone can make informed decisions. Radio Rattlesnake may not seem like a big deal in the broader scheme of things, but it actually is. It's the only station of its kind operating anywhere on the planet. And the news you put out has a way of getting around. You might be amazed at how many people are tuning in to what you are doing."

"OK," I said slowly. "I'll call Maggie. If she agrees to your terms, I'll arrange for a meeting at your convenience. Up here at the house would probably be best. That way we could make sure nobody else knows you're involved. How does that sound?"

"All she has to do is say when," Big Al said.

As it turned out Maggie said she'd be at the house as soon as she could get there. I could tell she was excited to meet our mysterious high-level news source. But she also appeared adamant about protecting his identity. I didn't really know Maggie that well, but if Big Al was willing to trust her, I would too.

When I hung up, I called Tina and Melissa and told them we were going to have a summit conference at the house. They had managed to keep Big Al's true identity a secret as promised, and I didn't think he'd mind if they participated in the conversation. They arrived a half-hour later, just ahead of Maggie.

We were all assembled in the living room when Maggie came through the front door. Big Al stood up from the sofa as she was led in by Aunt Trish. Maggie seemed confused when she saw Al. She apparently knew of him and the wrecking yard. But she didn't yet understand what he was doing there.

"Maggie," I said, standing between them. "This is Alfred Wertheimer, the captain of the Fortune's Fool."

She blinked while this sank in. Then her eyes grew wide, and she took a step back. I rushed over to catch her in case she fainted. "My god," she said, with a hand on her collar bone.

"No ma'am," Big Al said amiably. "Just a humble spaceship captain." The joke seemed to help Maggie get some of her composure back.

She smiled, somewhat embarrassed by her reaction, and reached out her hand. "Margaret Gonzales," she said. "Station manager at Radio Rattlesnake."

"I'm very pleased to make your acquaintance," Big Al said, bowing slightly.

It was all pretty exciting. Questions were flying around, fast and furious. They were coming mostly from Maggie, but Melissa and Tina weren't shy about weighing in either. Everyone wanted to know what had led up to the situation that existed now, with the bluecoats in control of the ship and the planet and what came next.

How things had gone on Planet Earth was common knowledge by now. Whether it was hypnosis or osmosis or whatever, everyone had a basic grasp of what had transpired on Planet Earth in the century and a half after the 1950s that led up to the building of the Fortune's Fool. We were all aware of the sad chronology of events that had made it necessary for us to leave our home planet--how extreme temperature fluctuations in the early 21st century led to massive storms and the melting of the polar ice caps which caused extreme coastal flooding and population displacement. We knew about how global conflicts had accelerated and worsened. How wars were eventually fought not just over territory, or political or religious differences, but for the means of basic survival--food, medicine, clean air, and water. And we knew about how global plagues had ravaged the planet, killing more than half the world's population.

We knew the ship had left Earth orbit in March 2204 after a century under construction, the product of a joint effort by the newly reconciled world powers. We knew the ship had survived the 250-year journey from Earth essentially without incident. That is, until the recent Xenecorp rebellion. And now here we were.

After Kurt had poured Big Al and himself some expensive bourbon, Big Al explained the ascendancy of the corporate guilds. The manufacturing sectors, their management hierarchies, and the political leadership of the guild-related precincts on the ship had joined forces and consolidated their power in secrecy in the preceding decades. They had developed their own advanced militias, ostensibly to ensure law and order in their cities and territories. But in actuality, they were building a formidable fighting force to eventually take on the Federation and replace its agenda with their own.

"How could that have happened?" Maggie wanted to know. She had her Big Chief writing tablet out and had her pen poised. Big Al didn't seem to object.

"It happened under our noses," said Big Al with a self-effacing shrug. "It may seem naive now, but the Federation elected to take a hands-off approach to managing the corporate guilds. It was believed people tended to do better, both at their jobs and in general, without constant monitoring and supervision. We accepted at face value their claims that they were now part of the team, that they shared our goals and our vision for starting a new civilization on Epsilon 4 that would avoid the pitfalls of the old one. In our defense, we had close to 250 years of experience of peace and harmony behind us relative to the corporations. They'd done what was asked of them and had given us no reason to suspect they were preparing to mutiny this late in the game."

"So the corporations had been broken up when we all left Planet Earth," Maggie said.

"That's right," Big Al said. "There was little doubt that the mega-corporations and the political and economic institutions that supported them had played a significant role in the catastrophes that befell Planet Earth, though there was plenty of blame to go around. A repeat of that on Epsilon 4 was the last thing we wanted. On the other hand, we needed the help of those same corporations and institutions to build and maintain the ship. There was no existing alternative and no time to create a support structure from the ground up that could meet the demands of the Phoenix Project. It was agreed by everyone concerned at the outset that the conditions of corporate involvement required that they defer to the Federation in all matters of policy and leadership. Those were the ground rules. They would perform a supportive function on the ship and nothing more."

"What happened to the people on Planet Earth that didn't make it onto the ship?"

"We don't know for sure," Big Al said with a resigned sadness. It was obviously a subject that pained the captain. "We remained in contact for as long as we could after the ship left. The news was not good.

"You might be surprised to know that given the opportunity to leave on the ship a lot of people elected to stay on Earth. In fact, we had a hard time finding volunteers to join this project at first. Most considered it too risky. Given the choice between staying on good ole terra firma, even as bad as things had gotten, or heading off into the unknown on a two-century plus journey that no one would live to see the end of, the vast majority of likely passengers chose the former. And tell you the truth, we were less than confident we'd ever make it. Nothing on this scale had ever been attempted before.

"It wasn't until these last dozen or so years when we could actually see the planet on our long-range sensors, that there was cause for optimism. We could finally confirm the planet was real, and that it would more or less conform to our expectations. In retrospect, it still seems like a miracle we made it."

"So tell us more about Xenecorp," Maggie asked.

"A measure of autonomy was guaranteed to the contractors from the get-go as an incentive for signing on. They made the most of it. Their cities eventually became more extravagant and luxurious than ours in the Federation.

"So Xenecorp started as a bunch of people hired to work on the construction of the ship, and later, to service and maintain it."

"Essentially, yes. Most were industrial contractors who knew how to build on the kind of scale that was needed. And as things grew more dire on Earth, soldiers from the United Global Armed Forces were assigned to help build the ship and its systems. These were skilled workers, for the most part, trained in the construction and use of military hardware and support technologies that could be repurposed for Project Phoenix. A lot of those same soldiers volunteered to become crew members when the time came for the ship to depart on its mission."

"How many soldiers are we talking about?"

"Well over a million. They were less risk-averse than many of their civilian counterparts. Plus, they'd already been working on the ship, some for years, and so were already invested in the project. They were disciplined workers, accustomed to taking orders."

"What kinds of work did they do?"

"They were charged with overseeing and maintaining the infrastructure aboard the ship for the duration. What they did involved everything from calibrating quantum systems to the repair and maintenance of the mega machinery that's kept us going for the duration, including life support, climate control, food production, waste processing, and recycling. They were integrally involved in the nuts and bolts of keeping us on track. And to their credit, they carried out their duties admirably."

"So the Federation ran the ship?"

"That's right. We were a group of scientists, inventors, researchers, software developers, systems specialists, and social engineers tasked with seeing to it that everything ran smoothly on the ship on the long journey from Planet Earth. The Settlers' welfare was always our first priority. It may be that we were so focused on maintaining the Stacks that we failed to notice little things that could have warned us of what was to come."

78

Not Quite Human

"**C**an you tell us more about what we're dealing with here," Maggie said. "We know next to nothing about who's taken over our planet. From what you've said they have ambitions to recreate the kind of corporate culture that existed back on Earth on Epsilon 4, which valued profit and power above all else. We know they have expensive tastes and a seemingly bottomless supply of gizmos for sale to anyone who can afford them. And from what I've heard, they need us as a labor force to sustain their extravagant lifestyles." She shot me a quick glance. "At least until they get their automation up and running. But who are they? They're obviously in charge here, but aside from the checkpoints early on and the police squads patrolling the big cities, there's been almost no face to face contact. Just a smokescreen of propaganda."

The request seemed straightforward enough, but Big Al grew pensive. He took another sip of his bourbon. He seemed to be considering how to respond. I suspected he was trying to decide how much he wanted to tell us.

"They're. . .enhanced," Big Al said finally.

"You mean they pump iron?"

"Metaphorically speaking, yes," said Big Al. "They're more machine than human."

We took that in, mouths open.

"And that may well be part of the problem," he continued. "Over time the members of the guilds on the ship agreed to being modified, the stated goal being they'd be able to perform their tasks more efficiently over longer periods of time. It happened gradually. Their labs had made amazing strides in bio-engineering. Truly incredible. It started with implants to enhance stamina, physical strength, and dexterity. But eventually, there was the wholesale replacement of physical functions with manufactured components. Entire body systems, including all the organ groups, were swapped out for artificial ones. The benefits were many. Vulnerability to sickness, disease, and injury all but disappeared virtually overnight. Lifespans increased. Drawbacks appeared to be minimal. But there was a price to be paid. We're witnessing the results now. They've forfeited the bulk of what made them human in the process."

Everybody was stunned.

Finally, Maggie spoke. "What do you mean exactly?"

"They became. . . ," Big Al paused to collect his thoughts, ". . .almost entirely mechanical. Think hedonistic robots. They resemble human beings. And they function like human beings. They have the same aspirations as human beings and are prone to the same failings. When they worked, they were focused on work. No argument there. They did their jobs and did them well. When they weren't working, they played. Played hard. They lived what they considered the 'good life.' Acquisition and winning has always been in their DNA and continues to be their primary motivator. Much like it was with the upper echelons of the developed nations on Planet Earth before the big crash. Only now there's even less empathy, if that's possible."

"And they want to what? Turn this planet into their playground?"

Big Al scowled, something I hadn't seen him do before. "All this is virgin territory to them. They can't wait to put their stamp on it. Down here there are unlimited resources, and there's plenty of room to branch out. This is the Promised Land, as far as they're concerned. Ripe for the picking and the plundering. Just before we arrived in orbit, they'd begun claiming Epsilon 4 rightfully belonged to them, not to the Federation or to the Settlers. They asserted they'd put in more time and energy than anyone else in getting us here, so they were entitled. It's not true, of course. Everyone did their fair share to get us here. But it did serve as an effective public relations ploy to rally the troops and to justify their actions. It's also beside the point. The singular goal of this mission was to establish humanity in a new environment and to give it the best chance at survival. Favoring or rewarding one group over another once we got here was never part of the bargain. It's always been about you, the Settlers, first and foremost."

"So they lost touch with the original purpose of the mission."

"Yes. Don't be fooled by their overtures—and I doubt you are. As much as they may pretend to be concerned about your welfare, they're in it for themselves above all. They're fully prepared to use this planet up like they did the last one. It may take them a while. Centuries, a millennium perhaps, but with enough determination, they'll do it, I have no doubt."

"Bastards," Grandpa Kurt interjected, taking a mighty swig of his drink.

"It wasn't always like that," Big Al said. "There was cooperation at first, or so it seemed. We started out with a common goal, at least on the surface of it. Everybody did their part. But somehow that got subverted along the way. I can't tell you for sure when that happened. It's possible the 'enhancements' had something to do with it. And the social and political insularity of Xenecorp aboard the ship. 250 years is a long time. Time enough apparently to forget promises made and agreements signed. And time enough, as we've seen, to create a formidable fighting force to back up their claims and intentions.

"On the bright side, we managed to hold them off until we had you firmly established on the ground."

"How is that a good thing?" Maggie asked. "They followed us down here and took over. There wasn't a thing we could do to stop them."

"That may appear to be true," Big Al said, taking off his cap and scratching his scalp. "But things are a lot different for them down here compared to the ship. They're having to learn how to maneuver in an unfamiliar environment, just as you are. Down here they're separated from all their elaborate support systems and structures. And they're less adaptable than you are. They're accustomed to moving along well-worn paths, doing the same routine tasks, year in and year out. Like I said, they're used to taking orders. It's ingrained. They lack both the flexibility and the imagination you have. Original thinking was never part of their programming. Add to that the fact that right now we have them tied up trying to maintain control of the ship, and you've got what adds up to a fighting chance, regardless of appearances."

79

Humans, More And Less

"Are you in touch with the other Federation members on the ground?" Maggie asked, looking up from her writing pad.

"Constantly," said Big Al. "If I wanted to, I could raise a good-sized fighting force on short order. Also, we still have enough of a presence on the ship to warn us if an attack is imminent down here.'

"Would you have enough manpower to take back the cities?" Grandpa Kurt asked.

"We're pretty evenly matched on the ground right now, but we don't want to begin any kind of major campaign," Big Al said. "Our priority is to keep civilian casualties to a minimum. If that gives the other side a strategic advantage, so be it. They don't have similar scruples. And because they're entrenched in the cities here, they'd be difficult to roust without causing a lot of collateral damage and loss of life. So we've got to find a way of prying them loose without resorting to a direct assault. If you folks get caught in the crossfire and take significant casualties, we might just as well have stayed on Planet Earth. Without you, none of this—the journey, the settlements, all the time and effort invested—is worth a damned thing."

A nagging suspicion was tugging at my mind. I'm not sure why. There was no real evidence to support what I was thinking. But I had to ask.

'You said the Federation forces and the Xenecorp forces were evenly matched," I said carefully. "How could that be? That is, unless you have similar enhancements? *Is* the Federation also enhanced?"

Surprisingly, a smile spread on Big Al's face. It was a look of admiration.

"Smart girl," he said. "You were paying attention. Yes, the Federation forces are enhanced with similar bio-mechanical means as Xenecorp. The augmentation process dates back to a time when Xenecorp and the Federation still seemed to be in sync. Most of those enhancements wouldn't have been possible without the participation of our Federation scientists and medical staff. Until relatively recently, there was a free flow of information among all parties. But even when that was no longer the case, progress continued on both sides of the corporate/command divide. We got better at certain functions. And they got better at others. They focused on military-related upgrades, while we tended to excel at medical research—things like longevity and mental and sensory acuity. Unfortunately, under the current circumstances, that gives them a bit of an advantage."

I was trying to process this superhuman versus superhuman scenario. All I was seeing in my mind were comic strip fights. "Pow!" "Wham!" "Crunch!" "Slam!"

Finally, Maggie spoke up. "So," she said. "Can you give us some idea of the extent to which the Federation and Xenecorp are mechanical as opposed to biological now?"

Big Al paused to scratch his chin. "On average?" he said. "The Federation is at about 96%"

"96% mechanical?" Maggie exclaimed incredulously. "You mean the Federation fighters are all but 4% machines?"

Big Al nodded. "On average. The exact amount varies. The choice to adopt the upgrades was a personal one for us. It was up to the individual. For Xenecorp, the upgrades have always been mandatory across the board. Those folks weren't given a lot of choice."

"What are the proportions for the Xenecorp forces?"

"Closer to 100%," he said.

"Holy shit," said Maggie articulately.

There was more, and I knew it. The silence drew on.

"What about you, Al?" I asked at last. "Are you also upgraded? Are you also 96% mechanically enhanced?"

"You bet," said Big Al with a disarming smile. "Given the option, just about everyone on the ship elected to receive the enhancements. We've been getting implants and upgrades regularly for most of our lives. We're marvels of modern science, we are. All of us."

I'd often wondered how many generations had come and gone outside the Bubble to get us to this point. How many captains had helmed the Fortune's Fool, for instance. "How long has it been since any of you died?" I asked.

"None have died," Big Al said. "Or been born, for that matter. It was important to the mission that we maintain the numbers we had when we started out. We couldn't have the population of the crew start to get out of hand. We are, all of us, original crew members."

"You've been alive for 250 years?"

"Over 250 years if you factor in the years spent growing up on Planet Earth before we left. But you see the attraction. Becoming more or less immortal meant we'd live to see the end of the journey, something that was never even imagined when we started the trip. It was a monumental boost to morale. And there were other benefits as well. There was no need to raise and train succeeding generations of crew and support staff, for example. Everyone just got better and more experienced at what they did as time went on."

"Are you really immortal?" I couldn't help asking.

"Lacking any serious mishap we could, theoretically, go on forever," Big Al said. "There have been a few deaths due to accidents over the years, but not a significant number. At least until the current fighting began."

I turned to look around the room. Everyone--everyone *human,* that is--was as stunned by these revelations as I was, as I could plainly see. "No one outside the Stacks was born on board the ship," I said in a daze.

"Yes," said Big Al without apology or regret. "Only repaired, upgraded, and reassembled."

A jarring thought hit me. "Those of us from the Stacks are human though," I said quickly. "Aren't we?"

"Absolutely," said Big Al. "100%. No one has interfered with your physical development in any way. That would have defeated the whole purpose of the Phoenix Project."

"So we are mortal," I said.

"Yes," said Big Al. "Dozens of generations have come and gone in the Stacks. Birth and death have proceeded without any involvement on our part. It's all been completely natural."

I was probably the only one who noticed the small hesitation as he said this. I don't know how, but I knew he was thinking about our mutual friends who were in a category all their own. Paul, Des, and Cherry.

"I have a related question," Maggie said. "What about the wars? How many people in what you call the Bubble died in the fighting?"

"Very few," Big Al said. "We saw to that. It would have been a terrible waste to recreate the carnage that the wars caused. And it was entirely unnecessary. Thanks to LPRM we could realistically recreate the experience of fighting in great detail. The dedicated gamers among our staff excelled in that area. But those of you in The Bubble who went off to fight, invariably emerged from duty unscathed, to return to their civilian lives as before. They may have known or thought they knew people who had been killed or injured in the war, but those casualties were strictly functions of the program. No lives were sacrificed in the interests of realism. That would have been unconscionable and would have run contrary to our greater purpose here, which was to get as many of you as possible to Epsilon 4. We manipulated the outcome at least to that extent."

80

Alternatives

Time went by as we munched the cookies. A chill had settled over our gathering as we contemplated the fact that Big Al and the rest of the crew of the Fortune's Fool, Federation and Xenecorp members alike, were mostly not human. It made our whole enterprise on Epsilon 4 seem a bit more lonely and that much stranger.

"Not to worry," Big Al said cheerfully. "We may not be completely human anymore, but the Federation in general and I, in particular, are dedicated to one thing above all else. And that is that this mission succeeds as conceived by the Designers. That you, the settlers of this planet, survive and thrive. That goal supersedes all others. And I can promise you we shall do whatever is necessary to achieve that goal."

We all sat there, not looking at one another, grappling with our own thoughts. Trish hopped up from the sofa to retrieve the only antidote to despair we had under the circumstances: more chocolate chip cookies and milk.

"So what happens now?" Maggie asked.

"Now we wait," said Big Al. "There are options available. But they'll require time to put into effect. We won't let them follow through on their grand designs. You have my word on that."

"But in the meantime, our fellow settlers in the cities are going through the ringer," Grandpa said. "They're being brainwashed, bombarded with propaganda."

"Believe it or not, that's a good sign," said Big Al. "It means

Xenecorp hasn't given up on basic persuasion techniques. That's certainly better than the alternative."

"And what would that be?"

"Mandatory administration of drugs to enhance receptivity, for one, followed by progressively stronger forms of coercion. Increased curtailment of freedom of movement would certainly be on the agenda. Curfews, house arrest, and so on. Ultimately, I suspect they'd resort to imprisonment, separation of families, and worse. It's likely they'll make examples of people who are slow to adopt the party line. In other words, they'll introduce methods that have been used by despotic regimes throughout history to get people to do what they want them to. Right now they're still trying to woo you."

"So what is the plan going forward?" I asked. "Didn't you say that a lot of your people are here on the ground now?"

"Many, but not all," said Big Al. "Our strategy is to keep them occupied. That includes looking for openings to return to the ship and keep fighting. We want Xenecorp up there as much as possible and off the surface. We want their attention focused on us and not on you."

Big Al looked around at all of us with kindness. I guess we looked pretty spooked. It was going to take more than chocolate chip cookies to come to grips with the situation.

He looked fondly at his glass of bourbon, studying the golden color. "Old habits die hard," he remarked and, downed the rest of his beverage. Then he pushed himself up into a standing position and smoothed down the front of his Hawaiian shirt.

"I'd best be on my way," he said. "If anything happens that you should know about, I'll be in touch. Oh, and thank you for the cookies. And the spirits."

We rose to follow him to the front door with more unanswered questions. We watched as he got into his truck and drove away.

"If we're fighting evil robots, at least we know that we've got good robots on our side," said Melissa. "I guess there's some reassurance in that."

Nobody said anything. We were all still wrestling with the notion that Big Al was 4% human. I think the news was the biggest shock to Grandpa Kurt, who considered Big Al his best friend. I could tell he was mentally going over their history together, reviewing everything in light of this new information.

It was a lot to take in on top of everything else. We were in a place that looked like home but wasn't. It was a copy of a copy. We'd been on a huge spaceship for centuries, ignorant of the fact that we were living in a simulation, reliving a carefully curated piece of history. We'd been rats in a lab, every detail of our existence monitored and manipulated to preserve the illusion of real life on a real planet. Now we'd discovered we were pawns in the struggle between two groups of superbeings vying for control of our destiny. Which superbeings won would determine our future. Either we would live our lives in relative freedom under the watchful eye of benevolent overseers. Or we would be slaves to a master race of machines.

What we did in the meantime really seemed pretty irrelevant. We could rebel, conduct little raids here and there, blow things up, and otherwise try to provoke the tiger, but the outcome of the war would be decided by forces beyond our control. Or so it seemed.

When I aired my misgivings, Maggie said, "What we decide to do could still make a difference. That's what the radio station's all about. We don't just throw in the towel. Look at it this way. If the Federation and Xenecorp are still close to being evenly matched, it might take us puny humans to tip the scales. So I think it's as important as ever for us to continue to pay attention. And apply pressure wherever we think we can."

"You're right," I said. "I was just sulking. What do you think, Grandpa?"

"I don't think this changes anything," he said. "We're here now. This is our home. So it's here we make our stand. The history books are full of stories about the struggle against tyranny and oppression by regular folks like us. Take the American Revolution, for example. Not to mention the rebellions around the world that ended colonial rule. There's nothing new about having to fight for our freedom."

"So what do we do?"

"We do what we're already doing," said Maggie. "We'll carry on setting up our mobile broadcast station. After that, we'll start broadcasting."

"What about what Al just told us?" I asked her. "Are we going to broadcast that, too? All of it?"

"He didn't expressly tell us not to," she pointed out. "I don't think he would have told us what he did if he didn't expect us to take his story and run with it, do you? He let us interview him on the condition that we protect his identity. We'll keep his name and identity out of it, of course. The information will come from a 'highly placed anonymous source.' And what a story this'll be. It'll be the biggest scoop since the invasion. Bigger even."

I was inclined to agree.

81

The Rotary Gig

The girls helped me haul the nifty new generator, which weighed next to nothing, the solar panels, and the antenna that was the size of a serving tray into the garage, so we could inspect everything and see if we could get it hooked up.

It was exactly as Big Al had said. You literally just needed to hit the "on" button on the generator. Lights flashed, there were a couple of beeps, and that was it. It had set itself up. No additional wiring or electrical outlets needed. We positioned the panels and the antenna on the roof of the ambulance and secured them there. We had a working system right off the bat.

Maggie left, agreeing to check in with us the next day. She wanted to bring the rest of the staff up to date on what we'd learned. Then she intended to work on her report. She had plenty of material to work with for our first mobile broadcast. I could only guess at the kind of impact the news would have. But I had the feeling it was going to be big.

Before they split, Tina and Melissa reminded me about the benefit the Roadrunners had agreed to play for Radio Rattlesnake at the Rotary Club that night. I still had a couple of hours before it was time to pack up my music gear and head over. I planned to make those hours count.

The ambulance needed a decent tune-up to be up to snuff. No

problem for yours truly with an assist from Grandpa Kurt. Grandpa Kurt already had the hood up when I joined him.

"It'll need hoses and belts, too," he said, squinting into the depths. "And it probably won't hurt to replace the distributor cap and the wiring harness along with the plugs. I'm thinking a day to go over everything, depending on whether we've got the parts here or have to order them."

"I'll get on the horn and tell the radio folks."

"I'll do some diagnostics to figure out what else we'll need," Kurt said. "And then I'll call it quits for today. After all that's happened I'm on overload. I think I need a nap." Grandpa was not one to nap. But I knew where he was coming from, so I didn't give him static about it

"Are you sure you don't want to come to our show tonight? You could bring Trish. It's one of our more respectable venues," I said.

"I'll think about it," said Grandpa Kurt. "I'll be sure to let Trish know, in any case."

I was looking forward to the gig to blow off a little steam. I suspected I wasn't the only one.

Judging from the number of cars in the lot, it was going to be a good turnout. More money for the station, I thought as I hauled my amp and guitar out of the back of the Rex.

I couldn't think of the Rotary Hall without thinking about Paul Galahad, Des, and Cherry. I wondered where they were now.

I held my breath a little when I walked into the darkened interior of the venue through the front door, my first encounter with Paul and Des vivid in my mind. No sign of the dynamic trio. The night was still young though.

Tina was already there, setting up her drums on the raised stage.

"Our first gig since the invasion," she reminded me. "What did you think of the bluecoat parade the other day?"

"I heard about it," I said. "Were you there?"

"Nope. I was lying low on the Rez, waiting to see how things would shake out. Everyone there was packed up and ready to leave in a hurry if things got dicey. I was worried they were looking for the radio station."

"Me too," I said. "I went over to the Legion Hall to check up on them and ended up helping clear the place out. Nobody knew what was going to happen."

"All for show, I guess," Tina remarked, thumping the kick drum a couple of times. The sound boomed out into the empty venue like a howitzer.

"Once we get the mobile station together," I told her, "we won't be sitting ducks anymore."

Tina smiled that dazzling smile of hers. "I like the ambulance idea," she said in admiration. "And that snazzy gear. Very cool."

Melissa arrived with her new electric bass and amp. No tuba tonight.

The place was filling up as we dialed in our sound. There was electricity in the air. I knew it was going to be quite a show.

By the end of our first set, I don't think there was one person in the room not dancing. The place had been cleared of tables and chairs all the way to the back wall. The interior of the venue was basically one big dance floor. As we ran down our repertoire, all we saw was a sea of sweaty bodies in front of us moving and grooving. Tina was letting loose like there was no tomorrow, belting out the hits and our originals.

I was still getting used to Melissa's sound without the tuba. But I have to admit the Fender electric bass she had strapped over her shoulder was an attention grabber, especially with the stage lights reflecting off it. Talk about futuristic. You didn't see a lot of electric basses around. I wondered if they'd become as popular as Fender's electric guitars. The amp filled the place up with bottom end like you wouldn't believe. Plus, without having to blow into the tuba all the time, Mel could sing harmonies behind Tina. She had a really sweet voice. It felt like a whole new band.

82

A Familiar Face In The Crowd

At the break, I spied Grandpa and Trish off to the side. I hadn't noticed them from the stage and figured they'd just gotten there. I went over to talk to them.

"Good show," said Gramps. "I could hear you as soon as we got to town. Especially that thumping bass."

"I'll take that as a compliment," I said uncertainly.

"Darned tootin'," Gramps said amiably and sauntered off to find some refreshments.

"I'm glad you came," I told Trish. "I know it's not exactly your scene."

"You gals are amazing," she said. "This is powerful stuff you're doing. Nobody'd mistake it for Perry Como, but that's not necessarily a bad thing. I can't help but be impressed."

I was glad she got it. She'd always been as supportive of my activities as any mother could be, and I was grateful. I kept her company until Gramps got back.

Scanning the crowd, I saw a familiar face. It took me a moment to place it. When I realized it was Gillian, the warrior woman, I did a double-take. She was dressed like a civilian, with a white blouse and a knee-length pleated skirt. She even had on bobby socks and saddle shoes. It was kind of a shock to see her in that get-up. She stood out because of who she was and the fact that she was taller than anyone around her. Otherwise, she fit right in.

I excused myself from Trish and went over.

She had a lopsided grin on her face. "Love the show," she said.

"You like rock 'n' roll?" I said. I couldn't hide my surprise, figuring our music would be ancient to her, as far removed from her as we were from Bach.

"I've always loved rock 'n' roll," she said. "Especially the early stuff. I still listen to it on my time off. It'll never go out of style."

"So rock 'n' roll won't be a flash in the pan like everybody says."

"Not even close."

I couldn't help but reflect on what Big Al had told us that afternoon.

"I talked to Big Al," I said. "I mean, Captain Wertmueller." I waited and let the silence speak for me.

"He told you," she said simply. "About us."

I nodded. "He did," I said.

"And?"

"And I don't know," I said honestly. "I don't know what to think. I'm still digesting it. In a way, it just makes you all that much more incredible. You're human, but mostly not."

"Nicely put," Gillian said with a smile.

"I don't mean to offend you,"

"I'm not offended, believe me. It's validating. In our own minds, we're still 100% human, you see. We don't think of ourselves as machines at all."

I don't know why, but what she said made me a little sad.

"I can't get over that you like our music," I said to change the subject.

"There are quite a few of us that love rock 'n' roll," she said. "Xenecorp? Not so much. They hate anything that isn't computer-generated. It's a good litmus test, if you need to figure out who's who and what's what. Just ask about their music preferences." She laughed. "Probably the reason they haven't shut down your radio station is that you play so much rock music on it. They can't bring themselves to tune in long enough to figure out whether you might pose a threat."

83

The Underground

We did our second set. Off to the side, I could see Grandpa kind of tapping his toe. Trish was more proactive, dancing around this way and that. It felt good to see them there. I could pick out the radio station DJs in the crowd, including Maggie who was flailing around with her partner.

The show was more than just a gig. It was a chance for people to come together and talk to one another about what was happening in the world. With the usual means of communication through the airwaves cut off, gatherings like this offered a unique opportunity to exchange ideas and information face to face. So far these occasions had been few and far between. I resolved to do what I could to change that.

At the end of the second set, I approached Maggie, who introduced me to Lou, her dance partner.

"We've got to do this more often," I said.

"I was thinking the same thing," Maggie said. "Maybe this could be a once a week thing. What do you think?"

"I'd be up for it," I said.

"We could start advertising dance parties when we have the station-on-wheels up and running. It would be a great way to bring people together on a regular basis without raising any red flags to anyone else listening in." She nodded vaguely in the direction of the ceiling.

"Sounds like a plan," I said cheerfully. "I need to ask Melissa and Tina. But I'm pretty sure they'll be on board."

"I haven't seen Big Al here," Maggie said, looking around. "Maybe robots don't like music."

"Just the evil kind," I said. "I have it on good authority that rock 'n' roll has fans in the Federation."

"Do tell," said Maggie.

At the end of our third and last set, I spied Cherry among the crowd. It just seemed to confirm that this really was the way to go for people to reconnect.

"Whatcha been up to?" I asked when I got over to her.

"Settling in," she said. "Like everyone else, I guess."

She looked a lot better than the last time I'd seen her. Her cheeks were rosy, and she looked stronger than the wan, lank-haired young blonde I'd first met. That she'd brought Grandpa Kurt back from the dead proved that she had been much more powerful than she had appeared to be, even then. But I suspect that selfless act had cost her. I didn't know firsthand, but I imagined working miracles could do that to you.

"You look great," I said. In fact, she looked stunning.

"I'm really glad we're off the ship," she said. "I need to be on the ground. Otherwise, I start to fade."

"What do you think of this place?"

"The Rotary? It works."

"I mean this planet."

"I love it," she said gleefully. "It's my kind of place. Everything's new, geologically speaking. There's some serious volcanic activity here. It's everywhere you look."

I wasn't as attuned to volcanoes as she appeared to be, but I suspected she was right.

"How about that invasion?" I said.

"Pathetic," she said. "They want to destroy this planet as fast as they can. Like the last one."

"How are Paul and Des holding up?"

"They're doing fine. They've got a beach shack north of town under the palms away from everyone, just the way they like it."

"I'd sure love to have Paul sit in with us again some time."

"You never know," she said with a fleeting smile. "I never expected him to get up on stage last time. But he did apparently. I heard about it after the fact."

The inevitable question percolated up inside my skull. "Is he? Are they? Are you?"

"Are we what?"

"You know. Like the Federation and Xenecorp folks. Robots. Is that how you all have lived so long?"

She gave me a quizzical look. "Us? Robots?" she said. "Are you serious?"

I could see I was way off the mark. "Sorry," I said. "I didn't mean to offend."

"No offense taken," she said. She went back to chewing her gum and looking around the venue as it emptied out.

"But since we're on the subject." I couldn't help myself. I really wanted to know. "How does it work? This immortality business?"

She gave me a piercing look that rattled me. It was like she was peering into my soul, trying to decide how much to tell me. Then she relaxed. "It's really no big deal," she said. "Paul and Des have their own scene going. You could ask them. But I can't promise they'll tell you. They have quite a history together, those two. I'm not like them. Not a robot. No. Just. . .something else. Maybe someday you'll understand. You're a little different yourself, aren't you?"

She said it like she was talking about something besides the obvious, my physical characteristics and the work I did. It didn't make any sense to me. What did she see that I wasn't able to? Thinking that she might know something about me that I didn't made me uncomfortable. This seemed to amuse her. But she obviously didn't seem inclined to explain what she meant. She just clammed up and grinned that Cheshire Cat grin.

I was used to not understanding things by now. I let it go.

"I've started helping out at the radio station," I told her. "You may have heard of it. Radio Rattlesnake?"

"Sure," she said. "'The last real radio station on the planet.' Isn't that their motto?"

"We're building a mobile unit," I told her. "With Big Al's help. It should be ready in a day or two. Say, you wouldn't have any interest in working in radio, would you? They're looking for DJs."

Cherry looked at me. This time I was the one grinning. The shoe was on the other foot. I didn't let up. I just let the silence drag on.

Seeing that I was serious, she finally said, "I'm not sure what I could do. Maybe a slack key guitar show? I don't know. Let me think about it. I'm working on a little side project of my own right now."

"Really?"

"It's performance art, you might say. My debut on Epsilon 4."

"I can't wait to see it," I said. "When and where's it going to happen?"

"Oh, you won't be able to miss it, believe me," she said as if her thoughts were suddenly far away. "When you hear the bang, you'll know it's begun."

I'd been surveying the crowd while she was talking. But when she made that last cryptic remark, I turned to face her and discovered she was nowhere to be seen. It was as if she'd vanished into thin air.

I saw that Grandpa Kurt and Trish were just about to depart. The last of the attendees were filing past them at the front door. I strode over.

"Great show," Trish said. She looked flushed from all the dancing she'd done, and about ten years younger because of it.

"I'm glad you liked it," I said.

I regarded Melissa and Tina packing up on the stage.

"Listen," I told Trish and Gramps. "I'd better go collect my gear. They'll want to lock up here pretty quick. I'll meet you back at the house. I'm really glad you came."

They gave me a hug and turned to go out the front door.

Meanwhile, I hopped up on the stage and started packing my stuff alongside Melissa and Tina.

"We did good," I told them.

"I heard this might turn into a regular event for us," said Melissa. News traveled fast.

"They want us back again next week," I said. "If we're up for it."

"Sure," said Tina. "Anything for the cause." I couldn't tell if "the cause" was rock 'n' roll or the resistance. Happily, with this gig, we were engaged on behalf of both.

On the way home that night I kept thinking of what Cherry had said and wondering what she might have in mind as a debut performance. If she could sing, she hadn't shown any evidence of it so far. A cotillion, maybe? She didn't strike me as the type.

I liked Cherry, though I was a little awed by her. Knowing she'd be sticking around, at least for a while, gave me something to look forward to.

84

Shell-Shocked

We had a gig scheduled on the Rez on Wednesday the following week. I left the repair shop early that afternoon. Ted had been trying to get me to work full-time now that classes at the JC were officially suspended. But between what classes there still were, the radio station, rehearsals, and our gigging schedule, my time was pretty much taken up.

Invasion or no, we were still writing new songs. And as the radio station went mobile, the band became a regular feature on the station, doing interviews and even playing acoustic sets from time to time with Melissa on tuba again and Tina on the skin drum, just like old times. If you didn't know we had just landed on an alien planet and were occupied by a machine-made invading force, you might think we were having the time of our lives. And the strange thing was, we kind of were. Life definitely wasn't dull.

The mobile station worked like a charm. Not only could we park in a different part of town every day, or every hour if we felt like it, our range had improved tenfold, thanks to Big Al's contributions. The battery pack never needed charging due to the tray-sized panel collecting sunlight on the roof of the truck. We discovered the weird flat broadcast antenna fastened next to it was strong enough to reach Tucson-by-the-Sea, fifty miles to the south. But we weren't ready to go full power with it just yet. We weren't interested in drawing the scrutiny of our robot overlords. Nevertheless, we decided to expand our broadcast reach to a 20-mile radius.

Our play schedule was still heavily weighted to rock 'n' roll, what of it was available. New music coming out had slowed to a trickle since the invasion. Releases by the big names—Jerry Lee, Little Richard, and Johnny Cash—had all but dried up. By now everyone knew that the stars of the day were stand-ins, not the real thing, but that the voices on the recordings and the recordings themselves were genuine.

Before the invasion, it had been agreed that new releases would be apportioned out at the historically appropriate time by broadcast archives located in the major cities. But now that Xenecorp controlled the airwaves, that policy had gone out the window. Xenecorp had no interest in allowing new music to be released from the vaults, let alone new rock 'n' roll. You could say it was not high on their priority list. So at the station, we were stuck playing what we had in stock or what new music we could dredge up through back channels and underground sources.

These being rapidly changing times, adults as well as kids were tuning in to Radio Rattlesnake. It didn't hurt our audience numbers that Xenecorp was polluting the airwaves with their obnoxious blather, driving anyone with a pulse to our corner of the radio dial. We continued to be the only station folks could rely on for news and information about the status of the occupation or local happenings in general. We kept on telling it like it was. It really was no contest.

We were all holding our collective breath and wondering when the other shoe would drop. It was clear to anyone with half a brain who tuned in for more than five minutes that we didn't give a fig about the party line or the "official" version of events. That seemed proof enough that Xenecorp didn't, or couldn't, care enough to bother with us. Maybe it was true that they were so allergic to rock 'n' roll that they refused to tune in long enough to find out if we were subversives or not. Or maybe the Federation actually was keeping them occupied enough so that they didn't have the time or energy to monitor us. Maybe it was some combination of the two.

All we knew was that they had left us alone so far. It continued to feel to most of us at the station that we were leading charmed lives. How long we'd be allowed to go on doing what we were doing was anybody's guess. At least now we were ready and able to move in a hurry if and when things heated up thanks to Florence (for Florence Nightingale), our converted ambulance.

"They could squash us like a bug if they wanted to," remarked Jay, who had the 9 to noon show Monday, Wednesdays, and Fridays.

No one could disagree with him.

"I think the only thing keeping them distracted is their war with the Federation," Maggie said, recalling what Big Al had told us. "They don't have the resources and manpower available to chase down every rebel down here on the surface. We're on the back burner, as long as the Federation can hold out."

Maggie had done her report on what Big Al had told us. It had gone out over the airwaves the previous week. The furor that followed was pretty much what we'd expected. People wandered around, shell-shocked. You could see it in their eyes wherever you went. Everyone had been prepped and primed for the bombshell about the end of Planet Earth and our subsequent trip across the galaxy by whatever psych tech had been employed on the ship. But there was no such buffer in place to mitigate the revelation that we were caught in the middle of a war between two species of robot.

The Wednesday gig at the Rec center on the Rez went off without a hitch. We'd played there at least a dozen times in the past. It was always a festive occasion when the Roadrunners came to town. This time was no different. It was Tina's home turf. Everybody knew who she was and who we were. They always welcomed us with open arms.

But I admit there was another reason I enjoyed playing the Rez. I was looking forward to seeing Danny again. He was such a strange kid. But in a good way. I didn't have a "thing" for him, not like that anyway. He just seemed to me like he was from a whole other planet. And that's saying something because all of us actually were, one and all, on a whole other planet.

293

What was different about him? He just knew things. He knew, for instance, that our band was destined for stardom before any of us had an inkling. And he knew the attack was coming before anybody else did.

85

fireworks

We were sitting on the ridge above the Rec Hall after the show, Danny and I, gazing up at the night sky over Epsilon 4. It was beautiful, despite its strangeness. The sky was much clearer here than it was along the coast because of the decrease in humidity at this elevation. For that reason it was the perfect place to stargaze.

The Fortune's Fool was up there too, as pretty as any moon you could imagine. If you let your eyelids droop, it was easy to think we were still on Planet Earth, in Hawaii or Tahiti, or the ship's version of that, which was all we knew.

The reality of life on Epsilon 4 did feel more real. Maybe it was because of the quality of gravity that existed here. There was a solidity, a weight to the experience of being on the surface of a real planet that the simulation we'd grown up in lacked. But on a night like tonight, bygones could be bygones. We were here, at our destination. Having two suns in the sky during the day remained an awe-inspiring sight, the novelty of which had yet to wear off. But as I could attest, the nights were pretty spectacular too.

We were far enough away from the ocean that the air smelled mostly of volcanic rock. Even so, there was the faint scent of tropical wildflowers on the breeze overlaying the faintly metallic odor of the lava. Silhouetted against the night sky many miles behind us was the peak of the local volcano, white smoke billowing against the velvety deep blue of the starry canopy.

"It's happening," Danny said levelly, out of the blue. There was the force of certainty in his voice as he sat staring straight ahead.

I looked at him. I don't know what I'd been expecting, but it wasn't this.

I gazed in the direction he was looking. There were flashes of light in the sky above us and down Tucson way. There was no sound. It was like a Fourth of July firework display seen from too far away to be heard.

Below us, tribe members emerged from their houses and stood outside gazing at the light show. As near as I could tell, there was a firefight taking place in the sky between us and the ship. If you looked closely, you could just make out the outlines of aircraft firing at one another. It was impossible from this distance to tell the Federation forces from Xenecorp.

Pieces of debris began to shower down around us. At first, it sounded like a hail storm off in the distance. But as it drew nearer to where we were, you could hear the distinctive crunch and whine of metal as it slammed into the lava crust, sending up plumes of rock and dust. Soon we were enveloped in noise, and it was deafening.

Danny was already on his feet. "Come on," he shouted over the din, extending his hand to me. "We gotta find cover." It was only a matter of time before something hit us.

Below us, folks had awoken to what was happening and moved about quickly and purposefully collecting gear. The sound of car engines revving reached us. Everyone was heading for the caves.

I thought about making for the Rex. But it was on the other side of the settlement, too far away. The strikes were getting closer all the time. Something exploded uphill from us, showering us with lava sand and small stones.

"This way," Danny said.

We ducked down into the crevasse below the hill we'd been perched on. We followed a narrow sandy pathway away from the tribal center. The sky was now streaked with falling debris and smudged with smoke. It seemed to be everywhere now, hitting around us like mortar fire. Shrapnel made of metal chunks mixed with pieces of broken lava rock flew in every direction. I could only hope that Grandpa Kurt and Aunt Trish were doing what we were doing—finding shelter. It had been our agreement that we'd meet up at the lava tubes in case of emergency.

A piece of metal the size of a Volkswagen smashed directly in our path, sending a blizzard of stinging sand in our direction. Danny yanked me against the vertical rock wall as the cloud of debris blew past us and down the corridor.

"Holy shit," I said. I didn't often cuss. But our close call seemed to warrant it.

Danny peeked out from behind the rock wall and started forward. "All clear," he told me. "There's a cave I know up this way. It's not far."

We carefully skirted the steaming crater that the space junk had created in the middle of our trail and continued on for another couple of hundred yards. A canyon wall appeared before us. In it was a hollowed out area. We ducked inside, hearing the detonation of pieces of metal above and all around us.

"We'll be safe here," said Danny.

I wasn't completely reassured. "Do you think people will be OK in the tubes?"

"Hard to know," he said. "Some of this stuff raining down is pretty big. Bunker buster big. But you'd have to be pretty unlucky to get caught right underneath something that size."

Seeing the worry on my face, he said. "They'll probably be heading way back in those lava tubes. It's what I'd do. The further back they go and the safer they'll be."

I had to be content with that. It was frustrating not to know how Gramps and Trish were doing. But out here we were totally cut off.

It seemed like hours but was probably no more than thirty minutes before the flashes in the sky tapered off. The smoke of burned electronics and molten metal hung heavy over the landscape like a dense fog. An eerie calm descended.

"Most of the wreckage is out over the ocean now," Danny observed. He was studying the falling debris that was visible from our vantage point. The deluge was slowly moving out over the water away from us. "I think we're safe for now."

"You ready to chance going back?" I asked.

Danny paused like he was assessing something inside himself before nodding consent.

We ventured out into the open again, retracing our steps until we came to the ridge we'd started from overlooking the community center. It was dark and quiet down below, everybody seeming to have taken cover. At least everything seemed to be intact. There were no signs of damage to the structures as far as we could see.

We hiked down the hill and past the community center building. The Rex was waiting in back where I'd left it, my music gear safely tucked inside.

"I need to go check on my family," Danny said. "You going to be alright?"

"I think so," I replied.

"See you in the tubes?"

"OK," I said. I turned the ignition, put the car in gear, and peeled out of there.

86

No Time for Romance

When I arrived at our rendezvous point in the lava flows, I was glad to find that the gang was all there. Grandpa Kurt, Aunt Trish, Tina, Melissa, and even her mom and dad were all huddled in a large cavern off the main drag. There was activity everywhere as the folks from the Rez and elsewhere reunited with family members and settled into their respective digs.

The remnants of dozens of destroyed space fighters were still visible in the upper atmosphere, moving west out over the ocean. The planet's two suns had set long ago, but the debris was high enough to be lit by solar rays, transforming the pieces and particles into sparkling confetti. It was festive, if you didn't know the source.

A haze of acrid fumes from smoldering debris nearby wafted into the lava tubes after us, making life in the tubes less pleasant all around. But storm clouds gathering on the horizon to the east promised some relief.

The first raindrops began to fall as we settled in.

"We were starting to get worried," Aunt Trish said.

"I went for a walk with Danny after the gig," I said. "We were on the ridge when the fighting started, but we managed to get to shelter."

A look passed between Melissa and Tina. But I didn't feel the need to justify myself. Let them think what they would. Danny and I were friends. And as far as I was concerned, it didn't get any better than that. I had no interest in his privates. Or anyone else's for that matter.

I guess it was kind of ironic. Here I was, singing about love and romance every week with the band, and me being probably the least romantic person I knew. I was cool with that. The high drama of relationships had been all around me since junior high. I had decided early on that that particular brand of lunacy wasn't for me. Maybe it would catch up with me later like everybody said it would. But right now I honestly didn't feel like I was missing out on much.

Melissa's dad and Grandpa Kurt were huddled around a battery-operated ham radio inside the entrance to our cave. I moseyed over to where they were sitting.

"We've been listening to the station," Grandpa Kurt informed me. He didn't need to specify which one. There was only one station as far as most people were concerned.

"What are they saying?"

"The action seems to have been confined to the sky," Melissa's dad chimed in. "There's nothing happening on the ground so far. No enemy troop movements reported out of Tucson or anything like that. There were some injuries related to the falling debris. But so far no fatalities reported."

"Does anyone have a clue who won?"

"Nope," said Kurt. "I wish there was someone around who could give us the lowdown. That sure would be handy right now." He stretched and gave me an innocent look.

Kurt wasn't about to give Al's identity away, even though Melissa's parents were the only ones present who didn't know the real scoop. Namely, that the undisclosed high-level source interviewed by Maggie for Radio Rattlesnake was Big Al of Big Al's Wrecking and Salvage and also captain of the Fortune's Fool. Thanks to Maggie's report, however, everyone now knew about the Federation and Xenecorp being "enhanced" life forms, if the term "life" even applied in this case anymore.

I said as nonchalantly as possible, "Since it looks like the fighting's done for now, I think I'll pop back to the house and drop off my gear. Otherwise, it'll get baked when the suns come up tomorrow morning."

Both Grandpa and Trish pretended not to be thrilled with the idea of me heading out again at this hour. But they turned out not to be too difficult to convince. They wanted a status report on the fighting as much as I did.

"I'm going with," Tina said, jumping up from her perch. "I'll help you carry your amp."

"Me, too," said Melissa.

Her dad looked at her skeptically. 'Hold on a minute there, girl," he said. "Exactly how much help do you figure Rose will need with her gear? Far as I can tell there are two pieces of gear and three of you."

Grandpa Kurt caught his eye, and he relaxed a little. "Just come right back, OK? And be extra careful. It could still be dangerous out there."

"We'll be back before you know it," I said.

87

Good Greys

Melissa parked her dad's car at my house. There wasn't enough room in the Rex for all of us with my guitar and amp still in the back, so she had convinced her dad to let her use the Buick. There wasn't much Melissa's dad would deny his daughter. That wasn't hard to understand. She was a great kid who never got into trouble and got straight A's in school. We all knew we were on a mission to see Big Al without anything being said.

We caravaned back to my house. I got my gear out of the Rex and stashed it in my room. Then the three of us piled into the Rex and started toward town, Melissa riding shotgun and Tina tucked in behind the front seats.

"Ever thought about rigging a temporary seat back here?" Tina said. She was curled up on her side behind us looking none too comfortable.

"I'll work on it," I promised her.

The rain was coming down pretty steadily now, and the landscape was pitch black. I had my parking lights on so as not to attract unwanted attention. I had to concentrate on not running off the road, especially on turns. It was a relief when we saw the town's lights ahead of us.

"Do you think they'll start going at it again?" Melissa asked.

"Anybody's guess," I said.

In fact, aside from the odd chunk of mangled metal at the side of the road, there wasn't much evidence that anything had gone down earlier that night. Then again we couldn't see more than 15 feet in any direction.

The lights of the town were muted in the downpour. Otherwise, everything looked the same as before. I decided to risk turning on my headlights once we were in town. It must have been about three in the morning by now, and not surprisingly there was no traffic out. I imagined everyone hunkered down at home either asleep or waiting anxiously to see what would happen next.

We made a beeline for the wrecking yard. The place looked deserted, just as it had on my previous visits. And yet Big Al, as often as not, had turned up. So I pulled in close to the front gate and turned off the engine and headlights. We got out of the car and walked up to the chain-link fence.

To our amazement, a Grey emerged from the office hut. It came straight toward us. We drew back warily as it approached the fence. We moved back even further when it started to futz with the big padlock on the inside of the gate. We were ready to bolt in an instant. Yet something about the calm intensity of its focus kept us from panicking. The chain loosened and the gate swung slowly open. Now there was nothing between us and the Grey.

We stood there, not sure what to do. Instead of coming out after us, the Grey stayed inside the open door. There was something gracious, even noble, in the way it carried itself. It seemed to be waiting for us to enter, like the doorman at a hotel. We were too dumbstruck to respond right away. The Grey seemed to grow impatient and pantomimed walking in through the gate, so we dumb humans would get the idea. It was actually pretty funny.

We weren't quite ready to trust the thing, so we just stood there, gawking at it. We were saved by the office door opening and Big Al walking out. He started to wave us through.

"It's OK," he said. "That's Archie. You don't need to worry about him. He's friendly."

We sidled through the gate, never turning our backs on the Grey, who stood off to the side like any good concierge.

"I'm sorry I couldn't come out sooner," Big Al said. "I had some business to attend to. Come in. Come in."

We entered the shed and were led into the back room. We were stopped dead in our tracks by the sight that greeted us. First there was the intense light emitting from within. When our eyes had had a chance to adjust a little, we saw the place was brimming with shiny metal tables and sophisticated looking electronic equipment lit by high-intensity lights that reflected off the sleek surfaces. The whole enterprise looked immaculate, like the kitchen of a fancy big-city restaurant, or an emergency operating room.

I'd never realized just how big the place was. We'd only ever been in the front section where the reception counter was. At the time, I just assumed the storeroom at the back would be dark and dinghy, filled with grease-stained parts and accessories purloined from old wrecks. But I'd never dreamed it could look like this. There wasn't a speck of rust or old motor oil anywhere to be seen.

Stranger still was that a lot of the machinery was being manned by Greys. There were probably a dozen humans there as well.

We stuck to chairs near the entry.

"Welcome to our temporary command center," Big Al said expansively. "Let me guess, you've got questions for me."

88

Field Command

"What are the Greys doing here?" was the first thing I could think to ask.

"They're helping out," said Big Al. "They're an advanced species, as you know. They piloted a spaceship to Earth well before manned space flight was remotely possible for us. At the time, it was the stuff of science fiction. They've got an aptitude for numbers. Hardly ever need a computer."

"But I thought. . . ."

"I believe I mentioned there are good Greys and less good Greys," said Big Al mildly. "Once upon a time they'd been ready to give us humans the benefit of the doubt. But that was before they were used and abused by the military. They were almost universally treated with hostility back in the days of first contact. Many of them weren't willing to forgive and forget. The ones that like to aim their guns at us fall into that category."

"Wait," I said. "Are they artificially enhanced, too?"

"They are," said Big Al. "Archie and his team agreed to work for us not long after they were discovered stowed away on the ship. They could have stayed hidden, but I think they just got bored with how slow we were to catch on to what to them were the most rudimentary principles of long-distance space travel. They were invaluable in getting us as close to the speed of light as we got. The trip would have taken centuries longer without them.

"Working alongside us, they had access to the same technology we were discovering and using to prolong our own longevity. It turned out their biology was enough like ours that they could adapt it to their needs with a few tweaks here and there."

Tina spoke up, "This is very interesting and all," she said. "But what gives with the light show tonight? Who won?"

"The dog fight you witnessed today ended in a virtual draw," said Big Al. "Of course Xenecorp would tell you different. They trounced us, if you pay attention to their broadcasting. I'm sad to say there *were* a lot of casualties. But they were about equally distributed between both sides."

We took this in.

"Are you and your families OK?" Big Al asked. "How's Kurt?"

"We're all in the lava tubes," I told him. "Grandpa and Trish are fine."

"What's happening with Maggie and the station? I liked her report. I think she did a fine job of delivering the essence of what I told you. And she did it without giving me and those of us on the ground away. Admirable."

"We've been able to reach tons more people with your generator and transmitter donations," I said. "They've been a huge help."

"Glad to hear it," he said.

"I'm not sure where the station is right now," I said. "Probably down some dark alley or side street. They're constantly on the move."

"Just as it should be," said Big Al.

He looked where we were looking—at all the gleaming tables and fancy electronic gear everywhere. Big Al smiled. "We had to make room for our electronics," he explained. "Right now the automobile parts are stored out back, behind the shed. Don't worry, I can still fulfill any automotive needs my customers might have. But I'm looking forward to the day when I can devote my full attention to the business again, instead of having to deal with this nagging war. It's no fun for any of us."

"Speaking of which," I said.

"Of course. Let me give you an update, though there's not much new to report," he said. "I'd appreciate it if you continue to keep our location, and my identity, confidential. The wrecking yard has been a good cover for us. We'd prefer it if that didn't change anytime soon. Agreed?"

"Absolutely," I said. Melissa and Tina were nodding in agreement right along with me. "So what exactly is the situation?"

"It's still a stand-off on the ship," he said. "It's been back and forth. Today's battle hasn't changed a lot. What you witnessed today was the fighting on the ship breaking out into the open. But right now the struggle continues out of sight on the Fortune's Fool as before. It's far from over up there, unfortunately. How are things looking in Rattlesnake Junction?

"OK," I said. "There was a serious downpour of space junk. But we didn't see any real damage on our way in."

"That's good," Big Al said. "We're hoping it stays that way. It may be best if you stay up in the hills for the time being. There's a good chance there'll be more incidents like the one you witnessed tonight before this is over."

"What are the prospects, sir?" Melissa asked politely. "What are the chances of you gaining the upper hand?"

"That remains unknown," said Big Al. "But not to fear. Xenecorp will not prevail in this conflict. We are determined to do what is necessary to keep up our end of the bargain. I consider it a sacred trust."

"Are the people in the cities going to be safe?" Melissa asked. "I mean couldn't Xenecorp still turn on them? Hold them hostage?"

"The more time that goes by, the less likely that is to happen. I know it's tough for the people in the cities right now. Very unpleasant indeed. But they need to hang on a little while longer."

"What can we do to help?" I asked.

"Just stay safe," Big Al said. "This is no time for heroics. The important thing is that you stay alive so that you can carry on when all this over.'

He straightened up and the seriousness of his demeanor seemed to fall away. A grin spread across his face. "My advice to you, ladies, is to keep rockin'," he said. "I don't think there's anything you could do that would be more important than that."

The rain had let up as we drove back into the hills. The silence and lack of traffic on the roadway at that hour were kind of spooky. This was what the aftermath of an attack might look and feel like. Nothing but blackness everywhere.

I think all of us sensed that this was the calm before the next storm. And I wasn't just talking about the weather.

89

Rock Revolution

By now the Roadrunners had become a symbol of the resistance. Since the major radio and TV stations were busy transmitting Xenecorp rubbish, a lot of our programming was taken up on the down-low by the major centers on the planet and passed along, first by ham radio and later by smaller local stations like our own. But we were among the first. As such, we became the early standard-bearers of free speech and a free press under an oppressive regime.

And because I was now a staff member at the station in my free time and didn't have a lot of ideas for a show, I ended up interviewing the Roadrunners a lot and playing our music, along with a generous sprinkling of the pop hits of the day. Most of the heavy lifting in the news department was being done by Maggie and other staff members. Unless of course, like tonight, I actually had a pretty solid scoop of my own to present.

The Roadrunners had developed more popularity and notoriety than we had any right to expect. With the cities locked down, the musical giants--Elvis, Jerry Lee, Little Richard, and Chuck Berry-- just weren't getting the kind of rotation they had gotten before. Their music was sealed up in the vaults, inaccessible to anyone who might care about it. Consequently, our music was given equal weight to the big hits of the recent past, both on our own station and on other stations like ours around the world.

This meant that we were now one of the biggest acts going, even though we'd never played or even strayed much beyond Rattlesnake Junction. We had fans among Africans, Asians, and Europeans, as well as in the Americas, north and south, and Indians, both American and Eastern. Someone had once said it was all about being in the right place at the right time. We were living proof of that. To be fair, we were getting pretty good. But we weren't Elvis. Nobody would ever be Elvis, except maybe Paul Galahad.

In my defense, I did my best to play the greats whenever I did a show. And I wasn't the only one. Music was a big part of what the station did. But there wasn't the kind of saturation by the big acts that had gone before.

What happened was our humble records started to sell. They sold like crazy.

If we'd dared (or been allowed by parents and such) to book a tour, we could have taken over. But these were not normal times. When had they ever been? At least before, in our ignorance, in our safe and secure fifties dream, we'd had at least the illusion of normalcy. Now we knew better. And right now, everyone was lying low. There wasn't a lot of touring going on. There wasn't a lot of entertainment of any kind to be found.

Right now, we were it. For better or worse Radio Rattlesnake was the cultural standard-bearer. It just so happened they had a DJ named Rose Thorne on their staff, who also happened to play electric guitar in an all-girl combo called the Roadrunners. It's amazing the sneaky way destiny works sometimes.

Big Al had said that rock 'n' roll annoyed the heck out of Xenecorp. So I figured we were doing our part for the resistance. It was a part we were used to playing. Even in the good old days aboard the Fortune's Fool, I felt like we'd been bucking prevailing trends. It was hard to believe now, but there was a time when rock 'n' roll was a thorn in the side of the establishment. Now some might say I was a Thorne in the side of Xenecorp. It might have been my old combative side coming out, but I kind of liked that notion.

Did the music really distract the powers that be from getting hip to our rebel-rousing and subversive broadcasts, even if the only reason they were subversive was that we were telling the truth? I guess we'll never know for sure. But I like to imagine that the brand of music we played on the station was like a Flying V, a phalanx as the Romans called it, that plowed through everything in the way of the message getting out.

A walkie-talkie connection all the staff members shared told us Radio Rattlesnake was parked off a little-traveled dead-end dirt road north of town. We tracked down the van just before daybreak and told our story to the producer of the early morning show while she took dictation. Naturally, any specifics about Captain Wertmueller's identity or whereabouts were omitted.

The news we had gleaned from Big Al about the Federation and Xenecorp duking it out to a draw over our heads the previous night went out later that morning.

90

Back To School

Rattlesnake Radio kept on broadcasting. So far there had been no indication that Xenecorp knew we existed. But that didn't keep us from discussing the possibility at every opportunity. It was like an itch we couldn't keep from scratching.

"Nothing's changed," Grandpa Kurt insisted. "We aren't a threat. We aren't even on their radar. We're no more dangerous to them than a moth flying around a streetlight.

I wish there was more we could do. Surprise them somehow. Do something they aren't expecting."

'We are doing something," I reminded him. "We've got the radio station. It's a rallying point. If everybody's up to date on what's going on, we all stand a better chance of getting through this. Right? Al told us our main responsibility was to stay alive, so we could take up where we left off when all this is over."

"He's right," Grandpa Kurt conceded. "It's just hard to sit here and do nothing."

"You're not doing nothing," I said. "You're The Mechanic. You're keeping Radio Rattlesnake on the road. That alone should earn you a special place in history."

We ate on in silence.

"Our best hope is that the Federation can turn the tables on these guys," I said quietly. "It's maybe our only hope."

We were still doing band practice on campus. As the days went by without another dramatic celestial firefight, we found ourselves gravitating to campus more often. I never thought of myself as an avid student. But ironically, having the option of attending classes ripped away from us, inspired an interest in learning like never before. Knowledge became a living, breathing thing, something that could potentially help us understand and counteract what was going on.

There were a growing number of classes being offered informally at the school: math, chemistry, biology, history, and political science. The humanities classes met mostly as discussion groups, an opportunity to share information and vent frustrations with the state of things. Even so, reading lists were handed out. Books were critiqued and discussed. We could almost imagine things having returned to normal.

Now that the Roadrunners were relatively famous, we were feeling the pressure to try to live up to our stature as a "global" band. It was kind of hellish once the novelty had worn off. At first, it kept us up at night, trying to imagine how we were supposed to act and even what we were supposed to be doing musically. It almost did us in. We started having disagreements. Every decision was fraught with implications for our future.

It took us a while, but we finally started to see the humor in it all. We were this tiny band in an obscure corner of this new world that had achieved massive popularity, mostly as a fluke. When we realized that what we had could just as easily evaporate overnight, we decided the best course was to just be ourselves, come what may. We were a trio of teenage girls who had become friends and loved to rock. Everything else was just a distraction. We promised each other we wouldn't lose sight of that again.

There were more important things to worry about.

91

Bomb Shelter

now that Rattlesnake Junction was a seaside community, my bandmates and I had gotten into the habit of going to the seashore. It was nice to drive down to the ocean and get our feet wet after rehearsals. I guess you could say we were starting to go native. But we were in the tropics, right? And the ocean was only a twenty-minute drive from campus

It was December according to the new calendar. But December was no different from July weather-wise. Down at the water's edge, it was as warm and as muggy as ever. The days were a couple of hours shorter than they had been on the ship's version of Planet Earth. But that wasn't a major hurdle. Everyone adapted.

We were on the sand after a rehearsal when the next firefight started. This time the action was west of us, out over the ocean. Since it was far away, we watched it from the shore with a certain amount of detachment. Also, it was daytime. Fighters shooting each other out of the sky was not nearly as impressive during daylight as it had been at night. In fact, you had to shield your eyes and look closely to tell something was happening at all. Most of the debris that yielded to the pull of gravity touched down so far offshore that we could neither see nor hear the splashes. The explosions sounded like distant thunder.

We could see silvery, bullet-shaped fighters taking off from Tucson to the south, and I wondered again if there was some way we could sabotage those fighters during the lull between attacks. Wrecking the planes near Tucson would not have much of an impact overall. But if we could coordinate an attack across the board somehow. . . . It was worth thinking about.

"The fighting's getting closer," Melissa said.

She was right. The sound of the explosions was getting louder. And now we could see spouts of seafoam where pieces of metal and machinery hit the water.

"We'd better make tracks," said Tina, already in motion.

We drove back up to campus where the girls had their cars parked and agreed to meet back in the caves.

The fight ran into the night, raining space junk around town and across the countryside. Now we could see streams of fighters going to and from the Fortune's Fool, whereas earlier they had all but been invisible. The Tucson spacecraft had been joined by fighters from other locations on the surface, probably the other major centers. As before, it was impossible to know who was who at that distance.

The fighting went on for three days. We spent the duration in the tubes. I'd been reading up on the history of World War II, and this was an opportunity to experience firsthand what it was like to wait out the blitzkrieg in the bomb shelters of London. It was not a pleasant experience.

The three of us had stuck together during the ordeal. When the fighting finally stopped, and we were pretty sure it wouldn't be starting up again soon, everyone emerged cautiously from underground.

Our first order of business of late, when something major went down, was to try to locate Big Al. While Grandpa and Trish headed back to the house, the girls and I made for town in the Rex.

When we got to the wrecking yard all was quiet, as usual lately. But this time we had no luck raising Big Al or anyone else, alien, human, or machine. The place really was dead this time around, or so it seemed. We stood gazing through the chain-link fence for what must have been half an hour, before pulling back.

It was at that moment that I caught sight of movement among the stacked cars.

It was a Grey. Friend or foe, I couldn't tell.

The thing was waddling toward us. There was no weapon in sight, which we took as a good sign. It just kept coming.

We held our ground, ready to beat a retreat at the first sign of hostility. But the little guy just stopped on the other side of the fence a few feet from us. It looked at us with what looked like exasperation, like it wanted to say something but couldn't find the words.

We waited.

Finally, with a voice that sounded like a creaky door hinge, it started to speak.

"Stand by," it said.

THE POWERS THAT BE

92

Standoff

ehind the Grey, Gillian, Amazonian warrior woman, appeared. She scanned the surrounding area and, deciding there was no immediate threat, came up to the gate and started to work the lock.

In a minute we were back inside the office/shed/warehouse, also known as the Federation command center on Planet Epsilon 4. We were seated in folding chairs in front of the counter in the reception area in a small semi-circle. It was quiet. There was apparently no one else in the facility. And everything behind the service counter was dark.

"It's started," Gillian announced. "Captain Wertmueller thought you'd want to know."

"What has started?" I asked.

"The push to take back the ship. All of us are back on the Fortune's Fool. All of Xenecorp's there too."

"Everybody?"

"I'm the only crew member still on the surface right now."

"Why take the fight to the ship?" I asked.

"A couple of reasons," she said. "First and foremost, we can't risk having you caught in the crossfire. The second is that the ship is essential to all enhanced personnel, Federation and Xenecorp alike. It's where we're strongest. Any needed structural repairs can be done on the fly. And it's where we get our batteries recharged. Literally."

319

We took in this news in silence.

"So how do things stand? What's the status of the fight?" Tina asked.

"Neither side has a clear advantage. Xenecorp took over the ship's command center after we prepped the planet and got you all safely down to the surface. But the Federation still controls its share of the resources on board, including a lot of the military hardware. The corporation, of course, has its own stockpile. We may have a slight advantage in terms of numbers. But Xenecorp has some advanced tech they've been hiding that'll make them tough to beat."

"Why doesn't Xenecorp just take us hostage and get it over with?" Tina asked. "If we're so important in the scheme of things?"

"We'd both know it would be a bluff," Gillian said. "They need you. We know it, and they know it. Without you, it would take them much longer to create the infrastructure they need for their survival here on the surface. With your participation, it might take them a few years to get up and running. But without you, it could take decades. And during that time they'd be vulnerable.

"They're scrambling to make this little revolution of theirs work. And we're scrambling to contain them.

"There must be something we can do," I said.

93

The Counter Offensive Begins

As it turned out, there was quite a bit we could do.

The first thing on the list was to track down Radio Rattlesnake. The ambulance was parked along the waterfront this time, less than ten minutes from the wrecking yard. We told the producer and the DJ on duty that we had an important update on the most recent attack and the war in general.

A call went out to the station manager, Maggie, and we all agreed to meet in town at Henrietta's. Maggie and the three of us settled into our usual booth at the back of the café.

"So you have it on good authority that both sides are off-planet right now?" Maggie asked.

"That's what Gillian told us," I said. "She's a big shot with the Federation fighters. It sounds like the decisive battle is being waged right now over our heads. It's all hands on deck."

"OK. So what now?"

I said, "Gillian didn't come out and say we couldn't or shouldn't help the war effort. She was cagey about it. Our safety was her first concern, she said. But I think what she was implying was that we might have a role to play, if we chose to. That's the way I interpreted it." I looked to Melissa and Tina, and they both nodded in agreement.

"We don't know what kind of toll Xenecorp's tactics has taken on our brethren in the cities or if they'll help us at all. But I figure we have to try."

"What are you thinking?"

"The first thing to do is to get the word out that Xenecorp has evacuated the cities. We have to impress upon everyone everywhere that this our chance to take back control. A chance we may not see again."

"Do you have a suggestion as to how we might do that without alerting Xenecorp to our intentions?" Maggie asked.

We tossed some ideas back and forth. Most of these involved coding our message in such a way that it would appear harmless to anyone listening in. But that seemed woefully inadequate to the urgency of the situation.

"To hell with it," Maggie said finally. "Let's just put out a universal call to arms and be done with it. Let's raise the alarm. We'll keep broadcasting the message until everybody's up to speed. None of this tiptoeing around business. We need to make sure as many people as possible get the message. This is it. The time to act is now."

I couldn't fault her logic. "If we can cripple their facilities on the ground, their fuel depots and landing strips and anything related to maintaining a presence on the ground, that'll buy us time should they decide to return to the surface," I said. "Once that's done, I think the next move would be to take back the TV and radio stations in the big cities."

"Getting the big media outlets back would be a big step forward," Maggie agreed. "Right now there's still a significant lag time between when our broadcasts go out and when they're relayed to the rest of the planet. Things have gotten better recently. But it would be so much better if we could reach everyone at once, especially if we end up going hand to hand with a vastly technologically superior force."

No one knew how Xenecorp would react to our broadcasting initiative. But we were past caring what the response might be. If the Federation was making its move, so would we. The important thing was to strike soon and strike hard.

Another way word was getting out was by good old telephone. Wires had been painstakingly strung from city to city and country to country, thanks to the Federation's resettlement initiative. To them, it was the oldest technology imaginable. But they were into authenticity in replicating the fifties for those of us from the Stacks. An unintended benefit of wires was that they resisted eavesdropping by anyone scanning for radio transmissions.

So as the call to arms went out over Radio Rattlesnake, any specifics regarding strategy could be discussed on the phone and plans made accordingly. It became quickly apparent that the hardware that Xenecorp had stockpiled near the major urban centers was unguarded and vulnerable to attack just as was the case in Tucson and Phoenix. A coordinated assault was decided on, the idea being to hit the storage depots simultaneously in as many locations as possible.

One of our main concerns was that our city brethren had been so demoralized by what Xenecorp had done to them that they would not be in any shape to retaliate. We were wrong about that. Xenecorp's propaganda tactics had only left everyone righteously pissed off.

Even countries where autocrats still ruled expressed a willingness to join the fight. One result of Xenecorp rule was that the corporation had displaced the dictatorial regimes in places like the Soviet Union, Africa, and South America. Now with Xenecorp gone, at least momentarily, there was a power vacuum created which was being filled by popular leaders who had no interest in seeing the old oppressive regimes reinstated. New allegiances and alliances were being forged out of the ashes of old dictatorships worldwide. There was a renewed sense that we were all in this together, human beings fighting on equal footing for the freedom of the species. If we won, maybe things would go right back to the way they had been before. But somehow I couldn't see it. I suspected, if we got out of this alive, things would never be quite the same.

It was generally understood that we might have one shot at this. After that, we could only hope that the Federation prevailed. Everyone was scared, of course. No one wanted to contemplate what might happen if the Federation failed and Xenecorp returned. Would they pulverize us with their ray beams when they saw what we had done?

To their credit, the cities chose to fight as one alongside us. Most everyone had come to the realization by then that to live under Xenecorp would mean dying a slow death anyway. If we were going to die, why not die fighting for freedom?

94

Raiding Party

I drove Melissa and Tina back to my house where they had their cars parked. We agreed to meet again at midnight outside the wrecking yard. We weren't planning on sitting this one out.

I found Grandpa Kurt in the garage as usual. He had the radio on, tuned to Radio Rattlesnake.

"So the revolution starts tonight," said Grandpa, looking up from a wiring harness he was working on.

"Looks like," I said as casually as possible.

"They're calling for a strike at midnight," Grandpa said, repeating what he'd heard on the radio. "I hope you and the girls aren't thinking about joining any kind of raiding party. It could be dangerous."

"Wouldn't dream of it," I said, hoping I was maintaining a straight face as I said it.

I sneaked out of my bedroom that night at 11:30, my getaway planned. I'd go out into the garage through the kitchen. I'd quietly open the garage door. Then I'd put my car in neutral and let it roll down the hill until I was going fast enough to start the engine by cramming it into gear. Though I'd never tried it, I figured it should work despite the automatic transmission. I'd wait until I was far enough away from the house not to be heard when the engine kicked over. Then I'd continue on into town.

What I hadn't figured on was Grandpa Kurt sitting at the kitchen table as I came through.

"I wouldn't miss this one either," he said without any preamble.

I could see I wouldn't be going anywhere without him. Not that I minded, really. Grandpa Kurt had always been a reassuring presence on the adventures of my childhood. But I was as concerned about his safety as he was about mine. His hospital stay and the episode in the garage were still fresh in my memory.

He had on a canvas jacket, old jeans, and heavy-duty work boots. There was a backpack on the table. The stock of a rifle was sticking up out of it. I released a sigh. He was loaded up and ready to go.

"What's in there?" I asked, pointing at the backpack.

"Some things we might need. Wire cutters, an acetylene torch, flashlights, sandwiches, a canteen. Oh--and a couple of handguns, a sawed-off 12 gauge, and a few sticks of dynamite."

"Dynamite?"

"Always good to have a few sticks around just in case."

I didn't bother to ask in case of what.

We were on the road in ten minutes.

"Isn't Trish going to worry when she finds out we've flown the coop?"

"I left her a note," Grandpa said. "Told her we'd be back sometime tomorrow. I told her not to worry about you 'cause I'd be chaperoning." He seemed pretty pleased with himself.

Since Grandpa was going to be included in our activities, we took the Studebaker. The girls were out in front of the wrecking yard as planned. With them were a dozen or so guys from the Rez. I recognized her brothers and Danny among them. The rest I'd seen at our gigs and later when everyone took cover in the lava flows.

As my headlights raked over them, everybody swung into action, moving toward their trucks and pickups. We just fell in line at the back of the caravan without coming to a complete stop.

The Big Boom came as we were driving toward Tucson. It shook the ground and continued to shake the ground until the trucks in front of us were jumping around like water droplets on a hot griddle. The night lit up like daylight.

At first, we thought Xenecorp was back to give us holy hell, maybe drop an A-bomb on us or something. But when our vision cleared, we saw that it wasn't a bomb that had gone off. It was the volcano that had exploded. It was blasting molten lava thousands of feet into the air with a fierce hissing noise, punctuated by dull detonations that continued shaking the earth as far as the eye could see.

Everyone was speechless.

The last thing Cherry had said to me after the Rotary gig floated into my mind. "When you hear the bang, you'll know it's begun." Could this be what she'd meant? It couldn't be. Nobody could predict a volcanic eruption weeks before it happened. At least, nobody human.

What I said was, "We could hardly ask for better cover for what we have planned tonight, wouldn't you say?"

"That's for sure," Grandpa said in amazement. "The timing couldn't be better."

95

Gathering At Ground Zero

When we reached the outskirts of Tucson-by-the-Sea, we saw we weren't the only ones on the road that night. There was a bumper-to-bumper stream of traffic heading toward the Xenecorp depot from all directions. It was further proof that Xenecorp's propaganda strategy had not had as much of an impact in the cities as we'd feared. We fell in with the stream of cars and trucks.

When we got to where the WWII military hardware was stored, we saw that people were busy appropriating the old machinery for the cause, hot wiring jeeps, cargo trucks, and even tanks. Warehouses and storage sheds were being raided for artillery shells, rifle ammo, explosives, and any other ordinance that could be found. Newly armored and armed, they then merged with the greater traffic flow toward the brightly lit area in the center of everything, the spot where Xenecorp stored those of its fighters still on the surface, its fuel, and its stash of specialized gear, the function and purpose of which remained a mystery to us. Not that it mattered much. Anything that belonged to Xenecorp was fair game, ripe for vandalizing if we could just figure out a way to get at it.

The force field that protected the equipment was still in place. Nothing seemed to have changed. Attempts had already been made to try to breach the perimeter to no avail.

During the process of experimentation with the force field someone made the discovery that if you could lob something high

328

enough, you could get it over the invisible barrier. This immediately presented a number of possibilities. The tanks and artillery seemed a good option at first but were quickly dismissed. These all featured excessive range. The trajectory of the shells would carry them over the facility entirely and into the ocean. Mortars fared better. They dropped where they were supposed to but were insufficiently powerful to cause any real damage to the shiny objects inside the protected area. They might have dented or scratched the fighter planes, but not so you'd notice from where we were standing.

Frustration was growing. People were milling around, restless. There was all this pent-up energy to do something, but we were stymied.

It was right about then that we heard the sound of bomber engines starting up behind us. Someone had managed to get one of the old B-29s sitting along the peripheries of the storage area to kick over. Amidst cheers from the crowd, the bomber's engines revved and the beast separated from the sea of aircraft and military transports around it. It taxied toward the main highway, the one we'd come in on, raising a cloud of dust and dirt in its wake. Ahead of the aircraft, the vehicles on the roadway parted like the Red Sea, making way by rolling out onto the hardened lava beyond the shoulder.

As the vintage World War II aircraft gathered momentum, the engine's whine increased to ear-splitting levels. It continued to gather speed as it lumbered down the highway away from us into the night, the light from the erupting volcano playing along its metal shell until it was out of sight. We heard the sound of the engines change, and we knew more than saw that the four-propeller Boeing was in the air.

"We'd better get out of here," Grandpa Kurt said, "if they're thinking what I'm thinking."

To confirm Grandpa's suspicions, the blaring of a bullhorn split the night advising everyone to get as far away from the depot as possible.

"This facility is about to be bombed," came the announcement. "I repeat, this facility is about to be bombed. Vacate the area immediately for your own safety."

There was a mad scramble as people ran for their cars and trucks. The area near the fenced-off perimeter cleared faster than I would have thought possible considering the turnout. We were lagging behind because Grandpa Kurt just wasn't as fleet as he used to be, especially since the surgery. We did manage to get to our cars by the time we heard the World War II bomber coming back our way, growing louder and louder on the final approach.

Piling into the Studebaker we hauled bananas, chasing the line of tail lights shrinking on the highway ahead of us. The bomber loomed out of the darkness above us like a phantom bird of prey and roared over the car with a couple of hundred feet to spare, its bay doors wide open. In the rearview mirror, I could see massive bombs tumbling toward the ground.

96

Divine Intervention

saw the conflagration in the mirror as the bombs exploded. It seemed like the whole horizon was in flames. The shock wave slammed into the Studebaker from behind, propelling us forward as if Godzilla was using us for field goal practice. I fought the wheel to keep us on the road. It was touch and go for a few seconds.

Though the blast was impressive, it was anybody's guess whether our archaic firepower had succeeded in causing any significant damage to the depot. But something else was happening that had nothing to do with exploding bombs. Fissures had begun to appear along the roadway. Bright seams of molten lava became visible in the cracks. Looking into those seams was like looking into another world.

I glanced in the rearview mirror in time to see a huge section of the landscape simply disappear from view behind us. A massive hole opened up where the Xenecorp equipment depot had once been. The hole was filled with spewing and spitting lava. Everything in the facility sank beneath the rising tide of glowing liquified rock. The circumference of the hole advanced outward rapidly as the surrounding ground crumbled and was consumed by the newly formed lava lake. The Xenecorp fighter planes and gear were no match for the superheated molten rock. I caught glimpses in the rearview mirror of shiny aircraft going nose up and then dissolving as they sank slowly backward into the fiery quagmire.

I mashed the accelerator on the old Studie, trying to outpace the collapsing ground. It was going to be close. But I wasn't worried. Something told me we'd be alright. The only way I can describe it was that I sensed an intelligence at work here. As impossible as it might seem, I was convinced that Cherry was behind what was happening, and I doubted she'd want to hurt us. Cherry, the volcano goddess.

All around us the hills were alive with lava streams. But the highway we were on remained untouched.

Grandpa, who had not gotten to know Cherry the way I had, said, "I hope to hell Trish is OK, and that the house is still there."

"I have a feeling they will be," I told him as reassuringly as I could. "Everything's going to be OK."

I must have sounded pretty certain because he gave me a funny look. But he didn't try to argue. He just turned in his seat next to me and gazed at the surreal landscape we were passing through, his expression unreadable.

Meanwhile behind us, Mel and Tina were gazing in wonder at the scene unfolding all around us. The molten rock cast the night in an eerie red-yellow glow. Surprisingly, or maybe not so surprisingly, the lava flow had entirely missed the town of Rattlesnake Junction.

And sure enough, our house, when we got there, was untouched. The lava activity had slowed to a trickle by now. The eruption was ending as quickly as it had begun. I mentally sent a salute Cherry's way. You did it, girl, I thought. You did it.

The lights were on inside the house. We found Trish sitting at the kitchen table in her robe, nursing a cup of coffee when we came in. We were like bedraggled soldiers returning from the war. She got up to grab us sodas, anxious to hear how the night had gone.

"Did you see the volcano?" she asked. "I was so worried about you."

Grandpa was shaking his head. "It took out the whole facility like it was made to order," he said. "Never seen anything like it in my life."

"There was an explosion that shook everything," Trish said. "I thought at first Xenecorp was back. But then I saw the eruption up on the mountain."

"It's funny," I said. "But I don't think we were ever in any real danger out there. The volcano was on our side."

Everybody looked at me like I'd gone daft.

"I mean, the only thing destroyed was the Xenecorp storage site, right?" I said. "It was very. . . ."

"Serendipitous?" Trish supplied helpfully.

"That's the word," I said.

I didn't want to have to go into what I knew and sensed about Cherry. And I especially didn't want to have to explain that she had been responsible for bringing Grandpa Kurt back from the dead. This wasn't the time for any of that.

"Why don't you stay over tonight?" Trish said to Tina and Mel. "The guest room has two twin beds in it."

The girls nodded. I could see they were minutes from falling asleep just standing there, just like I was.

As we all trundled off down the hallway, I could hear Grandpa launching into detail about the evening's escapades for Trish's benefit. Unlike us, he still seemed wide awake.

97

A New Day

The world was still there when I awoke at 10 the following morning. Or as much as I could see of it.

Kurt was in the garage and Trish was tidying up the kitchen.

"Is everything alright?" I asked.

"So far," said Aunt Trish. "Dad's been out in the garage listening to the news all morning. He'd be the one to ask."

Grandpa Kurt was jubilant when he saw me. "Look," he said. "A few of the old radio stations are back."

"That's great," I said, stifling a yawn. Rattlesnake Radio's reign as the go-to station on the planet was bound to come to an end sooner or later.

Grandpa turned down the radio and turned to me. "People everywhere have taken back control of their cities," he said. "It's a little chaotic out there right now, but interim governments are being set up. Elections are pending, even in some places that have never had free elections before. Power struggles are going on, especially in former dictatorships in Africa and Asia. But that's people being people. It's messy. With the power vacuum Xenecorp left behind, it's going to be crazy for a while. But at least this time it's humans versus humans. It's like everybody's coming out of a trance and trying to take up where they left off."

"More like awakening from a nightmare," I said. "And there's been no response from Xenecorp?"

"Nope. Not yet anyway."

"I wonder how things are on the ship," I said, "how Big Al is doing."

Grandpa nodded solemnly. "We can take it as a good sign there's been no retaliation," he said. "It could mean the Federation is keeping the company busy enough so they don't have time for us puny humans."

"I sure hope that's true."

"Anyway, for the moment life goes on."

"That means school could be back in session soon, I guess," I said unenthusiastically. It had been fun learning when it was all kind of underground. Just going to class had seemed like a revolutionary act. Not to mention we could study whatever we pleased.

"Yup," said Grandpa Kurt. "Pretty soon you'll probably be busy working at the garage again, too."

"And playing, don't forget," I added quickly. The prospect of playing again was the only glimmer of light in an otherwise humdrum future right then. Rock 'n' roll had quickly overtaken my other interests and vaulted into first place. Fixing cars at Ted's had become just a job for me in the last year or so.

It's funny how quickly the threat from overhead was placed on the back burner. But it was understandable, I guess. People just wanted to get on with their lives. Even living on an ocean where once there had been only desert sand wasn't nearly as disruptive as you might expect. I'd even started to think about taking up surfing. On this day it felt like we'd won, never mind that the bad guys had left of their own accord.

Still, in the back of everyone's mind was the possibility that Xenecorp could come back at any time. If they rode back into town, guns blazing, we wouldn't stand a chance. We'd be back at square one. The cities would fall, and the rest of us would be living in fear for our lives like before. Not to mention that finding their precious toys destroyed, Xenecorp just might be cranky enough to cause some real damage.

98

Extravaganza

But right now there was cause to celebrate. An impromptu gig was quickly arranged, where else but at the Rotary Hall? It was a place known by young and old and where everyone felt comfortable. It had become the town meeting place. News could be exchanged. Fun could be had. Steam blown off.

The Roadrunners, as a band of global repute thanks to Radio Rattlesnake, were now the default house band of the resistance. Due to our considerable fame, if not fortune, we were prevailed upon to do the show that night.

The evening was noteworthy for a few reasons. First, it seemed like everyone in town was there. The crowd quickly filled the parking lot and spilled outward into the surrounding streets.

Secondly, our show was being broadcast live on Radio Rattlesnake. The now-familiar ambulance was parked close to the back door of the facility, cables snaking from it into the hall. Consequently, anybody who had a radio within our newly increased broadcast range could tune in the show. It solved the problem of how to include as many people as possible in the evening's festivities. With the windows rolled down, Radio Rattlesnake could be heard blaring out of just about every vehicle in a fifty-mile radius of the Rotary Club.

Or so I'm told. All my concentration was taken up with playing my guitar. That's one of the disadvantages of being a performer. You don't get to throw away your cares and let it all hang out like everybody else. For those of us on stage, it was a work night. A fun work night, granted.

Unbeknownst to the band, the program was piggybacking off Radio Rattlesnake and being transmitted to the major urban centers of the world. That meant an audience for our humble live show that numbered in the millions. It's a good thing we weren't clued in. I'm not sure I could have gotten my fingers to move on the fretboard if I'd known.

Grandpa Kurt and Trish were there, which was always reassuring, as were Melissa's parents, along with Tina's family and what looked like half the tribe.

Thirdly, and probably most significant to me personally, was the appearance in the crowd of the dynamic trio—Paul, Des, and Cherry. I couldn't wait to bombard Cherry with questions, but it would have to wait. I was otherwise engaged at the moment.

That didn't mean I could resist the opportunity to invite Paul Galahad, also known in the smallest and most exclusive of circles as Elvis, the original Elvis, up to the stage to do a number. Together we collaborated on a rousing rendition of Jailhouse Rock, if I do say so myself.

Needless to say, the performance brought the house down. Without knowing it, people were being treated to a glimpse of the real deal. And it just tickled the heck out of me to be in on it in any shape or form. I could see confusion in the eyes of some. How could someone of somewhat advanced years be so plugged into this kind of music? But they dug it in spite of themselves. How could it be otherwise? It was that voice. The voice that launched millions of records. You can't fake something like that.

We couldn't leave it at one song. We did Don't Be Cruel as a follow-up and ended with All Shook Up. It's lucky I'd done my homework and knew all the Presley material that had been released so far. Melissa was a huge fan, so no problem there. And Tina, who was kind of a female Elvis herself, knew exactly where all the stops and starts were on her drums.

The show was the stuff of legends. Or would be if we lived long enough to wax nostalgic about it. But I can't tell you what a relief it was to know that Paul, Des, and Cherry were around. If they were here celebrating with us, there had to be hope. I didn't know the secret to their longevity or what other powers they might possess, but it felt to me that as long as they were around we could make it through whatever roadblocks fate or Xenecorp could throw in our way.

At that moment, on this night, all was right with the world, this strange new world we'd been planted on with the hope that we'd find a way to save ourselves and our species.

99

The Volcano Goddess
And Her Friends

When the cheering had died down and the room began to clear, I left the stage to look for Cherry. Paul had ducked out of the hall with Des after his performance. It was clear he was uninterested in attracting more attention than he needed to. But I could tell that he'd enjoyed his time on the stage. He'd departed with a wink in my direction.

I found Cherry outside in the parking lot, staring up at the sky.

"See anything?" I quipped.

"Nothing yet," she replied enigmatically.

"The volcano," I said, as nonchalantly as I could. "Was that you?"

She shrugged modestly.

It was still a shock when she confirmed it. "How?" I managed when I found my voice. "How did you do that?"

"Do what?" she said, turning to look at me.

I suddenly felt like a fool. How could she have had anything to do with the eruption? There was no way. Still, I couldn't let it rest.

"I remember Big Al saying something about you having a connection to the active volcano in Hawaii. Kilauea."

"Oh? And what did he have to say?"

Maybe it was my imagination, but she didn't seem pleased.

"Nothing beyond that, really." I didn't want to get on the bad side of this chick. One thing I had learned was that there was way more to this girl than met the eye.

In spite of it all, I persisted. "Didn't you mention a debut performance. Something like when I heard the bang, I'd know it had begun, whatever 'it' was? Are you telling me that what happened last night had nothing to do with you? It was just a random event?"

Suddenly, she broke into a huge smile. "I was pulling your leg," she said, chewing her gum again a mile a minute. "Yup. I did it. It was me. I was responsible. Happy now?"

I sputtered something inane.

"I *am* connected to volcanoes, just like Al said. Volcanoes and I go way back."

"You can cause them to erupt?"

"Sure," she said. "What of it?"

"Nothing," I said. "Nothing at all." She was starting to seem a little surly again. "But I would really love to know how you did it. I mean, how do you make something like that happen? It's a natural phenomenon. We aren't supposed to be able to control an eruption, any more than we can control an earthquake or a hurricane."

"And yet I know people who can do all those things," she said mildly. She seemed to enjoy tormenting me. "Well, 'people' might not be entirely accurate."

"And you're one of those 'people.'"

Again, she shrugged.

"My God!" I exclaimed.

"Goddess actually," she deadpanned.

"Right," I said. "Volcano Goddess." I was way out of my depth here.

"It's really no big deal," she said. "I don't usually put on demonstrations like that. But you know the saying about extraordinary times calling for extraordinary measures. On the other hand, you'd do well not to piss me off."

"I'll keep that in mind," I said, uncertainly. Shit, I thought. What had I gotten myself into here? There was some reassurance in the fact that she appeared to be on our side.

"Of course I'm on your side," she said as if reading my mind. "Robots make lousy disciples. You know I'm kidding, right?"

"What's your connection to Big Al?"

"We've known Big Al for a long time. Since before all the enhancements and such. We trust him. And by extension, the Federation. More so than Xenecorp. I know what the corporations and their political hacks did to the planet. I was there."

I didn't know what to say to that, so I didn't say anything.

"Are you in touch with Big Al, you or Paul or Des?"

"Sure," she said.

"How's the war going. Up there?"

"Back and forth. Still too close to call," she said. "That's why there hasn't been any sign of Xenecorp down here on the surface. Preoccupied, you might say."

"How? How can you know what's happening up there? Do you have some kind of direct line to the ship?"

"I don't look like this all the time, you know," she said. "This modest form is convenient for you and me to interact. Plus, it's useful when I'm in the mood to dance around without destroying anything. Most of the time I'm not localized like this. I have a lot of leeway in what I can do and where I can be."

"Were there others like you aboard the ship?"

She gave me a quizzical look. "That depends," she said.

This time it was me who was puzzled. "On what?"

"On how much they know about themselves," she said. "There might well be other gods and goddesses around, sure. But what good does it do them if they don't know it?"

I took this in.

"Earth was dying," Cherry continued. "Paul and Des signed on for the trip. I decided to tag along. Can you imagine how boring it would have been to just sit around and wait the million or so years it would take the earth to recover? If you factor in the extra eons necessary for life forms to evolve, let alone something I could hold a conversation with, we're talking about hundreds of millions of years. Maybe a billion or more."

"I see your point."

I thought it over a moment. "I think I get it about Elvis--Paul, I mean. But what is it about Des that interests you? She looks like nobody I've ever seen, that's for sure. Is she one of those other gods and goddesses you mentioned?" Getting this information out of her was like pulling teeth.

"How can I put this?" Cherry mused. "You've heard of vampires?"

"Sure," I said. "There's Bela Lugosi. But that's just in the movies."

She said nothing.

"Vampires just exist in the movies," I said, suddenly panicked. "Right?"

Cherry puckered her lips and made a noncommittal lateral movement with her head.

I swallowed. "She's a vampire," I said.

"A reformed vampire," Cherry clarified. "She hasn't been active as a vampire in a long time. But the potential remains."

It took me several minutes to digest all this. It was a lot to take in.

"So, is that why she doesn't age?"

"Yup," said Cherry. "And Paul too."

"HE's a vampire too?" I said incredulously.

"Just enough to be immortal, more or less," said Cherry. "In order to be a bona fide vampire, he would have had to actually kill someone. He never did, of course. It just wasn't in his nature."

"Do they sleep in coffins?"

"Nope."

"They don't seem to have a problem with sunlight either," I said.

"Yup. That took a bit of work on Des' part. She inoculated herself with small doses. But again, that was all a long time ago. They're in a class by themselves, really. There's nothing quite like them anywhere in my experience. And my experience covers a lot of ground."

"I can see why you'd find them interesting," I said finally, trying to catch my breath.

"Not only that," Cherry said. "But they turned out to be the most amazing humans. I would have missed them if they'd gone off without me. So I came along. Besides, you never know when you might need the services of a goddess. Right?" She gave me a wink.

"So last night," I said. "That was you earning your keep?"

She laughed. Then fire, literally, flared in her eyes. "I don't need anyone's permission or approval to do what I do," she said ominously. For a moment I was expecting another eruption.

She seemed to grow calm again. "They helped me on the crossing," she said soberly.

"Paul and Des. And Big Al?"

She nodded solemnly. "I wouldn't have made it without them," she said.

I watched a couple of late departures from the parking area. When I turned back, Cherry was nowhere to be seen.

Some instinct caused me to turn toward the top of the yet unnamed volcano in the distance. A rumble issued from the mountain and a cluster of molten lava rock sprayed into the air over the caldera like firework rockets, highlighting the surrounding area. A parting gesture? I don't know if I'd fully come to terms with the idea that Cherry was a volcano goddess, THE volcano goddess. But there'd been too many coincidences lately for me to dismiss the possibility.

I hoped it wouldn't be the last time I'd see Cherry. I had the feeling it wouldn't be.

100

Questions

I went back to the stage to get my gear. Mel and Tina were nearly finished packing up, and the dais area was clear except for my amp and guitar, which was propped up on a stand, reflecting the footlights along the front of the stage nicely.

After a last trip to their cars with their gear, Mel and Tina strolled over.

"Spill," Tina said. "It was that girl from the standoff on the ship, right? I hardly recognized her. She's been doing something right. She's a knockout."

In more ways than one, I thought. I wasn't ready yet to explain to them who or what Cherry was. Volcano Goddess? I could just barely believe it myself. They'd seen enough on the observation deck of the Fortune's Fool, to know she had some serious pull. She'd had a bunch of fully armed Xenecorp fighters quaking in their boots. But to try to explain that she was a stowaway goddess was a bit more than they were ready to hear, I was pretty sure, and more than I was ready to impart. "She's a fan," I said.

Tina and Mel eyed me skeptically. "Uh hunh," they said in unison. But to their credit they let it go.

It always took time for us to decompress after a show, so I suggested we go for a milkshake.

"Sam's?" Mel suggested.

"Sure," I said. Sam's was a drive-in diner on the outskirts of town which, like Sally's where Melissa worked during the summer, offered curbside service. Unlike Sally's, Sam's had indoor seating, featuring a dozen red vinyl booths as well as a lunch counter. The place was open 24 hours a day.

Melissa and I left our cars in the Rotary Club lot, and we took Tina's Ford Fairlane. The place was jumpin' when we arrived. A bunch of people from the Rotary gig had had the same idea.

We parked and made our way to the front door. Whistles and friendly greetings abounded as we walked into the joint. After tonight's show, the holdouts around town who hadn't yet heard of the Roadrunners now seemed to be clued in.

Most of the action was curbside. People were tuned into Rattlesnake Radio in their cars while they munched their fries and sucked on straws that drilled down into frosty malts and shakes.

Coming into the diner area, we caught snippets of our concert coming from transistor radios propped up on dining tables all around us. Apparently, somebody at the hall had recorded our performance, and now it was being rebroadcast. We happened to have arrived at the point where Paul Galahad was doing his trio of songs. People were eating it up along with their fried food, riveted to their radios.

We found an empty booth and placed our orders.

'OK,' said Tina. "You don't want to talk about your blonde friend, the one you were talking to after the show. That's OK. But what can you tell us about the guy who calls himself Paul Galahad? He's something else. For an old guy."

Tina didn't miss a trick. She would make a good attorney someday if she had any aspirations in that direction. Luckily for the band, she didn't. I figured all three of us would have it hard settling into a traditional job or profession when the time came. We'd been ruined by rock 'n' roll.

"I know they're different," I said diplomatically, trying to buy some time. I was doubtful that what Cherry had told me was intended to be general knowledge. On the other hand, Tina and Mel were my best friends. They'd been privy to secrets in the past and hadn't said a word to anyone else. I leaned in. "They're vampires," I said in a low whisper.

Tina almost fell out of her chair, laughing. It was a most unTina-like display. Melissa was a little slower to respond, but pretty soon she was laughing too.

I looked around surreptitiously. "I'm serious," I hissed.

They stopped laughing. They'd been shaken up enough lately by things once taken for granted proving not to be true to dismiss the idea out of hand. "Vampires?" Melissa said quietly. "Like Bela Lugosi?"

I nodded. "At least Des is," I said. "Paul's only partway there. But yeah. That's the gist of it."

"Holy shit," Tina said. She wasn't laughing now. "And the blonde, what was her name?"

"Cherry."

"Cherry told you this?"

"Yup."

The girls mulled this over. They'd seen enough to know that what Cherry said shouldn't be taken lightly.

"So how did that happen?" Tina wanted to know. "How did they become vampires?"

"She didn't give me the details. All I know is that it was way before the ship left Earth."

"So that makes them. . . ?"

"Hundreds of years old."

The girls were quiet. Finally, Melissa said, "At least they're not robots. There's a lot of that goin' around."

"I couldn't see a robot singing and moving around like that," Tina said. "There's just no way."

"And Cherry. She's not a vampire?"

"Nope."

"What is she then? She doesn't look older than fifteen."

"Looks can be deceiving. She's the oldest of all."

"How do you figure?"

"She's the volcano goddess."

101

The Social Experiment

She told me disruption was one of her specialties," I informed them, recalling the details of our recent discussion. "There's no underestimating what a well-timed eruption can accomplish, she said."

It took a couple of seconds for this to sink in. "The eruption the other night. That was her?"

I nodded. "She told me it wasn't the first time she's done something like that," I said. "In Hawaii, where she's from, she once helped to roust a power-crazy vampire. She did it to save humanity, she said. And to help Paul Galahad. She said that's what cemented their connection way back when. They've been fast friends ever since."

There were still small clusters of people here and there in front of the Rotary Hall when Tina dropped us off. We agreed to meet again for rehearsal the next day. I waited until Melissa had followed Tina out of the parking lot before heading for my car.

The atmosphere was hushed in the mostly empty parking lot. Now that the wild celebrating was done, reality returned. We'd experienced nearly 24 hours of freedom. Would we get another 24?

As I walked to my car, Danny sidled up to me.

"That was an amazing show you put on tonight," he said.

"I think it was the timing more than anything," I said. "We just played our usual gig. The crowd did the rest."

"You wanna go somewhere and talk?" Danny said. He seemed nervous.

"Sure," I said. "Where do you want to go?" I knew what he was going to say before he said it.

"How about the drive-in diner? Sam's?"

Talk about awkward. I didn't mention we'd just come from there. I looked up at the sky. "Sure," I said. "I could use a Coke."

When he didn't make a move to head for his car, I got the message. "And why don't we take my car?" I said, with feigned cheerfulness. "I could bring you back after." I suspected he wanted to show off a little to his friends, show up at the drive-in with the girl guitarist in a hot rod. It didn't matter that it wasn't his own.

"Hop in," I said. I liked Danny. Otherwise, I would have left him in the lot choking on smoking rubber. I didn't like the feeling of being used. Maybe that's why my romantic life was non-existent. There was a weird give and take involved in relationships that I didn't get. Nor did I have the patience to try to get it. Maybe I was getting cynical in my young age. But so far I hadn't caught on to what all the fuss was about. I wasn't going to let any guy lead me around on a leash, no matter how cute he was or how much he thought of himself.

What a minute, you say. Hadn't I made a name for myself singing corny love songs, albeit with a muscular backbeat? But songs aren't real. It was a mistake to think they were. In my opinion, you were buying yourself a heap of trouble confusing the two.

From where I was sitting, it looked like kids were getting into that kind of trouble left and right. And the strange thing was, they didn't seem to mind, even when it all turned to pucky, which it inevitably did. After a lot of gnashing of teeth and pulling of hair, they got over it. Mostly, I guess.

Well, that wasn't for me. If I could circumvent that, all the better. I was sure I'd be saving myself a lot of wasted time and energy.

So why was I going back to Sam's with Danny, having just been there with the girls and stuffed myself to the gills? Curiosity. That's all. Call it a social experiment.

102

Ghost Girl

The drive-in was just as crowded with cars and people as it had been twenty minutes before. Were these people ever going home tonight? It was like everyone was partying like it was their last night on the planet. Maybe it was.

I got the same treatment walking back into the diner as I had earlier. People waving, a couple of wolves whistling, unintelligible shouting, and multiple thumbs up. A few whispers were added to the mix when Danny appeared. If tongues were going to wag, let 'em wag. People had started to wonder about me. I'd been wondering about myself for a while. But I wasn't in any hurry to clarify where I stood along the cosmic yin/yang continuum. That is if, in fact, there was any clarifying to be done. I had a reputation as an equal opportunity hard ass, earned or not. I tended to make the most of it.

Some of the guys were looking at Danny with new respect. I could tell he was puffed up. Cool by association. I think that was his plan all along. OK with me. I wouldn't have done half the things I'd done in my life if I worried about what other people thought.

All the booths were occupied, but I spotted a couple of empty stools at the end of the lunch counter. We perched.

"It's not what you think," he said.

"What do I think?"

He laughed and didn't say anything further. As the silence dragged on, I began to realize that maybe I had underestimated him.

"You may have heard about the one The People call Grandmother," he said finally. "Up at the reservation?"

"Some kind of medicine woman," I said. "Sure. Can't hang around the Rez for long and not have heard about Grandmother."

"She talks in the old way. Metaphorically, you might say."

I was starting to get goosebumps. I couldn't remember the last time I'd gotten goosebumps.

"She was at a tribal meeting a few nights ago. She said she'd had a vision about the Sky People. 'The ones with no spirit', is the way she put it. There were good Sky People and bad Sky People and, of course, they were in conflict. She said she saw a white girl with red hair in communication with the good Sky People. She was a kind of intermediary. Grandmother called her Ghost Girl.'"

I looked at him, waiting for more.

"She said this 'ghost girl' was going to be a powerful leader someday. That she would be elemental in driving the soulless Sky People away."

He just looked at me as if he were waiting for the pieces to fall into place.

"What?" I said, getting self-conscious.

Danny just laughed.

"Maybe you could enlighten me about what that's supposed to mean," I said, starting to get a little irked. "I'm a little slow on the uptake when it comes to the finer points of Indian lore."

Danny laughed again as if this were the funniest thing he'd heard all day. There was definitely more going with this guy than met the eye.

"Here's what I think," he said. "I think you're the ghost girl in Grandmother's vision. You're the intermediary who communicates with the robots in her story or parable or whatever you want to call it."

"And I'm supposed to be instrumental in driving away the Sky People?"

"That's the way I interpreted what she said."

I looked at him for a beat. "And, let me guess, there's nothing about how this great feat is supposed to be accomplished by this red-headed girl?"

Danny chuckled again, more in admiration this time I liked to think. "You got it," he said. "Grandmother did not specify. She's like that. She tends to know more than she's letting on. My take is that's because she doesn't want to interfere with destiny. She believes it's best if things are allowed to play out as they will."

"Great," I said, unable to conceal a note of sarcasm.

"She also talked about a trio of super-beings," Danny went on. "She called them the Thunder Tribe. They appear as two adults and a young person. But the young one is the older of the two."

Goosebumps. Again. I had the feeling I knew who the Thunder Tribe was, but I kept a straight face. I didn't give anything away.

"They're ageless. Immortal. Ring any bells?"

"Sure," I quipped. "I know lots of people who fit that description."

Danny wasn't interested in my attempt to be cute. He didn't even smile.

"OK. I'll bite," I said after a moment. "Supposing I do happen to know, let's say, an unusual family? What's their part in all this?"

"They're a stabilizing influence, according to Grandmother. They're like guardians. There's some kind of pact they have with the good Sky People. An agreement. They're important to the future of the settlement. They're overseers. Spirit protectors."

Holy shit, I was thinking. This conversation was giving me the heebie-jeebies.

I looked at him. "And this is why you're here? Grandmother sent you so that you could tell me all this?"

"Are you disappointed?" Danny said with a twinkle in his eyes.

103

A Late Night Visit To The Rez

"**S**he wants you to visit her," Danny said.

"Oh? When?"

"The sooner, the better, she said. She believes something's about to happen, and whatever's going to happen will happen soon. 'All will be decided by the third sunrise' was the way she put it."

"The third sunrise after what?"

"I was thinking it had to do with what happened the other night," he said. "The volcano erupting and all. It's the kind of reference point the elders might seize upon. They're big on natural phenomena."

"OK," I said. "If yesterday was day one, that would mean we're talking about the day after tomorrow."

"I don't know for sure," said Danny. "Better to be on the safe side and go soon."

"Soon?"

"Now."

"Now?" And here I'd been looking forward to getting a good night's rest after the show. I still needed to catch up on sleep from the night before.

He sat there stone-faced, all traces of humor gone. He waited.

"I need to stop by the house," I said, "let Grandpa and Auntie know where I'm going."

"Sure."

"Grandpa may want to come along."

Danny shrugged. Apparently that wasn't a problem. "I'll follow you to your house," he said. "Then I'll lead you to where Grandmother lives."

A half an hour later I was driving up the slope toward the reservation in the Rex, Grandpa Kurt next to me.

"And you're going to the reservation at 2 am why again?"

"Danny said it was important. He said the old medicine woman the tribe calls Grandmother wanted to see me right away. She had a vision he thought applied to me and what she called the Sky People."

"The Sky People?"

"You know," I said nodding upward. "The robots. The Federation and Xenecorp."

"OK," said Grandpa neutrally.

"She also seemed to know about Big Al's friend, Paul, and his entourage, Des and Cherry. Danny said she called them The Thunder Tribe."

"Sounds ominous."

"She seemed to indicate they were on the good side. Our side. Protectors or such."

Grandpa Kurt nodded. "I'll go along with that. They seem like good people. And if Cherry was somehow responsible for the eruption last night like you said. . . ." Grandpa fell silent. "And whatever the old lady has to say can't wait until tomorrow?"

"Danny was pretty adamant. Things are supposedly coming to a head in the next couple of days, according to the old woman. I got the feeling that nobody says no to her. She calls and you come."

"But that only applies to the tribe, I'd think."

"So maybe I'm just a little bit curious about what she has to say, OK? She seems to believe I have a role to play in what's going to happen. She calls me an intermediary between us humans and these Sky People."

"Well," said Kurt. "You're the one who's had the most contact with Big Al lately. That's for sure. If he's one of these Sky People, then that much is true. And you've had a role in this since you found that tunnel up the arroyo."

"You ready for this, Gramps?" I asked him as we continued to follow Danny onto the Rez.

"Ready as I'll ever be," Grandpa replied with a sigh.

104

Grandmother

t was quiet as the grave at the tribal center. We kept going. I
followed Danny's tail lights for another mile or so north. He pulled
up in front of a tiny house off by itself on the lava flows about a
hundred yards back from the graded dirt road we'd driven in on. I
pulled in next to Danny.

Grandpa reached for the door handle.

"Remember, Grandpa," I said, putting a hand on his arm. "You
agreed to stay in the car. Danny said Grandmother will only see me."

"Yeah, yeah," Grandpa said grouchily, relaxing back in his seat.
"Ears only. I get it. I'll be good."

"I'll fill you in on what she says," I said, getting out of the car
and closing the door carefully behind me. The quiet was so absolute
here at this time of night that I didn't want to disrupt it. The blackness
of the lava merged with the blackness of the night so that it took a
moment to distinguish where one stopped and the other started. The
Fortune's Fool had set in the sky a couple of hours before, so the
only light came from the twinkling of stars through a slight haze of
humidity that blew in from the ocean far below.

Danny was standing at the end of the walkway that led to the
front door. "You think you can find your way back home from here?"
he asked.

"You're not coming in?" I said, surprised and maybe a little
nervous about facing the formidable Grandmother on my own.

"Nope. This meeting is just for you. You'll be fine. She's really a sweet old lady." I think he sensed my jitters about this strange late-night rendezvous.

"OK," I said. "And you really have no idea what this is about?"

"Nope," he said. "None at all."

"Well, thanks for bringing me out here," I said. "I guess I'll be seeing you around."

"Sure thing," he said. "Maybe we'll have a chance to catch up later."

I didn't know if he was just being encouraging or really meant it. He might have been smiling as he walked back to his car.

I took stock. There was a soft light coming from the window facing the road. It seemed friendly enough, no jack-o'-lanterns in sight or anything. I straightened up and strode up the path to the front door. I knocked.

When the door opened, I was surprised to find a woman facing me who couldn't have been much older than me. She had on a new looking buckskin shift tied at the waist with a wide belt studded with silver and turquoise. The light tan tunic was covered with intricate designs made with tiny multi-colored beads. It looked like some kind of ceremonial getup. Her long hair was jet black, like Tina's. It was tied at the back by an ornate turquoise and silver clasp and dangled to her waist.

She turned without a word and led me into a small living room next to the entry. It was crammed with all manner of religious icons and lit by a dozen or so candles. The statuettes and framed pictures were both Christian and pagan as far as I could tell. Men and women from exotic cultures I couldn't identify were featured too. Mother Mary was everywhere. My family didn't attend church on a regular basis, but she was hard to miss. There were also several faded photographs of American Indians from long ago.

Tucked in among the photos and statuettes and surrounded by them was a very old woman. She was tiny and wrinkled, her skin as brown as a walnut. At first, I mistook her for a wooden statue herself. But then her face creased into a toothless smile.

The woman who had ushered me in took a seat in a folding chair across from the old woman. Grandmother motioned for me to sit in a similar chair directly behind me. I sat.

The old woman regarded me. She bowed to me as deeply as she could manage in the threadbare upholstered armchair she was in. She seemed thrilled to see me. I didn't know how to react, so I smiled back at her and bowed to her from where I was sitting. It was all a bit awkward. I didn't know what was expected of me.

The old woman began to say something. She went on for a long time.

When she was done saying her piece, the younger woman turned to me and said. "Grandmother is honored by your presence. She welcomes you into her abode."

"Thank her as well," I said lamely.

The old woman said something.

The young woman translated. "You have a question," she said.

I have many questions, I thought. This was all I needed at 3 in the morning. A riddle.

The old woman spoke again.

The young woman translated. "You have carried a question with you your whole life long," she said.

Oh. That question. I swallowed. This was getting personal pretty quickly. "I was raised an orphan," I said. "And I guess I've always wondered about my birth parents—who they were." My throat felt dry, and it came out as more of a croak.

The old woman noticed my discomfort and had her assistant pour me a cup of tea from an earthenware teapot that rested on a tray made of woven grass at her elbow. I took the cup that was offered and sipped. It was some kind of herbal brew. It tasted like the desert smelled. Not unpleasant.

The old woman spoke. The young woman started to translate. I don't know how, but I already knew what the old woman was saying. When I stopped listening to the words, which I didn't understand,

I found I could tune into the meaning behind the words. It was the strangest thing. But what she said surprised me even more.

"You have never had parents," the old woman said. "You are your own parents."

105

The Song Of The Earth

was speechless.

"You are self-creating," the old woman continued. "Eighteen years ago you decided to adopt the waking sleep that is called life. You understood that by entering this life, you would forget who you were. But you did it anyway. You made the choice to be mortal and to live as a mortal. And you have, although you were never physically born."

She paused and took a sip of tea, her eyes never leaving my face.

There was a pitched battle being fought inside me. On one side was the Voice of Reason, telling me there was no truth to what she was telling me. There couldn't be. And on the other side was a part of me that knew she was right.

When I could speak, I said, "Who am I really then? Who was I before I was born."

"You are the Mother Spirit of Planet Earth. That is your true identity. You are the one people referred to as Gaia. A long, long time ago."

The name was unfamiliar to me. I was pretty sure I'd never heard it before. Mother Spirit of Earth? I started shaking my head like I had a bug in my ear. What was she talking about?

"You are the Earth goddess gone into exile. You left when our planet could no longer sustain life. You have blessed us with your presence on the great crossing, first only in spirit and now in human form."

"If this is true, then why don't I remember any of it?" I said.

"That was your choice," Grandma continued mildly, as if it were perfectly normal to have a bewildered earth goddess drinking tea in her living room in the middle of the night. "You have your own reasons."

"OK," I said. I noticed my hands were getting clammy. It was unlike me to get a case of nerves like this. "If you had to guess, then."

A wide smile from Grandma. "It is obvious that you wanted to experience life as a human in this time of transition. And maybe it's just as simple as that. Mankind is making a new start in a new place among the stars. Maybe you wanted to experience that in physical form. But I also believe you will want to assume your true form again eventually. You will want to merge with the essence of this new planet, for that is why you came here. You see, it is only with your participation that this place can become a true home again for mankind."

I just sat there. I admit it gave me a thrill to think that as an immortal I might be in the same company as Paul, Des, and especially Cherry. But it wasn't real. None of this could be true. I was an ordinary girl who loved cars and rock 'n' roll. On a good day, I was a decent guitarist. That was all. What can I say?

"Here there are no traditions," Grandma went on. "There is no history, except what we brought with us. By coming here you are breathing life into an otherwise barren piece of rock floating in space. You are bringing Spirit to a place without spirits or gods or goddesses. You are destined to become the Soul of this planet, just as you once were the Soul of Planet Earth. It is right that it should be so."

"Am I ever going to remember any of this? Who I am, I mean?"

"By becoming human you have chosen a life with a beginning and an end. There may be times, perhaps, when you will glimpse your true potential. In those moments you will see that what I am saying is true, even if you may not entirely believe it now. But these moments may be fleeting. It doesn't matter if you do not remember everything. It is enough to live your life, a day at a time, just as every other human does. Awareness of your totality will come again later, when you leave this form behind."

"In other words, when I die," I said. "What happens then?"

"You will again be who you were, who you have always been. Everywhere at once. In the rocks and the soil. In the sea and the sky. You will contain the spirit of the plants and trees and all the creatures here, those we have brought with us, and those who were already here. Only with your presence can this place become a true home for us all. Only with you here can this world become a replacement for the one that was lost. You are the Song of the Earth."

I opened my mouth, but no words came out.

Finally, I found my voice. "If what you say is true, what can I do to save us from Xenecorp? What good is knowing any of this when I'm powerless to change what's going on."

"It is not your purpose to alter the course of history," said Grandmother. "It is your purpose to experience your human life, with all its frailties and vulnerabilities. Well, maybe not all." The old woman chuckled at that. "You are already somewhat unique, are you not? You are She Who Loves To Go Fast." She slapped her right hand onto the palm of her left hand with a sound like a shot. And then she chopped the air with her right hand to indicate rapid movement. If I was in any danger of falling asleep, which I wasn't, I would have fallen off my chair. "You are She Whose Music Unites the People. You have done much already to bring the peoples of this planet together, regardless of their own cultures and traditions. You have inspired many with what you do and so have aided them in their struggle to make a life here.

"And you are not entirely alone. There is the Thunder Tribe. You sense the one you call Cherry is like you. And you are right. To us, she is Thunder Woman. The Goddess of Earth Fire." A memory of Cherry calling us "sisters" surfaced in my mind. It was starting to make sense. If I could accept what I was being told. If I could believe even an iota of what the old woman was saying.

As it was, I could only take her word for it. I didn't really feel any different than I had moments before. I had no special powers that I knew of. I knew how to get a car running and how to get some gratifying squawks out of an electric guitar. But that was it.

"What's going to happen to us?" I asked. "Can you see the future? Are we going to survive? Will we be free or will we become slaves?"

"None of that is written yet," said the old woman. "It is the nature of our existence as mortals not to know certain things. But you can be assured about one thing. The Earth Goddess can never die. And regardless of what happens, the human spirit will survive. It will find a way."

106

The Easter Bunny

"Well," said Grandpa. "What did she say?"

"She said I was the Earth Goddess. Something like that."

"That's all? Ha. I could have told you that!"

I looked over at him.

"Just kiddin'," he said. "OK. That's a nice thing to hear, I'll bet. Even at 3 in the morning."

"Sure," I said. "Except I don't feel like the goddess of anything. What good is it if I don't know it? She could have told me I was the Easter Bunny for all the good it's doing me."

"You *are* the Easter Bunny," Grandpa said. I could tell this was all a big yuk to him. "You've always been my Easter Bunny."

I gave him another look.

"OK," he said. "Let's just say, for the sake of argument, that you were this almighty goddess she says you are, wouldn't that make you the Easter Bunny too? It stands to reason. I mean you could be pretty much anything you pleased, couldn't you?"

I didn't honor this with a reply. Instead, I stayed focused on the dirt road in my headlights. On top of everything else, I'd have to clean the car when I got home. I always did when I visited the Rez.

"Being this Earth Goddess must come with some perks," Grandpa Kurt said. "I mean. . . ."

"Just give it a rest, Pops," I said. My patience was wearing thin.

The lateness of the hour and the fact I hadn't slept much lately were conspiring to turn me into a righteous grump.

I didn't know what to make of my visit with Grandmother. My first thought was, too bad Cherry wasn't around. It would have helped to be able to run this by a bonafide goddess, see what her take on all this was. Unfortunately, Cherry wasn't around.

"Did she say anything else about Big Al's friends, Paul and Des and Cherry?"

"Nothing new."

"Well, I'd say the fact that she knows about them at all means she must know what she's talking about. At least to some extent."

"Somebody could have told her," I said.

"Somebody? Like who?"

I didn't have an answer for that. Mel and Tina knew about Paul, Des, and Cherry. But Mel didn't hang around the Rez, except when we were playing there. Tina would know Grandmother, of course. Everybody on the Rez did. But somehow I couldn't see Tina spilling the beans, even to a tribal elder. It just wasn't her style. She was the proudest, stubbornest, and most tight-lipped Indian I knew, when she wasn't singing her head off.

"I don't suppose she gave you any hints about how all this was going to shake out? The robot wars? Our chances of surviving on Planet Epsi?"

I looked over at him. "Planet Epsi?" I said. "Cute."

"Got a better name?"

"Not offhand," I said. "And nope. If she knew about the future, she wasn't telling. She said we'd have to work that out on our own."

"It's better we don't know," he said with finality. "Would it help if she'd said we were all doomed?"

"I guess not."

"You're darn right. It would just depress the heck out of us. We'd sure be no better off for it."

"This is some sh. . . crap we've got ourselves in," I blurted out. The whole situation was starting to get to me. Why couldn't Xenecorps just kiss off and leave us in peace to try to forge a new life for ourselves? It was bad enough that we were trillions of miles and two and a half centuries away from our home planet.

If I had unlimited powers that's what I'd do, I thought. I'd decree a sanctuary here, free from outside interference, where the human race could rise or fall based on the choices it made from now on. No evil robots to contend with. No worrying about who would come out on top in the war going on in the sky and what it would mean for our future. Of course, if I had unlimited powers, I'd fix up Planet Earth and transport us all back there in the blink of an eye. But I guess it didn't work like that. Humanity was stuck with the future it had created for itself.

We'd royally messed up last time. Would we blow it again here? Or would we as a species have learned something? I guess how you saw the prospects depended on whether you were a glass-half-empty or half-full kind of person when it came to human nature. For better or worse, we'd come this far. We were here now. Pessimism wasn't going to get us anywhere.

Grandpa was probably right on why Grandmother might play it close to the vest, provided she really knew something we didn't. Inside information, good or bad, wasn't going to help us in the long run. It might even prove a detriment. We'd have to make our own choices and live with them, just as we always had. And hope that things worked out in our favor.

107

Bad News

I barely made it home, I was so tired. I immediately went to my room and collapsed.

I slept till close to noon the following day. There wasn't anything planned beyond rehearsal at the college later that afternoon, so there was no reason not to ease into the day. Work had been slow at Ted's since the occupation. And my next stint at the radio station wasn't until later in the week. But now that people were driving to and from Tucson again on a regular basis, work would start to pick up again soon, I figured.

That is, if things worked out. I remember what Grandmother had said about everything being resolved on the third day. So we had another day to go, if Danny had been right in his calculations. She'd also told me I was a self-created goddess. So I didn't know how seriously to take her predictions.

Grandpa Kurt regarded me with mock amazement when I finally showed up in the kitchen. "It's Sleeping Beauty," he said. "Make yourself some breakfast. I'm about to make myself a sandwich for lunch."

"A glass of orange juice would be fine," I said, heading for the fridge

"What?" Grandpa said. "That's not like you. You gotta eat something to keep your strength up. Especially if you're Queen of the Universe."

"Earth Goddess," I corrected him.

"My point is nobody's going to take an undernourished goddess seriously. How are you going to get your minions to do your bidding?"

I had to chuckle at that. It really was basically a joke. I didn't believe I was a goddess any more than Grandpa did. When I'd studied myself closely in the mirror that morning, I saw that nothing had changed. I was still the freckle-faced kid of yore with the flaming red locks. Even when I'd tried puffing myself up and showing my muscles, it didn't help.

"So what's on the agenda for today, Goddess Rose?"

"Practice," I said. "But not until 4."

"What say we mosey on over to the wrecking yard in the meantime and see if the Captain's turned up. If he's not there, there might be someone around who can fill us in on the latest up top."

"Sure," I said. I was starting to feel my appetite returning. So I began rummaging around in the fridge for some eggs. Grandpa already had a loaf of bread out on the countertop for his sandwich. "I think I will fix myself a bite after all," I said.

"That's my girl," said Grandpa with a smile. "Care for some toast?"

"Sure," I said.

He popped a couple of slices into the toaster.

A half-hour later we were on our way over to Big Al's Wrecking and Salvage in the Rex.

As usual of late, the place looked deserted. But appearances can be deceiving we'd learned. It took a while to raise someone. When we succeeded, it was Archie, the Grey. Or maybe just *a* Grey. It was hard to tell one from the other. It didn't have a ray gun pointed at me. That was the important part. It waddled around the side of the office building and came to a halt, looking at us. It seemed to want to say something. But there was no sound forthcoming.

We held our ground, Grandpa and I at the fence and the Grey near the office. About a hundred feet separated us.

After five long minutes, the Grey disappeared behind the building again. Grandpa and I looked at each other. Was that all we were going to get?

We were about to turn away and head back to the car when the front door of the office opened. Gillian appeared. She looked battered. She was smudged and scraped and her fatigues were ripped. She came toward us.

"What's happened?" I asked, suddenly alarmed. "What's going on?"

"It's not looking good," Gillian replied. "Things haven't been going well on the ship."

"How come?"

"It boils down to their tech being better than our tech. What can I say?"

"Xenecorp is winning?" I asked, incredulous.

Gillian nodded her head. "I won't kid you. It's starting to look that way. We've given it our best. But we're down to our last fighters now. We don't know how long they can hold out. I'm afraid it's just a matter of time before our lines of defense cave."

"How much time?"

"Hours. A day at the most."

I'd still been harboring hopes that the Federation could pull it off, that it would come through for us. The alternative had been too awful to contemplate.

We stood facing each other through the chain-link fence. A warm breeze was blowing in off the ocean. All was quiet in this corner of town. It was hard to believe there was a war raging over our heads and harder still to acknowledge our lives were about to change profoundly for the worse.

"What about Big Al," I asked. "How is he?"

"He's inside," Gillian said evenly. "He's not in good shape."

"Can we see him?"

"I'm not sure it would be a good idea. He's pretty beat up. We're trying to fix him. But it'll take time. Time we may not have."

"Can we at least talk to him?" Grandpa said. "We don't need to stay long. Please?"

"Wait here," Gillian said. She disappeared into the office.

She reappeared a couple of minutes later. "It's alright," she said. "You can go on in."

108

Field Hospital

There was a lot of activity in the warehouse section of the building. As before, the weathered and somewhat dingy look of the front office yielded to blinding lights in the back portion of the building, reflecting off stainless steel surfaces throughout the large room. The place had been transformed into something resembling a combination surgical arena and medical laboratory.

"We've turned it into a field hospital," Gillian explained.

There were curtained cubicles along the outside walls that could have been makeshift hospital rooms. Elsewhere, people, or what looked like people, were hauling boxes and equipment toward open double doors at the rear of the facility, up a ramp outside, and into the cargo hold of a waiting a space shuttle backed up to the building.

"We don't have a lot of gear to work with down here," Gillian continued. "Everything we need is basically on board the ship. But we no longer have access to the repair and restoration facilities on the Fortune's Fool. So we've been doing the best we can with what we have here."

"It looks like you're vacating," Grandpa observed.

Gillian nodded. "We're wrapping up operations here on the surface. To stay much longer would be too risky for you. We can't have that."

"But where will you go?" I asked.

"We're going back to the ship. We're going to take everyone that's left down here and prepare for one final push."

"But if you're losing. . . ? It's suicide," I stated.

"We'll hold out as long as we can. We are sworn to protect you to the very end. And that's what we'll do."

She turned away from us. "Captain Wertmueler is over there," she said, indicating a curtained cubicle adjacent to the open rear doors with a nod of her head. "Go on in through the drapes. Just bear in mind your visit will have to be brief. We're leaving as soon as we're loaded up."

Grandpa and I just nodded. We were dazed by all the activity and by what we'd just heard. The prospect of Xenecorp winning was starting to sink in. It was not a happy thought.

We found ourselves in front of the screened-off room. We drew back the curtains to find it contained one bed, the back raised. In it was Big Al. His Hawaiian shirt had been replaced by something that looked like a hospital smock. Instead of saline solution, there were bags of something that looked like hydraulic fluid hooked up to IVs going into his arms. The sight made me cringe. For a moment I thought I'd be ill. I still hadn't quite come to terms with the idea that Big Al was mostly robotic.

He was motionless, staring off into the distance. Aside from that, he looked his usual self. There was no damage visible. But then most of him was covered.

Someone who could have been a doctor approached. "His electronics and voice box are damaged," he told us. "He may have trouble communicating."

Big Al became aware of our presence next to him and moved his head to look up at us.

"It's good to see you both," he said. The voice was weak, barely audible.

He nodded to two chairs next to the raised bed. We sat.

"Looks like this may be the last time we get to talk," he remarked without preamble. "I just wish we had more time together. It's been an honor to know you," he said, acknowledging Grandpa. "And it's been a real kick to know you." He managed a weak smile in my direction. "We did our best to live up to our end of the bargain. We really did. But it looks like you'll be on your own a little sooner than expected."

Nobody said anything. This was it, I thought.

"I'm going to need somebody to look after the family business for me," Big Al said. It took us a moment to realize he was talking about his wrecking and salvage operation. "Would it be too much to ask you to find a good owner for me? I know it's a big request. All I ask is that you maybe try to find someone who'll carry on the tradition, if such a person exists. It would have to be a junk junkie like me." Again the weak smile. "The happiest times of my unnaturally long life were spent right here. That pile of junk out there has been my treasure. Maybe I feel such affection for it because we share a similar pedigree. Makes sense, doesn't it?" He laughed again, but it devolved into a cough.

"Consider it done," Grandpa said without hesitation. "We'll take care of it for you, whatever it takes. You don't need to worry about that. We just wish. . . ."

"No need to get all maudlin on me," Big Al said wryly. "It is what it is. You guys are going to have some changes to adjust to in the near future. I feel a little guilty about asking you to do this on top of everything else."

"Don't give it a second thought," Grandpa said. "We'll do you proud. I promise."

"I know you will," Big Al said. "You already have."

A group of people that looked like technicians had shown up and surrounded the bed, waiting expectantly.

"It looks like it's time to face the music," Big Al said, acknowledging them.

He couldn't have helped but notice our sad faces.

"Now, now. No need for that," Big Al said. "I've lived longer than I had any right to expect. Keep in mind I'm 96% machine. You wouldn't mourn your toaster or your washing machine, would you? I'm basically no different."

"You're not a toaster or a washing machine," I said quietly. "You've been our friend, and we're going to miss you."

109

Preparations

I think we were in a state of shock as we drove home. It wasn't just the idea that Xenecorp would be back in full force. It was seeing Big Al laid low like that, barely able to speak above a whisper. He'd always been this larger than life character. Maybe he wasn't exactly alive like us. But somehow he represented the best of us. He was courageous, noble, and good-humored. He was someone you could rely on. Someone who would always come through, if it was at all in his power.

The fact that circumstances had proven beyond his control, didn't diminish any of that. It just made him more human. As was his love of the wrecking yard and the way he cared about his friends, especially Grandpa and The Thunder Tribe, as I was beginning to think of Cherry, Des, and Paul. He had been the most important person on the ship, and yet he chose to live a humble existence far away from the trappings of power. We felt privileged to know him.

"What do we do now?" I asked Grandpa.

"We go underground," he said. "In the tube tunnels like before or somewhere else. Farther up the hill, maybe. Try to stay off the radar. Better to live free hand to mouth, I'm thinking, than have everything be provided and be a slave."

It was pretty much what I'd been thinking, too.

"Let's make a few calls when we get back," Grandpa continued. "You'll probably want to let your friends at the station in on the latest.

Folks need to know it's time to prepare for the worst and decide how they're going to deal with it."

"I've got a feeling when people realize how things are going, we're not going to be the only ones heading for the hills," I said. "I hope there's going to be enough space underneath that volcano for all of us."

"I don't think space in the tunnels is going to be the main problem," Grandpa said. "The question is, what is Xenecorp going to do? With the Federation gone, there's nothing to prevent them from coming after us."

"I think everybody will understand the need for secrecy," I said. "Maybe we can keep it quiet."

"How long can a thousand people stay hidden, let alone a hundred thousand or more? They'll find us eventually."

We drove on. When we arrived at the house, the suns were starting to light up the eastern horizon. On Planet Epsi the sunrises were as interesting as the sunsets. The twin suns showed up within minutes of each other at opposite ends of the horizon. They were further away and therefore smaller than what we were used to. This was a good thing. We would have cooked otherwise. But even after these many months, it was still impressive to see them peek over the horizon like two wide-spaced, but somehow friendly-looking, headlights.

I immediately took to the phone and called Maggie Gonzales at the station. I described the scene at the wrecking and salvage and the evacuation in progress. And I told her about our talk with Big Al and the shape he was in, knowing the word would go out in a matter of minutes.

In the meantime, Grandpa had awakened Trish, and they were already well into collecting the last few things we'd need to make a go of it in the tubes longer term. We hadn't bothered to unpack from our last visit to the tunnels, so the process went quickly. Some of our camping gear was still in place in the caves--stuff like kerosene lamps, tents, bedding, and canned goods--in case we needed to beat a hasty retreat.

I wondered how Tina and Melissa would handle the news. I

gave both a call. It was early yet and neither had heard the Radio Rattlesnake broadcasts that morning.

They dealt with the news better than I had. While I hadn't wanted to confront the possibility of failure, they seemed to have at least considered it. We agreed to meet in the tubes later that morning, deciding it was probably the best place to await further developments.

Maggie and the gang at the station knew all about the tubes and planned to park Florence, the ambulance, nearby in case they needed to head for cover in a hurry. It was generally assumed that Xenecorp would commandeer the media outlets first thing, like they had last time. Factual news reporting would go underground again, with Radio Rattlesnake taking up the slack as before. By now this state of affairs was so familiar to us that the few days of freedom we'd had seemed like an aberration, not the norm. Except that the Federation would no longer be around to back us up and serve as a buffer against the damage the Xenecorp might do.

110

Exodus

Telescopes were trained on the Fortune's Fool in hopes of detecting a clue as to what was going on and what would come next. Even with binoculars, you could see that bay doors were open all over the surface of the ship, and shuttles and fighter craft were swarming. We couldn't see who they were at this range. But from what Big Al had told us, it was a safe bet they were Xenecorp making ready to descend to the surface to reclaim the planet.

I wondered where Big Al was, and Gillian. Were they still alive? Or had they already become casualties of the war?

By midday, it looked from the ground as if Xenecorp was mounting a cleanup operation on and around the Fortune's Fool. There were still flashes of weapon fire among the fighters circling the ship. But these were becoming few and further between as we looked on. The end was near. It wouldn't be long now before Xenecorp turned its full attention to the planet and us puny humans.

We were getting reports from all over to the effect that mass exoduses were underway from the cities and towns on the surface. People couldn't get out of town fast enough.

Tucson was emptying out. Through our binoculars, we could see lines of cars and trucks, bumper to bumper, on all the available routes out of the city. Most were heading inland toward the volcano. A few were traveling north toward Rattlesnake Junction. And some were headed northeast in our direction. Finding us and the Rez folks occupying the tunnels in the lower elevations, they drove on looking for points of entry into the lava tubes higher up.

From morning to night the caravan of cars and trucks poured out of the big city and fanned out into the surrounding countryside. Only at sunset did the traffic flow begin to subside. The sound of revving engines echoed across the hillside as drivers struggled to navigate the tricky lava flows without getting bogged down.

Anyone not in the driver's seat was gazing skyward in dread and anticipation. the Fortune's Fool was over the ocean by now, lit up by the twin setting suns. It was as heart-stoppingly beautiful as ever. The contrast between the dazzling sight and the prevailing mood couldn't have been greater.

I don't think there was anyone anywhere who didn't have mixed feelings when they beheld the Fortune's Fool in the night sky. It was undeniably spectacular. Unlike Planet Earth's moon, it never went through phases, but was always full. It was so bright that except on particularly stormy or foggy nights, you could easily drive at night without headlights and even go swimming or shoot hoops.

Next to this was the knowledge of what the ship actually was and what it represented. It was a mechanical conveyance that had transported us a fair stretch across the galaxy. It was a constant reminder of how we'd been duped (for our own good, of course) and that our true home, Planet Earth, was no longer habitable. Consequently, the experience of seeing it up there was bittersweet at best.

Added to the mix was the precariousness of our situation as humans on an alien planet. We'd been here less than a year and the novelty hadn't worn off. No one knew if we'd survive even without the threat that Xenecorp posed. We were at the mercy of forces beyond our control. And right now our future was being decided in the evening sky over our heads.

All there was to do was wait.

III

Endings And Beginnings

The suns had set when the sky exploded.

One moment the Fortune's Fool was a dazzling, glowing orb out over the ocean, reflecting the last rays of daylight. And the next it was gone, replaced by a haze of silvery confetti that stretched from horizon to horizon.

To say the ship was destroyed was the understatement of the year. It was atomized. The blast reduced the ship to a metallic mist that would be visible in the upper atmosphere for weeks to come.

All traces of Xenecorp and the friendly machines that had overseen our crossing from our home world had been obliterated. Whether the combatants had a soul and consequently whether they had actually been "killed" would be a subject of debate for decades to come. And with the Fortune's Fool gone, any fantasy anyone anywhere might have entertained of our species one day returning to Planet Earth was laid to rest once and for all.

Those of us who'd had the good fortune to know Big Al and, in my case, Gillian mourned our loss. The group of us who remembered the Greys was smaller. Those of us who had encountered them weren't quite sure how to feel about their passing because we hadn't known what to make of them while they were alive. Friend or foe? Apparently both.

Everyone to some extent missed the Fortune's Fool, even

knowing that most all aspects of our lives onboard the ship had been an illusion. Still, New Arizona would remain in our memories, as close an approximation of our original home as we would ever know.

Mixed in with all that, was a sense of relief. A sense that we had collectively dodged the bullet. There were only a few of us that had experienced actual contact with members of the Federation. To most, the Federation remained an abstraction, a benevolent presence working behind the scenes to ensure our safe passage. Added to that somewhat vague knowledge, at least to most humans, was that the Federation members had been robots—the "good" ones.

But what stuck in the minds of most people was the nightmare of Xenecorp's occupation. Xenecorp would always be remembered as the "evil" robots, a vestige of the kind of disregard for life that had facilitated the destruction of Planet Earth in the first place. A cautionary example of what could happen if myopic self-regard was ever again allowed to set the agenda.

All this by way of saying that the mood on Epsilon 4 was, for the most part, jubilant. The robots, one and all, were no more. It was just us chickens down here now. If we were going to be destroyed, it would be us doing the destroying.

Naturally, a grand celebration was called for. And as the go-to band for the resistance, the Roadrunners were booked to play. The new football stadium behind the college was decided upon as the concert site. It was by far the largest venue around, with bleacher and lawn seating to accommodate everyone in Rattlesnake Junction and plenty more besides. Lucky thing too because folks were heading over from Tucson and some from as far north as Phoenix to join in the festivities. It was going to be the Rotary Hall times a thousand.

When the day of the concert rolled around the parking lots on campus were jam-packed. The overflow fanned out for hundreds of yards in every direction on the smooth, hard-packed lava around the arena. The event had sold out quickly, so only a fraction of the people parked out on the lava had tickets. Once again it was up to Radio Rattlesnake to make sure anyone with a radio who didn't have access to the live show could participate in the festivities from wherever they were. As it turned out, that included just about everyone else on the planet.

Was I happy it was over and the threat gone? Sure. I hadn't been looking forward to having to kill myself if Xenecorp caught up with us. But at the same time, I felt slightly ill. We humans are a sentimental lot, I guess. I couldn't help but miss Big Al and my hero, Gillian, the Warrior Woman. They were a part of me and probably always would be.

If Grandmother up at the Rez had been right, and I happened to be this great Earth Goddess underneath my scrappy, no-nonsense exterior this might be a good time to switch into goddess mode. I figured that even if a goddess couldn't bring back loved ones from the Great Beyond, she wouldn't care so much or want to change things that couldn't be changed. But the fact remained, I had no idea what it was like to be a goddess, nor would I likely know until some time in the hopefully distant future when I no longer had a body to worry about. And tell you the truth, I was in no hurry to find out.

The gig of all gigs was coming up. This time we'd be televised, I had learned. I had to get with the program or the girls would never forgive me. I'd never forgive myself.

112

The Celebration

When the show started there were more people in the stadium than I'd ever seen together in any one place in my life. In addition to the packed stands, the entire field area was occupied by people in neat rows of folding chairs. And none of that took into account everyone in their cars in the surrounding hills or, for that matter, all the people listening in on their radios or watching TV.

It was a Thursday. Not that it made any difference. I drove over to the venue early to get set up and hopefully do a soundcheck. Tina and Melissa were already there. Besides the band, there was a squad of carpenters busy putting the finishing touches on a stage that looked to be the size of the deck of an aircraft carrier. Meanwhile overhead, technicians defied death to climb high into the scaffolding to adjust the klieg lights and secure a column of PA speakers the likes of which I don't think anyone had ever seen before. Thick cable bundles snaked this way and that. Boxy TV cameras were being rolled in along the sides of the stage. A couple of camera operators had their cameras trained on us from cherry pickers out in the audience seats several rows back from the stage. They wove around in front of us like the antennas of a giant insect. Great. Was I going to need to start worrying about how I'd look on TV on top of everything else?

Maybe. Was I going to? Nope. Too late anyway. I concentrated on tuning my guitar.

Besides us, the construction crew, and the TV and sound technicians, there was no one in the stadium. Yet.

When we had our gear set up on the stage, we launched into a couple of songs to loosen up. The PA wasn't live yet, so we did a few numbers at low volume, making sure we were able to hear Tina's vocals over our instruments. Everything was going to be mic'd and then sent out through the speaker towers. All we could do was hope the sound engineers knew what they were doing.

It felt good to be playing. Lots better than sitting around waiting for the show to start.

While we were doing our soundcheck, Maggie arrived with the Radio Rattlesnake crew. I knew the office staff and most of the DJs. Everyone was here, scrambling to run audio lines out to Florence The Ambulance, parked outside the stadium proper somewhere. Maggie acknowledged me with a wave. It was clear to both of us there wouldn't be enough time to talk before the show. That would have to wait until later.

About an hour before showtime, people began filing into the stadium. Grandpa Kurt and Trish, being VIPs, were among the first audience members to be let in. They appeared in the wings at stage left. I ran over to greet them. It was time to quit rehearsing anyway and settle in to await our cue.

From a bench on stage we all watched the twin suns angling toward the west. The upper atmosphere smudge that was all that was left of the Fortune's Fool was clearly visible. It was a silvery shroud in the evening sky. Nothing was said.

The atmosphere in the stadium was hushed at first. But gradually a low roar began to build as more and more people filed in. At about ten minutes to showtime, it looked like every available seat in the place was filled. The air vibrated with the chattering of thousands of people. The anticipation was palpable.

At six o'clock sharp Maggie stepped up to the microphone at the front of the stage. "Good evening, ladies and gentlemen," she began, her voice booming out into the vast space and echoing off the distant bleachers. "Welcome to the biggest house party this planet has yet seen."

The stands erupted. All the pent-up anxiety of the past months was released in a flood of cheering, clapping, and whistling. Our humble gig would mark the moment we humans took back control of our destiny. What happened from now on was up to us.

When the applause died down, Maggie continued. "Today's program will feature a concert by one of our very favorite bands. Unless you've been living under a rock this past year, you know who they are. If you don't like rock 'n' roll, cover your ears. We are proud to present Rattlesnake Junction's very own Roadrunners!"

Judging from the applause, it seemed just about everyone in attendance was a fan of rock 'n' roll, at least for today. We launched into our set even though the clapping wasn't showing any signs of letting up. I can't say we weren't just a little unnerved by the number of people we were playing to. I think we all secretly just wanted to get through our set and get off the stage.

As it turned out, our nervousness started to evaporate after the first couple of songs. And as we kept at it, we actually got to the point where we were enjoying ourselves. It helped a lot that we were well-rehearsed. The only things that were different, really, were the size of the venue and the size of the crowd. And because we were greeted with wild enthusiasm after every number, these ceased to be a problem.

Coming up on the two-hour mark, the girls and I could have kept going. We'd already done our entire repertoire twice at this point. They didn't actually have to drag us off the stage, but almost.

I can't overstate how much it helped that everyone was so excited. I couldn't kid myself that it was all the music. We were just there. We happened to be the focal point for the excitement and relief everyone was feeling. This was a community effort, maybe a global effort, but that was too big to contemplate right then. We just let the cheering and clapping carry us along.

I know it was just my imagination, but I felt like I left my body for whole songs at a time during the second hour of the performance. In those moments it was like I was floating above the stage, looking down on it and the stadium from high above. The feeling was like standing on a super high cliff. It was kind of scary really, at first.

After that first bout of vertigo, I started to get accustomed to the sensation. I started to relax. It was like I was this tiny person on this massive stage wailing away on the guitar. And at the same time I was this really big person observing everything from way up in the sky. There were moments when it felt like I was cradling the entire planet in my arms as if it were an infant, and I was singing a lullaby to it, enveloping it in sound. I felt an affection for everybody and everything that was overwhelming. Tears began streaming down my face. Divisions disappeared. The fear and uncertainty of the past several months was a distant memory. Healing was happening, here and now. I could feel it.

We were going to be alright on this rock a trillion miles from home. I was as sure of that as I'd ever been about anything in my life.

113

The Thunder Tribe Returns

e sat on the front edge of the stage after the show, watching the stadium gradually empty out. None of us seemed in any particular hurry to leave, including Grandpa and Trish. The band had played for over two hours, and we were drained, but in a good way. I, for one, had no desire to pack up my gear and head for the car just yet. It was enough to sit there and let the glow of the moment wash over us.

We watched as technicians milled around us, taking down the PA and collecting microphones and cables. While they worked, we sat.

Something shifted in the quality of the air. I became aware of a familiar presence behind me. I knew who it was before I turned to find Paul Galahad, Des, and Cherry standing there. They were smiling, even Des. Though no one said anything, Paul's lopsided grin seemed to say, "You done good, kid."

I started to rise, but Paul motioned for me to stay put. They joined us, dangling their legs over the front of the stage, just as we were doing, and looked out over the sea of mostly empty chairs and bleacher seats. The work crew behind us was busy dismantling the speaker rigging while technicians ran back and forth across the stage area behind us, hauling cables and electronic equipment back into the wings from whence they had come. There was a lot going on. But the noise didn't quite reach us. It was as if we were in a world of our own at the very front of the stage, enveloped in a sphere of silence.

Finally, Paul Galahad spoke. "You brought the house down," he said. "It was one for the ages."

I got butterflies. "Thank you," I said, basking in the glow of validation from the highest level.

After a moment, I said, "I'm so sorry about Big Al."

Paul just nodded. And we sat for a while without saying anything.

"I've been thinking about what happened," he said finally, gazing into the distance.

I waited for him to continue.

"This may have been what Al had in mind all along."

"You mean blowing up the ship?"

"That or something like it."

"How do you figure?"

"His job was done. He'd gotten us here. But over the course of the journey, things had changed. No one had figured on the advances that would make it possible for the entire crew to survive the trip and then some. I personally know he never imagined he'd live to see the end of the mission when we started out. So now he was in a bind. How to carry out his goal of noninterference AND somehow reckon with the fact that the crew had lived long past its expiration date and would still be around well into the future? I think what happened with Xenecorp just confirmed what he'd already come to realize. He couldn't have it both ways. One group or the other would survive. But not both. And of course, being Big Al, he made the right choice. He chose the Settlers."

"How did the founders or designers or whoever imagine things would play out once we got here?" Grandpa Kurt asked.

"They figured several generations of ship's crew would have come and gone by the time we arrived, with the last of these being responsible for getting us to the surface safe and sound. The plan was to assimilate the last generation of ship's crew into the Settler population with a minimum of impact. It would have required extensive deprogramming, but it was part of the deal. It was generally accepted that everyone, crew and Settlers alike, had to have the same starting point for assimilation to work. Neither group could have an advantage over the other."

"They agreed to dumb themselves down," Tina said, "by forgetting 250 years of scientific advancements?"

"In order to be able to participate in the colonization process, yeah. It was a sacrifice they were willing to make."

We were all waiting for more.

"When this thing with the Company happened, it just confirmed what Big Al had already been thinking. Only now it wasn't just speculation anymore. Under the circumstances, he knew he'd have to act decisively if he wanted to save the Phoenix Project. And that's what he did. With that last major offensive against Xenecorp prior to the explosion he succeeded in luring the remaining enemy fighters off the planet and up to the ship to make a stand. And, well, we know the rest."

"Wouldn't it have been enough just to get rid of the bad guys?" Mel asked.

"I think he figured it would have been too risky to have robots around for the longer term, even the good kind. It would have run counter to everything the Designers had envisioned for the Settlers. Everything they'd done--LPRM, the isolation of the Stacks, the Bubble, all of it--they did to create a clean slate for humanity, completely free from outside influences. Their intentions were clear on that score. There could be no justifying having a bunch of enhanced humans running around no matter how you rationalized it. What ended up happening may not have been Big Al's plan at first. But he'd had a lot of time to think things over on the journey. As the decades rolled on, and he and everyone else onboard started with the implants, he must have known it was a devil's bargain. What would happen once the ship arrived? That was the big question. In the end, he stuck to the original plan. I'm sure, knowing Big Al, that there was never any question in his mind. He would do what needed to be done to save the settlement. Even if it meant destroying himself and the entire population of enhanced humans in the bargain."

"Everyone opted for immortality even if it meant becoming not human anymore," Melissa said as if thinking aloud.

"Something like that," Paul gave a dry laugh. He gave Des a quick, unreadable glance. "I think he knew the bill was going to come due at some point. He got to choose the moment. The last-minute threat that Xenecorp posed would only have reinforced his resolve."

"Did you know about his plans beforehand?"

"Not really," he said thoughtfully. "But thinking back to the conversations we had toward the end, I knew something was going on with him. In retrospect, I think he was working out how to do what he was about to do."

"What did he say?"

"Nothing specific. He'd started reminiscing a lot about the journey from Earth and questioning how he might have done things differently. I'd never known him to second guess himself. He was always focused either on the present or on the future he wanted to create for you. I don't know. It all added up to him clarifying things in his own mind. He was getting ready to close up shop."

I nodded. I remembered Big Al that last time we saw him at the yard. He'd been resigned. It had seemed understandable under the circumstances. He was injured, and he was facing what seemed like an unwinnable battle. But there might have been more to it.

'He knew it was over," I mumbled.

"Excuse me?"

"Nothing," I said. "I was just thinking about the last time we saw him. Just before he was carted away on the gurney."

Grandpa Kurt spoke up. "Let me get this straight. You're saying his strategy these past few weeks was to get both the Federation and Xenecorp on or near the ship before it blew. He wanted to keep everyone who didn't belong on the surface together in one place, including himself."

Paul nodded. "Sounds about right."

No one said anything for several minutes. In the meantime, the work behind us continued unabated. The speaker towers were being brought down in sections, and the stage was starting to empty of gear and cables. None of us noticed.

"In that case, I guess we owe him a debt," Grandpa said, without much enthusiasm. "Doubly for all he did getting us here in the first place."

Everyone nodded solemn agreement.

I think we were all mad at Big Al for taking himself off the board like that. I, for one, hated it that he was gone. I wasn't ready to forgive him for that, I couldn't help it. It was going to be a sore spot for me for a long time to come.

Paul stood, and Des and Cherry followed suit. "Really enjoyed the show," he said, trying to shift the somber mood. "It reminded me of Aloha From Hawaii, except I got to see it as a member of the audience. Again." He laughed. The laugh was replaced by a wistful kind of smile.

I nodded as if I had a clue what he was talking about. There was a lot I didn't know about Paul Galahad. Like how he had gone from being Elvis, the biggest star on the planet, to being Paul Galahad, a guy nobody knew, and why. It was just one of the many mysteries surrounding the Thunder Tribe. I hoped one day I'd know more.

Paul leaned in toward us as if in confidence, squinting out into the now empty arena. "Listen," he said. "It's going to be alright. All of it. The band's got a bright future ahead of it. In fact, we all do. It's what Al wanted for us, and now there's nothing standing in the way of that happening. We don't want to miss out by dwelling on what's past and can't be changed."

His words had an effect. He was someone speaking from experience. We thought about the gig we'd just played and the audience reaction to it and started to feel a little better.

He straightened up then. "Time to get moving," he said. Cherry stood behind him, chewing her gum like her life depended on it. "Anything you need, don't hesitate to call. If any career-related questions come up, chances are I've been there. Maybe I can help." He produced gold embossed cards from his shirt pocket and handed them to Tina, Mel and me.

The cards said simply, "The King" next to a small skewed illustration of a crown. Underneath that was the phrase "career consulting in popular music." At the bottom of the card was a telephone number.

"The King," Tina said with a grin. "Modest."

"It's kind of a private joke." He flashed Des an apologetic look. He seemed embarrassed. "It's Cherry's idea," he said. Behind him, Cherry was smiling ear to ear. "Now, she may genuinely believe my experience as a singer qualifies me to offer real-world advice to up and coming performers. I'm ready to give her the benefit of the doubt on that. But I suspect this is mainly an excuse for her to hang out with you all. She figures you'd be my only clients since nobody here knows me from Adam. Anyway, this is where we can be reached."

He straightened up. "Y'all take care, you hear?" He said it with that soft drawl of his. "You showed 'em how it's done today," he added, addressing us girls. "It won't be the last time. Count on it. Whatever you do, remember to enjoy the ride." Then he swept off the stage with Des and Cherry in tow.

Kind of like royalty.

114

Complications

"So how does it feel?" Danny asked me after I confided in him what Grandmother had told me. "Do you feel any different?"

We were at the counter at Henrietta's, pulling on chocolate malts. I'd gone back and forth about telling him and decided it couldn't hurt. If I couldn't quite take it seriously myself, I couldn't expect anybody else to.

"Not really," I said. "And I don't plan on changing my wardrobe any time soon to look like Wonder Woman."

He laughed. "You could ease into it. Start with the tiara. Then add the cape and go from there."

I punched him in the shoulder.

Still, I couldn't help but remember the amazing sensation of floating above the stage. It had felt pretty real at the time.

Danny nodded solemnly. "That was an amazing show you put on today," he said soberly. "The best yet, in my opinion." Danny had been to a number of our gigs. He seemed sincere.

"Why, you are too kind, sir," I said, going for Scarlett O'Hara, but sounding more like Betty Boop. I decided mimicking accents wasn't my thing. "Tell you the truth," I said in my normal voice, "I thought I was going to lose my lunch the first couple of numbers. But after a while, the butterflies went away, and we all settled into a groove. On balance, it felt pretty good. People seemed to like it."

"That's an understatement," he said. "So what's next for the Roadrunners?"

"Keep writing songs and recording them. Maybe do some touring. It would be fun to see what the rest of this planet looks like."

"Are you going to keep taking classes at the JC?"

"When I can," I said. "But going back to school full time may have to wait."

"Wait?"

"The girls and I want to see how this music thing plays out. I guess that's our priority right now."

Danny didn't say anything. But I could tell he was a little disappointed. I realized something right then. I cared about what Danny thought and felt. When did that start to happen? In the lava tubes? The night of the firefight above the Rez? It kind of caught me by surprise. I wanted to say something flip. Instead, I said, "Listen, I'll be back. I've got family and friends here and so does the rest of the band. I can't see us staying away too long. There aren't enough cities and towns on the planet to keep us busy playing for more than a couple of months at a time."

Danny looked over at me more hopefully.

"Maybe you could come visit when we go out on the road," I said. I didn't know where that came from, but I meant it. I wanted to keep hanging out with Danny. And something told me I'd miss him if I couldn't.

I can't tell you how strange that realization was. I'd seen relationships come and go around me all through high school and into college. It had all seemed pretty abstract. Until now.

Here we were drinking malts at Henrietta's, something I'd done a hundred times before. But today it felt different. It felt. . .romantic.

This is ridiculous, a part of me thought. Cornier than a bag of Fritos. That part of me was all for getting up and marching right out of there without a backward glance.

But another part of me knew that wasn't going to happen. I'd never been the kind to run away from something because it wasn't what I was used to. And I had to admit it felt good just to be there with Danny, doing nothing in particular.

I knew he liked me. You can just tell these things. And I guess I kind of liked him back. And maybe he could tell that too.

But even though he probably knew, I still had to say, "Let's not lose touch, OK?".

"OK," he said, with a slight smile.

And we left it at that.

Lying in bed that night, I was hearing all those goofy teenage love songs with new ears. The Teddy Bears, "To Know Him Is To Love Him", Ritchie Valens' "Oh Donna," and the Elegants' "Little Star" were playing nonstop in my head. And don't forget the Penguins. Did I imagine myself as the Earth Angel they were singing about? Maybe. It worked better in a song than "Earth Goddess." But it was in the ballpark, I figured.

I was showing all the symptoms. Here I was not sleeping, for instance, thinking about my conversation with Danny at the soda fountain and getting fluttery. I sensed that things could get a little complicated from here on out. But that wasn't enough to put me off. Besides, I was pretty sure I could take Danny in a straight fight if it came to it. If he got out of line I'd have him in a headlock pronto. What was there to worry about?

Danny was a friend, I told myself. And you can't have too many friends, right?

115

Journey's End

It was amazing how quickly things returned to normal when the robots were gone. It wasn't long before it was business as usual in Rattlesnake Junction--and elsewhere, I'm guessing. The only difference was there was no moon to light the night, just a sea of stars overhead.

Gazing up at the nighttime sky I tried to pinpoint where Planet Earth was, or at least where the solar system might be. Everyone had a vague notion, but unless you were in astronomy class at the college and had easy access to their telescope, you'd have a hard time getting a clear view of our former sun.

I tried to imagine a time in the future when we'd have the ability to make a quick and easy flyby of our home planet to see how things had evolved while we were gone. I reminded myself that at least a million years had passed on Earth in our absence, thanks to Einstein and relativity.

What would it be like now on Earth? If the atmosphere had made a comeback, there might be green rolling hills covered in dense forests. I imagined thousands of miles of unspoiled coastline. The roads would long since have been erased, buried under layers of sediment and plant life. The towns and cities would have crumbled to dust ages ago and become one with the soil.

I wondered if a few pockets of humans might have survived here and there, against the odds. If they had, they'd be living a Stone

Age-like existence. There might be tribes of hunters and gathers on the plains. Tree dwellers in the forests nibbling on nuts and fruits. Maybe some basic agriculture here and there. But there was little doubt that nature would once again reign supreme. And Man, if he still existed, would be living alongside the animals and birds and reptiles. The idea that one could be of greater or lesser importance than the other would have made no sense.

Maybe it was best that we never went back, if it was only to spoil everything all over again. We were better off on this volcanic continent, on this new world. Here, at least, there wasn't that much to spoil. Not yet anyway.

It was interesting how easily I adapted to the idea that mankind had succeeded in destroying its original home after the shock had worn off. Having come of age in the fifties, I'd been used to thinking that America was invincible and that the world as we knew it would always be there. But knowing what would happen over the next few centuries, it wasn't that hard to see that all the elements of the future catastrophe were already there if you knew where to look. The wilderness was shrinking year by year. As the number of cars on the highways and byways increased, air quality was starting to become an issue, especially around the big cities. No one but some nature nuts and a few college professors seemed worried about the direction things were going in.

Now history was starting all over again. What had happened there wouldn't necessarily be what would happen here. This was the beginning of a new story for all of us. Our chance to make things right.

And if future generations were inclined to backslide into the same old behavior patterns and traps, there would always be the specter of what had happened on Planet Earth to serve as a warning. Or so I hoped. It was hard to overestimate mankind's capacity for self-delusion.

But right now life was good. We'd made it this far. Maybe Big Al had been right in doing what he did. Maybe the demise of the robots would be a blessing in the long run. This way, we'd be relying on ourselves from here on out. If it all went south, there'd be no one to blame but ourselves.

But this wasn't the time for doom and gloom. It was a time of celebration. A time of optimism and hope for our future. With Xenecorp gone, things were looking up. We really did have an amazing new home, pristine and unspoiled. Tropical beaches as far as the eye could see. Volcanoes to explore. And practically the whole of the interior of the continent to chart. There was enough space here so nobody would be stepping on anybody else's toes for a long time to come.

Time, space, and a fresh start. That was the legacy of the Fortune's Fool. That was the gift we'd been given.

I learned to surf.

I couldn't see a Hawaiian shirt without thinking of Big Al. But even the memory of the brawny red-faced man at the wrecking yard began to fade in time. When I thought of him, it didn't matter to me that he'd been more machine than man. To me, he was and would always be Big Al, as full of life as any human I had ever met.

We kept our promise to him to look after the wrecking yard. But instead of looking for a buyer, Grandpa and I decided to take over the business ourselves. Aunt Trish quit her job at Legal Services and started to manage the office. She was terrific at keeping things organized. The business thrived.

As to any trace of the benevolent robots who had safely shepherded us to this new place, none remained.

We were still riding the high of being an internationally known band a year later. Since everyone was well aware by now that our current musical idols were imitators and that the real ones had been dead for centuries, the field was wide open for up and comers like the Roadrunners to stake a claim. The notoriety we had gained as the band of the resistance gave us an advantage in the post-Fortune's Fool world. We were as well-positioned for world domination as anyone else on the music scene. And that's kind of what happened.

We were traveling a lot, so my time helping out at the wrecking yard became limited. With a pang of regret, I finally gave up the job at Ted's Auto Repair. And my attendance at classes up at the college became sporadic at best.

Through it all, Danny and I remained fast friends. Though he never did join us on the road, I'd see him when I was home. And though neither of us was particularly pleased about being apart for long periods of time, we accepted that as a current fact of life. He seemed genuinely happy for me and the way my life and career were going. I think he understood that it was important for the band to make the most of it while we had the chance. We all knew it could go away at any time.

The girls and I talked about going back to our studies when we'd made our fortunes and retired from the music business at the ripe old age of twenty-five. Who'd want to be playing rock 'n' roll after that anyway? Right? It was hard to conceive.

In the meantime, life was as exciting as it had ever been. We were going places as a band. We loved what we were doing. Life was good. And we were ready to live it to the max.

Epilogue

Seen from space the ocean was vast. It dwarfed the single continent that cleaved it in two, north to south. Even now, a few years after the planet had been settled, the only evidence of the existence of humans was the clusters of lights that appeared at night along the edges of the continent's surface. The larger cities were clearly visible, while lesser towns appeared as faint luminous smears along the coasts. The massive uninhabited interior loomed dark and mysterious.

Besides the light emissions from the cities and towns, radio and television waves were constantly being dispersed into space. The technology was rudimentary at best. A spaceship equipped with the most basic receivers could easily pick these up and decode them.

A ship that hovered just beyond the reaches of the planet's gravitational pull did just that. It was more a pod than a ship actually, an invisible speck in the darkness of space high above the planet, undetectable by anyone on the ground.

An occupant sat in the captain's chair, tapping his toes to the sounds that were emanating from small speakers on the command console. He reached forward to turn up the music. The song being played was "No Particular Place To Go" by Chuck Berry.

The occupant couldn't help but smile at the aptness of the song as it applied to his current situation. Was he wistful at not being able to participate in the vital culture that was emerging on the surface? To the casual observer, it would certainly seem so. For the most part, he gave every indication of being inordinately pleased with what he was hearing through the speakers and what he was seeing through the pod's visor. His was the pride of a doting father reveling in the first steps of an infant child.

He liked to think that was at least partially the case.

He did indeed feel an enormous sense of satisfaction at how well human civilization had adapted to this new environment. And he was justifiably proud of the part he had played in ensuring mankind's safe passage from Earth and its chance at a new start. This had been his charge. And he was at peace with the fact that his part in the great endeavor was over and that he was no longer essential to the continuation of the settlement process.

He had done all he could. That he had survived the blast was nothing short of a miracle and no fault of his own. It certainly hadn't been intentional. He'd been in the pod monitoring the conflict at some distance when the destruct sequence countdown had reached zero. Amazingly, the pod had survived the powerful blast that had obliterated the ship. Though the hull now resembled nothing so much as a shitake mushroom, it had not been compromised during the explosion. The propulsion system, on the other hand, had not fared as well. Since that fateful day, he'd been adrift in a craft that was essentially dead in the water miles above the planet.

All that was left for him to do was to await the inevitable. Eventually, the onboard systems would run out of juice and begin to shut down. Two things could happen then. He would either drift aimlessly further out into space, he and his craft becoming lifeless pieces of interstellar debris. Or he would be drawn down into the planet's atmosphere to become a shooting star, a cinder, long before he reached the ground. But given his current trajectory both of these options could be a long time coming.

The intervening years had given him time to think. During that time a third option had presented itself which involved an activity near and dear to his heart: mechanical restoration. He needn't accept his fate passively. With a few repurposed parts, the pod might become functional again. The thought cheered him. This craft was of a manageable scale. At bottom, it wasn't that much different from those old cars he'd been so fond of. Vastly more sophisticated, granted. But it, like them, could be retooled, rebuilt, and made to rise again from the ashes.

All he'd require was time. And he had plenty of that. Things could proceed as they had for years under the present circumstances before he fell out of orbit in one direction or the other. Decades even. He could afford, for instance, to wait until all who might remember him on the surface were gone. That way no one (including his own conscience) could accuse him of meddling. He took this business of noninterference as seriously now as he ever had.

Nevertheless, he often found his mind wandering. And during his musings he often imagined himself returning to Rattlesnake Junction and the wrecking yard one day. If the yard had been abandoned or fallen into neglect, he saw himself returning it to its former glory. If it was still a going concern, he might see if he could acquire it somehow and take up where he had left off those many years before. But he was getting ahead of himself.

He shifted slightly in his chair and turned his head. He saw hanging along the wall of the cabin a dazzling array of Hawaiian shirts. He leaned back and admired his collection, a smile on his face.

There was a chortling noise at his elbow.

Big Al nodded. "You're right, my friend," he said. He glanced over at the diminutive gray-skinned creature in the chair next to his. "Getting this crate up and running would expand our options, that's for sure. We wouldn't necessarily have to wait an eternity. We could find ourselves a nice little town where no one had a clue who we were. We could get you a disguise. Pass you off as my nephew, say."

There was some chortling in reply.

"Niece? OK. Whatever you prefer." He gave his companion an uncertain look. "At any rate, we could set up shop in a foreign location to start. Maybe deal in cultural artifacts for a while. I hear the Europeans and the Asians have some great junk. Eventually, we could make the transition back to cars. But that would be further down the line."

More chortling.

"Rattlesnake Junction?" Big Al mused as if the notion hadn't occurred to him. "I suppose. There wouldn't be much harm in heading back to Rattlesnake Junction when there's no one left who would know who we were. Do what we like to do best. Collect old cars and strip them down for parts. Become a part of the community again. Only this time we'll do it right. It won't just be a sideline. No more ship's captain bearing the fate of mankind on his shoulders."

Again, chortling.

"Yes we did, didn't we?" said Big Al with a grin. "We got it done. We took the hit. A big one, I admit. But considering how well they're doing down there, it's hard to have too many regrets. I frankly don't think things could have worked out better for the Settlers and for the Phoenix project in general if we'd planned it this way all along. It turns out Xenecorp did everyone a favor by forcing my hand. Does that seem insensitive?"

More chortling.

"I know I'm a robot," Big Al said, indignantly. "You are, too. That doesn't mean we don't have feelings. I miss my people every day, and I know you miss yours. But we had a good run, didn't we? And way more time to enjoy life than any of us had any right to expect. We did what we came to do. It was time for us to get out of the way and let things take their natural course. Sure. There might have been a more elegant solution. But this is the way things worked out."

Chortling redux.

"That's for damn sure," Big Al said, with a laugh that shook his belly. "We went out in a blaze of glory, didn't we? Like Butch and Sundance. There's something to be said for that."

He turned back to the awe-inspiring view of the planet through the wide window at the front of the craft. They'd give it a few years, he thought. It might take that long anyway to get the pod up and running again. But Archie was right. They might not need to wait for decades. If they made a go of it in another place, in another part of this world, they might be able to dive in again sooner than they'd imagined. It would just be Big Al and his diminutive sidekick, a pair of tumblin' tumbleweeds, bunking under the stars, and then blowing into town off the lava flows when the time seemed right. The classic fresh start. Maybe in Shanghai to kick things off.

He wondered how Kurt and his daughter were doing. He knew he'd be tempted to look in on them once he was down on the surface again. But he'd have to resist that temptation. Better no one knew he was still around. It would only complicate matters. Another secret to be kept. The alternative was to risk celebrity. And he definitely didn't want that.

No. They'd bide their time. They had both learned a thing or two about patience on the great crossing. They'd watch and wait.

Chuck Berry was replaced by Sheb Wooley singing "Purple People Eater" on the console intercom. Suddenly Archie became animated, gyrating wildly to the beat, arms flailing. This was clearly one of the alien's favorite tunes.

Again Al had to smile to himself. He was grateful for Archie's company. Without him the seemingly endless days in confined quarters would have been unbearable. True. Archie couldn't carry a tune to save his life, and he had no sense of rhythm to speak of, but he was one hell of a poker player. Even a couple of centuries into their acquaintance, his expressions were still all but unreadable, which meant he had no discernible tells. Nevertheless, he remained an unending source of amusement to the former captain of the Fortune's Fool. And despite the poker face, he was fairly certain the alien thought similarly of him.

From his perch high above the planet, Big Al could observe mankind's progress in the new world, sharing in its triumphs and tumults, if only from a distance. He'd never stopped caring about his passengers on the long haul from Earth. And his affection had only deepened after he had opened the wrecking yard and started meeting those few remarkable individuals that would eventually become his closest friends. None of that was likely to change anytime soon. And why should it?

He was 4% human after all.

Printed in the United States
by Baker & Taylor Publisher Services